DUNGEON CRAWLER CARL

Titles by Matt Dinniman

Dungeon Crawler Carl Series

DUNGEON CRAWLER CARL

CARL'S DOOMSDAY SCENARIO

THE DUNGEON ANARCHIST'S COOKBOOK

THE GATE OF THE FERAL GODS

THE BUTCHER'S MASQUERADE

THE EYE OF THE BEDLAM BRIDE

KAIJU: BATTLEFIELD SURGEON

The Shivered Sky Series

EVERY GRAIN OF SAND

IN THE CITY OF DEMONS

THE GREAT DEVOURING DARKNESS

Dominion of Blades Series

DOMINION OF BLADES

THE HOBGOBLIN RIOT

THE GRINDING

TRAILER PARK FAIRY TALES

DUNGEON CRAWLER CARL

MATT DINNIMAN

ACE

New York

ACE
Published by Berkley
An imprint of Penguin Random House LLC
penguinrandomhouse.com

Copyright © 2020 by Matt Dinniman
"Backstage at the Pineapple Cabaret" copyright © 2024 by Matt Dinniman
Penguin Random House supports copyright. Copyright fuels creativity, encourages diverse voices,
promotes free speech, and creates a vibrant culture. Thank you for buying an authorized edition of
this book and for complying with copyright laws by not reproducing, scanning, or distributing any
part of it in any form without permission. You are supporting writers and allowing
Penguin Random House to continue to publish books for every reader.

ACE is a registered trademark and the A colophon is a trademark of
Penguin Random House LLC.

Library of Congress Cataloging-in-Publication Data

Names: Dinniman, Matt, author.
Title: Dungeon crawler Carl / Matt Dinniman.
Description: First Ace edition. | New York: Ace, 2024. |
Series: Dungeon crawler Carl ; 1
Identifiers: LCCN 2024011863 | ISBN 9780593820247 (hardcover)
Subjects: LCGFT: LitRPG (Fiction) | Novels.
Classification: LCC PS3604.I49 D86 2024 | DDC 813/.6—dc23/eng/20240322
LC record available at https://lccn.loc.gov/2024011863

Dungeon Crawler Carl was originally self-published, in different form, in 2020.

First Ace Edition: August 2024

Printed in the United States of America
1st Printing

Book design by George Towne
Interior art on pages v, 12, 228, 432: Vintage Black Texture © 316pixel/Shutterstock
Interior art on page 1 by Matt Dinniman
All other interior art by Erik Wilson (erikwilsonart.com)

This version of Dungeon Crawler Carl *is dedicated to the star of one of the greatest, most inspiring, most amazing survival stories of our time.*
Fiona.
Fiona the hippo.
Yes, I am dedicating this book to a goddamned hippopotamus.

Sorry, Mom.

Rome will exist as long as the Coliseum does;

when the Coliseum falls,

so will Rome;

when Rome falls,

so will the world.

The Venerable Bede

DUNGEON CRAWLER CARL

1

THE TRANSFORMATION OCCURRED AT APPROXIMATELY 2:23 A.M.,
Pacific Standard Time. As far as I could tell, anyone who was indoors
when it happened died instantly. If you had any sort of roof over you,
you were dead. That included people in cars, airplanes, subways.
Even tents and cardboard boxes. Hell, probably umbrellas, too.
Though I'm not so sure about that one.

I'm not gonna lie. You guys who were inside, probably warm and
asleep and dreaming about some random bullshit? I'm jealous. You're
the lucky ones. You were just gone. Splattered into dust during the
transformation.

It was a Tuesday, and the calendar had just ticked over to January
3rd. A terrible winter storm had descended on North America, and
half the country was buried in snow and ice. In Seattle we didn't have
too much snow that night. But it was well below zero, which was
unusually cold, even for January.

I'm sure in other parts of the world where it was warmer and not
in the middle of the night, many more people survived. Many more.

I also bet most of them were probably wearing more clothes than
I was at the time of the incident. And those assholes were smart
enough not to go into the light.

Me, I didn't have a choice. Like I said, it was below freezing. I was
outside. And I was wearing boxers, a leather jacket, and a pair of
pink Crocs sandals that barely fit me.

I was also holding a crying, scratching, squirming, and spitting cat
named Princess Donut the Queen Anne Chonk. She was a tortoise-

shell Persian cat worth more than I made in a year. My ex-girlfriend called her Princess Donut for short. I just stuck with Donut.

So let me back up about ten minutes. I won't bore you with too much backstory, but some of these details may be important.

My name is Carl. I am twenty-seven years old. After a stint in the US Coast Guard, I ended up working as a marine tech, fixing electrical systems for rich assholes and their party boats. I, up until a few days before this started, lived with my girlfriend in our apartment in Seattle.

Her name was Beatrice. Bea. She went to the Bahamas for a New Year's thing with a bunch of friends. She didn't tell me her ex-boyfriend went along with her on the trip. I figured it out pretty quick when I saw the picture of her sitting on his lap on Instagram.

I don't like drama, and I don't deal well with it. Whether she was actually cheating on me or not, it didn't matter so much. She'd lied. So I called her up, and I told her we were done. I promised I'd have all her stuff ready for her to go when she got back. No drama. No fuss. But we were done.

She'd asked her parents to come get the cat, but they lived on the other side of the Cascades, and nobody was getting through any of the passes with this weather. So I promised I'd look after her until Beatrice got back.

So, let me tell you about Donut the cat. Like I said, she's one of those fluffy, flat-faced cats that look like they need to be sitting on the lap of a Bond villain. Bea and I shared a two-bedroom apartment, and one of those rooms was dedicated to the cat if that tells you anything. More specifically, the room was devoted to Donut's Best-in-Show ribbons, her Best-in-Breed ribbons, and countless trophies and framed photographs of her sitting on a table, looking all fuzzy and pissed off while Bea and a judge stood behind her. Bea probably had fifty of the pictures. She'd won a mess of ribbons and trophies and photographs pretty much every time Beatrice took Donut to an event. And Bea took that damn cat to a show almost every weekend.

Her whole family was into raising and showing Persian cats. Me, I didn't really know much about that whole cat show world. I didn't want to get too involved. Like I said, I don't do drama.

And let me tell you something about cat people. More specifically, cat *show* people.

Actually, never mind. Fuck those guys. All that's important is Bea and Donut were a part of this whole world I didn't want anything to do with.

I never considered myself a big fan of cats. But, if we're being truthful here, I *liked* Donut. That cat did not give two shits about anybody or anything, and I could respect that. If Donut wanted to sit on my lap while I was blasting away on PlayStation, then she sat on my damn lap. If I tried to pick her up, she hissed and scratched and jumped right back up there. And then she looked at me with a squished face that said, *What're you gonna do about it?*

I'd been tempted, more than once, to throttle the thing. But I'm not an asshole. Plus, I could respect the little monster's tenacity. Some of my buddies would give me crap about it, me spending all this time with a fuzzy cat that was probably worth more than I would make in a year, but I enjoyed it. I enjoyed having that ball of fuzz sitting in my lap.

One of Beatrice's ironclad, this-is-not-negotiable rules was no smoking in the apartment. So after our fight and breakup, I'd made a point of smoking as much as I could. I know, immature. But it was freezing outside. Donut didn't seem to like the smoke too much, and the smell clung to her hair. So, as a compromise, I would crack the window when I smoked.

So when I woke up at about 2 a.m., having been startled awake by a dream, I decided I needed a smoke. I pulled out my pack, cracked the window, and I lit a cigarette.

Donut, who had been sleeping right next to me on the bed, decided at that very moment that she wanted to—for the first time in her feline life—go outside and explore. She jumped up on my shoulder, and she leaped out the second-story window onto the tree outside my apartment. Just like that. I'd had that window open dozens of times over the past year, and she'd never even given the window a second glance. But tonight, on the coldest night of the year, the furry asshole decided to Lewis and Clark her way out of the apartment.

She scampered down the tree, sniffed at the sidewalk a few times, and then promptly realized it was cold as fuck. Her adventure over as quickly as it began, she rushed back up the tree and stared at me over the five feet from the window to the branch. The adventure all drained out of her, Donut decided not to risk jumping back inside. So instead, she decided to start howling at the top of her lungs.

I spent the next several minutes cursing at the cat, trying to coax her back inside. I opened the window all the way, sending gales of ice-cold air in the previously toasty apartment. The fuzzy black-and-beige-and-white cat just sat there, bitching and howling so much I feared one of my neighbors might wake up and shoot her.

I'd left my boots in the dryer all the way in the building's basement. I didn't know where the hell my running shoes were. So, in a momentary decision I would quickly come to regret, I squeezed my feet into a pair of my ex-girlfriend's Crocs, pulled a heavy leather jacket on, and I rushed outside to grab the cat. A part of me kept saying, *Screw it. It's not your cat. Let the fucker freeze.*

But, like I said, I'm not that much of an asshole. As much as Beatrice deserved it, she loved that damn cat. And poor, stupid Donut wouldn't stand a chance out here in the cold. Not for long.

Plus, again, the cat was right there, howling like someone was eating her children in front of her.

I rushed down the stairs, and I jumped outside, rushing to the tree that sat between the sidewalk and the building. I immediately regretted not taking the time to put proper clothes on. The cold, windy air sank its claws into my legs and feet.

Donut was right there, sitting on a tree just out of reach, looking between me and the open window into the apartment. She continued to howl. A light popped on in an apartment on the first floor. I groaned. Mrs. Parsons. Grumpy, I-like-to-file-complaints Mrs. Parsons.

"Donut!" I said. "Come on, you little shit!" I held out my arms.

The cat could jump into my arms. It was something I'd trained her to do. I could shake a bag of cat treats, and she'd jump right up there. I could make a *pspspsps* sound, and she'd sometimes jump up on my shoulder. I cursed myself for not bringing cat treats out with me.

The window on the first-floor apartment slid open. "What in god's name is going on out here?" Mrs. Parsons called, sticking her head out the window. The old woman had her head wrapped in some sort of towel, making her look like a swami. Her beady eyes focused on me. "Carl, is that you?"

"Yes, Mrs. Parsons," I said. "Sorry. My cat got out, and I'm trying to get her in before she freezes to death."

"It looks like you're the one who's going to freeze to . . ."

Mrs. Parsons never finished the sentence.

Slam.

It happened so fast.

The building smashed down to the ground. I watched it happen. The seven-story apartment building was there one moment, and then it was gone. But it hadn't disappeared. I was looking right at Mrs. Parsons when it went down. It was like the building was a massive tin can that had been crushed by a giant cosmic boot. I saw it, and I heard it. Wind rushed at me, and it was instantly dark outside. The streetlamp just to my left was gone. The buildings all around me were gone. The cars on the street were gone, too.

Everything was gone except the trees and the bicycles in the bike racks, and Marjory Williams's moped, which was still booted by parking enforcement.

I looked around, the freezing weather momentarily forgotten. In the dark, overcast night, I could barely see anything. In the distance—a distance I could now see thanks to the lack of buildings—a fire burned.

There was utter, complete silence.

"What the hell?" I said, spinning in circles.

A couple random things remained. Like the bike rack. The stop sign was there, but the street sign next to it was gone. It didn't make sense. Where the cars were parked on the road, car-shaped indentations of dirt appeared, as if they'd been pulled down toward the center of the Earth, being ripped directly through the asphalt.

Donut jumped into my still-outstretched arms. I looked at the cat, not knowing what to do or say.

"What the hell?" I said again.

All that remained of my building was a rectangle of churned dirt and rocks.

And then I saw it, right near my feet.

It was Mrs. Parson's head. In the dark, it was hard to discern. But I immediately knew what it was.

It hit me, at that moment. The sudden shock of the buildings was one thing. But there were people in those buildings. It was almost everybody in the damn city. Hell, even most of the homeless people were in shelters. There'd been a whole thing on the news about them rounding everybody up because of the extreme cold. It was two in the damn morning on a Monday night. Everyone would be in bed. And that meant everyone was dead!

I kept spinning in circles like an idiot, not knowing what to do. I felt sick to my stomach. Donut started to squirm, having decided I was useless. She clawed at me, but I wouldn't let the cat go.

Then came the voice. A male, robotic voice.

It spoke in my mind. The voice was like a physical thing. A spike in my brain scratching me. It wasn't speaking English. But I understood the words. As the person spoke, the text also appeared floating in front of me.

Surviving humans, take note.

"What?" I said out loud. "What's that? Who's there?" I kicked at the floating words with my foot, and the too-small Croc went flying.

I hopped over and quickly shoved my foot back in. The words moved with me, floating just a few feet in front of my face.

Even the letters weren't in English. They crawled down, not across the screen. But I knew them, understood them like I'd been reading the language my entire life.

Per Syndicate rules, subsection 543 of the Precious Elemental Reserves Code, having failed to file a proper appeal for mineral and elemental rights within 50 solars of first contact, your planet has been successfully seized and is currently being mined of all requested elemental deposits by the assigned planetary regent.

Every interior of your world has been crushed and all raw materials—organic and inanimate—are in the process of being mined for the requested elements.

Per the Mined Material Reclamation Act along with subsection 35 of the Indigenous Planetary Species Protection Act, any surviving humans will be given the opportunity to reclaim their lost matter. The Borant Corporation, having been assigned regency over this solar system, is allowed to choose the manner of this reclamation, and they have chosen option 3, also known as the 18-Level World Dungeon. The Borant Corporation retains all rights to broadcast, exploit, and otherwise control all aspects of the World Dungeon and will remain in control as long as they adhere to Syndicate regulations regarding world resource reclamation.

Upon successful completion of level 18 of the World Dungeon, regency of this planet will revert to the successor.

A Syndicate neutral observer AI—myself—has been created and dispatched to this planet to supervise the creation of the World Dungeon and to ensure all the rules and regulations are properly followed.

Please pay careful attention to the following information as it will not be repeated.

Per the Indigenous Planetary Species Protection Act, all remaining materials—estimated to be 99.999999% of the sifted matter—is currently being repurposed for the subterranean World Dungeon. The first level of this dungeon will open approximately 18 seconds after the end of this announcement. The first-level entrances will be open for exactly one human hour and one hour *only*. Once the entrances are closed, you may no longer enter. If you enter, you may not leave until you have either completed all 18 levels of the World Dungeon or if you meet certain other requirements.

If you choose not to enter the World Dungeon, you will have to sustain yourself upon the surface of your planet, and this may be the last communication you receive during your lifetime. All previously processed matter and elements are forfeit. However, you are free to mine and utilize any remaining and naturally occurring resources for your own benefit. The Borant Corporation wishes you luck and thanks you for the opportunity.

For those who wish to exercise their right of resource reclamation, please take note.

There will be 150,000 level one entrances added to the world. These entrances will be marked and easy to spot. If you so choose to enter the first level of the dungeon, you will have five rotations of your planet to find the next level down. There will be 75,000 entrances to level 2. There will be 37,500 entrances to level 3. 18,750 to level 4. 9,375 entrances to level 5 and 4,688 entrances to level 6. The number of available entrances to the next lower level will continue to decrease by half, rounding up until the 18th level, which will only have two entrances and a single exit.

Crawlers who choose to enter the World Dungeon must find a staircase and descend to the next level down before the allotted time is up for that level. Once the time has passed, the level will be reclaimed and all remaining matter in the level, organic and inanimate, will be forfeit. Generated loot and other matter that is not gathered and claimed may be placed in the Syndicate market.

Each lower level will have a longer period of reclamation. Additional rules come into play once any crawlers descend to the tenth floor. These rules will be explained when and if any crawlers reach this level.

If you so choose to enter the World Dungeon, it is highly recommended you immediately find and utilize a tutorial guild. Multiple tutorial guilds will be seeded throughout the dungeon on levels 1 through 3.

If you have any additional questions, or you wish to file an appeal, such requests must be submitted in writing directly to the closest Syndicate office.

Thank you for being a part of the Syndicate. Have a great day.

My brain could barely parse any of what the voice had said, so bewildered was I at everything that had just happened. I could no longer feel my legs. I had been outside much too long, and I was in serious danger of freezing to death, of losing toes to the cold. I had to get inside, and I had to do it now.

But there was no inside anymore. There weren't even any cars. I eyed the fire that continued to rage a few blocks over. I needed to get over there, and fast. I turned, and I started to shuffle-run.

The wind, which had been a light breeze before the buildings all disappeared, was now a constant, freezing gale that stank of the ocean. Donut twisted in my arms, scratching at me, trying to get free. She chomped onto my shoulder, but my jacket protected me. I clutched the cat tighter.

Was this a dream? Had I accidentally been dosed with some sort of hallucinogen?

World Dungeon? What the actual hell? What did that even mean? My mind continued to race. I immediately thought of *Path-finder* and *Dungeons and Dragons* and other games I hadn't played since I was on active duty. I couldn't see a single damn person. I was surrounded by only the sound of the wind.

A horn, like a trumpet, sounded, blasting through the night air. I stopped dead, looking around. What now? *It's the dungeon appearing,* I thought. *This is happening. Holy shit, this is really happening.*

Less than a hundred feet to my left, right in the middle of what had once been a thrift store, a spotlight burst into the air. I saw an additional spotlight appear about a mile away. I turned, and I saw a few more littered throughout the city.

Even from this distance, I could feel the warmth radiating from the brightly lit hole in the ground.

I didn't think about it. My head still swam with all the information that had been thrown at me. The pink Crocs barely fit on my feet. The distant fire was farther away than I thought. I had seen firsthand what hypothermia did to people.

So I turned toward the light, and I ran.

PART ONE

2

DUNGEON FLOOR 1.
TIME TO LEVEL COLLAPSE: 5 DAYS.

AN ORNATE STAIRCASE LED DOWN INTO THE LIGHT. EACH STEP AP-peared to be made of wrought iron, and the whole thing was wide enough to accommodate twenty people walking side by side. Glowing warmth radiated from the hole. I took a step, falling down a little farther than I anticipated. My footfalls echoed into the brightness.

This was a city of almost a million people, and I was the only one here.

Donut, who had stopped fighting, clutched onto my shoulder and started growling as we descended toward the bright light. Welcome, glorious warmth beckoned me deeper. My legs and feet, which I hadn't been able to feel, were now starting to burn. I hadn't been out in the cold long enough to sustain any real damage, but I was frost-bitten to hell.

The stairs seemed to go on forever. The iron steps were carved in an odd pattern depicting what could've been fish. Or maybe demons. The almost Asian-looking carvings gave me an uneasy feeling. These stairs weren't here just a few minutes ago. *This whole thing is made of the buildings and cars and people of the world.* Who did this? *How* did they do it?

By the time I reached the bottom of the stairs, the temperature had risen to a humid, balmy 80 degrees Fahrenheit or so. The metal stairs ended at a marble floor and a hulking door that stood about thirty feet tall and was just as wide. The wooden arched door was carved in the shape of a massive fish demon, like the stairs.

I looked up at the double doors.

"What the hell is this thing?" I muttered.

As I stared at the door, an information box popped up over the door. The box appeared so suddenly and unexpectedly that I stepped back. It was like I was in a game, or maybe wearing special contact lenses that popped up informational tooltips. It even had a little X in the corner to close it out.

This is a rendition of a kua-tin, the dominant species of the Borant system and principal owners of the Borant Corporation. Make sure you recognize these guys. There'll be a test later.

Was that last part supposed to be a joke? I focused on the X in the corner and mentally closed the box.

Huh, I thought. I looked up at the carving again and I felt something, almost like a slight haptic tingling in my brain. The information box popped up again. I closed it.

Weird. I could control the information with my mind. I could open information boxes on certain items by focusing on them. I could close the boxes by mentally clicking the X with my mind.

That means they're in your head. Maybe this isn't really happening. Maybe you're asleep, and this is all some sort of high-tech simulation. Like in the Matrix *movies.*

The pain in my warming-up legs and feet reminded me that simulation or not, it didn't matter. Not when I could hurt.

With my one free hand, I pushed at the door. It opened easily inward, revealing a long hallway lit by multiple torches. The hallway was just as wide and tall as the door, more like a tunnel for a double-lane roadway than for someone to walk through. In the distance I could see several branches leading off the main hall. A blinking light appeared near the first branch. It seemed to be a sign of some sort, but I couldn't read it from here.

"Oww," I cried as Donut chomped down on my hand. I dropped the cat, and she bounded forward into the hallway. She stopped about ten paces in, looking around with a confused, startled look on her face.

I stepped toward the cat, and the doors slammed behind me. The light from the entrance room cut off and was replaced with a dusk-like dimness.

Welcome, Crawler. Welcome to the First Floor.

This was a new voice. It was male, sounding overly enthusiastic, almost like a game show host. It wasn't the same person or speaker from the original announcement. The words appeared floating before me and were simultaneously spoken in my mind. Unlike the tooltip-like box, I wasn't able to close it out. This was more like subtitles.

A timer appeared in the upper right of my vision. It was at **4 days, 23 hours, and 48 minutes** and counting down. I, again, swiped at the characters. They didn't go away. I closed my eyes, and the information disappeared. It was unsettling and it gave me a slightly queasy feeling to my stomach.

Donut remained in her spot several paces in front of me, but the chunky cat was swiping at the air in front of herself. *She sees it, too,* I thought. *Holy crap.* Whatever this was, it was happening to the cat just like it was to me.

"Donut," I said, calling to the cat. "Stay with me."

The cat, being a cat, ignored me. But as I looked at her, I felt that same almost imperceptible tingle I felt when I'd looked at the door. I focused more tightly, and an information box popped up over the cat.

Crawler #4,119. "Princess Donut."
    Level 1.
    Race: Cat.
    Class: Not yet assigned.

I took a step forward, painfully aware that I was wearing Crocs that didn't fit.

More text assaulted me.

> You have been designated Crawler Number 4,122. You have been assigned the Crawler Name "Carl."
>
> You are assigned the race of Human. You are currently level 1. You may choose a new race and class as soon as you descend to the third floor. Your stat points have been assigned based on your current physical and mental profile. See the stat menu for more details.

Menu? I wondered how to pull a menu up. But before I could even try to figure it out, I was bowled over by a wall of text.

> Congratulations! You've earned your first achievement: Crazy Cat Lady.
>
> You have entered the World Dungeon accompanied by a cat. Ahh, isn't that sweet?
>
> *Reward*: You've received a Bronze Pet Box!

> New achievement! *Trailblazing* Crazy Cat Lady.
>
> You are the *first* crawler to have entered the World Dungeon accompanied by a cat. You must really love that thing. Too bad you're both probably going to die a horrible death at any moment. Or maybe not. Look at the prize you just received!
>
> *Reward*: You've received a Legendary Pet Box!

> New achievement! Early Adopter.
>
> You are one of the first 5,000 crawlers to enter a new World Dungeon. Sucker.
>
> *Reward*: You've received a Silver Adventurer Box!

New achievement! Empty Pockets.

You didn't bring any supplies. None. You know you still gotta eat, right?

Reward: You've received a Bronze Adventurer Box!

New achievement! Why Aren't You Wearing Pants?

You entered the dungeon wearing no pants. Dude. Seriously?

Reward: You've received a Gold Apparel Box!

New achievement! Unarmed Combat.

So. You just gonna waltz right into something called a "World Dungeon" and you're not even going to bring a weapon? You're either braver than you look, or you're just an idiot. Good luck with that, Van Damme.

Reward: You've received a Bronze Weapon Box!

New achievement! Loner.

You entered the dungeon without any human companions. Didn't anyone teach you there is safety in numbers?

Reward: None! Haha. You are so dead.

I stared at those last words as they faded away.

You are so dead.

Donut was, again, swiping at the air.

"Menu," I said out loud. Nothing happened.

"Stats." Nothing.

How the hell was I supposed to look at my information? It said I'd "received" multiple . . . what? Loot boxes? That's sure as hell what it sounded like. Which meant I had some sort of inventory. I remembered something from the initial announcement, something about finding a tutorial guild. I looked up at the neon sign about a hundred meters down the dark tunnel. Would that be it?

· I started to shuffle-jog down the tunnel toward the blazing sign. I passed Donut, who sat upon the ground, licking her paw and rubbing it against her forehead. After a moment, the cat seemed to sigh and decide to follow.

The neon sign read **DA TUTORIAL GUILD** with an arrow pointing down a thin, dark alleyway. I shuffled to a stop. The swish of my footfalls echoed in the large, empty tunnel. I peered into the darkness. It was pitch-black in there.

Behind me, Donut meowed with concern.

I stepped into the alley.

New achievement! Fall into an Obvious Trap.

    Reward: Well, if there's a heaven, and if you haven't been too much of an asshole, maybe they'll let you in. Because you about to meet your Maker.

Three lights flipped on, blinding me. I covered my eyes and took a step back. Something mechanical hissed, and what sounded like a steam engine roared to life. I heard laughter, high-pitched and squealing.

I turned, and I ran. Both of my pink Crocs went flying as I turned down the main tunnel, heading away from where I'd come down the stairs. Donut yowled and rushed after me.

I hazarded a look over my shoulder and saw the contraption rocket out of the alleyway, almost crash into the far wall, and then slowly start to back up and turn, facing me.

The machine was the size of a tractor and ran on treads, like a tank. The thing was built out of mismatched rusting hunks of metal, and it looked as if it would fall apart at any moment. A spinning spike-covered wheel dominated the front of the death machine. On top of the tractor three green-hued humanoid monsters stood, screaming and pointing in my direction. Each of these monsters looked to be about four feet tall and was dressed in leathery rags. One appeared to be wearing a kitchen pot on his head. He grunted and screamed as he worked the controls for the tall machine. Black smoke billowed from several pipes. The spinning wheel whirred even faster as the machine righted itself and started barreling toward me.

A tooltip popped up.

Goblin Murder Dozer. Contraption.
A goblin-built, steam-powered machine designed to mow down and slaughter unsuspecting dungeon crawlers. I hope you're up-to-date with your tetanus shots.

Three more tooltips popped up over the three riders. Two of them read:

Goblin. Level 2.
Small, green, and smart. What goblins lack in physical strength, they make up for in pure spunk.

The third goblin, the one with the pot on his head and driving the machine, had a different description:

Goblin Engineer. Level 3.
Engineers. The incels of the goblin world. They have a hard time finding a date, which makes them extra angry. If there are any females in your party, they will attack them first.

I didn't have time to think about the stupidity of the jokes or the fact I was, for the first time, looking upon a group of real, live monsters trying to kill me. I rushed down the hallway and reached another junction. I could go three ways: forward, right, or left. Right was another half-lit hallway about half as wide as the last, but still plenty big enough for the goblins to follow. Left led into a tight, dark hall that'd be way too thin for the bulldozer.

The obvious choice would be to flee down the dark hallway. I paused. It was *too* obvious of a choice. I sensed another trap. I couldn't go straight because the next junction was too far away, and the machine would catch me for sure.

I turned right. Donut followed, choosing to stay by my side, which was very un-Donut-like behavior.

This hall was only as wide as a regular road with a smooth, fifteen-foot ceiling. Green lichenlike growths glowed on the brick walls and ceilings, giving the tunnel an odd glow. Behind me, the goblins squealed as they struggled to maneuver the murder dozer. The thing had a wide turning radius, and it would take them at least a minute to pursue.

Ahead, another group of junctions appeared. But just before the intersection, I spied a single plain wooden door built into the wall. A simple sign was attached to the wall above the door. The words were painted the same color as the dark red bricks of the wall, and I could barely read it. It read **TUTORIAL GUILD**. The words were in that same odd language.

The moment I read the sign, a glowing green box appeared, highlighting the name.

New achievement! You've Discovered and Read an Official Dungeon Sign.
Wow. You can read. Whoopee.
Reward: All official dungeon signage will now be highlighted and easier to spot. Nearby guilds will appear on your minimap.

A minimap? I really needed to figure this out. Behind me, the murder dozer had gotten stuck on the corner, and one of the level two goblins was shouting and beating on the pot helmet of the engineer with what looked like a stick. The third looked at me and shook a fist.

Would they follow me into the guild? I didn't know. I grasped the brass door handle and tried to turn it.

It didn't open. Locked.

"What the hell?" I said. I banged on the wooden door.

"Hey," I called. "Is there anybody in there?"

The two level two goblins seemed to give up on waiting for the bulldozer to negotiate the tight turn, and they hopped off and started jogging toward me. They were unarmored, but both wielded what appeared to be wooden sticks with a pineapple on the end of it. They'd catch up in a minute. Next to me, Donut started to growl and hiss.

From behind the door I heard the rattling of chains and turning of locks. The door cracked, only pulling open part way. A single chain remained, keeping the door from opening farther.

A bearded ratlike creature appeared in the doorway. I could barely make out his features, but he was about a head shorter than me. So taller than the goblins, but not by much.

"Whaddya want?" the voice said. "You mobs ain't allowed in here. You know that!"

"Hey, this is a tutorial guild, right? The thing said I was supposed to go in here."

The eye widened as it looked at me.

"You're . . . you're a crawler? Wait." The rat creature stepped back as if to get a better look at me. I was immediately reminded of Master Splinter the rat sensei from *Teenage Mutant Ninja Turtles.* "You are! By his left tit, we opened up and I didn't even notice! I must have slept through the announcement. Nobody tells old Mordecai anything! There used to be a newsletter. It was delivered every few cycles, reliable as can be. But then it just stopped. Budget cuts, I'm guessing. They're always cutting corners. I thought we weren't opening for another two years!"

"Hey, let me in!" I interrupted. I turned to face the two goblins who jogged to a stop. One moved to my left; the other moved to cut off my retreat.

"Open the damn door!" I cried.

One of the goblins said something to the rat man behind the door, whose name appeared to be Mordecai. I couldn't understand the goblin language. It was grunts and squeaks. Mordecai responded in the goblin language. They both laughed.

"Sorry, Crawler. You took too long," Mordecai said through the chained door. "I can't open up if there are mobs directly outside. Rules are rules."

"*I* took too long?" I said. I moved to a fighting stance. One of the goblins feinted, swinging at me with his club. The pineapple at the end of the club fell off when he swung it, and it hit the ground with a splat. The goblin cursed and kicked it away. I took a step back. Donut stood between my legs, hissing and spitting.

"At least tell me how to open these damn loot boxes!"

Mordecai was silent for a moment, as if he was contemplating on whether or not to tell me.

"It's in the Awards and Boxes tab of your inventory menu," the rat man said. "But you can't access it yet, kid."

"How do I get access to the inventory menu, then?"

The second goblin—the one who still had a pineapple on the end of his stick—swung at me, missing by a wide margin. Up close, the goblins looked much like they did in movies and video games. Short, green, mostly bald with pointed ears, angular faces, and sharp teeth. I briefly wondered on that. It seemed the aliens, or whatever, knew a whole lot about Earth mythology and lore.

Far behind him, the murder dozer had finally backed up properly and had straightened out. It rumbled down the hallway toward us.

"Yeah, you gotta complete the tutorial."

The pineapple goblin swung at me again. I waited until the club passed the apex of its arc and stepped in. I hit the goblin square in the nose with a jab and then a left hook to its right temple. It crumpled to the ground in a heap. A bar appeared over the creature's head the moment I hit it. A health bar, I realized. It hadn't appeared until it took damage. The bar went down more than halfway, turning from green to red. The goblin had more than half of its life drained.

I'd clocked it pretty good, but not that good. It was like I'd just punched a ten-year-old.

The second goblin looked at his friend, open-mouthed, then turned and ran back toward the dozer.

My fists ached. I hadn't been in an actual physical fight in years. Most of my time as a coastguardsman was aboard a cutter as an MK—a technician. I was never involved face-to-face with any sort of real law enforcement. That said, most people I encountered who'd never been in the service didn't realize that we trained as much as we did. People thought of us as glorified lifeguards. They had no idea how much we trained in hand-to-hand combat.

"How the hell do I do that if you don't open the door!" I yelled as I kicked the downed goblin in the ribs. I felt a satisfying *crunch*. "Can't you just let me have access now?"

"It doesn't work that way, kid," Mordecai said. "We can't just have untrained crawlers wandering around the dungeon, you know. Besides, you can't open boxes unless you're in a safe zone. And unless you're a complete idiot, you can probably guess you're not in a safe zone right now."

The goblin's health bar had moved deeper into the red, but he wasn't dead yet. A distant part of me seemed horrified that I was planning on killing this thing. Despite his weapon, he was incredibly easy to hurt. But one glance up at the bulldozer, which had stopped to pick up the second goblin, relieved me of any potential regret. I put my hands on either side of the unconscious goblin's head and I smashed down on the stones. I smashed down again and again until the health bar completely drained away.

"Hey, hey!" Mordecai yelled. "Hey, stop!"

"Whose side are you on anyway?" I asked, whirling on the creature.

But then I realized the rat wasn't talking to me. "You can't come in here!" he was saying, his back now turned.

Donut. He was talking to the goddamned cat. She had decided she'd had enough of this hallway and wandered into the guild through the cracked door.

A whole wall of **New Achievement** notifications appeared along with a couple other, new notifications, but instead of auto-playing like they did before, they appeared as little messages in the upper left of my screen. I sensed I could mentally click on them, but not now. The AI or whatever the hell was running this circus seemed to know that right now was not an opportune time to cover up half my line of sight with game bullshit. Not with the real danger barreling down on me.

"Open the fucking door!" I cried.

"Kid, get your creature!" Mordecai said, turning toward me, a strange hint of panic in the rat's voice. "I'll get in trouble if they find out I let a crawler sneak in against the rules."

"Open the door," I repeated. "Look. It's clear, but it won't be in about five seconds. Let me in!"

The door slammed, the last chain rustled, and then it opened all the way. I rushed inside just as the murder dozer barreled by, rolling directly over the bloody corpse of their friend. The brakes screamed, but the dozer continued its forward momentum, sliding on the body as it smeared down the hallway. The two goblins turned and met my eyes as I flipped them both off. They squealed in rage as I slammed the door.

3

THE MOMENT THE DOOR CLOSED, A NOTIFICATION APPEARED.

> Tutorial Guildhall
>> This is a Safe Zone.
>> Warning: level timers are still active.

"I shouldn't have let you in," Mordecai said, wringing his furry hands. I examined the rat creature. He wore a black vest and blue pants. He had a pair of well-worn sandals on his feet. An info box popped up.

> Mordecai—Rat Hooligan. Level 50.
>> Guildmaster of this guildhall.
>> This is a Non-Combatant NPC.
>> Hooligans are the smartest, fastest, and ugliest of the Rat-Kin race. While not as roided-out as a Rat Brute, or as *Imma fireball yo ass* as a Rat Shaman, Rat Hooligans offer the best of both worlds. They are physically strong, and they have a decent grasp of magic.

I closed out the box. Through the door, I could still hear the screech of goblin machinery just outside.

I mentally clicked on the first of several information boxes cluttering my vision.

Error. You may not access this until you have completed the tutorial.

All the boxes disappeared, swooping away into a single folder item that started to blink.

I stood in a wide room about the size of a classroom. A fireplace and bed dominated one side of the room. Several shelves dotted the walls on the left half of the room, filled with random objects and a few framed photographs of birdlike creatures. The other half of the room was nothing but a well-worn and oval-shaped gray carpet and an empty desk. A half dozen classroom-style chairs lay scattered about. I turned back to the door.

"Is this the only way out of here?" I asked.

"What?" Mordecai asked. The rat wasn't paying attention to me. He was focused on the cat.

"Yo," I said. "Morty. Is this the only exit?"

"It's Mordecai, kid. And yes, yes. Of course."

"Are those green assholes going to still be waiting for me when I get out of here?"

Donut jumped up on a high shelf and knocked a vase over. Ash spilled out.

"Mom!" Mordecai cried, running to the shelf, shooing the cat away. He reached up for the shelf, but he couldn't reach. "Damn this body." He turned back to me. "Can you just grab that thing for me? Get him out of here?" Mordecai sneezed. "I think I might be allergic."

I didn't think he was sneezing because of the cat but because of the gray cloud of dust that had formed around the spilled ash.

"Holy shit, man," I said. *Be careful,* I warned myself. *He doesn't seem too tough, but he's level 50. That's gotta mean he's a powerful bastard.* "Can you help me? Are they going to wait for me or not?"

"Yes. No. Probably. Well, it's complicated. One might wait. But one will definitely go back to their clan and call the others. You smashed that poor goblin's head right in. Give them an hour and the whole family will be out there."

Across the room, Donut discovered the fireplace, which crackled merrily. The cat sat in front of it, lifted her leg, and started licking herself.

Shit. "Okay," I said. "Don't you dare lock this door."

I grasped the handle and went back outside.

I barely had time to hear the rat say, "You're tracking my mother's ashes all over . . ." before I slammed the door.

The goblin tractor had overshot the doorway by about ten meters and was in the middle of a wide turn, trying to come back the way it had come. The engineer had driven the tractor right into the wall. The spinning wheel sparked as the spikes shredded against the stone. The dead goblin remained smeared over the tiles. The corpse looked more like a party-sized sausage and green pepper pizza that had been run over a few times.

Both of the remaining goblins had their backs turned to me. I sprinted toward the vehicle.

The murder dozer had a small ladder near the back. It looked as if it was made of bones tied with rope. One of the goblins would turn at any moment. I had to get them now. If one of them got away and warned the other members of its "clan" or whatever, I'd be screwed. I *needed* this tutorial guild, so I only had one choice.

The jagged bones of the ladder ripped into my bare feet as I pulled myself up. I stifled a cry. I jumped onto the top of the metallic, whirring contraption.

The murder dozer screamed so loudly that neither had noticed me. The whole top of the machine was nothing but a fur-lined recessed hole with benches running the length. Despite the fur, the ground was hot on my feet, almost burning. It smelled of scorched tar and animal musk. The machine could probably carry about fifteen or so goblins, not including the driver, who had a seat up front. A dozen levers and spigots and vibrating handles extended from the floor in the cockpit area. The controls all vibrated and bounced up and down. The pot-wearing goblin sat in the seat, screaming and grunting something as he twisted and turned and pulled on levers. Smoke billowed and steam hissed from multiple pipes. The whole machine vibrated like a boiler about to blow.

The smooth, rocky ceiling of this tunnel was much lower than the long main hallway leading off the stairs. When I stood to my full height, I could reach up and touch it. Barely. It still amazed me, the idea of an entire world made up of these hallways and paths.

I rushed forward and grasped onto the regular goblin, who still clutched his pineapple-less stick in his hand. The creature barely weighed anything, surprising me. I picked him up as he grunted in surprise. He unsuccessfully attempted to hit me with his stick. With all of my strength, I threw the goblin forward. He rocketed out of the passenger area of the dozer.

The screaming monster sailed directly over the head of the engineer, who was only now starting to react. The flying goblin crashed onto the tunnel wall, then bounced back, landing directly on the spinning front blades. A spray of red showered over the both of us.

The final goblin snarled, and quick as a whip pulled a small, curved blade from a sheath on his side. He jumped from his chair and rushed at me.

Oh fuck.

The monster moved much more quickly than I anticipated, surprising me. I had to remember this was a different class than the last two, and he was a level higher. Two levels higher than myself.

This was a dumb idea. What was it that Bea always said? *"You just jump headlong into things without thinking it through"*?

I kicked at the goblin with my bare foot. With nobody at the controls, the tractor continued to whine and shred at the dungeon wall. The vibrations got worse by the moment. Soon the whole thing was bucking like a washing machine with a rock inside it.

The goblin was yelling something at me in its guttural language.

"You're in my world now!" I yelled back at him. "You need to speak *my* language, you weird green piece of shit."

To my surprise, the goblin grinned. I could tell he understood me. The little monster switched the knife back and forth between hands. "*You're* not speaking your language," he said. "You're speaking Syndicate Standard, you idiot slave. They programmed it into your brain. Do you really think you'll survive past . . ."

The goblin never finished the sentence. As he was distracted with his own soliloquy, I leaped forward, snatched the pot off his head, and clobbered him with it. Sharp little teeth went flying. The goblin stumbled. I smacked him again. He careened off the side of the tractor. His health bar appeared after I'd smacked him the first time, but it was still well in the green. He splatted to the ground, groaning. His knife went flying.

I peered over the edge. The goblin lay on his back. The tractor continued to spin and buck, but it was edging in the opposite direction. The goblin's health was still three-quarters full, but he'd had the wind knocked out of him.

The goblin started to sit up and I threw the pot at him. To my utter astonishment, I clobbered him right in the forehead. He cried out, his hands reaching to grasp the new wound.

I gauged the distance. It wasn't very far. Like maybe seven, eight feet. I'd done that plenty of times as a kid.

What the hell? I jumped off the murder dozer, aiming both feet toward the chest and stomach of the still-recovering goblin.

I'm not sure if I mentioned this earlier, but this is important information right here. I stand six foot, three inches tall. I weigh about 230 pounds, and while I wasn't in nearly as good shape as I was while I was on active duty, I'd been hitting the gym three times a week for years, building my muscle mass. I'd always been blessed with one of those bodies that naturally held muscle well. My dad was a linebacker. Hell, even my mom was five foot ten. And *her* dad had played center for Oregon State before becoming a prison guard.

So, what I'm getting at is that I'm a large dude. I have a lot of bulk. The goblin was small, and he had hardly any mass at all. The effect of me jumping onto him from high above was like someone smashing a fat jelly donut with a sledgehammer. The little dude didn't have a chance. Goo spurted out of the goblin from every orifice.

The murder dozer started to whine even louder. I looked down at what I'd done, and I suddenly felt sick to my stomach. More notifications appeared on my screen. A tooltip popped up, appearing in my peripheral vision. I turned to look.

Goblin Murder Dozer—Boiler Breach Imminent.

A countdown timer appeared below the text. It was at 12 seconds and counting down.

Son of a bitch. It's gonna blow.

I turned back toward the room, a mere thirty meters down the hall. Was that too close? I didn't have time to think about it. I ran, slipping and sliding on the tiles as I booked it back to the room. I ripped open the door and jumped inside. I slammed the door and braced for impact.

Bam! The world shook. The door bucked, throwing me forward onto the floor of the guildhall. My ears rang. But the door held, and I didn't seem to be otherwise injured. Donut was in the corner of the room, poofed out and hissing.

"What the bloody hell did you do, kid?" Mordecai asked, looking over me at the door. "That gate is capable of holding back a kinetic strike from a star destroyer. I'd never seen anything shake it that much."

"Huh," I said, sitting up. My ears continued to ring. "That goblin bulldozer thing got stuck against the wall, and then it blew up."

Mordecai nodded slowly. "A boiler breach, then. The local shaman probably enchanted it in case it ever exploded. It would have focused the energy from the blast at the closest non-goblin. You're lucky you were behind that door. A focused explosion, even a small one, has a lot more energy than you might think."

Having decided the commotion was over, Donut left the corner and returned to her spot in front of the fire. Her normally poofy exterior remained extra puffed out, and her tail swished up and down. I could tell the cat was pissed off.

"Your creature crapped in my mother's ashes," Mordecai said, shaking his head. "This is so not worth it. Not worth it at all."

"So, Mr. Training Guild," I said, leaning against the wall. My feet ached. My heart continued to thrash in my chest. I was covered in goblin blood. It felt as if I had raw hamburger meat stuck between my toes. I shuddered. *I need to get shoes. Shoes and pants.* "What the hell is going on? What's with the dungeon? Is everyone really dead? How do I work this shit?"

A million other questions popped into my head. I knew he could probably snap and break me in half, but I had an overwhelming urge to grab the rat man by his stupid vest and shake him until all the answers tumbled out of him. "Also, who the hell are you? Why are you here? What's really . . ."

Mordecai held up his hands. "Okay, okay, slow down, kid. I know you're confused. I've been in your position. All will be explained. That's why I'm here. But before I start, I need to explain something to you two." The rat looked over at the cat, who glared back at him. "My name is Mordecai, and I am what's called a Non-combatant NPC. I am like you. I'm a person whose world was displaced. This was many, many solars ago. I was a dungeon crawler just like you. I made it all the way down to floor 11, and I knew I would never make it any farther than that. Once you descend to floor 10, you're given several options to exit the dungeon. The deeper you go, the better those options are." He walked over to the shelf with the upset vase, and he picked up a framed photo of one of the bird creatures. He handed it to me. It looked remarkably like a normal framed photo. But the material was peculiar, and the photo was cut oddly, oval-shaped with the corners lopped off.

"That's what I really look like. This is a photo of my brother. I was born a skyfowl, but I became a Changeling when I reached floor three of the dungeon. I switch form every time my guildhall is moved."

Mordecai continued. "When a dungeon first opens, I work in a guild such as this. Later on, after the third floor collapses, my room here is transported to a much deeper level, and my form is changed again. I spend most of my time working a magic guild, which is a place one can go to pick spells and train if they've chosen a magic-based path. Though over the years I've only had a handful of people actually make it that far. Most crawlers don't make it past the tenth floor."

"So, a Changeling is a shapeshifter?" I examined the picture. I couldn't tell if it was a photograph or a painting or something else. The eyes of the image seemed to bore into me. It was a golden eagle–like creature. Wings, angel-like, were folded on its back.

"Yes," Mordecai said. He sighed. "They re-created my home for me, including all my possessions, when I decided to become a guild-master. I had but a few moments to grab anything I wanted before they evaporated it all. Now, every time I move to a new world, they change my shape. It's something different every time, but it's always a type of mob from the current floor of the dungeon. I don't know why."

"I don't believe any of this," I said. "So you're aliens? You're all from a different world? Then how does the game or whatever know how we talk? Some of those last notifications mentioned Jean-Claude Van Damme and incels and steroids!"

Mordecai nodded. "You're getting ahead of yourself. Each dungeon is specially built for the world it inhabits. And they spend a lot of time . . . *a lot* . . . of time making sure the locals understand the game and the notifications. They go for authenticity. I'm not really supposed to tell you any of this stuff, but I figure if you're going to be stumbling around out there, you need to know what's happening."

"I still don't know what's happening," I said, frustration rising further.

Mordecai shook his head. "You humans are all the same. This is the seventh or eighth human-seeded world, and it's always the same. You always want to know why. Why can't you just accept your circumstances and move on? My people, the skyfowls, we generally last much longer than you humans. You know why? Because we roll with it."

I didn't say anything for several moments. There was a lot to parse there. "Human-seeded world?" Did that mean that conspiracy-spouting asshole on TV with the crazy hair was correct? That humans weren't unique, but a crop, left to grow unattended until, until . . . *this?*

Mordecai saw my look of bewilderment and sighed. "Okay, okay. I'll give you the quick version," he said. He pulled a seat and sat down. He gestured to another chair situated in the center of the round carpet. "You might as well get comfortable."

4

"THERE ARE SIX BASIC STARTER SPECIES THE SYNDICATE USES TO seed worlds. Humans are one of them. They find a compatible world, sprinkle the humans on there, wait a couple thousand years, and then reveal themselves to the largest settlement. They usually do this as soon as civilization starts to take hold, but long before any sort of industrial revolution. As long as there's a working government, this counts as 'First Contact.' In a legal sense, I mean, which gives them leave to wait a couple thousand additional years, come back, and strip the planet dry."

"How?" I asked. "It all happened in a second!"

Mordecai shrugged. "Technology beyond your understanding seems like magic. So as far as you're concerned, in this place, it *is* magic. It's like that *Wizard of Oz* movie, but you'll never get to peek behind the curtain."

"You've seen *The Wizard of Oz*?"

"Guildmasters prepare for years for each new dungeon world. Kid, I have been preparing for this longer than you have been alive. The advance team arrived in your 1930s, I believe. Whenever that book came out, *The Hobbit*. I left the last system and entered the prep phase in your year 1964. I know this world and your customs just as well as you do. I even once got to shapeshift into a human and go out into the world. I went to a Blockbuster Video and stole a bunch of James Bond tapes. I was so happy once you guys started digitizing everything."

"How long have you been a guildmaster?"

Mordecai shook his head. "You don't even want to know. So anyway, your planet defaulted on claiming Earth as a sovereign entity. You had 50 local years since first contact, and first contact was several thousand years ago. Whenever those pyramid things were built. The Borant Corporation has a huge backlog of worlds to mine, and your time is now."

My head swam. "So, they're taking all of our minerals?"

Mordecai nodded. "Sort of. Borant deals in rare *elements* and the like. What they end up mining will fit on a single transport. I don't know too much about that part of the process. The elements involved are unimportant. It's a big universe out there, and there are plenty of places to mine. That's not why they're really here. While Borant does make a profit on the mining, the real money is in the game. The dungeon."

"How?"

"Are you kidding? The Syndicate consists of over three billion independent star systems. Every season, a new *Dungeon Crawler World* debuts across the net. Quintillions of citizens of the Syndicate become obsessed with the Crawl."

"Wait, so this is like a TV show? Like *Survivor*?"

"Oh, I loved that show. And as far as you're concerned, yes, it's a show like *Survivor*. But it's more a *Running Man* situation than a *Survivor* one."

I leaned back in the chair. *I'm on an alien television show. Holy shit.*

Bea had always wanted to be on television. She'd tried out for countless reality shows. Me? I'd rather have a hot poker stuck through my eye. I briefly wondered where she was, and if she was alive. *Probably not,* I decided. It'd been just past 5 a.m. in the Bahamas when it had happened, which meant she'd probably been asleep in her hotel. Probably in bed with that asshole. And if by some miracle she had survived, there's no way she'd have gone into one of those tunnels.

"So are there people watching right now?" I asked, looking around.

Mordecai put his hands together. "I will get to that in a moment.

It doesn't look like anyone else is going to be joining us anytime soon, so let's get the tutorial started."

Mordecai's right hand glowed for a moment, and I felt that haptic buzz in my brain. Across the room, Donut hissed and batted at the air.

You have been granted access to the Crawler Menu.

My world blinked, and several items appeared in my vision. A long green bar—a health bar, I realized—appeared in the top right. It pushed the timer down a notch. That blinking folder remained in my top left. A small minimap appeared in the bottom right.

"You just received a notification," Mordecai said. "That's called a crawler notification. There are a few different kinds, but that type will only be seen by you. There are also system messages, which everyone sees no matter what floor they're on. Those may be in different voices. There are also floor-specific notifications, et cetera."

"I have a blinking box in my top left," I said.

"Those are game and status change notifications. Probably from your fight outside a few minutes back," Mordecai said. "Don't click it yet. We'll get there. First, I want you to focus on the map on the bottom right. Look right at it, and make sure you're thinking about looking at it."

I did as he asked, and the map got bigger, increasing to fill my entire vision. It was a simple blue-and-gray map showing the hallways and a few random doorways. Most of the area around us wasn't filled in. It only showed the area we'd walked, pushing out about twenty meters in every direction. A green dot sat in the middle, right in the guild. Two additional dots appeared, a blue one and a white one. I focused on the blue dot, and a note appeared above it:

Crawler Princess Donut.

The white dot read:

Guildmaster Mordecai.

The whole room glowed yellow, and when I focused on it, it read:

Tutorial Guild.

A trio of X's appeared outside in the hallway. I mentally clicked on one.

Corpse—Level 2 Goblin.

I mentally clicked away, and the whole map shrank back to normal.

"Good, good," Mordecai said. "So, you're the green dot, the blue dots will be other crawlers, white dots will be NPCs such as myself, and mobs will be red. There are a few other kinds, but you'll figure those out along the way. By the way, no other crawlers or mobs can see your menus, but while you're inside this guild, *I* can see what's on your screen. You are already adept at opening and closing, which is good. Now try focusing on the map again. With your mind, pinch it smaller. And then move it across the screen. That way you can customize your HUD."

It went on like this for a while, him explaining how to open and close menus within my display. I could just think about it, and a whole menu system would pop up, giving me access to several folders. Once I got used to the weirdness of it being in my head, the system was quite intuitive.

The first menu was player stats. Like I mentioned earlier, I've played a handful of computer and tabletop RPGs over the years, so this section wasn't too surprising. My stats were:

Strength: 6
 Intelligence: 3
 Constitution: 5

Dexterity: 5

Charisma: 4

According to Mordecai, I couldn't directly adjust these stats. Not yet. I received three stat points every time I leveled up, but I couldn't distribute them until I picked a race and class. And I couldn't do that until I reached the third floor down. For now, these numbers went up and down on their own based on my inherent, real-life phys-ical and mental attributes. He also added the typical adult human averaged between three and five for each of these first five stats, so my six in strength was good.

I could find items and potions that would either temporarily or permanently adjust these numbers, but for now, there wasn't much I could do about them.

"Why do we have to wait until we go down to the third floor before we get to pick a class?" I asked.

He shrugged. "It takes a lot of energy to run this whole opera-tion. I think they figure if you manage to make it to the third floor, you're worth the investment to transfigure. Class is easy. But chang-ing your race takes some doing. You're being fundamentally changed at the cellular level. That's a lot of effort for someone who's just going to get eaten by a flytrap on the first floor."

I hadn't thought about it until that moment. *I can change into a different type of creature.* If this was a computer game, I'd do it in a second. I never played humans in games if I could help it. But per-manently changing myself into something different? The thought made me ill. It was something I'd have to think about and deal with when I got there.

I grumbled a bit about that three in intelligence. Yeah, I never did too great in math, but I never considered myself a slobbering idiot, either. I could fix most anything electrical after studying it for a bit. My friend Billy Maloney, now that guy was an idiot. Just last week we'd come out of a bar, and he'd peed right on a cop's bicycle while the cop was giving someone else a ticket for drunk and disorderly. *That* guy deserved an intelligence of three, maybe two.

Billy is dead. He was still in jail. He'd had a warrant for failure to appear, so they'd taken him in. *He's dead like everyone else in the world.* I pushed it away.

After I complained about my intelligence score to Mordecai, using the Billy example, he said, "Intelligence told you that bike belonged to a police officer. *Wisdom* told you not to urinate upon it. We all have a wisdom stat, but it doesn't appear on that list. It used to, but they discovered changing one's wisdom greatly changed their personality, so it's no longer adjustable. I do not know what this Billy's intelligence is, but I guarantee his wisdom is not a five. Worry not about an intelligence of three unless you're seeking a magic-based class. Your best bet is something that focuses on strength."

That mollified me while Mordecai moved me to the next menu.

"This next screen is the single-most important menu in the entire game. Your life depends on these numbers."

It was called Ratings. I clicked on it, and the list took me aback:

RATINGS
Views: 0
Followers: 0
Favorites: 0
Patrons: 0

Apparently the first level of the dungeon was off-limits to live viewers, so these stats wouldn't move until I descended to the second floor.

As of right now, no viewers had access to anything that was going on. However, Borant would release an edited highlights reel over the next day or so. If I managed to get shown during the "premiere" of the show or any of the regular update episodes, it would be like hitting the lottery. Featured crawlers always gained billions of views and millions of followers right out the gate.

Given the sheer number of people in the world, I seriously doubted I was going to be featured, so if I wanted to survive, I needed to have what Mordecai called "Chutzpah" and "The 'it' factor."

"You need to stand out. You can't just kill that shambling acid impaler and walk away. You need to kill it with style, with excitement. Maybe you can come up with a catchphrase. During my crawl, I managed to accumulate almost 30 million followers and four patrons. That's the only way I survived."

"Excuse me, a shambling what?"

"A shambling acid impaler. The second floor will be lousy with them. They trounce about on four legs, are green, hairy. Spit darts at you that melt your skin off. Awful creatures."

"Jesus Christ," I said. I still felt as if this was all a dream.

Mordecai snapped. "Hey. Kid. Pay attention. The monsters aren't important. Well, they are. But this part especially is more important."

"Okay, okay," I said, waving him along. "Keep going."

He went on to explain how viewership worked. Once I hit the second floor, watchers from across the universe had the ability to tune into any crawler they wished. Borant would continue to air highlights. So the longer I survived, the better my chances at getting featured. Anytime someone watched me for just about eight seconds or so, it counted as a view. This stat didn't help or hurt me, but it was a good indicator of how "interesting" I was.

"You might not like it," Mordecai said, "but pay careful attention when I tell you this. Obtaining patrons is crucial to your survival. There is plenty of great loot in the dungeon that'll help you survive, but the best loot comes from benefactors. Patrons. Views lead to followers. If you're being followed, it means the viewer has bookmarked your crawler ID. They can look in on you whenever they want. Following leads to favorites. If you're favorited, that's a good thing. It means the viewers are getting live updates on your stats and condition. They get notifications if you're fighting. If someone has favorited you, they really want to know how you're doing. Viewers only get a certain number of favorites, so consider it an honor.

"But," Mordecai continued, "ultimately, it's all about the patrons. Lots of favorites will always lead to patrons. Patrons are *usually* organizations, not individuals. They'll see someone has a lot of favorites, and they'll sponsor you. It's an advertising thing. They sponsor you by purchasing boxes for you. There are dozens of types of boxes, and each type of box has six quality tiers. Bronze, then Silver, then Gold, then Platinum, then Legendary, then Celestial."

"Yeah," I said drily. "You wouldn't let me open my boxes yet. Can I do it now?"

"Hold up, kid," Mordecai said. "We have a process here. We'll get there in a minute." He continued. "Most patrons can only afford, or are willing to, send you silver or gold boxes. Bronze boxes tend to be crap, but anything higher usually has some good stuff in it. Some of the richer patrons may even send you platinum boxes, though the cost for them has got to be astronomical. That said, patrons are the only ones who can send what are called benefactor boxes. Those contain the rarest items. So even a Bronze Benefactor Box is better than a plain Gold Adventurer Box. A benefactor box may contain items from the patron's home world. You will never find a pulse rifle or automated power armor in any sort of box in the World Dungeon, but it's possible to get one from a patron. Does that make sense?"

"None of this shit makes sense," I said. "But yes, I understand what you're saying. I'm on an intergalactic game show, and I have to be an obnoxious show-off in order to get eyes on me. And once I do have eyes on me, I might get a loot box with toilet paper in it. Does that about sum it up?"

Mordecai clapped his rat hands. "Yes! But toilet paper is complimentary. Restrooms are liberally populated throughout the map. It's the only place the viewer cameras can't follow you."

"Are you serious?"

Mordecai nodded. "Oh, I'm serious. The last dungeon Borant managed didn't have rest areas, and the crawlers were pissing and crapping all over the place. Crawlers lose viewers when they're shitting in the middle of a hallway. It's gross."

"And what does Borant get out of this?"

Mordecai's demeanor changed. It was a subtle thing, but he stiffened slightly. His voice took on an oddly formal tone.

"In addition to the mining income we already discussed, the Borant Corporation receives advertising dollars, a stipend from the Syndicate government, and a commission on every credit spent by patrons." He waited a moment, a long moment, before adding, "Also, it should be noted that every time a crawler mentions the name of either the interstellar government or the organization sponsoring the current crawl, the system AI will record the interaction for review. If it is found a crawler is disparaging either of these two entities, especially while on camera with live viewers, the crawler's experience may be 'accelerated.'"

I nodded. "Got it." I had no doubt that "accelerated" meant nothing good.

We spent the next several minutes going over a few other menu items. I had a health menu like in other games. Overall health was a single green bar, but in the menu, it was a more extensive pie chart. It indicated any active conditions and debuffs plus I could drill down to specific areas. Healing was sped up in the dungeon. I had recently been cured of several issues I didn't even know I had, like abrasions at the bottom of my feet and on my hands, frostbite, and the start of an infection from when Donut had bitten me. Health ticked up on its own slowly, based on my constitution level.

Also, if I went down a set of stairs to the next floor, my health points would instantly fill all the way up on their own. Another way to heal myself was via spells, potions, and scrolls. But there was no respawning.

Dead was dead.

After that was my skills menu. This section just went on and on and on. There seemed to be an infinite number of pages. If I didn't have the skill, I couldn't read what it said. It was still listed there, but the words were blurred out. Literally hundreds of pages would scroll by before I saw anything. Mordecai had me change the view to skills I did have, and that list was just as long. I had things like **Breathing: 3. Walking: 4. Operating a Sony Brand RMVLZ620 Universal Remote Control: 1.** The list just never ended. He had me uncheck a box, and most of those skills disappeared. What was left was still several pages long. Then another check, and anything with a skill of one or two disappeared. What was left were things like **Unarmed Combat: 3, Basic Electrical Repair: 6, Swimming: 4.** Nothing was over five other than Electrical Repair. Most everything was three.

"This is a good start," Mordecai said. "I'm impressed, kid. You're proficient with several Earth weapons, all firearms. But since you didn't bring any, you'll want to train with some of the dungeon-based weapons. We'll see if you have anything good in any of the boxes when we get to it."

"And you'll train me how to use them?"

"Nope," Mordecai said. "Not my job. There are guildhalls scattered around that'll help you level up the skills—especially magic ones. But the best way is always to practice."

"Is there a store?" I asked. "The AI thing said something about a store."

"That's when you reach the third floor," Mordecai said. "There's a structure to the third floor, and random stores will start populating the map after that. You can also trade with other crawlers or friendly mobs, if you can find any. Mobs on the second floor will start dropping gold."

Next was the magic menu, which was complicated as shit. It was also one of the most surreal parts of this adventure so far. I was given a simple healing spell and a pool of mana points that appeared in my top right underneath the health bar. Because my intelligence was only three, I only had three magic points. The healing spell cost two. Magic points naturally refilled about one every hour.

I had a hotlist of ten spaces along the bottom of my screen, and there I could add potions or spells or other special items. Mordecai had me place the healing spell in spot number one. I could mentally click it to cast it. The spell was only a level one basic healing spell, and it would heal about 20% of my health.

He made me try it, even though my health was already at the top. I cast the spell, and my whole body glowed red, my magic bar went down by two-thirds, and nothing else happened.

"If you were injured or sick, you'd feel much better after that," Mordecai said.

A voice boomed, interrupting the tutorial. This was yet another speaker. Not the game show host that usually spoke, but a distinctly female voice. She spoke almost casually, like a manager addressing a store filled with employees just before they opened for business.

Hello, Crawlers! The dungeon is now sealed. We have a diverse group joining us this season, and we are very happy to have you here. We had just under 13 million human crawlers make it through the gates and into the dungeon. We are already down to under 10 million. A quick note, the entrances to the second floor will not open up until the introductory episode of *Dungeon Crawler World* tunnels, which will be in approximately 30 of your hours. Once that happens, the entrances to the second level will populate. There will be no lag time for the appearance of additional levels. On behalf of the Borant Corporation I wanted to thank you for volunteering, and I wish you all good luck and a happy crawl.

Ten million people. It was more than I expected. But still, three million additional people dead in a matter of minutes. The number was so huge, it lost meaning.

The announcement made me think of the way the dungeon was set up. The 5-day countdown timer continued to tick away.

"Do we get five days before they destroy each floor?"

Mordecai shook his head. "No," he said. "It's usually more each floor down. Later on, it'll depend on a lot of factors, such as ratings, how many crawlers are left, et cetera. But they usually add about five days each time. So you'll probably have ten days for the second floor and then fifteen for the third. The countdown doesn't start until the previous floor collapses."

"How hard is it to find the staircases?"

"It can be tricky. It's not too difficult for the first few levels, but you'll want to focus on finding items or skills that'll help you find the next entrance down. This first floor is huge, as you can imagine. It's almost the size of the surface of your planet. They won't tell you this, but it's not all connected. It's not like you can wander about and run into someone from China. That'll change once you hit the third floor. You'll see if you survive that long. Starting on the fourth floor, each level will have a random theme and will encompass significantly less area. Entrances will stop populating in random places. They'll be guarded. You'll have to complete quests or defeat bosses to get to them. I had barely made it to floor 11. And when I saw what guarded the entrances to level 12 . . . I knew it wouldn't be worth it."

"What was it?" I asked.

He shook his head. "It doesn't matter. It'll be different here. It's different every time."

From there we resumed the tutorial. We went over the party menu. If I had been accompanied by a group of people, we could manage our party in this menu. Party members shared experience and were able to access a group chat feature. Anyone who entered the dungeon at the same time as anyone else was automatically grouped together, and as a result, I had a party of two. Me and Donut.

The cat continued to lounge in front of the fire. It appeared she'd fallen asleep.

"So, my cat," I said. "The system has given her a crawler name and designator. Does that mean she's getting all these special achievements and loot boxes, too?"

"Yes. Any biological creature above a certain weight who enters the dungeon is assigned a crawler ID. But one needs at least an intelligence of two to qualify for training, and if you can't do training, your inventory doesn't get turned on, which allows you to access your boxes. Otherwise, they're designated as pets. All the other ones, like wild animals who happen to make it inside, very rarely make it past the first floor. We'll get to the pet menu after we open up your inventory, which is the next step."

Now that we'd put about twenty minutes between my earlier mention of Borant, I wanted to continue our previous conversation.

"Before we do that, I have a couple questions about the people running the show."

He paused. "What is it?"

"Are they always listening?"

"Listening, yes. Paying attention, not necessarily. They expect a certain amount of . . . gnashing of teeth . . . amongst the crawlers. And we NPCs are required to say the name of the organizers multiple times during the training, so we're mostly ignored. Mostly. You really need to be careful once you start collecting followers. They know they're sadistic assholes, but they don't want you saying it on camera. They take their image quite seriously."

"I'm no math expert, but when the dungeon opened, there were tons of the glowing entrances in my city. They said there were only 150,000 of them seeded around the world. It seemed like . . . too many for my area."

"They have certain benchmarks they try to reach. The AI closely monitors the launch of the game, but there are loopholes. The entrances are rarely distributed equally. Ten million crawlers upon the sealing of the dungeon is pretty typical. So however it happened, it wasn't on accident. Like I said, they spend a lot of time preparing for each dungeon."

"Yeah, you mentioned that," I said. "You've been here for decades. Does this show really only air once every 90 years or so?"

"No, not at all," Mordecai said. "Different corporations run each season, which appear about every two and a quarter of your years. My employer usually has about five forward teams working at any given time, and they get chosen to run a season about one in fifteen."

"So with different corporations running each season and different worlds, uh, crawling, then is every season vastly different?"

"Oh yes. The Squim Conglomerate chooses a different game completely, for example. It's a Battle Royale–style fight. An entire world, and it all comes down to one champion. It's good for ratings, but it doesn't make them much money from what I understand. My company is known for making the most elaborate, most entertaining dungeons."

Wonderful. "And you?" I asked. "Are you stuck here for the rest of your life?"

"No," Mordecai said, smiling sadly. He looked down at the framed picture of the eagle creature I had placed on the floor. "This is my last tour. Once this nightmare is over, I become a full citizen, I receive a moderate stipend, and I am free to make my way into the universe."

"Will you go back to your home planet?"

"No," he said. "It's not open to me."

"What about the people who didn't go into the dungeon on your world?"

He paused. "We really need to get back to the tutorial."

"Okay, but what if someone won the dungeon, made it past level 18. The message said if that happens, they gain control of the world. Maybe your world is under control of one of your people."

The rat creature grunted. "Remember how I said I made it down to the eleventh floor?"

"Yeah."

"A handful of crawlers over the centuries have made it that far. One once made it down to 13. One. He died within a half hour of hitting the floor. He was a human, like you. But from another human world. That's the deepest anyone has ever delved, kid. Level 13."

5

"I'VE JUST ACTIVATED YOUR INVENTORY," MORDECAI SAID, WAV-
ing a hand. "This season Borant is trying something a little different."

"Different good or different bad?" I asked, pulling up the menu.

The only thing listed was a handful of loot boxes with **Ready to
Open** next to them.

"Last season, it was a slot-based system. It allowed one to carry
multiple items, but it was limited in capacity and had standard
weight limits. This season, each crawler is given a dimensional inventory and AI cataloging system."

"What does that mean?"

"It's a good thing. Basically, unlimited storage. And if you can
physically lift it off the ground by yourself for about four seconds,
you can put it in your space, no matter how big it is. The only rule
is you can't store living creatures. They will immediately die. Also,
the storage is time locked, so food doesn't go bad. That's a big one.
We had an issue last season with crawlers starving to death. Watching thousands of lethargic, unmoving players as they waited the
timer to run out . . . Yeah. It was no good, so Borant fixed it. Disease
and starvation don't make for compelling drama."

He produced a single glass bottle. It was small, like a third the
size of a Coke bottle. It was red with a cork in it.

"Pick it up and place it in your inventory. A gift from me to you."

I picked it up and examined the item's properties.

Standard Healing Potion.

Increases your health by at least 50%. Doesn't cure poison or other health-seeping conditions such as succubus-inflicted gonorrhea. So remember to wrap it up, bucko.

I pulled up my inventory menu, and an **Add Item to Inventory** button appeared. I clicked it, and the potion vanished. It appeared in my inventory list, which now had both a Potions and a Healing submenus. I mentally clicked on it, and the potion reappeared in my hand.

"Good, good. If you add the potion to your hotlist, you'll drink it without having to actually drink. Remember this, because some of these potions taste like shit. If you straight pull it from the normal inventory, you'll have to pop the cork and swallow. Potions and other like items stack up to 999 a slot, so it's best to stick them in your hotlist. And that's pretty much it. There are a few other quirks regarding inventory, but you'll figure them out along the way."

I put the potion back and then added it to the hotlist next to my healing spell.

"Okay," Mordecai said. "Let's take a look at your current notifications. . . . Holy tits!"

"What? What?" I said, alarmed, looking around. Donut looked up from her spot by the fire and yawned.

"You have a Legendary Pet Box! Why didn't you say so?"

I just looked at him. The urge to punch him in the face returned.

Mordecai shook his head. "Legendary right when he walks in," he grumbled. "Okay. Yes, yes, you do have a lot of boxes. Okay, now that inventory is active, you can pop up your missed notifications. Let's take a look."

I had a line of the notifications. I clicked on the first one.

New achievement! You've Inflicted Damage on a Mob.

Hopefully it won't hit back!

Reward: It's probably going to hit back.

New achievement! You've Killed a Mob!

You're a murderer! He probably had a family!

Reward: You can now gain experience. Get enough of it, and you might even go up a level.

New achievement! You've Killed an Armed Mob with Your Bare Fucking Hands!

Holy crap, dude. That's kinda fucked up.

Reward: You've received a Bronze Weapon Box!

New achievement! You've Killed a Mob a Higher Level Than Yourself!

You're getting the hang of this. Don't let it go to your head.

Reward: You've received a Bronze Adventurer Box!

New achievement! You've Entered a Guildhall!

Congratulations. You know how to open doors.

Reward: That sense of fulfillment you feel? That's reward enough.

New achievement! Podophilia!

You've used your bare feet to crush and kill an opponent! Hey! That's my fetish! Seriously. Keep doing it, and you'll be rewarded. This will help.

Reward: You've received a Gold Shoebox!

New achievement! Boom!

You've caused a wall-shaking explosion within the dungeon! The last time the walls shook like this was when your mom came over for a visit.

Reward: You've received a Silver Goblin Box!

New achievement! Level Up, Baby!

You've received enough experience to gain a level.

Reward: Leveling up is your job. You don't get rewards for doing your job.

Underneath those were a few additional notifications:

You've gained a skill level!
  Pugilism Level 4.
  The art of beating the shit out of your opponents with closed fists.
  Each level of this skill increases your bare-knuckle damage by 25%.

Level Up! You are now level 2.
  Three stat points gained.

Several other skill-based notifications flashed and disappeared before I could read them, likely thanks to my tinkering with the menu earlier. My inventory glowed, and I clicked on it. Several additional loot boxes now appeared on my list.

"You may only open boxes in safe areas," Mordecai said. "All guildhalls are safe areas, but not all safe areas are guildhalls."

"Will they be hard to find? The safe areas, I mean."

"The safe rooms will always appear on your map, even if they're within the fog of war."

"Fog of war?"

"If you haven't visited an area, it won't show the specifics of the hallways, even if it's in the range of your minimap. The fog of war covers places you haven't yet visited. The safe rooms will have restrooms, sleeping cubicles, and some will even have food and fountains with healing potions. Getting to them might be hard, but you'll always know where they are if you get close enough."

"Is there a time limit for staying in one?"

"Nope. But don't forget the level itself is going to collapse in on your head after a certain amount of time. The only way to survive is to keep moving deeper."

"Okay," I said, rubbing my hands together. "Hopefully there are some pants in one of these things. Let's start cracking them open."

"Okay," Mordecai said. "You have 10 loot boxes. That's a lot, but not a crazy amount. Usually people come into the tutorial with two or three. You can hoard them, but when you do decide to open them, you can't pick and choose which ones to open. It's an all-or-nothing thing. There's no real tactical reason to hold on to them since you can't sell or transfer unopened boxes. Also it's important to note that while it's possible to receive unstable or damaged loot, you'll never receive outright cursed loot in a box. But that doesn't mean everything is safe to try on. Always read the descriptions before you activate or wear something. Always, always. No exceptions. Okay, here we go. It's going to open them by tier."

The ten boxes all popped out of my inventory and appeared floating in front of me single file. The first few boxes were about half the size of a military footlocker. Each box had a label floating over it. The first to appear was bronze-colored and had a strange, hedgehog-like animal stenciled on the top.

Bronze Pet Box. (1/10)

The top popped open on its own. The box disappeared in a puff of smoke, and a single rolled-up piece of paper and a small pile of what looked like dry cat food appeared on the floor. Text appeared above each item.

Scroll of *Heal Critter*.
 Pet Biscuit x 10.

The items disappeared and entered my inventory. Before I could open the inventory box to read the description of the scroll, the next box appeared.

Bronze Adventurer Box. (2/10)
   Potion of Healing x 2.
   Common Fingerless Gloves.

After that was

Bronze Weapon Box. (3/10)
   Toad Cudgel.

The "toad cudgel" was a stick. It looked like a three-quarters-length baseball bat shaped by someone who only had a vague idea of what baseball was.

Bronze Weapon Box. (4/10)
   Poker.

This wasn't much better. It was literally a fireplace poker. A wrought iron stick with a screw-on point at the end.

Bronze Adventurer Box. (5/10)
   Potion of Healing.
   Potion of Mana.

These next two boxes were slightly larger and made of silver.

Silver Adventurer Box. (6/10)
   Poison Antidote x 2.
   Crawler Biscuit x 100.
   Torch x 20.

This next silver box looked distinctively different than the last. Like the goblin murder dozer, it appeared cobbled together with random hunks of silver-colored metal. A goblin skull was etched onto the lid.

Silver Goblin Box. (7/10)
    Dynamite x 5.
    Lighter.
    Goblin Pass.

The Goblin Pass took the form of the same goblin-shaped skull from the top of the box. The symbol appeared floating in the air. Instead of adding itself to my inventory, it flew and smacked up against my inner left forearm. I was still wearing my leather jacket, but I could feel it burning against my skin, like I was being branded. The brand also appeared on the exterior of the jacket. The pain quickly abated, and my jacket was otherwise undamaged.

It was time for the good stuff. These next two boxes were bigger yet and glowed with a golden light.

Gold Apparel Box. (8/10)
    Enchanted Nightgaunt Cloak of Stoutness.
    Enchanted Trollskin Shirt of Pummeling.

Beside me, Mordecai gasped the moment the two items appeared. I hoped that was a good thing.

Gold Shoebox. (9/10)
    Enchanted Toe Ring of the Splatter Skunk.

A toe ring? A goddamned toe ring? I needed shoes, damnit! Not a toe ring!

I was so irritated by this prize, I almost missed the opening of the final box. The Legendary Pet Box had the same symbol etched on it as the Bronze Pet Box, but this thing was three times the size. It was made of alternating, intricately carved silver and gold patterns. Clockwork gears spun with a ratcheting *click click click* as the box opened. A musical fanfare sounded.

Legendary Pet Box. (10/10)
    Pet Biscuit x 500.
    Enhanced Pet Biscuit.

"That's it?" I said as the final prizes poofed back into my inventory. "What the hell is an enhanced pet biscuit?"

Mordecai was looking between me and Donut.

"Yeah, kid. You'll want to give your cat that biscuit right now while you're still in the guild."

"What does it do?" I asked. I pulled it out of my inventory. It looked like a cat treat. It was small—smaller than my fingernail—brown, hard, and round with a crumbly texture. I doubted I'd be able to get Donut to eat it. While the cat was always stuffing her face with food, Bea insisted on giving her the wet stuff even though it got all over her face. Donut turned her nose up at most everything else.

I examined the treat's attributes.

Enhanced Pet Biscuit.
    So, it looks like a regular pet biscuit. It's not.
    Feed to your pet at your own risk. What's the worst that can happen?

"Uh, what does it do?" I asked a second time.

"The effects vary," he said. "Regular biscuits feed pet-based classes for a full day. The pets find them delicious. They smell them, and they'll just gobble them up. So make sure you only pull one out at a time. Enhanced treats have over 100 different possible effects. Half of them are good. The rest are . . . neutral . . . or decidedly bad. But if there's a bad outcome, your pet won't attack you if you feed them the treat while you're in a safe zone. Your pet will be teleported outside to a random place within a square mile of here. If you feed it to her while you're out on crawl, and she transforms into a toothed fleshbutcher, you're pretty much fucked. So you should definitely do it now. Either that or save it to sell later. It's worth a couple thousand gold."

Shit. I'd been avoiding thinking about this until now, but what could I do? Donut was a damn cat. It wasn't like she was a mastiff or anything, some sort of pet I could use as protection. Even if I could get her to follow me in the first place, she'd be more a liability than anything.

I felt an obligation to her. I was all she had left in the world. It wasn't logical, I knew. But if I could sell this tiny little treat for a lot of money, I could buy some really useful items. Like shoes and pants.

I rolled the cat treat in my fingers. As awful as it was, it would be best to . . .

"Ow!" I cried as Donut leaped up and ate the treat right from my hand.

Splat! The moment the cat hit the ground, she was transformed into a wet mess of flesh. She splattered like a hunk of hairy, jellied water.

"Donut!" I cried. "What the hell happened to my cat?"

Waiting . . . Waiting . . . appeared over the quivering, shaggy mass.

"Hmm," Mordecai said, coming forward to poke at the blob with his foot. It wiggled. "Transformation. Your creature is being changed somehow. It didn't teleport away, so it's not considered a negative result. Looks like we'll have to wait. I've seen this before a few times. It won't be long. Maybe five to ten minutes."

6

AS WE WAITED FOR MY MUTANT CAT TO EMERGE FROM HER BLOB, I examined my other loot. The fingerless gloves went onto my hands. Of the two weapons, I liked the feel of the cudgel more than that of the poker, which felt like it would bend and break the moment I hit something with it. I examined the cudgel's properties. The game show host AI described it using a caveman voice.

Toad Cudgel
Big stick for bonking. Bonk toad. Bonk mob. Bonk girlfriend and drag back to cave by hair.

I wondered if the metal pot was still out there. It'd be better than this bullshit.

I placed my hand on the symbol branded onto my jacket. An info box popped up.

Goblin Pass.
It's a tattoo! On your forearm! Now you'll never get a good job!
Note: Pass tattoos cannot be hidden unless you purchase a cover-up sleeve. Will show through any armor you may wear.
Removes automatic goblin hostility. Allows for free passage through goblin-controlled territory in the dungeon. Warning: Holding a Goblin Pass will cause natural goblin enemies, such as fairy-class creatures, to deal 20% more damage against you. Still, it looks kinda badass.

I grumbled that the system didn't give me a choice. It just burned it right onto me. I didn't have any tattoos, and I'd never really wanted one. Most everyone I knew had plenty, but I'd never liked the idea. My old man had been covered in them, and it wasn't ever something I associated with being cool.

The black, leathery, and hooded nightgaunt cloak weighed almost nothing. It appeared to be made from the wing of some sort of demon creature. The skin was stretched between rows of long, body-length finger bones. When I put the hood up, I noticed it had pointed ear things on either side.

Enchanted Nightgaunt Cloak of Stoutness.
    The wearer of this cloak gains +4 to Constitution and becomes resistant to poison and ice-based attacks. In addition, the cloak adds Anti-Piercing resistance to all worn armor. It also makes you look like a dollar store Batman. Warning: If a Nightgaunt spies you wearing this, they probably won't be too happy with you.

"This is an extremely valuable cloak," Mordecai said. "But the shirt is better. Much better."

Enchanted Trollskin Shirt of Pummeling.
    The wearer of this shirt gains +7 to the Regeneration skill. In addition, all melee-based damage debuffs such as Stun, Knock-back, Disarm, and Out-of-Breath are negated. The shirt is also quite stylish. Maybe a little too stylish. Unlike most monster-skin apparel items, this shirt will not grant a negative reaction amongst trolls. In fact, lady trolls might just want to haul you away for some one-on-one time if they see you in this.

"That shirt is one of the best under-armor garments for tanking," Mordecai said. "A level seven Regeneration skill means you're back to full health pretty quickly after taking damage. In as little as two minutes. Finding it was a lucky break. This is something that would be in a platinum or legendary box."

"You don't have to tell me twice," I said. I pulled off my jacket and slipped the short-sleeved shirt on. It felt cool to the touch and form-fitted to my skin. A couple notifications appeared. I put the leather jacket back on and then added the cloak. I felt a quick rush of power course through me as my constitution rose from five to nine.

> New achievement! Loot!
> You're wearing something you found in the dungeon.
> *Reward*: You're now a handsome son of a bitch. That's reward enough.

> New achievement! Oooh, Magic!
> You're wearing magical gear for the first time! You're a wizard, Crawler!
> *Reward*: You've received a Bronze Adventurer Box!

The box contained another torch and a pair of healing potions, leaving me with a total of six. I still didn't have any pants. Or shoes. I was wearing a jacket, a cloak, and boxers. I shook my head. I examined the last item, the toe ring.

> Enchanted Toe Ring of the Splatter Skunk.
> Imbues wearer with +3 Strength and gives +3 to the skill Powerful Strike. Also, it's a toe ring. It's probably uncomfortable and it makes you look like one of those hippie assholes who sit around in a field juggling and Hula-Hooping all day.

"Powerful strike is a good skill," Mordecai said. "Each level multiplies your damage when you're not wielding a weapon. So at level three, each kick or punch does three times the damage it normally would. With your Unarmed Combat skill and the Pugilism skill, your fists already do much more damage than either of those weapons. You might want to consider a monk class, which will enhance that further."

"So, I could be like a ninja?" I said. I sat down and slipped the toe ring on. It adjusted itself, sliding easily onto my filthy, bloody index toe on my right foot. Like the description warned, it was uncomfortable. I'd never been a jewelry guy. I hopped up and down, trying to get used to it. I felt my strength rise by 50%.

"And just like that, you're almost as strong as any human who has ever lived," Mordecai said.

I received another snarky achievement for putting on jewelry, but no reward.

I started to fiddle around within my skills menu. Despite the heavy filtering, there was a lot of information in there. There was literally a skill for everything. The menu had a search box. I typed in **Frogger**, just to see what would happen. Growing up, my old man had an original stand-up *Frogger* video game machine from an arcade. I had spent hours and hours playing the game when I was stuffed in the basement. My mom locked me in there a lot. Whenever my dad had his friends over, they'd smoke and drink and get loud, and my mom didn't want them "being a bad influence" on me. So instead I stayed downstairs with no television or internet and that damn machine.

The top score one could get on an original machine was 99,990. The game never ended, so you could keep playing past that, and the score would cycle over and over. My record was 879,460.

Sure enough, it popped up.

Frogger—1981 Video Game Cabinet Version (result hidden due to filters)
  Skill: 8.

I grinned at that. I wondered why that skill was hidden by the filters, but things like **Lacing Boots—Skill: 3** wasn't. It probably only included skills useful in the dungeon. I doubted there would be a *Frogger* machine in one of these hallways.

But that wasn't true, was it? Assuming it hadn't been tossed in a landfill, that old *Frogger* machine was down here somewhere. At least the atoms of it or whatever. This dungeon was literally made out of items built by human civilization. I sighed. It was hard to comprehend.

"Really, Carl," a new voice said. It was female, sultry yet pompous at the same time. "If you're going to insist upon wearing that hideous cloak in public, you might want to do yourself the dignity of putting pants on first. I just can't fathom why Miss Beatrice hired you in the first place."

I looked wildly about for the speaker, expecting to find someone dressed like a medieval princess.

Instead, all I saw was the cat.

7

"UH, DONUT?" I SAID, LOOKING DOWN AT THE CAT.

Mordecai stood beside me, mouth agape.

Despite being nothing but a pile of goo just a few minutes earlier, the cat appeared to be exactly the same as before. Maybe she had gotten a little bigger, but not by much. Either way, she was still decidedly a cat.

Except for the talking part.

"First off, Carl, my name is 'GC, BWR, NW Princess Donut the Queen Anne Chonk,' and I'm going to have to insist you call me by my proper title. I will accept just Princess or even Princess Donut but *not* if we are in the presence of high company." She looked at Mordecai as if he was something she had just vomited upon the floor. "I suppose Princess Donut will do for now."

"I see what's happened," Mordecai said after a moment. "You're partied with her, so you can see for yourself. Pull up her stats."

I clicked on the party menu, and then I clicked on Donut's stats.

Strength: 11
Intelligence: 11
Constitution: 2
Dexterity: 8
Charisma: 25

"What the hell?" I said. She was stronger and more intelligent than me. And her charisma was just ridiculous. "What happened?"

"Her stats *were* all one. All except dexterity, which was always eight, and charisma, which was five. Whatever buff you gave her kept her race but changed her stats. Hmm, let me look. . . . Yes, it's like I thought. Look in her health menu. It shows conditions."

I clicked over, and under **Buffs** it read:

Enhanced Growth.

   After an initial boost to four random stats, all additional levels will automatically grant +1 to Strength and Intelligence. Charisma will gain +2 per level. No additional stat points will be received upon level up.

"Wait," I said. "So she's getting four stat points per level instead of three?"

"Yes," Mordecai said. "And she doesn't have to wait until she picks a class before they disperse. But that boost is a double-edged sword. She's forever stuck with a constitution of two and a dexterity of eight unless she can find some gear that will enhance it or if she picks a race and class that change it for her. But even then, the points will still distribute as indicated." He grunted. "With a charisma like that, she should consider a bard-based class. Two points every level is going to add up fast. I'm immune to the effects of her charisma. Same with you and other crawlers. But all the other NPCs and mobs won't be. For the first several floors, that number is huge. Bigger than you realize."

"But how can she talk? She's still a cat!"

"I am right here, you know," Donut said. "It's quite rude to talk about me as if I'm not in the room. And if you must know, Carl, for me, I hear your speech as it should be heard. And you hear mine as that disgusting monkey grunting you call English. I imagine this other creature hears it as squeaks and vermin hisses. This whole translation system is quite elegant, I must admit."

"I'm gonna have to start the tutorial all over," Mordecai said. "She's not a pet anymore. She's now classified as a regular crawler."

"Not necessary. I heard everything you said to my manservant," Donut said. "Now wave your hand and grant me access to my prize boxes so we can get this farce rolling."

"Manservant?" I said.

"He's a little slow," Donut said to Mordecai. "Intelligence of only three. Sad, really. But he's been with the family for a while now, and I just can't see myself letting him go."

"I've activated your menus," Mordecai said. "Oh, wow." He looked at me. "She received a Legendary Quadruped Box for being the first cat to enter the dungeon."

I watched as a group of loot boxes lined up in front of her just as they had done with me. She only had five of them. Three bronze ones with a couple healing potions and torches. Next was a Silver Adventurer Box that contained a book and a pile of pet biscuits. The note over the book read:

Tome of Magic Missile.

Next came the legendary box. The symbol on the front was of a lion thing. Only a single item came out. A small jeweled tiara. The cat-sized crown glittered with smoky dark gems. The deep purple stone in the center swirled internally with clouds, as if the center was liquid.

Enchanted Crown of the Sepsis Whore.

"That sounds ominous," I said.

"Wait until you read the description," Mordecai muttered. The item disappeared into her inventory. The cat sat down and started to groom herself.

"Are boxes custom-tailored to the person?" I asked as I pulled up the party menu. I quickly found I couldn't examine items in Donut's inventory. Only items she had equipped.

"Sort of," Mordecai said. "You'll receive items that can be used by your race, but not necessarily your class. So a human barbarian might receive a necromancer staff."

Donut glowed a bright red.

Mordecai turned to the cat, raising his hand. "Ah, Princess Donut, I see you taught yourself the *Magic Missile* spell already. That's good, good. In case you didn't know, tomes will permanently teach you the spell, and scrolls will just cast it once. That other item you received is quite valuable and powerful. But it is also a very dangerous item. Before you decide to put it on, you should take special note that it—"

Poof! The crown magically appeared on her head.

Mordecai lowered his hand, sighing.

"How the hell did she do that?" I asked. I'd had to manually put on my cloak and shirt.

"She's a quadruped, so she has a different user interface than you. She can perform many actions directly from her menu."

Now that it was equipped, I could examine the tiara's properties.

Enchanted Crown of the Sepsis Whore.
    Who's a dirty girl? You're a dirty girl!
    This is a Fleeting item!
    This is a Unique* item!
    Imbues wearer with +5 Intelligence, grants the user +5 to the Good First Impression skill. All attacks, including magical attacks, now have a 15% chance to inflict the Sepsis debuff.
    Warning! (Seriously, though. I'm going to say this again.
    WARNING! Read this shit before you put it on.) Placing this crown upon your head permanently places you within the royal line of succession for the Blood Sultanate on the ninth floor of the World Dungeon. Removing this item *will not* remove this status. Royal members of the Blood Sultanate will be required to slay the Sultan and *all* other members of the royal family before descending to the tenth floor. You'll only want to wear this if you're a bloodthirsty raging psychopath.

"That . . ." I began. "I'm not so sure you should've put that on."

"It's purple," Donut said. "Purple is my color. Do you know how many purple ribbons I've won? Do you know what it takes to get a purple ribbon?"

"What does 'fleeting' mean?" I asked Mordecai. "And why is there an asterisk by 'unique'?"

Donut had received a few more boxes from learning the spell and putting on the tiara. It was all low-tier potions and torches. She sorted through the items now, hissing with displeasure each time she received another torch.

"'Fleeting' means it'll crumble to dust the moment she takes it off. If that happens, another crown will be generated somewhere else in the dungeon. Now that it's on her, don't let her take it off. If another crawler gets the crown, it'll just be one more person you'll have to kill to get off that floor."

The idea of having to fight actual people hadn't occurred to me. Would that really happen? The thought of it made me sick. I looked at Donut.

"What the hell am I going to do now?" I asked, shaking my head. The tutorial was over, and I knew it. We'd have to go back out there.

"It's quite simple, really," Donut said. "You need to assist me to this 18th level so I can exit this hellscape and resume my rightful place as liege. I am assuming this rat creature won't be able to travel with us"—she lifted her paw and pointed it at me—"so you have been promoted from manservant to bodyguard. Congratulations, Carl."

Princess Donut has named your party The Royal Court of Princess Donut.

Princess Donut has changed your title to Royal Bodyguard.

Princess Donut has changed her title to Grand Champion Best in Dungeon.

"Really?"

Mordecai laughed. "She has the highest combined stat total, so she's the designated party leader. As such, she has more control over the party menu. Don't worry. The titles don't mean anything." He paused, suddenly serious. "Listen up, kid. She's quite a bit more powerful than you are right now, so you'll want to stick together. At least until you get to the ninth floor. That . . . that will be a challenge. You can always leave the party. That crown is on her head, not yours."

Donut walked up to the door and scratched at it. It opened on its own.

8

AND WITH NO ADDITIONAL FANFARE, WE LEFT THE GUILD AND struck out into the dungeon.

"By the way," Mordecai said as we left. "Now that I've successfully trained both of you, if you enter any additional training guilds, you'll be transported back to this room. I'm now your registered guide, so feel free to come back here if you have any additional questions. You'll lose access to me once you hit the fourth floor."

"Yeah, take care," I said. "Good luck out in the universe once this is over."

Mordecai looked at me sadly. "Yeah, good luck to you, too." He grasped my jacket and met my eyes and then whispered, "It's not worth it, no matter what they tell you. Not until floor 12, and even then, negotiate as much as you can. Remember that."

He slammed the door, and my mind reeled. What did that mean? Was he saying it was better to die than to take whatever exit they offered on floors 10 and 11? Did that even matter? Floor 10. Who was Mordecai kidding? Three million people had died in this place in the very first hour. I wasn't expecting to survive until the next floor opened up.

"Okay," Donut said, "here's what we're going to do. You're going to walk that way, and if we get attacked by anything, you protect me."

"Wandering aimlessly? That's the plan?" I asked.

"We have approximately 29 hours before these aliens air their television show. That means we have 29 hours to do something absolutely spectacular. But," Donut added, "first we need to find you some pants. I will not be presented to the universe in such a fashion. I can just see the comments now on the Martian social media." She mocked an alien voice. "'Beautiful cat, Blorg. But why isn't her body-guard wearing pants?'"

I sighed and started moving down the hall. We headed back the way we'd come before, back toward the main thoroughfare. This entire area was scorched black from the explosion of the goblin dozer. The smear of blood from where the dozer had run over the goblin remained. Everything else had been destroyed in the explosion.

"You know, you're not wearing pants, either," I said after a moment.

"Nor am I wearing a cloak that makes me look like I won a participation trophy at the special needs comic con, Carl. I'm a cat. Cats don't wear pants. Don't be so droll."

We came to the junction, and I warily looked around the corner. I didn't see anything. This hallway was lit by torches, not the green lichen, so it was much brighter. It seemed completely abandoned in either direction. We stepped out into the wide tunnel.

"Now, I know your simple mind is telling you to just keep—"

"Okay," I said, turning on the cat. "I was struggling with this decision earlier, but this . . . transformation . . . or whatever has happened has made this much easier. I'm going to go that way"—I pointed east—"and you're going to go any other direction than that. Good luck."

"What?" Donut said. "You want to separate? I don't understand."

"Look," I said. "Mordecai said you're a lot more powerful than I am. Great. That means you'll probably be okay. More okay than me." I leaned in. "But I would rather just get this over with and get squished by a goblin bulldozer than spend another second dealing with this bullshit. Cats are assholes. I get it. But do you know why people like cats, despite their asshole-ness? It's because *they don't fucking talk*. If they did, and they were all like you, they'd all be extinct because we'd have killed you all by now." I pulled up my menu and tried to figure out how to remove myself from the party.

"Wait, Carl, wait. Don't. I'm sorry. Wait."

"What?" I said.

The cat sat on the floor. She seemed to deflate. "I'm sorry. You're right. I . . . It's just . . . Have you ever woken up from a long dream, one where you're one thing, and now that you're awake, it takes you a moment to realize that's not who you really are?"

I just looked at her.

"Okay, when I woke up back there, I had all my memories of all my time being me. Of sitting in that window looking outside, of watching television all day long, of all the hours in the carrier in back of Miss Beatrice's car traveling to those horrid yet wonderful shows, of being told what a princess I am. And then, suddenly, my mind looked back on all of it, and I understood what had happened. I *am* a grand champion, Carl. I'm supposed to act a certain way. But sitting in your lap, watching you get fragged over and over in *Call of Duty*? I liked that, too. I mean, you really suck at that game, but you keep playing. I didn't realize it at the time, but I liked that."

"So, what are you saying? That you're not a crazy, stuck-up, asshole princess?"

"Oh, I am a princess, Carl. But I'll try not to be too much of an asshole. I need you. And you need me, okay? Look, I'm really scared here. I don't want to be alone. And I know you, and you don't want to be alone, either. I saw you the other day, looking at the map on your computer, and then at those apartments on Craigslist."

"What do you mean?" I asked, but I knew exactly what she meant.

"There was that day when the passes were clear. You could've taken me back to Miss Beatrice's parents, but you didn't want to. You were looking at apartments, making sure they allowed cats. You were thinking about catnapping me."

I just looked at her. It's exactly what I had been doing, but I hadn't even admitted it to myself.

"It wouldn't have worked, by the way. Her dad would've gotten me back right away."

I sighed. That was true, too. Bea's dad was a lawyer out of Yakima.

"Okay," I said. "Let's keep moving." We kept traveling. The mini-map showed the cardinal directions, and we headed east. I kept an eye out for any special rooms or other dots.

"Yeah, anyway, I'm not wearing pants because you decided to jump out the window," I said after a few minutes of us traveling in silence. That reminded me, and I felt in my pocket. Yes! A pack of Marlboro Reds. I still had half a pack left. I still had my Zippo. I'd also received a lighter from that goblin box, so now I had two. I had the urge to pull the pack out right then, but I knew I probably wouldn't get any more cigarettes ever again. I had to conserve them.

"If I hadn't jumped out the window, we'd both be dead right now."

"Why did you jump anyway?"

"Stop," Donut hissed. "There's something down there."

We'd passed by multiple junctions and alleys. Everything in this maze was featureless so far. I saw no signs of life whatsoever. We stopped now by a thin alleyway, similar to the one that had hidden the goblin dozer. It was completely pitch-black in there. On my map, the alley led down to another junction, then several more tributaries. The map only revealed so much of the area, so I couldn't see past there.

There were no red dots or anything like that. Not that I could see. "What is it?"

Donut leaped up off the ground and landed on my shoulder. I suppressed an *oof*. She wasn't nearly as heavy as she used to be when she did that. Then I remembered my strength was much higher than before. She curled her long, fluffy tail around my neck and glared. A low growl escaped her throat.

"What? What do you see?"

Thwump! Thwump!

Two bolts shot out of Donut's eyes, one after another. They were like laser blasts from a sci-fi movie. I was so surprised that I almost fell backward. Instead, I just stumbled a little. I remembered she had that *Magic Missile* spell.

The first bolt hit the rocky wall of the alley, sending bits of rock and smoke showering. The second was better aimed and traveled the length of the tunnel before splashing against something that howled with pain. It was too far away for me to see what it was, but the moment the missile hit it, a red dot appeared on my map.

"Okay, there it is. Go get it," Donut said.

"Yeah, maybe next time wait until we know what it is before we start randomly shooting at it. What if that'd been a person?"

The creature made a deep rumble that was half bleat, half roar and started galloping down the alley toward us. Whatever it was, it was big.

"That's quite obviously not a person, Carl," Donut said.

Shit, shit, shit. The thing was really booking it now.

"Shoot another missile!" I said

A third magic missile shot forth from Donut, this one hitting it directly in the chest. The creature staggered and cried out in pain, obviously hurt. But it kept coming. In the moment it was lit up by the pulse blast, I could distinctly see what it was. I got a good enough view for the info box to pop up.

Bad Llama. Level 3.

It's a llama, but it's bad. If he were human, he'd be covered in prison tattoos and would be hanging out in front of the Circle K hitting on 14-year-old girls. They might be willing to sell you something if you have good stuff to trade.

You won't want to get hit by their spit.

"Goddamnit, Donut!" I cried, jumping back from the alleyway entrance.

A red baseball-sized ball of spit blasted out of the hallway and splattered across the floor. It sizzled where it hit, and the stones of the rocky floor turned crimson.

Lava. The llama was shooting lava out of its mouth.

I balled my fists. Mordecai had said my punches were more powerful than either of the weapons I had, but the idea of fighting a fucking llama with my bare hands was ridiculous. I had the fingerless gloves I'd received in a loot box, but they offered no armor protection.

"You're gonna have to shoot it again!" I said.

"I can't!" Donut said. "I'm out of mana!"

"Didn't you get a mana potion?" I cried as the llama emerged.

The damn llama was even bigger than I'd expected. It was as large as a horse. The creature had giant yellow buckteeth. It turned its scorched and tan-colored head to glare at me. One of its eyes had been blown off by the missile. Black-and-red ichor poured down the side of its face. It had the debuff **Septic** pulsing over its head. The powerful debuff was similar to poison. It worked faster, but it couldn't be stacked, and unlike poison, it could be healed with a simple healing spell or potion.

The llama's health was already about three-quarters gone. Donut howled and leaped off my shoulder as the llama reared back to spit again. The thing's neck glowed red.

I hit it with an uppercut and a left hook right in the face. I felt bones crunch. My left hand exploded in pain, and I didn't know if the crunching bones were in the llama's face, in my hand, or both. Probably both.

It grunted with surprise and unleashed its gob of spit just as its head turned away from me. I felt the heat of the lava ball sail over my shoulder. I stepped in and punched it again. A right jab directly in its glowing throat.

The creature dropped like a sack of hammers. It tried to cry out, but nothing but gurgling came out. I jumped back as the fur and skin around its neck erupted in red flames.

I had ruptured whatever the hell was in its throat that made the lava.

The llama continued to gurgle and make pitiful sounds as its health plummeted. A moment later, it was dead.

The lava around its throat started to rapidly cool, filling the hallway with an acrid, sulfurous stench.

My left hand was broken. It throbbed in pain, but thanks to my regeneration ability, it was already knitting itself. I pulled up my health menu and looked at the pie chart. I could zoom in on that specific injury, and it gave me a detailed explanation on everything that was happening.

My Regeneration skill did a triage of my injuries, healing the most important items first. It was just my left hand along with some abrasions on my right hand. I could adjust the menu and give healing priority to other parts, too. After a minute, I was good as new.

"I dealt 71% of the damage," Donut said. "It's telling me I get to pick loot first."

The corpse blinked, and an info box popped up.

Lootable Corpse. Bad Llama. Level 3. Killed by Crawler Grand Champion Best in Dungeon Princess Donut with an assist by Crawler Royal Bodyguard Carl.
   Poor Llama skin.
   Uncooked Llama steaks x 2.
   Baggie of trailer-park-grade meth x 2.

The skin disappeared from the inventory menu along with one of the steaks. The corpse's skin disappeared, leaving just a gross pile of muscle.

"Your turn," Donut said.

"Meth?" I said. I laughed at how absurd it was. I added the rest of the items to my inventory. My inventory added two new menus: **Food Items** and **Pharmaceuticals.**

I had a couple new achievements. One for looting a corpse and one for sharing experience. I received a pair of Bronze Adventurer Boxes. Donut got the same, plus a couple additional achievements for casting her first spell and finally killing something, along with killing a mob a higher level than herself.

"That was no good," Donut declared as we continued our trek east. "Sloppy. You can't be injuring yourself every time we get into a minor tussle."

"Minor tussle? We need to be more cautious," I said. "We can't just blindly stumble around."

"No, we need to level up," Donut said. "And we need to do it quickly. I'm starting to think this main road is not the best choice for traveling or fighting."

She jumped down a random hallway and I had to rush to keep up. A few turns later, and we were far from the main thoroughfare. Here, the walls were tighter and the ceiling much lower. The whole place glowed green from the lichen on the walls. Some of the halls curved and met dead ends. But thanks to the map, which built itself as we went, it was easy to keep from getting too lost.

The whole place was eerily barren. Occasionally I heard a screeching noise coming from the distance, and once I heard something that sounded like a man screaming at the top of his lungs, followed by gunfire. But it was far away, and I couldn't tell exactly from where. We traveled like this for what seemed like hours, not coming across anybody or anything except a few random tutorial guilds. And bathrooms. The bathrooms were everywhere.

It was the strangest thing. There seemed to be a bathroom door about once every quarter mile or so. Each doorway was different, and it appeared the doors were taken from actual bathrooms in restaurants and bars and buildings from around the world. Some had the symbol for men or women on them. One had a handwritten sign in what looked like Korean. Another had a note saying it was for paying customers only.

I opened the first four bathrooms we came across, and each one was the same inside. A silver toilet and a roll of toilet paper. No sink, no mirror. Just a toilet and barely enough room to sit down in. No matter how wide or thin the door was, the room was the same each time. After the third room, I began to suspect it *was* the same room. To test it, I took the roll of toilet paper and pulled it out, dipping the end into the bowl of the waterless toilet. The next one we passed, I opened it up, and sure enough, the toilet paper remained dipped in the bowl.

After I closed the door, I had Donut open it up. She could open and shut doors just by looking at them as long as she was close enough. She opened the door I'd just been in, but this time it was a knee-high cubicle featuring a litter box.

"Oh good, I gotta wee," Donut said, entering the room and shutting the door. She emerged thirty seconds later, trailing litter all over the place. She looked over her shoulder at me. "You should go. You look like you need to go."

What I really needed to do was sleep. The initial adrenaline rush from all of this was finally coming down, and I was exhausted. I'd only slept an hour or so before I'd woken up last night. *Last night? It was barely five hours ago or so.* In my health menu it listed me as **Fatigued**. It didn't cure itself with my regeneration. We had to find one of the rest areas. Mordecai said they were all over the place. We could set up a temporary base of operations there and explore the area cautiously and deliberately. This aimless wandering was going to get us into big trouble sooner rather than later.

A couple minutes later, we were beset by a group of level two rats. There were five of them, and the screeching, hissing creatures were about half the size of Donut. The monsters weren't too big, but the bastards were *huge* for rats. They bit and scratched, and one even inflicted me with a **Poison** debuff that only lasted for a second before my cloak canceled it out.

I ended up defeating them by punting them against the wall one by one. They hit the wall and exploded like water balloons. Their deaths were over-the-top, overly gory, almost like their bodies contained twice as much blood as they should.

Donut had leveled up to two after the llama battle. It appeared we received experience equal with the percentage of how much we participated in the battle. But the number wasn't exactly equal with how much damage we dealt. I suspected support activities such as tanking and healing also counted, though we didn't have nearly enough data to figure out if that was accurate or not. It also appeared that simply being in a party with someone and present at the battle garnered a nominal amount of experience. With the rats, I received nearly enough to level me up to three.

Donut, who hadn't lifted a paw to help me, spent the next five minutes bitching about how her "mentorship" should've counted for more experience.

The cat was definitely making an effort to be less abrasive, but she was still a cat. She had a reckless streak to her, and a quick mouth, often making quips before realizing what she'd said. But she was also showing very catlike signs of affection, too. One time I stopped and leaned up against a wall to rest, and she spent the time purring and rubbing up against my legs. I looked down at her, and she returned my gaze. "What?" she said.

By the time we finally found a safe room, we had participated in ten more skirmishes, all against rats and these large cockroach things called Scatterers. The bugs were the size of and shape of a loaf of bread. We didn't receive any additional loot of interest except multiple rat pelts, and one cockroach dropped an item called a Scatterer Carapace, which added itself to my Crafting Items menu. I killed every single one of them with my bare feet. I punted the rats and jumped on top of the cockroaches. The bug mobs crunched like potato chips under my feet.

While I did most of the fighting, Donut now made an effort to fire one magic missile each fight from the safety of my shoulder. Her skill level in the spell went up to three. I spent a moment examining her stats. My view was limited, but I could see she currently had a 17 in intelligence, giving her 17 mana points. Each zap of her spell cost five mana points. For me, the spell points regenerated very, very slowly, making magic almost useless. Donut regenerated much faster, at about one point a minute. I didn't know why she generated the points more quickly, but one a minute was still pretty slow. Most of these fights were decided in seconds.

I hit level three and gained a skill called Foot Soldier, and a second one called Smush.

The Foot Soldier skill increased the damage I dealt by kicking.

The Smush skill was . . . something else.

The voice reading the skill description was deeper, more throaty than usual. I could actually hear him breathing like he was a dude beating himself off while he said it.

Smush: Skill Level 3

> Killing with your feet. Your bare, beautiful feet.
>
> Taking your bare foot, placing it on top of a living, conscious life, and then pressing lovingly down until that life ceases to be. Is there a more noble way to kill?
>
> The amount of pressure you can bring to bear upon an enemy with your unshod foot is increased by 10% with each level of this skill.

I remembered the weird message I'd received before when I'd jumped on the goblin engineer. I'd thought it was just a throwaway joke, like most of the descriptions. But it seemed the AI—or whatever it was that controlled the game messages—really did have some sort of foot fetish. It was fucking weird.

"I guess we're not getting you shoes," Donut said after I made the mistake of describing the skill to the cat.

"Yes, we are. As soon as possible," I said.

"It sounds to me like the computer fancies you," Donut said. "Or your feet, at least. We'll need to take advantage of that. If the system likes us, then maybe it'll go easier on us."

"It makes me uncomfortable," I said.

"Being eaten by a bugbear makes *me* uncomfortable, Carl. So if your boyfriend ogling your tootsies keeps these easy-peasy bugs coming at us instead of more of those lava-spitting llamas, then you better buck up, get over your human male privilege, and take one for your princess."

"Take one for my princess," I muttered as she cackled with laughter.

I saw the safe room glowing green on the edge of the minimap, and we angled our way toward there as we continued to argue.

The Scatterers were becoming more frequent, and I knew the main nest had to be nearby. At least I hoped that was what was happening, and that Donut wasn't right. A single level four cockroach scuttled away at our approach, disappearing toward a large round cavern that was just past the entrance to the safe room. We didn't pursue it, choosing to head toward safety.

We entered the safe room.

9

ENTERING SAFE ROOM.

WE ENTERED THE ROOM, AND BOTH OF US STOPPED AT THE
entrance, gaping.

"What is this magical place?" Donut asked, jumping from my
shoulder, her tail swishing about with excitement. "That's the biggest cat tree I've ever seen!"

"It's not a cat tree," I said. "It's the playground."

We were in a fast-food restaurant. It was almost like a McDon-
ald's, but instead of everything being red and yellow, it was white
and blue. The playground with the massive slide and tunnel system
and ball pit was straight out of my own childhood. The signs on the
walls were in a weird language, Polish maybe. Pictures of plastic toys
from some cartoon movie indicated this month's prize inside their
off-brand Happy Meals. I couldn't remember the movie's name, but
I recognized the hippopotamus and ferret thing. The movie was new,
just released.

They had taken a complete, intact fast-food restaurant from some
random country and placed it here underground.

We'd come in through a main entrance. Large windows surrounded the empty restaurant, but the glass showed nothing but
solid wall beyond. Three large screens stood directly above the
counter where the menu would normally be.

But instead of a menu, the screens contained information about
the game in Syndicate common language. Donut bounded toward
the play area, disappearing into the colorful children's maze while I
read the screens.

The first was a countdown until the level collapse, which was in four days and 17 hours. The line below that read:

Countdown until the premiere of *Dungeon Crawler World: Earth*:
23 hours, 42 minutes.
Remaining Crawlers:
4,322,395.

I blinked at that. Holy hell. It had been 10 million just a few hours before. As I watched, the number just kept going lower and lower.

I looked down at my feet, which were bloody and covered in bits of bug chitin and that white goo that came out of the bigger ones. We'd been lucky so far. We'd found some good gear and survived several attacks. Weren't these other people working together? It seemed like too many people had died. I shuddered.

I swallowed and continued to examine the signs.

The next screen over read:

Leaderboard:
Leaderboard will populate upon collapse of the third level.

The third screen read:

Welcome to the Safe Room. You are on the First Level.
Rental Rooms currently available: 20
Rental Room price: 0 gold
Personal spaces will become available for purchase on the fourth level.
Food is available at this location.

Rooms available? I looked at the minimap, expanding it to fill my screen. The restaurant had three exits. There was the door we'd come in through; a second door on the opposite wall had a dotted line on the other side and an X over the door. I mentally clicked on it, and a box popped up.

Personal Spaces are not yet available.

That made it sound like I could buy an actual house or base of operations here. But if the floors kept collapsing, did that mean I'd have to buy a new one each floor?

Through the third door, which would've normally led outside, I could instead see a small hallway flanked by ten tiny rooms on each side. Mini hotel rooms, each no bigger than a closet. Sleeping spaces.

That's when I noticed the white dot on the map. I startled, realizing there was a creature standing right next to me, just behind the counter. I waved away the map and looked. A furry creature with a paper hat stood there, barely taller than the counter, which explained why I'd missed him. I examined his properties.

Tally—Bopca Protector. Level 63.

Caretaker of this Safe Room.

This is a Non-Combatant NPC.

Bopca Protectors are magical gnomelike creatures who exist solely to watch over Safe Rooms. They do everything from scrub the toilets to prepare your food. They are surly, smelly, and they never wash their hands.

I cautiously approached the counter. The hairy dwarf didn't move, like he was a statue. His hair was brown, but it had an odd, almost green tinge to it. The creature had so much hair on his face that I could only see his black eyes and his bulbous nose, which was covered with angry red veins. He smelled vaguely of wet moss. He wore a blue apron, a plain paper hat, and he had a name tag that read, "Tally."

"Hi there," I said.

"Do you wish for food?" he said, his voice louder than I expected. The creature had a Slavic accent. Not quite Russian, but close.

"Uh, what do you have?" I asked, looking back up at the menu board, which hadn't changed. "Is there a list somewhere? Sorry, I'm new here."

"Tally knows you are new here. This dungeon has just opened. It opened without warning, so Tally is not ready. But I am ready enough to make most food for human crawler. Tally is prepared, has been preparing for many of your years to make food for human crawlers." He leaned, rising up on his toes to look at Donut, who was bouncing about in the ball pit. "I am not prepared for cat. But I have milk. Is better than pet biscuit."

"Actually, she really likes yogurt," I said. "I'm not supposed to give her too much. Bea gets . . ." I paused. "Cats need meat to survive."

"Will you be renting room?" The creature barely moved a muscle when he talked. It unnerved me.

"Yes," I said. "I know our time is limited, but I need to sleep."

"I shall give yogurt to cat. I will have meat for cat when you wake. But I can make food for you now if you wish."

"Sure," I said. "You really have yogurt?"

"Yes. What is it you wish for?"

I realized, at that moment, that I was starving. "Is there anything you recommend?"

A pause. "You wish me to make food of my choice?"

"Yeah," I said. "Why not? As long as it's not any sort of fish. I've had enough fish to last two lifetimes."

Tally nodded by barely moving his chin. "What is your spice tolerance? One to five?"

"Uh, are we talking human spice tolerance? I like spicier, so four. But only if it's on a human scale."

"It is a human scale. Now sit. Open boxes. Wait. Tally will bring you food. Then you sleep." He placed a fast-food cup and a small paper bowl on the counter and then nodded at a row of self-serve soda machines before turning and waddling toward the back.

My choices at the soda machine were something called Hoop

Cola, water, milk, vodka, and something called Warka, which I determined to be beer after I tapped the lever. I was tempted by the beer, but I went with water. I filled the little bowl with water as well. I took a sip, and I was surprised at how cold, how pure it tasted. I shook my head and sat at a booth.

I'd received multiple boxes, including a Silver Adventurer Box for finding my first safe room. I spent the next several minutes sifting through the mostly useless loot. Potion, potion, torch, bandages—that was new. They stopped Bleed effects. I didn't know if my trollskin shirt stopped that or not.

It was all the same stuff except for a silver ring I found in the silver box. The ring gave me +1 to my constitution, bringing the stat up to 10.

Donut jumped up on the table while we waited. She drank a bit while I finished examining my loot. She had several boxes as well, including a gold magic item box she'd received for being one of the first 100 crawlers to level *Magic Missile* up to level three.

In the box were 25 potions of mana restoration and a collar charm. The charm was a little silver butterfly. Donut squeaked in delight when she received it. It even had a little ring on it, so it'd easily attach to her collar. The charm jingled when it moved.

I shook my head. The game really was tailoring the prizes toward the crawler.

"You don't want to wear a damn bell around your neck. Do you know why people put them on cats? So the birds and squirrels can hear them sneaking up on them."

"It's adorable," Donut announced as the charm poofed onto her collar ring. "And I am wearing it."

I examined the charm's properties.

Talisman of the Slate Butterfly

Those who remember and commemorate the sad tale of the Slate Butterfly are given a boon by the fairies of the world. That story even made me cry.

Adds +4 to the Light on Your Feet skill. Adds +1 to Intelligence. Winged fairies will no longer be automatically hostile toward you.

I had no idea what the tale of the Slate Butterfly was, but I had to admit it was a good item. But was it worth the extra noise we would make? I didn't know. I wasn't exactly the king of stealth, either.

The Light on Your Feet skill simply meant she'd be able to pounce higher and farther. She was already a three in the skill when she'd received it, so the charm made her a seven. The moment she put it on, she went bounding back toward the play area and jumped all the way to the top of the plastic tubes, a leap that was twice as high as she'd been able to go before. She spent the next ten minutes with the zoomies, rushing around the play area like she had when she was a kitten.

Shit, that had been what? Four years ago?

"Hey," I called. "Be careful! Don't forget you still gotta land!"

Tally emerged from the kitchen holding two trays. He waddled from around the counter and placed them both on the table. "Eat."

Donut had a simple bowl filled with white yogurt. She returned to the table and sniffed it suspiciously.

"What is this?" I asked, poking at my food with a plastic fork. It smelled delicious.

"Murgh Vindaloo, spice level four. Boneless chicken cubes simmered in velvety sweet-and-sour vindaloo sauce. Also potatoes and other spices. It is on top of biryani rice, and I have also made garlic-and-spinach naan. I apologize I do not have lamb. They took my lamb for a mob in preparation for the second floor." He turned to Donut. "Also, Your Royal Highness, I have special-ordered a fresh salmon for your meal upon waking. I will have it properly prepared and diced and garnished for you later."

"*Your Highness?*" I said.

"Thank you, Tally," Donut said. "Oh, and, Tally?"

"Yes, Your Highness?" he asked, bowing slightly.

"Please make sure Carl and I have the best-appointed room for our convalescence this evening. That'll be all."

"I'm pretty sure they're all the same," I said. "Also, you don't want a room of your own?"

"Of course, Your Highness," Tally said, and turned away.

I looked at the cat, and she blinked and tilted her fuzzy head, her approximation of a shrug. "It's not my fault he sees me as royalty."

I took a bite of the food, and I immediately forgot everything else in the world. It was literally the most delicious thing I had ever tasted. I'd never been a huge Indian food fan, but holy shit. It was just the right level of heat. I devoured it in minutes.

Tally had returned to his post at the counter and remained there, unmoving.

"Dude," I said. "This was the best thing I've ever eaten!"

He nodded slightly.

"Are you going to be in all the safe rooms?"

"No," he said. "When this floor collapses, I will move to a random floor in the dungeon. When that floor collapses, I will move down until I am no longer needed." He didn't elaborate further.

"Well, I'm thinking we're going to stay here the next couple of days," I said. I fought the urge to lick the plate. Could he really make anything in the world?

The world is gone.

A wave of sadness washed over me, unexpectedly. I took a deep breath. I pulled out the pack of cigarettes from my pocket and was about to light one when a loud, but firm, "Nope," from behind the counter made me put it away.

"We can't stay here," Donut said. "We need to keep moving."

"I have an idea," I said. "I think there's a nest of those Scatterer bugs just next door. I say we spend our time here and try to clear out the nest. Surely we'll get some experience. Once the entrances to the next level down show up, we'll go searching for a staircase. But until then we have a spot to sleep, a supply of good food, and a nearby source of experience. I think this is a good place."

"Okay," she said after a moment. "But we need to come up with a snappy way to kill them. Something exciting, yet cute. Something with zest. I want on that show, Carl."

"We're not getting on the show," I said.

"Weren't you paying attention? Millions of followers! Loot boxes! We *need* to get on that show. Maybe we need a catchphrase."

I sighed.

10

I SLEPT MUCH LONGER THAN I PLANNED. THE ROOMS WERE SMALL, but not claustrophobic like the dungeon bathrooms or the racks in a Coast Guard cutter. The bed was more comfortable than I expected. The white cotton sheets smelled brand-new and faintly like laundry detergent. And while the halls of the dungeon were humid and stuffy, the temperature in the rooms was a bit chilly, just how I liked it. Donut insisted upon sleeping in the room with me. As usual, she slept on my neck.

I didn't dare take off my shirt or cloak, though I knew I was supposed to be safe. Once my head hit the pillow, I was out. I didn't dream, wasn't haunted by nightmares like most nights.

I awakened feeling refreshed and full of energy. I looked at the countdown time, astonished that I'd slept 10 hours straight. I hadn't slept that long without waking in at least five years. It took the literal end of the world to finally give me a full night's rest.

Donut yawned deeply and rolled onto her side as I sat up. "Go back to bed," she said sleepily. "I need several more hours. That is an order from your princess."

"Get up," I said. "Tally is making you food, remember?"

That perked her up.

The bathrooms in the restaurant had stalls for showers with soap and shampoo dispensers. There were also cheap disposable razors and shaving cream. I finally peeled my clothes off and took a long, warm shower. I stayed until the water no longer ran black. I shaved. There were no towels, however, and I had to drip-dry.

My internal clock was already broken. I knew it was nighttime again on the planet's surface, but when I saw the plate with bacon, eggs, and pancakes, I sat down and inhaled it all. It *felt* like breakfast time. It *felt* like a new day.

I wondered about those who'd survived but didn't go into the tunnels. How were they faring? Especially folks in the area of the winter storm. With no shelter, they'd have to build one from scratch. With no electricity, they'd have to make fires. And how much available food would there be? Probably not much. Even most of the animals like chickens and pigs were probably in coops and barns during the collapse.

Across from me, Donut was eating her third plate of salmon pâté.

I'd been deliberately avoiding looking up at the board, but I did now. 4,148,111. How soon before my number would be ticked away?

I tried asking Tally some general questions about the dungeon, but he refused to answer. He'd only answer questions directly relating to the safe rooms.

"If I buy a personal space, will it transfer from level to level?"

"Yes, it will," he said. "And from safe space to safe space. Also, it's best to buy all the accessories as soon as you can. Some of the items only upgrade when it goes down a level, so if you wait several levels before you purchase a crafting table, it won't get as strong as one purchased earlier."

Soon thereafter, we left to hunt for some bugs.

Outside, the hall was just the same as before. I looked warily about for red dots, but I didn't see any of the bugs. I stepped a bit from the entrance, and I pulled out a cigarette and lit it, sighing deeply. I counted, and I had nine left after this one.

"Really, Carl. Must you light that? You know how I feel about them."

"Jesus, Donut," I said. "You're worse than Bea."

"While Miss Beatrice and I don't always see eye to eye on certain policy decisions of the household, I must agree with her on this one. Cigarettes are disgusting."

"Well, there are only nine left, so you won't have to suffer—"

I stopped dead as the trio of Scatterers rounded the corner, chittering as they approached. It was two level twos and a level four that was larger than the others. This third bug was almost the size of Donut. I wouldn't be squishing this one with my foot.

Scatterer Brood Guardian. Level 4.

Cockroaches that have been baptized in rage and Monster Energy drinks.

Like its smaller brethren, the Scatterer Brood Guardian is a giant bug who wants nothing more than to fuck you up. Unlike his little brother, these guys are dangerous.

Shit. That doesn't sound good.

I really didn't want to fight this thing with my hands. Despite knowing I did less damage this way, I pulled out my toad cudgel and clasped it in my hand while Donut blasted the large cockroach three times with a magic missile. It hissed and rolled back a few times, its health knocked down by half.

"Want me to hit it again?" Donut asked. "I'll have to down a mana potion."

"No," I said, relieved that the missiles did so much damage. "I'll take it."

I stomped forward with my foot, crushing both the smaller roaches.

The brood guardian jumped back up and charged again. It was fast, but I was ready for it. It skittered forward, mandible-antennae things thrashing. I swung the cudgel down at its head. The rounded edge of my weapon bounced off the creature, which hissed and fell back.

The hit didn't appear to do much damage. Plus I had to awkwardly bend down to use it. I quickly switched to my poker to see if that'd be better. It charged again, and I stabbed with the iron stick. Its giant head knocked the poker right out of my hand, and it went flying.

This place has the shittiest weapons.

I stepped back and snap-kicked, hitting the roach right under its little semicircle head. It squealed. The kick did more damage than the magic missile. I swept forward, continuing to kick at it while it shrank back. Donut leaped off my shoulder with a hiss as I jumped in the air, coming down hard on its back.

The cockroach exploded like a balloon filled with coconut pudding.

"Goddamnit," I said, looking at the goo on my feet.

Donut crept forward and sniffed the remains. It didn't leave anything lootable.

"The level 4 ones aren't too hard to kill," Donut said. "Oh, he smells just awful."

I looked at the map. A couple curves of the halls led to the large room. It looked as if there was a door, too.

"Okay, this is what we're going to do," I said as I went to retrieve my poker. The damn thing was useless, and I shoved it in my inventory. "We'll wait until your mana refills. Then we're going to creep toward that main room and peek inside. If it's too much to handle, we'll run back here and rush into the safe room."

"The safe room door won't open if mobs are outside," Donut said.

"We'll be fast."

"That's fine," she said after a moment. "Just remember I can run a lot faster than you."

We ended up killing a couple dozen more of the level 4 Scatterers before we reached the door. We found a hit to the face with a magic missile just before it lunged would stun it. I'd punch down a few times and then stomp the head. Stomping the head almost always resulted in a critical hit. We received several vials of something called Scatterer Hemolymph, which looked like the white goo that came out of them when they died. The system identified it as an alchemy material.

Every once in a while, the Scatterer would get inflicted with Sepsis when it was hit by the magic missile. When that happened, it would turn and try to run off. It would usually collapse and die after it took about thirty steps.

Both Donut and I were level 5 when we got to the door.

For me, the higher levels didn't really mean anything. I received three stat points every time I leveled, but I couldn't distribute them yet. The only thing that helped was that my Pugilism, Unarmed Combat, Foot Soldier, and Smush skills were all level 5 now also.

Because of Donut's special buff, she was growing with each level up. Her strength was at 15. Now when she jumped onto me, I could feel the strength of her claws on my shoulder, even through the leather jacket and trollskin shirt.

"Do you have any sort of slashing skill?" I asked. "You know, something with your claws?"

"Of course I do," Donut said. "My Slice Attack is at level four, and my Back Claw is also level four."

"Okay, good," I said. "You can help if we get into trouble. Your strength is way higher than mine. You should get in there once your magic runs out."

The door at the end of the tunnel didn't have any sort of official sign on my minimap. We crept toward it, going as silently as possible. Donut's little bell jingled with each step. The room beyond was large and round shaped, probably about 1,500 square feet. The door itself was old and grimy with a doorknob that appeared to be hanging on by a single bolt. While it wasn't labeled on the minimap, there *was* a paper sign attached to the door written in Spanish. It looked like some sort of official notice. The sign was old and weathered, and it looked like it had been there awhile.

"*No entrar,*" I whispered, squinting at the sign. "I think that means 'do not enter.' The next part, '*por orden del Centro de Salud,*' I don't know. By order of something, I think. Can you read it?"

Donut just looked at me like it was the stupidest question she'd ever been asked.

"It doesn't matter," I whispered. "Okay. We're cracking the door and looking inside."

The doorknob didn't work, and the door wasn't fully latched. I pushed it open as slowly as I could. The door screeched, and I cringed.

The room was pitch-black. I couldn't see a damn thing. I heard rustling, so I knew there was something in there, but I couldn't see what it was.

Donut was standing completely still, her hair poofed out like when she was freaked out.

"What do you see?" I asked.

"There's a lot of level one and two cockroaches in there. Lots and lots of them. But there's other stuff in there, and I can't tell what it is. It looks like piles of garbage. It smells like that bag you take with you on those days that other guy comes over to the apartment. You know, like socks. But hundreds of them. I don't see anything else. Light a torch and throw it in there."

"Wait, what?" I said. "Are you talking about my gym bag? Some guy was coming over to the apartment when I was at the gym?"

"Focus, Carl. Light a torch."

"Actually," I said, "I have a better idea."

I couldn't believe it. Actually, I *could* believe it. It was my own fault. I should have broken up with her long ago. I felt like an idiot. I also suddenly felt very reckless.

"Get ready to run," I said as I pulled out the stick of goblin dynamite. The red stick was wet and sticky on the outside, like it was sweating. I examined its properties.

The game show voice whispered the description:

Goblin Dynamite.
    This stuff is especially volatile. It's so volatile, you probably don't even need to light the wick to set it off. It's so volatile, even loud noises might set it off. Keep it in your inventory until you're ready to use it. Be gentle and don't squeeze too hard or else you might get the . . .

The AI didn't speak for a good two seconds.

BOOM!

The AI shouted that last word in my head, and I almost pissed myself. I stood still for several moments, my heart thrashing.

"You are a fucking asshole," I whispered up at the air.

"Okay," I whispered to Donut. "Run now. I'm right behind you."

Donut scampered away as I carefully pulled my Zippo. I lit the long wick, which started hissing and popping like a sparkler. I tossed the dynamite into the room, throwing it as hard as I could. I turned, and I ran.

I prayed it wouldn't blow when it hit the ground.

11

IT BLEW WHEN IT HIT THE GROUND.

I'd chucked the dynamite a pretty good distance into the large room, but I was only a few steps away from the door when it went off. *Bam!* The sudden resounding concussion sent me flying. I hit the stone floor and bounced, sliding. The wooden door splintered, and a jagged hunk of wood ricocheted off my head. Stinking, billowing smoke poured through the entrance. Blood seeped from a cut deep in my scalp.

My vision flashed red, and I received a **DANGER LOW HEALTH** warning. But it quickly abated.

Behind me, I could hear the crackling of fire. I groaned, rolling onto my back as my health slowly kicked its way back up. I felt as if I'd been run over by that goblin bulldozer thing.

Donut appeared above me, looking down.

"Are you dead?" she asked.

"No," I said. "I don't think so."

"Then you better get up. Let's go see what we just killed."

I pulled myself up. Mordecai had said I'd be fully healed in two minutes, but two minutes was a long time when you were in pain. I had over a dozen healing potions now, but I didn't want to waste one just yet. Not when I didn't have to.

The room glowed red. I pulled a torch from my inventory. I went to grab my lighter, but a box appeared above the torch, asking if I wanted to activate it. Weird. It was different than the dynamite. I mentally clicked **Yes**, and the torch lit on its own. A half-hour timer

appeared and then faded as the bright dancing flames engulfed the
top half of the stick.

I paused at the entrance, peering inside. The room looked as if it
was the interior of a dumpster. Mountains of trash rose to the ceiling.
Multiple small fires burned, giving it a pulsating red glow. I tossed
the torch in, and the room lit up further.

I spied multiple bug pieces scattered about. My map populated
with about three dozen X's indicating bug corpses. I didn't see any
movement and red dots. I'd also received a ton of notifications, but
they were all in the folder.

"I think we killed them all. Do you see anything?"

"Nope," Donut said, strolling into the room. She stopped a couple
steps in, looking distastefully at her paw. She'd stepped on something that looked like a dirty diaper. "The only thing that smells
worse than trash is burning trash. You made a real mess of this
place."

I followed her in. Donut jumped to my shoulder and immediately
began licking her paw. I pulled up the notifications as we cautiously
moved deeper into the room. The ceiling was higher than out in the
hall, almost as tall as the main corridor. Piles of garbage filled the
room, stacked at least 15 feet tall. A black garbage bag was ripped
open at my feet, and I could see fast-food wrappers, soggy Spanish-
language magazines, and empty cans within.

Why would they transfer garbage into here?

I stepped gingerly as to not cut my feet, but I already felt as if my
feet were changing, becoming less sensitive to the bare ground. Before, I knew this would be pure agony. It was still uncomfortable,
but it was getting better. And it was happening much more quickly
than it would have before all this happened.

I'd received several skill upgrades just from that one move. Explosive handling. Dangerous Explosive Handling. Goblin Explosives.
In addition, I'd received another Silver Goblin Box for killing more
than 10 mobs with an explosive and a Gold Crowd Control Box for

killing more than 15 mobs with the same attack. I'd received a huge experience bonus for that, taking me almost up to level six.

I had one more notification, an achievement. I clicked on it.

"Do you hear music?" Donut asked, pausing her cleaning to look up at the ceiling.

New achievement! Boss Babe.

You have struck a blow against a dungeon boss and caused damage to it. Here's a fun fact. For crawlers who make it through the tutorial, this achievement is, by far, most often the last achievement they ever receive. Isn't that interesting?

Reward: Let's wait a few minutes before we decide on whether or not to waste a prize on you.

Shing!

The door, which moments before had been blown to bits, magically re-formed itself, locking us in the room. And just to hammer the matter home, silvery glowing bars of metal appeared, locking it in place one by one with a *clink, clink, clink*. Three skull-headed torches appeared, arising from the garbage heaps.

At the far end of the room, something rustled. Something big.

Music started playing, the sound filling the room. It was odd, intense, disjointed. It was like a harp playing with distortion with a heavy beat under it.

The ground rumbled as the announcement came.

Boss Battle!

You have discovered the lair of a Neighborhood Boss!

Put your game faces on, ladies and gentlemen! *Aaaand* Here.

We. Go!

The AI was louder than usual. He sounded like an announcer at a monster truck rally. Normally, I was only really hearing this stuff in my head. This time it was through an actual loudspeaker. It echoed, shaking the walls and the piles of garbage.

"Carl! Carl, I don't like this! Take me from here immediately!" Donut cried. She jumped from my shoulder and started scratching at the door, which would not open. "Carl, open the door this instant!"

I pushed myself against the back wall, waiting for the monster to emerge.

"Donut, get ready!" I cried. "Just start pumping it with magic missiles. Use your mana potions to refill yourself!"

Donut turned and panic-fired a missile, which bounced ineffectively against the sifting garbage pile.

"Wait until we see what it is first!"

The garbage exploded upward in a geyser of scorched trash bags. Bug parts and paper and food wrappers rained. A woman appeared, reaching into the air, screaming as she rocketed up like she'd been shot out of a cannon. She landed with a heavy crash twenty meters in front of us.

Donut and I looked at one another.

This was a human woman, about 35 years old, enormously fat. She wore a filthy and ripped T-shirt and no bra, and her skin was covered in open sores and scabs. A blue pair of sweatpants with the word "PINK" along the leg appeared to be stretched to their limits. Her black hair clung to her head in clumps. Like me, she wore no shoes.

She was also 15 feet tall.

She spied us cowering, and she screamed again.

Everything stopped the moment she screamed.

She froze, I froze, and Donut froze. The only thing that kept moving was my mind, which raced.

What the actual . . .

A mug-shot-style shot of my face in a round frame appeared floating in front of me, my name and level written under it. A second image of Donut appeared next to mine.

A huge **Versus** splattered into the air.

The Hoarder!

Level 7 Neighborhood Boss!

Trapped in her pile of rubbish, abandoned by society, the war inside her head has seeped out of her mind and infected both her body and her surroundings. Now nothing more than a garbage troll, the Hoarder is a horrific reminder of what can happen to those who fall out of the light! Protected by her minions, she'll do anything to keep her precious stockpile safe!

The woman's title—The Hoarder—appeared in a stylized metallic font with blood splattered around it. It was straight out of a fighting video game. The moment the description ended, we could all move again. The giantess finished her scream and took a few steps toward us, garbage cascading around her with each step.

Half of the woman's face was burned to hell. She had a health bar over her head, and it was already three-quarters gone. I'd cheated the boss fight, killing her minions and hurting her before it even began.

"Ayúdame por favor," the woman cried, reaching for us. Her voice was deep, beefy. Scared. The giant woman sounded terrified. *"No sé que está pasando. Me duele el estómago. No sé donde estoy. Por favor, tengo miedo."*

"Shit, I think she's a person," I said. "Like she was in her house when it happened, and they turned her into this thing. We should help her."

"Yeah, that'll be a no," Donut said. She shot a magic missile at the woman, who staggered as it exploded against her chest. The tattered remains of the woman's filthy T-shirt burned away, revealing pendulous, stretch-marked breasts that fell over a sagging, equally marred stomach. Her health barely nudged.

"Ayúdame!" the monster woman cried again. She made a gagging noise, and when she opened her mouth, a pair of level two Scatterers came out and charged at us, hissing.

"This is really disgusting," Donut said. She shot another missile at the woman, her third.

"Take a mana potion," I cried.

I punted a cockroach and then stomped the second. A bag of garbage softened the blow, and it didn't die. I stomped again. I cried out as a jagged hunk of metal tore my foot. The Scatterer hissed. *Fuck this.* I reached down and ripped its head right off the body. It came off with a *pop*, sending me flying backward. I hit the ground.

My hand grabbed something. I thought at first it was a bicycle chain. No, a leash. A metal chain-linked leash. The kind people used for really scary dogs. I snatched it up, pulling. It was still attached to the mummified remains of a large dog. It yanked out of the garbage like a monster leaping at me. *Jesus Christ.* I unhooked it and pulled myself to my feet.

"Okay," I said, looping the chain in my hand. The woman was scared, disoriented, and she obviously didn't want to be here. But she was also vomiting killer cockroaches at us. Our only real choice was to take her out.

"Distract her," I said. I ran around one of the big piles of garbage, one of the ones holding the skull torches. *Thwump.* Donut fired a missile.

"Hurry up!" Donut cried. "More cockroaches are coming!" The cat yowled. I saw her sail into the air, using her jump ability to land atop the pile I was running around. "Carl, this is not acceptable!"

I rounded the corner, coming at the massive woman from just behind her.

Another magic missile bounced off her chest. She staggered as two more Scatterers emerged from her mouth. She made this awful noise as they emerged, the sound of twenty people vomiting all at once. These were level four bugs, the larger brood guardians.

"I can't drink another potion yet," Donut cried. "It won't let me! I can't fire another missile for a minute!"

Shit. I didn't think about what I did next. I rushed up the pile of garbage behind the woman. My feet screamed as I stepped on what felt like broken glass. I looped the metal leash through the handle. I ran, and I jumped onto her back, slipping the loop over her throat. I slid off of her wet, greasy body, grasping the end of the leash with all of my strength as it pulled taut around her.

She gurgled and started thrashing about wildly. She stumbled backward, falling toward me. I scrambled to my feet, pulling. Her hands moved to her throat as she crashed down, splattering one of the Scatterers. Several other bugs filled the chamber now. Unable to easily get to Donut, they turned toward me while I pulled and pulled.

"You're doing it!" Donut cried.

"A little help here!" The bugs made an angry chittering noise as they descended on me. The poor woman gurgled and thrashed. Her health moved downward, slowly but steadily.

"My missiles aren't ready yet!"

A level four hissed and jumped at me. I kicked at it, and it skittered back. It lunged again and snapped, taking a bite of my leg. I screamed.

"Use your fucking claws," I cried.

"She's almost dead. You can kill them when you kill her!"

"*Goddamnit, Donut,*" I cried as a second cockroach bit me.

I stumbled forward suddenly, landing between the two Scatterers.

The chain had broken. I stared stupidly at the remains wrapped in my right hand. *Fuck.*

Thwump. Donut fired a magic missile. It must have let her drink another potion. A cockroach hissed and died. *Thwump Thwump.* The last two went into the woman. She still wasn't dead.

With the chain still wrapped around my hand, I scrabbled up and punched the head of the closest of the brood guardians. Its face exploded, showering me with gore. A notification appeared and minimized itself. I turned as the second jumped at me. I fell onto my back as it hit my chest, mouth thrashing at my neck, its barbed legs scrabbling. I ripped at the creature, and one of its legs came right off like I was pulling it from an overcooked chicken. It squealed in pain as I pushed it off me. I leaped at it, pummeling its back with my chain-covered fist. It shrieked and died. My knuckles ached. *I need brass knuckles. Real ones.*

I whirled around.

The Hoarder lay on her back. Her health bar was all but empty. Steam rose off of her. The broken half of the leash remained around her neck. I had to finish her off now before she puked more bugs. I scrambled toward her.

The woman's eyes met mine as I raised my fist.

"Lo siento si fui una mala persona," she said. She closed her eyes as tears streamed down the non-burned side of her face. The woman only had one misshapen tooth in her mouth. *"No quería que mi hija se enfermara. No quiero estar en el infierno. Por favor. Por favor envíame a Jesús."*

"I'm sorry," I said. I punched her right in the nose. I felt it give underneath my fist, almost like it was an aluminum can wrapped in clay. It crumpled and crunched deep inside. I punched again. And again. My fist burned in pain, and I took my own damage with each blow.

A minute later, and she was dead.

Once again, the world froze.

And the winner is, The Royal Court of Princess Donut!

Our two mug shots filled my vision with **Winner!** stenciled over them.

The remaining cockroaches all dropped dead. The door burst into shards. The music stopped. I leaned up against the stinking woman's dead body, and I tried not to vomit bacon and eggs all over myself.

12

"EXPLAIN THESE BOSSES TO ME," I ASKED MORDECAI. I FINGERED the chain wrapped around my right fist.

We found a tutorial guild about a quarter mile from where we'd killed the Hoarder. Her body had only dropped a single piece of loot, a scrap of paper called a Neighborhood Map. It didn't disappear when I looted it, and Donut was able to grab one for herself.

The moment I touched it, about a square mile of my minimap automatically populated. I could zoom out and see all the red dots in the area—there were hardly any now. A couple of rooms with white dots appeared, and upon closer inspection, they were all tutorial guilds, all with Mordecai inside. Other than Donut, there weren't any other blue dots visible in this area.

There was, however, the X of a corpse on the very edge of the giant neighborhood square, right on the edge of the main corridor. This X was different. It was twice the size and pulsing. I hovered over it, and it said, **Corpse of Crawler Rebecca W—Level 3.**

I didn't know how long she'd been there or how she died, but she'd been killed less than 200 meters from the safe room.

"Let's go loot her corpse!" Donut said the moment she saw it on her map.

"I want to talk to Mordecai first," I said. I noted the location of the closest tutorial guild, and we angled over there.

We opened the door to the guild to find Mordecai on his cot asleep. He had that photo of his brother cradled in his rat arm, and a pile of empty bottles littered the floor. The upset urn had been fixed, and the ashes all cleaned up.

"There are six main types of bosses," Mordecai said after we woke him up. His voice slurred ever so slightly, and I could smell the alcohol on his breath. "Neighborhood, Borough, City, Province, Country, and Floor bosses. There are also others, but those are called elites. You won't need to worry about them just yet."

"So that thing we just fought was the most common type of boss?"

"Yes," Mordecai said. "And now you'll know how to recognize their lair. It'll probably be pretty obvious to you from now on. The neighborhood bosses are the easiest to kill and easiest to find."

"Easy," I grumbled. My now-healed legs and fist still ached with phantom pain. "The one we fought, she was obviously a person from our world. Is it always going to be like that?"

I hadn't understood a word the woman was saying, and I was glad for it. I already had enough trouble sleeping. Mordecai didn't answer for several moments, like he was trying hard to think of a proper response. "No, not always," he said finally. "There will be a lot of . . . recycling . . . from previous iterations of the game. Some will be human stock, but most won't be, or even human from this world. Or they will be human, but it won't be as obvious."

"It was quite the disappointing battle," Donut said. "A Bronze Boss Box? That deserved a Legendary at least."

We hadn't opened our boxes yet.

"All bosses drop persistent loot, and their corpses stay there for any crawler to pick it up. A neighborhood boss will drop a neighborhood map, as you've discovered. Higher bosses will drop other public items, which I'm not allowed to tell you about yet. But," Mordecai added, "the ones who actually kill the boss also receive an achievement and a boss box. Bronze for Neighborhood, Silver for Borough, and so forth. Also, as you can now see, there's a bronze star after your name in all notifications. You'll get a star after each boss you kill."

"Are there harder bosses on this level?" I said. "It's not exactly fair. Most of us can level up, but we don't get anything out of it until we can distribute the points."

"The first three levels won't have any of the Province, Country, or Floor bosses, but there are some powerful bosses out there. They're meant to be taken on by larger groups than just two crawlers. You can't run from most boss fights, not on the early floors, so be careful."

"Okay, I'm opening my boxes," Donut announced, turning away.

I had 15 achievements and seven boxes to open, including that boss box and the Gold Crowd Control Box. While Donut grunted with annoyance at all the torches and pet biscuits, I turned back to Mordecai.

"Is it normal? This number of achievements?"

He nodded. "It's not normal to get that legendary box you did, but the first three floors are designed to drown you in low-tier loot and achievements and beginner skills. By the time you have to choose a class, you should have a good idea what's going to work for you. Once you hit the fourth floor, the achievements are harder to come by."

"A spell book!" Donut cried when she opened her Bronze Boss Box. I didn't have time to read the description before she glowed, indicating she'd already applied it to herself.

A moment later, Donut cried with rage.

Mordecai grunted with amusement.

"What is it?" I asked.

"Little one, you really must examine these items before you equip or apply them," he said.

Donut glowered. "It's a stupid spell."

"It's a very useful spell," Mordecai said. He turned to me. "She just learned a spell called *Torch*. It makes a curl of light follow you around. The more she uses it, the more powerful it'll become."

"It's a good spell," I agreed.

I pulled up my notifications. I was awash with odd skills, like a skill level increase in dumpster diving and jump attacking. One was particularly interesting:

> You've gained a skill level! Iron Punch level 3.
> When simple brutality isn't enough. Newsboy cap not included.
> With a skill like this, you can always find work as a 1920s street tough or a collection agent for a bookie.
> War gauntlets and lumpers will protect your hands and enhance your punching damage without losing your bare-knuckle bonus. Each level of this skill increases the enhanced fist damage bonus by an additional 10%.

If I was going to utilize my bare-knuckle skill, I really needed to find something to protect my fists. Breaking my fingers every time I punched something was not a good long-term plan.

My lower-tier boxes were all crap. The last three were more interesting.

> Bronze Boss Box. (5/7)
> Tome of Wisp Armor.

> Silver Goblin Box. (6/7)
> Stick of Dynamite x 5.
> Lighter.
> Satchel of Gunpowder.

> Gold Crowd Control Box. (7/7)
> Enchanted Spiked Kneepads of the Shade Gnoll Riot Forces.
> Scroll of Confusing Fog x 3.
> Potion of Iron Skin x 5.

"That tome is a good find, but it costs five mana to cast it, and you only have three right now. I would hold on to it until you decide what your build is going to be. It's quite valuable. Or give it to the princess," said Mordecai.

"I'll take it," Donut said, looking up at me. She didn't even know what it was yet. I read the spell's description.

Wisp Armor
    Cost: 5 Mana
    Target: Self Only
    Duration: 5 minutes + 1 minute per level of spell. Requires 5-minute cooldown.
    Surrounds your body with tendrils of light. While ineffective against physical attacks, this spell negates 75% of incoming damage from magic-based attacks. Provides temporary immunity to mind-control effects. Higher skill levels increase both effectiveness and duration. It also makes you look all wispy and ethereal and druid-like. A great spell to have if you're a club kid or trying to bang a vegan.

A magic protection spell. That would be useful. I'd hold on to it for now.

The scroll of *Confusing Fog* filled the room with a mist that only the mobs could see, and the Iron Skin potion raised my physical armor by 100% for five minutes.

The real prize was the kneepads. While they weren't pants, I was happy to finally have something to put on my legs. I pulled them out of my inventory and examined their properties.

Enchanted Spiked Kneepads of the Shade Gnoll Riot Forces
    Adds 10% Damage Reflect to all equipped armor.
    Cancels all Momentum-based attacks.
    Made of skin and fur and the spiky things from the back of Thorn Cadavers, these kneepads are both good protection and they're stylish. Stylish, that is, if your knees are cosplaying as hedgehogs.

The kneepads were built like slip-on knee bracers, so I pulled my feet through each one and pulled them up. They appeared much too small, but they magically adjusted. The spikes were thin, needlelike. Each spear was about eight inches long. They were retractable and appeared to only magically pop themselves out when needed. I hoped I wouldn't end up skewering my hand if I reached down to scratch my legs.

"Remember when I said you looked ridiculous before?" Donut said, looking me up and down. "Mordecai, darling. Is there a worst-dressed award for the dungeon?"

"Actually, yes. Sort of," Mordecai said. "After the main episode tunnels, a hosted special comes on where a couple commentators discuss the state of the game. They usually do a segment on weird things happening in the dungeon. They do a lot of contestant profiles and such. Sometimes when people win boss fights, they'll pull them out of the game for 10 minutes to do an on-camera interview. The show is almost as popular as the official program, though they'll never let you watch this one."

Donut's eyes got big as saucers. "They interview people?" She looked at me. "Carl, we need on that show. Make it happen."

I sighed. "That's not how this works, Donut, and you know it. And besides, I am not your agent."

"No, no, you're not. Miss Beatrice is my agent, and once we reunite with her, *she'll* make sure I get on that show. But she's halfway around the world. I figure we'll have to wait until the fifth or sixth floor before the dungeon shrinks enough for us to find her. I really hope we don't have to wait much longer than that."

I exchanged a look with Mordecai.

"Sure," I said finally. "Now let's get back out there."

13

THE FIRST THING WE DID WAS ANGLE OUR WAY TOWARD THAT
corpse.

I asked Mordecai if we'd be able to loot everything the dead
woman had, and he said yes, crawlers drop everything but the unopened loot boxes. Non-crawlers would also be able to loot her body,
but they wouldn't have access to her inventory, so the woman likely
had some items on her.

"Maybe she'll have some pants for you."

"Unless she's over six feet tall, then probably not," I said. Items
from the surface didn't magically resize themselves. Still, I held out
hope she'd have something.

"By the way," I added a few minutes later, "those magic missiles
of yours run out pretty quickly. You really need to start training
with your claws."

Donut didn't say anything for several moments. "I . . . I've never
done anything like that before. I'm scared of getting hurt. What if
it hits me back? I don't want to get hit back."

"How is it you can be so reckless and timid at the same time?"

"I can't control my instincts! I'm just a few generations shy of being a ferocious tiger stalking through the jungles."

"I've seen your pedigree," I said. "You're a few generations shy of
nothing. Also, your grandfather was also your uncle."

Both of us turned the corner, and there she was.

She was sitting, leaning up against a wall just off the main corridor. She was on the very edge of the Hoarder's neighborhood.

The woman was naked. She had no clothes, no gear at all. The manner of her death wasn't obvious.

She appeared to be about 30 years old. Slight. Asian. Her hair was pulled back into a ponytail. A full-sleeve tattoo of koi and a crane decorated her left arm. The bright colors of the tattoo suggested it was recent ink. She had several other, older tattoos.

"I think goblins came along and took all her stuff," I said. I examined her, popping up the info box.

Lootable Corpse. Crawler Rebecca W. Level 3. Killed by Crawler Frank Q.
   Apple Core.

I felt as if I was slapped. *Killed by Crawler Frank Q.*

That's when I saw it. A gunshot wound, right in her chest between her breasts, right in the middle of a moth tattoo. It'd killed her instantly, leaking hardly any blood.

"Oh goodness. This Frank Q gentleman doesn't seem like a decent person at all," Donut said.

I instinctively looked up at my map, looking for blue dots. There were none. Would the dots be hidden if the person was trying to hide? If I wasn't in the area of the neighborhood map, the red dots wouldn't appear unless I was right on top of them. But NPCs always appeared if they were within a couple hundred meters, even if they were around the corner. Could other crawlers hide from me?

Christ, another thing to worry about. A crazy asshole with a gun.

I was suddenly, inexplicably reminded of that day. The last day I ever saw my father.

You're a bully. You're a bully and nobody likes you. It's why Mom left.

I was expecting him to get angry, to hit me. But he never hit me, not once. The man just laughed and laughed, and that was enough. *I don't need you to like me. But you will respect me.*

The memory came quickly, out of nowhere. I didn't know why.

Nobody had died that day. Nobody had been hurt at all, not physically.

"Maybe Frank Q isn't a human," Donut was saying. "Maybe he's one of those cocker spaniels." She sniffed at the corpse. "Yes, this is definitely the work of a cocker spaniel."

I sighed. "She's been shot," I said. "Look. That's from a gun."

"Maybe the dog had a gun. If I had a gun in my inventory, I could shoot it."

"No, you couldn't. It wasn't a dog."

One of our neighbors in the apartment had a dog named Angel. A cocker spaniel. I couldn't remember the woman's name, but her dog was always barking her head off. Bea was friendly with the owner, and they were always chatting in the hallway. Every once in a while Angel would burst into our apartment, barking, running in circles. She'd pee on the floor and shriek-bark at Donut, who would sit atop her cat tree and hiss and spit and poof all her hair out.

"We need to be careful," I said. "Keep on the lookout for other players. If we come across any, don't tell them what gear we have. They can't examine it if they're not in our party."

"We are in a dungeon filled with killer cockroaches and drug-dealing llamas. Some imbecile with a gun doesn't scare me," Donut announced. "And they shouldn't scare you, either. We should hunt this vile killer down and bring him to justice."

"Weren't we just talking about this? And this guy doesn't scare me," I said. I looked down at the dead woman. I wondered who she was, why someone like her was outside at two thirty in the morning on such a night. *I'm never going to know her story. Nobody is ever going to know it.* I wondered how scared she'd been. Only to be killed by a fellow human. He'd looted her corpse, taking everything, leaving only an apple core. It made me irrationally angry. "In fact, I think you're right. I want to find him if we can."

I thought for a moment. "Okay," I said. "Let's stick to the neighborhood for right now since we have the map. We'll hunt down the remaining red dots. We need all the easy experience we can get.

Then we'll go back to the safe room and watch the premiere." Mordecai had said the show would air on the screens in the safe room. "After that, the stairs will open up. We'll go hunting for both the stairs and this guy."

"You're not scared of that guy? Really?" Donut asked, looking between me and the corpse.

"No," I said. "Not at all."

"Well, then, you're crazy. I don't like you being crazy. *I'm* scared of him. We need to stay away from him. What if he's like one of those murder hobos you hear so much about?"

"Just two seconds ago you said, and I quote, 'Some imbecile with a gun doesn't scare me!'"

"Yeah, that's when I thought you were being a pussy. I didn't realize you were getting all Charles Bronson *Death Wish* on me!"

"How do you even know what that is?"

"You two always leave the TV on when you go to work. I absorbed all that stuff. Miss Beatrice always leaves it on Lifetime and HGTV, and you leave it on that channel that plays *The A-Team* and Charles Bronson movies all day."

"We'll be careful," I said. "Don't worry."

Nearby, a group of three red dots was steadily moving through a hallway. The map didn't say what they were, but based on our earlier encounters, I guessed them to be more of the rats. I suspected we wouldn't see any more Scatterers in this neighborhood.

"Come on, Donut. Let's hunt."

14

THE PREMIERE OF *DUNGEON CRAWLER WORLD: EARTH* WAS EASILY
the most bizarre thing I'd ever witnessed in my life.

Apparently, alien television shows were presented in a completely
different way than a standard 2D television screen. Viewers were virtually placed within actual scenes, as they happened. This virtual
rendition and recap of the moments presented on the show were fully
experienced by the viewers, including the smells and physical sensations just short of feeling the actual pain.

However, Tally explained, many viewers didn't like the VR version of the action, so they watched using a method where they had a
bird's-eye view, and they could zoom in and out and switch angles
at will.

We didn't have any of that. The show streamed on the center of
the three televisions over the fast-food counter. Tally came out from
around the back to sit with us at the booth to watch.

4,006,002. That's how many people were left when the show
premiered. The number continued to steadily tick down while the
show aired. It made me sick to look at it, so I tried to tune it out.

"This is not good way to watch show," Tally announced as the
title appeared on the screen. The screen jerked around, like I was
watching someone play a game on Twitch. The view kept randomly
zooming in and out, sometimes focusing on nothing in particular.
Sometimes lights flashed for no reason.

It started with a commentator in the top right of the screen. I
stared at the orange-hued, four-eyed lizard-like creature as

he-she-it—I couldn't tell—breathlessly gave a recap of last season. The sound kept cutting in and out, and I couldn't tell why. The creature sounded like it had gravel in their mouth when they spoke anyway, and even though it was speaking in Syndicate Standard, I could barely make out what they were saying. It started with a shot of a planet that looked remarkably like Earth, but with the continents all jumbled up. It zoomed in on the planet, showing buildings that appeared to almost be made of plastic, all on stilts with round podlike mechanisms zipping about underneath. The collapse came, but instead of the buildings all sinking into the ground, they were swept away, rolling to the side like they'd been sucked up by an invisible vacuum.

Next came a view of a building that looked similar to the Roman Coliseum, only bigger. The arena had multiple floors, mazes, and a level filled entirely with water. On the exterior of the building, which appeared to be the size of an entire city, was written **The Squim Conglomerate Presents, Battle for the Planet Aryl.**

On the screen, thousands of furry, gorilla-like creatures screamed and rushed into battle against another group of similar creatures. Later, it showed a single heavily armored gorilla stick a spear into the throat of a smaller, gray-colored gorilla riding a massive pig thing. The word "**WINNER**" appeared on the screen.

The winning gorilla fell to his knees and appeared to start sobbing before the screen cut away. A round metal tube that looked like a barrel appeared on the screen for 15 seconds straight. There was no sound. Tally said it was a commercial.

"I do not like last season's version of game," Tally said, shaking his furry head. "They break the people into groups, tell them their loved ones will be safe if they kill others. Then everybody kill one another."

"Are they?" I asked.

"Are they what?" Tally asked.

"Are their loved ones safe if they win?"

"Aye, they are safe, but they are not safe. Is better dead. Squim saps the planet dry. It leaves planet, moves on. No more atmosphere. People live after the big fight, but they don't live. Not really. Borant at least gives people a chance. Tally's people had chance."

"So, you were a crawler, then?"

"No," Tally said. "Not all worlds are mined or picked for the show. Sometimes they come and offer to take people in exchange for not mining world. They came, and I went. This was very long ago."

"Shush," Donut said. "They're introducing us now."

Next came a view of Earth. Music swelled, sounding almost like mariachi with an EDM beat. Three lines of text scrolled across the bottom of the screen, all in different languages I couldn't read. Another two lines—one going up, one going down—scrolled on the right side, shrinking the viewing area. A generic, naked human male and female appeared on the screen, and the next 10 minutes were a discussion of human anatomy with an inordinate amount of time spent discussing male testicles and female ovaries. I still couldn't understand most of what the commentator was saying. Next came a long line of shots of Earth, focusing mostly on urban areas. It quickly became clear that the show was cherry-picking the shittier parts of the planet, showing shantytowns and garbage dumps. Bubbling pits of mud, and abandoned buildings. They were throwing in scenes from disaster films. I recognized a shot from the latest *Godzilla* movie. They were going out of their way to make Earth look like a nightmare.

Then came the people. They were showing people shooting up drugs, killing each other, a group of kids beating the crap out of another kid, a scene from the movie *Basket Case*, a dead horse for some reason, a scene from that serial killer movie that won Best Picture last year, an elderly woman crying, the kid from the "Charlie Bit My Finger" YouTube video.

"Wow," Donut said, shaking her head sadly. "I didn't realize Earth sucked so badly. Disgusting."

"That's not how it really is," I said. I paused. *Not is. Was. The world is gone.* "They're making it look like they're the good guys, saving us from ourselves."

Next came a sky-view version of the collapse, over a dense city I didn't recognize. Next was what appeared to be a CGI rendition of the dungeon forming below the Earth's crust. It only showed the first three levels, which was like an upside-down tiered pyramid.

The next forty minutes were nothing but scenes of people getting killed over and over.

The vast majority of people who entered the dungeon appeared to be from India and Africa and South America. Some of them were in massive groups of 1,000-plus people. I watched them trample each other as they ran from mobs I'd never seen, from spine-covered wolves to shapeless blobs of fire to floating, stingray-like creatures, which shot magic missiles from eye stalks, like the alien ships from *War of the Worlds*.

"Why did so many enter the dungeon?" I asked. *I* had entered because I didn't have a choice. Was it the same for the others?

Eventually, they started showing people surviving their encounters. A man with a broadsword cut through a group of floating eyeball things. A group of 10 people, armed with shotguns and bows and arrows, took down a nightmare pile of mouths and eyeballs and flesh. A borough boss, the screen said, the first one defeated. It quickly showed all 10 of their mug shots and listed the contents of the Silver Boss Boxes and the Platinum Weapons Boxes they'd received for the achievement. They'd all received magic tomes and enchanted ranged weapons.

Next, they showed a girl about 13 years old with a pair of rottweilers. I guessed she might be from South America somewhere. She wore an oversized soccer jersey that was yellow with a thick blue stripe running across it. The girl wore an angry, determined expression on her face.

The dogs ripped a cow-sized spider to shreds. Later, the same girl held a mace in her hand and had a full set of glowing silver armor. She'd kept the soccer jersey, wearing it over the armor like a tabard.

One of the dogs wore what appeared to be a chain mail sweater. The other had gained the ability to shoot lightning when it barked.

We were shown mug shots of her and both of her dogs. Her name was Lucia Mar. The dogs were Cici and Gustavo 3.

I still wasn't sure about the naming conventions. I guessed since I was the first Carl in the dungeon, I didn't have my last initial after my official name. And since this Gustavo was a dog without a last name, he had the three because he was the third Gustavo to enter the dungeon without a surname.

After that, it showed a quick rundown of several of the mobs, the images flashing by so quickly I could barely see any of them. I recognized goblins, Scatterers, rats, and dozens of the monsters shown in the earlier scenes.

And that was it. The announcer said something about staying tuned for a rundown of this season's rules and surprises and then something else about placing bets, but the screen snapped off and returned to the leaderboard image.

We just stared at the board for several moments.

"That's it?" Donut demanded, breaking the silence. She looked at me, incredulous. "After that epic battle with the Hoarder, we received no screen time. This is unacceptable!"

Before she could rant further, an announcement came. It was the same woman who spoke when the gates first closed.

Good job so far, everyone. We had 15 borough bosses taken out and over 1,500 neighborhood bosses killed. A pair of crawlers even came across a city boss, but that ended as you might expect. Losses are right on the projected track.

You'll be getting these announcements after each episode. A couple quick patch notes. The Fire Fingers spell should be safe to cast now. We've fixed the hallway bathroom bug. So, if you open the door, and someone else enters, they will no longer explode. Sorry about that. Reminder, however, hallway bathrooms are personal spaces, and they can't be shared. We also fixed the unlimited toilet paper bug. Now you're only getting one roll per floor, so if you waste it, you're on your own. We have a long list of fixes with the new inventory system that we're working on. For right now, the two big ones we've already patched are that you can no longer transport mobs to your inventory in order to kill them. Also, any momentum an item might have while it entered inventory will no longer be preserved. It's now safe to extract items you put into inventory while moving at a high rate of speed. Remember, this inventory system is a privilege, and it's not meant to be used as a weapon. While we love and admire your creativity, any unintentional exploits will be patched, so if you find something that has an unintended feature, don't get too comfortable using it.

We are now populating the staircases down to level 2. Remember, everyone. Only go down the stairs early if you absolutely have to. Once you descend to the next floor, you can't go back up. Also, we're trying something new this season. If you prematurely descend, you are held in stasis until the collapse. So those of you working on your social numbers, keep that in mind. Viewers tend to lose interest quickly, and you'll shed favorites if you're not accessible for a couple days before the floor above collapses. We recommend descending to the next level no earlier than six hours before the scheduled collapse. If you descend during that window, there will be no stasis involved, and you'll actually get a head start over those who came before you. Good luck. Let's have a great 30 hours until the next episode tunnels!

Now get out there and kill, kill, kill!

"Obviously we need to find one of these city bosses," Donut said. "That'll guarantee a feature the next episode. That's what we need to focus on."

I remembered the borough boss from the show. It had taken a group of ten well-armed crawlers to take it down.

"No," I said. "We need to find an exit."

I pulled up my map, hoping to see a stairwell appear somewhere in the neighborhood. There was nothing. I remembered reading once that the Earth was just under 200 million square miles. There would be 75,000 entrances down to the second floor. If these staircases were distributed randomly, we were fucked. Even if the first floor was just underneath the landmasses, and not the entire planet, we were still screwed. I was no math wizard, but I knew that meant the stairs would be hard to find.

Mordecai had said the staircase, like a safe room, would appear on the minimap, even if we hadn't explored that area yet. But even zoomed out, the map only encompassed a little more than a square mile. And when it was in normal mode, down in the corner of my vision, the map was a fourth of that. I couldn't just walk around with it zoomed out because I wouldn't be able to see anything.

We had three and a half days to find the staircase. We needed to cover a lot of ground.

15

TIME TO LEVEL COLLAPSE: 3 DAYS, 2 HOURS.

"WE'VE BEEN HERE BEFORE," DONUT SAID AS WE TURNED DOWN THE main corridor. "This is where we came into the dungeon."

After having explored much of the area, I was starting to see a distinctive pattern to the hallways. My apartment had been a little more than a half mile from the coast of the Puget Sound. The entrance I'd gone through appeared to be the very western edge of the map. The whole area was a giant grid of equal-sized squares, with the large, wide passages acting as the borders. While the interior halls and tunnels were twisty and mazelike, each section was still a perfect giant square. And within each square, there appeared to be four neighborhoods.

The Hoarder neighborhood was in the southeast corner of one of those squares. Directly west of that was the goblin neighborhood, right where we'd entered the dungeon. Across the hall was the domain of the llamas. Mordecai had said these first few floors weren't *really* covering the entire planet, and I could see now that he was correct, at least here. The dungeon was really just a condensed version of the city directly above, but more organized. I wondered what it was like in the more rural areas, if there were any entrances at all.

It appeared mobs didn't respawn in a particular neighborhood once you killed the boss, though mobs from adjacent neighborhoods had started to creep their way in. Also, the level two rats were just everywhere, though I never saw one in the main hall. They were nothing but a nuisance now. They'd see us, charge, and I'd either kick them or stomp them, killing them with a single blow.

Near the northern edge of the Hoarder's neighborhood, we started to run across a new type of mob: slimes.

After our first encounter with those things, we had to turn back. I couldn't fight them, not without any sort of protection for my hands. The first one we came across was a simple level two green slime. Donut and I had both already hit level seven by this point, and I figured it'd be simple as killing the bugs.

Kicking the green slime did nothing but burn my feet. I made the mistake of trying to punch the pig-sized blob, and it almost ate my arm off. As it was, I sank elbow deep into it, and my right fingerless glove dissolved right off my hand. The right arm of my leather jacket melted away.

It ended up killing itself thanks to my Damage Reflect ability. My arm was red and bubbling and screaming with pain by the time I pulled it out of the green gelatin mass.

I received an **It Burns, Dunnit?** achievement for that one.

Thankfully, the steel chain wrapped around my knuckles remained intact. In fact, the links appeared to gleam after the fight, as if they'd been cleaned.

I waited to heal, and we turned around, giving that neighborhood a wide berth.

It was then, as I gazed upon the next neighborhood over, that I got an idea on how to cover more ground as quickly as possible.

I pointed to the neon sign that remained blinking off the main corridor. **DA TUTORIAL GUILD**. It looked as it had when we first arrived. "We are headed in there."

DONUT: YES O.K. THERE WILL BE MONSTERS IN THERE.

"Stop," I said. "Please stop."

I'd made the mistake of showing Donut the chat feature of the party menu. One could click on the party's name, and a chat option appeared at the end of the list. For me, a virtual keyboard materialized floating before me, but after spending some time with it, I figured out how to just think the words while focusing on the chat window. Apparently Donut, as a quadruped, had a completely different interface.

When the messages came, they popped up with a haptic buzz in my brain, and it startled me every time. Donut spent a good ten minutes sending me message after nonsensical message until I finally told her to stop. She had, until now.

"Using the chat is quite enjoyable to me," Donut said. "Now I understand why Miss Beatrice was always on her phone. I wish it was connected to the internet. I think I'd have a lot of fun on the internet."

"It's good to have," I said. "But you don't need to do it when I'm right here. It hurts my head. Also, don't type in all caps. It makes it sound like you're shouting."

"Okay, fine. Be a grump," she said as we approached the alleyway.

Thanks to Donut's *Torch* spell, we didn't need to carry a light when we entered the pitch-black corridor.

I was expecting another goblin machine to be waiting for us, but the alley was abandoned. The place smelled of machines, oil, and pineapple.

"I'm okay with killing goblins," Donut said as we walked. "But I don't think there'll be stairs this close to the edge of the map. Remember what it looked like on the show? Each floor was smaller. I think we need to head east before we start seeing stairs."

"We're not going to kill the goblins," I said, indicating the tattoo on my forearm, which still appeared on the exterior of my intact left jacket arm. "Not if we don't have to." We eased our way down the alley, keeping an eye out for red dots.

It didn't take long. We turned a corner, and three level two goblins approached, all brandishing pineapple sticks.

"What is with the goblins and their fruit?" Donut asked as they approached screeching.

"I don't know," I said. "It's weird."

Before they got too close, I lifted my arm, showing the tattoo. "I have free passage through this area!"

The goblins all stopped at that. The moment I showed them the mark, their dots turned from red to white. They lowered their weapons and looked at one another, as if confused about what to do next. They started gibbering in their language. Finally, one turned toward me.

"Where you get that mark, human?"

I had a carefully prepared answer. Hopefully they would . . .

"He blew up one of your filthy tractors and smeared three of your friends all over the cobblestones," Donut declared. She pointed daintily south. "They're in that next neighborhood over if you want to scoop 'em up."

"Goddamnit, Donut," I whispered. The goblins stared at us with slack-jawed gazes of incredulity. "Let me do the talking. I'm the one with the brand."

"And I'm the one with the 37 in charisma," said Donut. "They're not going to care. Watch this." She started walking toward one of three goblins. "You, sweetheart," she said. "What's your name?"

"Uh, I don't . . ." the goblin began. "I don't think I have a name."

"Most unfortunate," Donut said. "Hmm. I'm going to call you B.A." She looked at the other two goblins. "And you guys are Face and Murdock." She looked back at me. "Remind me why we're here again?"

"I want to talk to some of the goblin engineers," I said.

"B.A., be a love and show us to some of your engineers. I do believe they're the gentlemen who wear culinary items upon their heads."

"Uh, okay. Yes, ma'am," B.A. the goblin said.

"Wait," Donut said.

"Yeah?" B.A. said.

Donut indicated the tiara on her head. "It's not 'ma'am.' It's 'Princess Donut.' You got that, B.A.?"

"Um, okay. Okay, Princess Donut." He turned and started marching farther north into the dungeon.

"What the actual fuck?" I hissed at the cat. "How . . . Did you know that was going to happen?"

"It's simple," Donut said as we walked. "Mordecai told me that the higher my charisma is, the easier it will be to get them to do what I want. As long as they can speak and their dots aren't red and they aren't a boss or a really high level, I can control them just like I control you. Mordecai says for the first four or five floors, I can talk anybody into anything. How do you think I've been getting Tally to give me five plates of salmon this whole time?"

As we walked, we passed several groups of level two goblins. We also saw a few types I hadn't seen before:

Goblin Bomb Bard. Level 5.
These bastards are more unhinged and sadistic than those guys who couldn't pass the psych exam to join the military. Bomb Bards are experts with explosives, and they strike with a variety of ranged attacks that'll blow your socks off. If the one you're looking at right now has more than half of his fingers, then he's probably very, very dangerous.

One of the bomb bards glared at us as we passed. The goblin, indeed, had all of his fingers. He tossed a small glass ball up in the air, catching it absently as we marched past. Each of the level twos on either side of him cringed each time the glass ball went up in the air.

We turned another corner, and we entered a large workshop. At the end of this room was a wooden door, and based on the minimap, I immediately determined beyond that door was the lair of yet another neighborhood boss. It appeared this next room over was almost identical in shape to that of the Hoarder.

I looked about the expansive workshop. We were surrounded by about 25 of the engineers and a smattering of others, including two level seven "shamankas" who stood guarding the far wall. The engineers all wore something odd on their heads, but it wasn't always pots and pans. One wore what appeared to be a hockey helmet. Another sported one of those padded helmets worn by boxers.

A massive steam engine dominated the western wall, and the engineers crawled about it like ants. Wheels and cogs whirled and chugged away. On the opposite side of the room stood a line of six parked goblin murder dozers. These also crawled with goblin engineers. Multiple tables covered with tools and giant greasy parts lay scattered about the room. A vast pile of coal stood in the far corner near the boss room.

One of the level sevens glanced in our direction and approached.

She was a female goblin, standing about five and a quarter feet tall, making her tower over the others. She had well-defined muscles and wore a jet-black robe. She carried a wooden staff that, oddly, also held a pineapple at the top, but this one was actually made of wood, a part of the carving.

The goblin's face was filled with piercings. There had to be fifty of them. She looked like one of those body-modification people who would appear on *Ripley's Believe It or Not!* It was hard to look at until you got used to it. The woman sneered, revealing sharpened teeth and a forked pierced tongue.

Goblin Shamanka. Level 7.

In case you're wondering, Shamanka is just a fancy way of saying female shaman. Goblin Shamans are the leader class of all goblin clans, second only to the War Chieftain or, more rarely, the Goblin Warlord. They are without humor and are said, as part of their training, to have to pick two of the following three actions in order to graduate Shamanka University: They have to fuck, cook, and/or eat their own parents. Most don't pick cook. And if that wasn't messed up enough, they specialize in Anguish Magic, a dark magic school designed to focus and enhance damage from other attacks.

"You may have a pass, but you are not welcome here, human," the goblin said. "Not in this place."

I took a deep breath. "I want to buy a vehicle from you guys. Or have you make me one really quick. Preferably something that I can negotiate down stairs, but I'll take what I can get. We have a lot of ground to cover, and I figured you guys could help."

The goblin looked at me as if I'd just asked her to eat a Twinkie out of my ass.

"You stupid, ugly excuse for a monkey. Do you really think you can just—"

"Oh, honey, can we discuss what's going on here?" Donut asked, interrupting the goblin. She waved a paw, indicating the jewelry in the goblin's face. "Is it like some sort of performance art? Do you wear all that metal because they made you eat your parents?"

The shaman looked at Donut, a mask of utter outrage on her face that started to melt the moment she met the cat's eyes. It was the weirdest thing. I realized the cat was casting a spell of sorts on the goblin, some sort of automatic charm effect.

"What?" the goblin asked, her voice totally changed. She, to everyone's complete surprise, sat cross-legged on the ground and leaned forward. She discarded her pineapple staff. "What did you say?"

"I mean, I guess I can see what you were going for. You have exquisite cheekbones," Donut said. "But your face looks like an overenthusiastic Brillo pad. That other lady shaman down there, she doesn't have nearly as many things in her face. Though, my word, she does have that unfortunate necklace made of bones, doesn't she? But we'll get to her later. So, tell me. Is it a daddy thing?"

The goblin didn't say anything for several moments, but then she put her face into her hands, and she burst into tears. "Yes," the goblin cried. "It's true." Donut walked forward and sat in her lap.

The other shamanka, alarmed at this new development, came running forward. But a moment later, the two magic users were on the ground, sobbing, clutching onto each other. The one with the bone necklace had a line of snot running down her face as she ugly-cried about having to eat her father raw.

Donut named the one with the facial piercings Rory and the other Lorelai.

"So, Rory," Donut asked after a few minutes of the goblins sniveling, "how about that vehicle my friend asked for? Is there something you can do for us?"

Rory wiped her face. "We cannot part with a murder dozer. They are much too valuable, and the chieftain would literally kill us. But I will have them make a human-sized chopper. One with a sidecar." She indicated a line of two-wheeled contraptions leaning up against the wall near the bulldozers. They appeared to be steam-powered bicycles. "But we can't do it for free. You gotta trade something."

"I have all sorts of stuff," I said. I pulled up my inventory. I selected the satchel of gunpowder, and it appeared in my hands. It was a heavy leather sack. I wanted to keep the stuff, but I wanted the transport more.

Rory thumbed over her shoulder, indicating a line of barrels right next to the giant machine. "We got funpowder." I hadn't noticed the barrels before. They all had "XXX" marked on them. Sparks were constantly showering off the giant steam engine. If one of those sparks landed on a barrel . . . "To offer goblins funpowder is like offering water to a piranha," she added.

This went on for a bit. I offered torches. Healing potions. Antidote potions. Both the pet biscuits and the crawler biscuits. All of it rejected.

My eyes caught something else on my list.

"How about this?" I asked, offering up the two baggies of meth.

Rory snatched them away. "Is this all you have? Two hits?"

Lorelai scrabbled at Rory's hand, coming away with one of the bags. The goblin opened the baggie, stuck a pinkie in, and had a quick taste. Her eyes grew wide. "This is dungeon made," Lorelai said. "He didn't bring it with him from the outside." She looked at me. "Where did you get it? Did they have more?"

"I'll tell you where to get more in exchange for that machine—one that won't blow up on us—plus coal or whatever you need to run it, and some of those grenade things your bomb bards carry."

"I don't know," Lorelai began, looking uncertainly at the other shaman.

"Do it," Donut said.

"Deal," Rory said.

Lorelai got up and started screaming orders at the engineers, who looked at her as if she had gone insane. The shamanka sent a blue bolt into the backside of one of the engineers, and they scrambled to work.

"Do you . . . do you want to come with us?" Donut asked Rory, her voice surprisingly gentle.

Donut still sat in Rory's lap, and she purred as the green monster stroked her hair.

The pierced goblin sighed. "I cannot. I can't leave the chieftain. He's terrible, soft even, but he's still leader of my clan. My family. And even if I could go with you, I wouldn't be able to leave this floor. If we climb down the stairs, we die. You get halfway down, and your body just dissolves. I've seen it myself."

"So you know how this works? You know what's happening here?" I asked.

The goblin nodded. Her face jingled when she moved. "I know enough. I know we are on the first floor. There are smart mobs, like us, and there are not-so-smart mobs. The deeper you get into the dungeon, the more are smart. In this borough, we are king. Us and the gnolls and the rat-kin and a few others. Most of the monsters aren't so smart."

"But do you know what happens in a couple days?" I asked.

"The floor collapses," she said. "Yes. But it is only you who dies when this happens. For us we go to sleep until the next dungeon opens. We will open our eyes, and it will be the same as it has been.

Just another day. But one of these days, one of these days we will wake up, and we will be deeper. That's what they tell us. Kill the crawlers, get better at killing, and you get to go deeper. And one day, eventually, we will be so deep that crawlers will never come, and we will finally have peace. We will have peace and a place to live and breed and have our little ones run free and not worry about killing for survival."

16

Goblin Copper Chopper with attached sidecar. Human-sized. Contraption.

Take a junkyard bicycle, add an unreliable steam engine, re-move all the bolts holding it together, replace them with chewing gum, and you get the idea. The preferred assault transport of Goblin Bomb Bards, what this contraption lacks in reliability and safety it makes up for in absolutely nothing.

I took a step back and admired the "vehicle." Like the description said, it looked a lot like a crackhead's bicycle. The framework was made of welded-together copper bits of varying patinas. Thankfully they'd made this one a little bigger to fit me, but even then, it was still probably a bit too small to be comfortable.

The two wheels were solid and black, made of some unknown material. The seat appeared to be an alligator skull with white fur lining the top, giving it the impression that the skull was wearing an Andy Warhol wig. The engine sat in the middle of the chassis, thumping. A hopper extended from the engine, opening up near the handlebars. I would have to periodically toss a lump of coal in there.

"What about the water?" I asked. "And how do I turn it off?"

"It's a permacube," the engineer said. "Won't run out until you die of old age. You don't turn it off. Just let it run out of coal. Toss in a lump, and it'll start up on its own after a minute. We don't use the lesser demons to run our steam engines like some do. This is just as good, and this baby will outlast you." He slapped the side of the bike, and the handlebars fell off, clattering to the ground. He cursed and bent to pick them back up. He started reattaching them to the frame with a wrench.

The detachable sidecar was nothing more than a bar, a single wheel affixed to a colossal spring, and another, smaller fur-lined skull that was supposed to be the seat. This skull looked like it was from some flat-headed orc creature. A pair of bones provided a backrest. Donut jumped up a few times, circled, sat down, then jumped off. She started demanding some changes of the engineers. They were currently painting the backrest purple after adding an extra layer of fur.

The bike was heavy, heavier than it looked. But thankfully, I could lift it off the ground for just long enough to be able to pop it into my inventory.

"It's not going to blow up on me, is it? That dozer thing exploded after it hit the wall."

"That dozer wouldn't have blown up if you had twisted the relief valve," the engineer said. He pointed to a pair of identical spigots on the side of the bike. "If it gets too hot, twist that one right there, and it won't blow. If the pressure is too high, twist the other one. Don't mix it up, or you make it worse."

"How will I know if it's too hot? Or if the pressure is too high? There are no gauges!"

He smiled, revealing a row of sharp teeth.

"Don't you worry about that, human. You will know. Just listen to the chopper. It will tell you."

The engineer had pointed at that stack of coal that reached the ceiling, telling me to grab all I could carry. I sneaked around the back of the heap and took a metric fuck ton of the stuff. I had three piles of 999 coal lumps before the heap started to look noticeably lower.

It was time to jet. Both Rory and Lorelai had disappeared while the goblin engineers worked. They reappeared now. Both of them were blitzed. Rory's eyes were noticeably slitted, and Lorelai danced seductively toward me as we prepared to leave.

"Wanna have some fun before you go?" Lorelai asked, grasping the front of my tattered jacket. Her breath smelled of rotten fish. She'd removed her bone necklace.

"Uh," I said.

"Oh, sweetie," said Donut, "as amusing as I would find it to watch Carl here disappoint yet another woman, we're on a schedule. Banging monster girls is not the narrative we're going for with this story. Maybe next time."

"Sure, but you look me up later, okay?" the goblin said. She reached up and booped me on the nose. "It'd be nice to fuck someone and not have to eat them afterward." She sighed and turned toward one of the bomb bards.

"You," she said. "Meet me in my chambers after lights-out. And take a bath first."

Rory handed me a bag. I examined it, and it was filled to the brim with dynamite and several types of small bombs and grenades. Remembering how dangerous this stuff was, I quickly added it to my inventory. I'd examine the items from there.

Rory turned to Donut. "Okay, we had a deal. Where'd you find the stuff?"

"The drugs?" Donut asked. "It's just one neighborhood over, on the other side of the road. We got it from one of those llamas."

"I *knew* it!" she said. She turned toward another bomb bard. "Gear up. They've been holding out on us. We're rolling on them in five."

I stood, bewildered, as all around me, the goblins—from the level two standard goblins to the engineers to the bomb bards—burst into a screeching frenzy of activity. The murder dozers growled like dinosaurs as goblins piled on. Four copper choppers similar to my own roared to life. The bomb bards all donned metal helmets with a German-style spike at the tip. The tips glistened, shooting sparks. The goblins could light their dynamite sticks and bombs just by raising them over their own heads.

One by one, the choppers and dozer transports rumbled away, filled with screaming goblins. A minute later, and we were alone in the room.

"Did that just happen?" I asked, spinning to see if we truly were alone. We were. "Did we really just start a meth war between the goblins and the llamas?"

"Yes, we did," Donut said. "Just like I planned. It went pretty well, don't you think?" She indicated the door at the far side of the room. "So, you want to go in there and kill their chieftain? I could really use another boss box."

I examined the large room we were in. The goblins had abandoned a ton of stuff. Just like that. I didn't see any weapons or armor. But there were piles of engineering supplies. Wires, cogs, dynamite, gunpowder—or, as they called it, "funpowder." Barrels of it. I eyed a simple cart used to transport the barrels from one area to the next.

"We need to loot everything we can," I said, looking around. *"Everything."*

"And then we kill the chieftain, right?"

I looked at the door. The last time we'd fought a boss, I'd had to pummel a scared woman to death. I could still feel her face crunching under my fists. We had no idea what was behind that door, but the support creatures of this area were significantly stronger than the ones guarding the last boss room. It'd be dumb to go in there. Really, really dumb.

Besides, it'd be the ultimate dick move after they'd helped us.

"Yeah, and then we kill the chieftain," I said.

Donut hopped up and down, her tail swishing. "This is going to make exquisite television."

17

MY INVENTORY HAD ABOUT 10 NEW TABS BY THE TIME WE WERE done clearing out the goblin workshop. I took another five piles of coal. We looted tons of tools, from shovels to wrenches to hammers. Most of them were much too small to use as weapons, but I would examine them all later to make sure. We had engineering supplies, coils and coils of wick, multiple types of explosives, about fifty gallons of various alchemical liquids, and a pile of those black disks they used for chopper tires. I even took all the tables I could lift. By the time we were done, all that was left were some of the bigger tables, the giant steam engine, a greatly reduced pile of coal, and a set of barrels with "XXX" on them, all placed neatly on the cart and tied down with a length of rope.

I'd managed to take almost a ton of the black powder, but it required me using the discarded leather sacks they had lying around. This stuff was distinctly the old-school, coarse black powder, not the more refined smokeless powder used in modern firearms. I wasn't quite strong enough to lift the barrels until they were less than half full. But when they did get that empty, I didn't put them in my inventory. Instead, I lifted the barrels and placed them on the cart.

We placed the cart in front of the door to the boss room. On top of the powder, I placed shovelfuls of nuts and bolts and other metal odds and ends. Then I placed the tops back on the barrels before an errant spark from the still-humming steam engine blew us all to hell.

Donut "directed" the action from the seat of her sidecar. I would put the chopper into my inventory before we proceeded.

"Do you think Rory and Lorelai will be mad at me?" Donut asked as we prepared the trigger. Unlike last time, I wasn't going to use plain goblin dynamite, which was inherently unstable. I found a blob of a C4-like explosive called "Hobgoblin Pus" that was detonated with an actual trigger. There was only a small amount of the material, but the description said it caused a big explosion. I had the sense that it was valuable, probably the real prize of this room. I was going to use it all. Next to the hobgoblin pus was a set of magical triggers. There were only three of the mechanisms, and I had to waste one in order to test it, to see how they worked.

The triggers were both genius and foolproof. You broke the tip off of the mechanism, which looked like a stick of underarm deodorant. You stuck the broken-off part into the explosive, and you pressed the button to set it off. Easy. The detonators were single use, but you could break off up to 10 pieces for each stick, so you could simultaneously blow 10 different bombs. It had a five-second countdown after you pressed the button. The description said the trigger had a range of about ten kilometers.

"Will they be mad? Probably," I said. "But Rory doesn't seem to like this boss guy too much, so who knows? I hope we never find out."

"Do you think this is enough?" Donut asked, looking over the four barrels. "I feel as if it's not enough."

I shrugged. "Black powder isn't really meant for blowing stuff up. But it's good at throwing metal. If he's in there and out in the open, we'll turn this guy into a pincushion for sure. But I doubt the explosion itself is going to be bigger than when that murder dozer blew up. Either way, if this doesn't kill him, more probably wouldn't, either."

The plan was a more refined version of what we had done with the Hoarder. From what I could see, the room that this war chieftain occupied was identical in size and shape to the one from the last boss battle. This was still the first floor, after all, so I doubted the guy was *that* powerful. We were going to open the door, push the cart in, close the door, run until we had several walls between us, and hit the trigger. If we killed the boss, we'd get a notification and a star by our names. If we didn't, we'd keep running. We'd pull out the chopper and put some distance between us and the whole neighborhood and forget this ever happened.

I'd put a hunk of the hobgoblin pus in each barrel, and I added the last of it to the top of the first barrel. I placed the detonator into the pus, sticking half out of it. I tried to make it look obvious, but not overly obvious. If the goblin chieftain had time to react, he'd hopefully spend his last moments digging the detonator out of this chunk of explosive, not realizing we had four more ready to go buried in each of the barrels.

It was a chickenshit way to do it, but I didn't care. Not when one got locked in the room with the boss otherwise.

"You ready, Princess?" I asked.

I stood directly behind the cart, poised to shove. I'd pulled it back a good ten feet, just enough to give me momentum. Donut would open the door using her menu, eyeball the room to make sure the path was clear, tell me to go, then slam the door after I heaved. Hopefully the floor would be flat enough for the cart to travel a good distance.

"Ready," she said. "I'm opening the door now."

From my vantage, I couldn't see into the room, but I heard the heavy creak of the door yawning open.

"Do it!" Donut cried.

I kicked my legs, and I crashed into the cart like it was a football sled. I'd greased the wheels, and the heavy cart moved quickly and easily. I shoved with all my might and watched the cart rocket into the room as the large door slammed.

Donut had already turned and was bolting for the exit on the opposite side of the room.

I scrambled up and followed. We'd practiced this part. We turned three times, making sure we were out of any line of direct blast. I didn't want to wait too long, but we had to put a few large rooms between us in case there was a shock wave that needed to be dispersed. We stopped at the prearranged spot, and I leaned against the wall, my heart thrashing. I pulled the detonator trigger from my inventory.

"Did you see him? Was there a giant goblin in there?" I asked.

Donut heaved for breath. "Yes. A huge. Ugly. Goblin. My word. I do not like running. He was sitting down, reading a book. Blow it, blow it good."

I jammed the button.

"There sure were a lot of babies in there, too," Donut said in that last moment before the blast.

18

"*GODDAMNIT, DONUT,*" I SAID.

We'd both been knocked over, but unhurt, by the shock wave. It'd been big, bigger than I'd expected. Dust cascaded from the ceiling. A terrible hissing noise followed the explosion. I suspected it was from the boiler of the giant engine. The whistling noise eased over the next several minutes. Occasional smaller blasts went off. But eventually even those stopped. An entire wall of notifications appeared, most of them achievements. But we had, indeed, killed the neighborhood boss. There was no fanfare this time, but another bronze star appeared by both of our names.

"Were there really babies in there? Like goblin babies?" I asked.

"Oh yes, there were a bunch of them. I only saw them for but a moment, but they were quite cute. Some of them were wearing little oversized jackets, like Baby Yoda. Adorable. I think you hit one with the cart. There were old ones and pregnant ones, too. Did you see your level? We're both level eight now. You're welcome." Donut looked up into the air. "We didn't get to see our faces all big. I suppose they don't do the boss-battle-graphic thing if you're not locked in the room with them. That's too bad. It's quite entertaining."

"Goddamnit," I said again. I was all about killing as many goblins and monsters as I could, but killing babies? That was pretty fucked up, and I wasn't sure how I felt about it. Actually, I knew exactly how I felt about it. It made me feel like an asshole. I didn't like feeling like an asshole. I stared at that blinking box of achievement notifications. I sighed. I didn't even want to click on the box.

"What?" Donut said, looking up with what appeared to be genuine curiosity. "It's not like they didn't have it coming. You didn't ask to be here. They're goblins! What kind of vile monster sticks babies in the boss room anyway?"

I shook my head. "We need to get back over there, grab the neighborhood map, and get our asses out of Dodge before the others return. They're probably on their way now. There's no way they didn't hear that. We'll go north, heading into the next neighborhood over."

The workshop had been completely obliterated. All that was left was blackened rubble. The lights on the walls were all out, but the entire north side of the room was a fifteen-foot wall of fire. The smoke billowed. I absently noted that the smoke was being sucked away into the ceiling. The dungeon masters were cheating, offering some sort of ventilation system. Otherwise this entire area would've been filled with black smoke by now. We could only take a couple steps into the room before it got too hot. I looked about. The large tables were just gone. Large chunks of stone had fallen from the ceiling. Donut jumped on my shoulder as I examined the room.

The boiler on the enormous steam engine looked like a baked potato that'd been peeled open with a bunch of copper sticks coming out from it, like tentacles. A steady cloud of angry steam still hissed from the interior of the wreckage, mixing with the black smoke. The room was ankle-deep in water, and the water sizzled and steamed as it came into contact with the burning wall.

"We probably should have taken all of the coal from that pile, not just half of it," Donut said. "We're not getting to that dead boss now."

She was right. The coal had ignited, and now our only way into the boss chamber was blocked off.

I was relieved. I wanted that map, but not as much as I didn't want to go in there. I didn't want to see the dead babies and other goblins. I felt sick thinking about it.

I noticed the line of white dots on the edge of my minimap headed in our direction. The dots wouldn't be white for long. Donut's charisma had ticked up to 39 once she hit level eight, but I doubted even that would be enough to save us once they saw what we'd done.

"Let's get the hell out of here," I said. I plotted out a quick escape, leading us into unknown territory. We'd have to fight through a quadrant we hadn't explored yet before we could get to another artery. Hopefully it wasn't filled with slimes or some other mob I couldn't handle. Maybe there'd be a safe room to rest in, to sit back and figure out all of these new achievements. From there we'd take the chopper and try to find a set of stairs.

"I must admit," Donut said as we jogged away. "I do like it when you blow stuff up. I like it a lot."

19

TIME TO LEVEL COLLAPSE: 2 DAYS, 18 HOURS.

New achievement! You *Monster*!

You have killed an infant! An infant!

Okay, okay. Unless you're a complete psychopath, we know you probably didn't wake up this morning and tell yourself, "Today is the day I'm going to slaughter a child." Well, let us put your mind at ease. All children mobs who die within this dungeon don't actually perish. They're transferred to a holding area where they're safe and treated nicely and gently until they can be reunited with their loving parents at the end of the season.

Feel better? Good.

Reward: These past twenty seconds, when your conscience started to ease? That was your reward. It was also a lie. That baby is dead, and it's dead because of you. You're totally going to hell.

You've also received a Bronze Asshole's Box.

New achievement! War Criminal.

You have killed more than 20 non-combatants in a single attack!

Question: What's the only thing standing between an innocent child and a happy, fulfilling life?

Answer: You. The answer is you.

Reward: You've received a Gold Asshole's Box!

WE'D FOUND A SAFE ROOM HALFWAY THROUGH THE NEIGHBORHOOD of the rot stickers. The monsters were small and round. They looked like little, black-hued raviolis that ran on the walls and ceilings and suicide-bombed themselves against you. All the ones we'd seen so far were only level one and two, but if they managed to stick themselves to your body, they'd explode. Each blast felt like getting hit with a sledgehammer.

The attacks also inflicted Take Down, an effect that was supposed to knock you on your ass. Once you hit the ground, I guessed, they'd swarm at your head and take you out. The little monsters were everywhere. Thankfully my trollskin shirt negated the Take Down effect.

Donut remained on my shoulder, shooting missiles at the creatures. A single blast took out several at a time. So far none had managed to get to her. She was quick that way. Despite all that happened, she was still a cat, able to jump out of the way at the last second. But just in case, I made her drink one of my Iron Skin potions, which upped her natural armor for several minutes. I drank one as well.

The rot stickers usually focused on me anyway, the bigger and slower target. One landed directly on my inner thigh and detonated before I could get it, the effect equivalent to being kicked in the nads by a horse. I did fall down that time. If I hadn't quaffed the potion, my leg and balls might've been blown clear off. I was only saved because of a well-timed missile blast from Donut.

Thankfully the raviolis made a loud, chittering noise when they approached, and it took them about three seconds to detonate once they attached to your body. Once we figured out how they worked, it was easy to smash and crush them before they did too much damage. As long as we didn't get surrounded by a giant group of them, we'd probably be okay.

This safe room was nothing like the last one we'd entered. This was more like a small waiting area at a dingy bus station or maybe a DMV somewhere. We still had the three screens and the larger bathrooms with showers. Plus a water fountain. A set of five cots with curtains around them lined one long wall. Two empty curtained areas appeared at the end of the row, and I wondered on that. Had they run out of cots? Or were they privacy areas for those who didn't want a cot? There was no attendant, so I couldn't ask.

My eyes immediately moved to the number flashing on the first screen.

3,594,517.

It had slowed its mad descent toward human extinction, but it hadn't stopped. It made a low, barely audible noise every time it went down. *Clink. Clink. Clink, clink, clink,* like water fast-dripping from a faucet.

I wondered how many of my fellow people had found a place like this and had given up. They were just hunkering down, eating, sleeping, waiting for it all to end. I shuddered.

The third screen read: **Limited services at this location. Take an experience cookie. One per Crawler per day. You deserve it.**

There was a plate on a table filled with what looked like chocolate chip cookies. Donut jumped up on the counter and picked it up with her mouth. She ate. A **+9.8 EXP** appeared in the air over her head, rising into the air with an audible *ping*, 8-bit-style. Being partied with her, I received the other .2 experience. She complained about me "stealing" her experience, and she tried to take a second cookie, but her mouth moved right through the plate like it wasn't even there.

I also ate one of the stale cookies, evening it out.

The 10 experience points were nothing. A single level two goblin was worth about 50, so this was mostly just a peculiarity of this specific safe room. It seemed every one of these rooms had something different and unique about it, and the weird cookies were this location's quirk.

Looking at the map, I guessed we had about half a mile to go before we reached the next artery. From there we would pull the chopper out of my inventory and head east in search of a set of stairs.

But first, rest.

We had about six hours before the next episode. We decided to take the opportunity to sleep. Afterward, we would watch episode two, and then we would leave. No more fucking around. We had two and half days.

In addition to the two baby-killing achievements, I received several more including multiple explosive-based achievements, rewarding me with several goblin boxes. We both got another Bronze Boss Box. I also got a Gold Looter Box for storing more than a ton of weight in my inventory.

I received multiple skill upgrades. All of my combat skills had ticked up thanks to the rot stickers, including my Smush skill. My Explosives Handling, Dangerous Explosives Handling, and Goblin Explosives skills rose to 5. I also received a new one:

IED Skill Level 3.
     It's one thing to take a grenade and toss it. But it takes a set of brass balls the size of basilisk eggs to actually build a bomb. Especially with the unreliable crap you find down here. Every level of this skill increases the damage yield of improvised explosive devices by 10% and decreases the chances of a catastrophic, premature uh-oh by half.

In addition, I received a pop-up that told me because my Explosives Handling skill was now five, I would receive additional information from all bomb-type devices when I examined them.

An entire new menu appeared in my interface. It was titled Demolitions Workshop. I clicked on it, but I received an error message.

You may only access this menu when you're standing in front of a Sapper's Table. You may purchase this workbench from a Safe Room store.

Interesting. That was something I'd explore later if we ever made it that far.

Donut received numerous skills and achievements from charming the goblins. She received something called a Silver Beguiler Box.

Donut opened her boxes first. She received the usual pile of biscuits and torches and potions. From the boss box, she received her first piece of armor. The beguiler box contained a tome called *Minion Army*. She also received the same two asshole boxes I'd received. The first contained a tattoo similar to the Goblin Pass I'd received earlier. The second silver box contained five potions called **Weapon Oil: Weeping Wound.**

She was *pissed* about the tattoo. Absolutely enraged. I hadn't seen her this upset since Angel the cocker spaniel crunched down and broke one of her jingly balls.

"What gives them the right to just defile me like this? What gives them the right!" she cried. "Oh my god! It's a disqualifying mark. It's a disqualifying mark, Carl! I'm damaged!"

The mark appeared on her back, just over her right shoulder blade. She'd screamed and hissed with outrage when it branded itself to her. It was hard to discern what it was. While it glowed through her fur, she had so much hair that it looked like nothing but a gold-colored splotch. I suspected I would get one, too, in a few minutes. I gently touched it, and it let me read the description:

Desperado Pass.
   Great. Now you're running with the type of kids who sit in the back of the bus. What would your mother say?
   This pass allows access to the Desperado Club.
   Warning: Holding a Desperado Pass negates the ability to obtain a Vanquisher Pass.

That was it. It didn't explain anything about what the hell that meant.

Donut continued to bitch about it for several minutes. Finally, she moved on. With a *pop*, the silver scale armor appeared draped over the back half of her body. It reached about halfway down to the floor.

I couldn't tell how it was attached to her, but it seemed to stay put. It was like a skirt, almost, though it didn't cover her stomach. It had a slot especially for her tail. She started turning in circles, trying to look at it.

"How's it look? How's it look? Does it cover the tattoo?"

"It's fine," I said as I examined its properties. "It doesn't cover the tattoo, not even close, but it looks great."

Enchanted Fae Scale Quadruped Crupper of the Fleet.
   Boy, is that a fucking mouthful. By the gods.
   +2 to Dexterity.
   Light and flexible, this scale armor is made from Fae steel. While not as strong as Elven mail or even good Orcish steel, it's the strongest alloy that fairy folk can wear. It's not the best protection, but it'll make your ass look oh so pretty.

The tome of *Minion Army* taught a spell that cost 50 spell points to cast. It caused hostile enemies to fight for you instead of against you. It was a great spell, but Donut only currently had 24 spell points, so it was useless for now. She tried reading the book anyway, but it wouldn't let her. Apparently you couldn't teach yourself spells you couldn't cast. She pouted for a good minute straight afterward.

"Don't worry," I said. "We'll either trade it in for something better, or you can use it later."

The last item she'd received was that oil, which was something one could apply to edged weapons to make the wound bleed longer.

It was my turn. I also received a ton of crap. More potions, more dynamite, another lighter, a couple smoke bombs, a couple more scrolls of *Confusing Fog*. I received no pants or shoes. I got the exact same items from the two asshole boxes, though my tattoo appeared on my goddamned neck. I couldn't even see it, but it burned as it was magically applied.

"It's a dagger dripping blood," Donut said, examining it close.

"My word, is it ghastly. Miss Beatrice is going to absolutely shit when she sees it on me."

From the boss box I'd received another ring of constitution, this one +2. I put it on my left ring finger, bringing my score up to 12.

From the Gold Looter Box I received a single item. A potion.

Skill Potion.

Drinking this adds a single level to the Determine Value skill. Hopefully now you'll realize all those *Magic: The Gathering* cards are nothing more than just meaningless pieces of paper, and you should have spent your money on something with actual value, like a treadmill. Or shampoo.

I immediately added it to my hotlist and drank. Nothing seemed to happen, but when I opened up my inventory, I had a new ability. While this first level of the skill didn't tell me the actual worth of any of the items listed there, it now allowed me to sort them by value, which I did.

The first item on the list was that tome of *Wisp Armor*. The second was the chopper. And after that was the single hobgoblin detonator I still had. The next several items were pieces of goblin equipment we'd looted from the workshop, including one of the tables, which was listed as an engineer's table. The list didn't include the items I currently had equipped. I suspected my trollskin shirt would be at the top of the list otherwise.

Finally done with our skills and loot, I decided to take a nap on the uncomfortable cot. Donut, still bitching about the tattoo, curled up with me.

You Monster.

I tried to pry the achievement out of my head. It was just another stupid joke. The game didn't care that I'd killed children. It *wanted* me to kill them. The room was set up for it to happen exactly as it had. We were supposed to kill or otherwise clear out the workshop. We were supposed to either blow up that room or do exactly what we did. It was a trap just as much as the bulldozer had been a trap. And those kids had been placed there, in that room, for that express purpose. They'd existed only to die. I couldn't blame myself, or feel guilty. Donut was right. This wasn't my fault. Not at all.

I looked up at the ceiling. Someone had carved their initials in the cheap tile. AMW. I wondered whose they were, and when they'd carved it. If they were alive now. This place had no signs, so I couldn't tell where it had come from. It didn't feel American, but I wasn't sure. It didn't matter anymore. This was a place from *my* world. A place these aliens had stolen.

"You're not going to break me," I said. "You might hurt me, or kill me, but you're not going to break me."

I turned on my side to sleep. On my neck, Donut cuddled closer. Her new skirt thing pushed into my skin, but it felt oddly comforting. She purred so loud it vibrated my teeth.

20

I WAS AWAKENED BY THE START OF THE SHOW ON THE TELEVISION screen.

"Day two," the orange lizard-like announcer was saying. It still spoke in that odd, barely recognizable version of the Syndicate common speech. It was like trying to understand someone speaking with a deep Cajun accent. Sure, they were speaking English, but to my brain, they might as well be speaking Klingon.

"Do you think we'll be on it this time?" Donut asked, scrambling out of bed to sit on one of the chairs. "We blew up half the dungeon! That's gotta count for something, don't you think? My word, I am so excited I could just wee. Actually, I do gotta wee." She scrambled from her chair and headed toward the women's room, which would have a litter box waiting for her.

But she rocketed back from around the corner just a minute later.

"Carl, Carl! He's here. He's in the bathroom! The *women's* bathroom. The killer! The guy who killed Rebecca W!"

I leaped to my feet. I immediately saw the blue dot on my map, right there.

How? Surely I would've noticed it the moment I woke up. I'd gotten used to keeping one eye on the map. I was always looking out for others. I mentally kicked myself as I rushed forward. I focused on the dot.

Crawler Frank Q.

That was him, all right.

"Come on," I said. I pushed my way toward the side hallway with the bathrooms.

We met in the hall, the man stepping out of the restroom, smiling apologetically. We came to a stop just a few feet away from one another. We just stared for a couple moments, sizing each other up. Donut stood between my legs and started hissing.

He was a tall man, lean, but not quite as tall as me. About forty. I pegged him as either military or a cop based on the way he carried himself. He was a white dude and he hadn't shaved in a few days. Good-looking, but not remarkably so. A Seahawks beanie covered what I guessed to be a bald head. He wore filthy ripped jeans and a black T-shirt. He was also equipped with what appeared to be football shoulder pads, but they were made of glowing black metal, obviously enchanted. The shoulders were spiked. It wouldn't let me examine the properties. He wore heavy boots, which I eyed jealously.

I assumed he had a gun hidden away somewhere, but I didn't see it now. Instead, he carried a massive battle-axe over his shoulder. The iron single-headed weapon looked well used. He also wore a belt with a line of throwing knives.

I examined his properties as he did the same to me.

Crawler #324,119. "Frank Q."
    Level 8.
    Race: Human.
    Class: Not yet assigned.

He did not have any stars by his name, which meant he'd never killed a boss. But he had something else.

Three skulls.

I knew exactly what the skulls were going to indicate even before I focused on them.

Crawler Killer x 3.

I suddenly felt very cold.

"Sorry, I didn't mean to startle your cat," the man said. He had an authoritative voice. Definitely a cop, or some sort of law enforcement. They taught you to speak that way in training. "That is a cat, right? I thought if I slept in the bathroom, nobody could sneak up on me. I didn't realize the bathrooms in the safe areas were different than the ones out in the hallways." He paused. "Where are your pants? And your shoes? Have you been walking barefoot this whole time?" He looked me up and down, alternating between me and the cat, a look of wry amusement. "Also, what's up with your name? Royal bodyguard?"

"So you were asleep in there, in the women's room?" I asked, ignoring his questions.

He paused. He tilted his head, as if deciding whether he wanted to answer or not. "Yeah," he said finally. "I hadn't slept in over 24 hours. I found this safe room, dragged one of those cots in there, and I passed out. I must've been out for 12 hours straight. Stupid, I know."

If that was true, then he'd have been asleep when we'd arrived. Hadn't Donut used the bathroom? I couldn't remember.

CARL: Donut, did you use the bathroom before we went to sleep?

DONUT: I DID NOT. I WENT IN THE HALLWAY BATHROOM BEFORE WE FOUND THIS ROOM.

"I never saw your dot on the minimap," I said.

"You don't see the icons of sleeping crawlers," he said. "Have you ever seen someone outside your party sleeping in a safe room? Their bodies become translucent. If you touch them, your hand moves right through them. Are you from Seattle? I'm still pretty close to where I came in, but I haven't been able to find any staircases down to the second level."

Donut, who had been hissing and growling this whole time, couldn't take it anymore. "You killed Rebecca W!" she shouted.

The man just stared at the cat for several moments. "Holy shit," he finally said. "I thought that's what I'd heard. A talking cat. This fucking place."

Donut hissed in response. Behind us, I heard the clash of steel on the television screen. They'd started showing the day's recap.

"Did you know her?" the man asked. "Rebecca Wong?"

"He admits it! The criminal has confessed!" Donut cried. "I'm gonna hit him with a magic missile." She jumped up on my shoulder and started to wiggle her butt.

"Wait, wait," he said. He took a step back and held up his hands. "I didn't . . . It's not what it looks like. I didn't have a choice."

"We didn't know her," I said. "We just came across her body."

He seemed to relax. "Look, I can explain," he said. "It wasn't just her. There were five of them. My partner got one, I got three, and you would not believe the thing that killed the fifth guy. It's a long story. Can you, uh, put down your cat?"

"Put me down?"

"That's not what he meant," I said. "Donut. Chill." This was the first living human we'd run across, and I wanted to get his story. I didn't trust him as far as I could throw him, but I wanted to hear what he had to say first.

Donut grumbled something under her breath.

"Where's your partner?" I asked.

He paused. "She's dead. Shot."

After a moment, I nodded. "Let's go to the other room. We're missing the show. We can talk in there."

"Okay," he said. He warily eyed Donut, who made a spitting noise. Her fur was completely poofed out.

"Did you see the last episode?" I asked.

"Yes," the man—Frank—said. He took a seat about 10 feet away, near the exit. He draped his left arm over the chair, trying to appear casual, but I could see his entire body was tense. "There's another rest area about three miles east of here. That one has a restaurant in it. That whole block is now overrun with thorny, creeping plants that will eat you whole. I found this place while looking for the stairs. The rot stickers outside pack a punch."

On the screen it showed a group of about 40 Middle Eastern men fighting a borough boss. The creature was an armored, elephant-sized, six-legged rhinoceros-like monstrosity with tentacles on its back. The tentacles seemed to have an ability that turned the men into stone. The monster had been hurt badly, but it ended up killing all 40 of the men. Half of them had been turned to stone. A moment later, the creature fell over and died. The display froze, and **Match Draw** appeared on the screen.

"Tell us your story," I said, "and then we'll tell you ours."

I kept one eye on the screen, which was showing one adventuring disaster after another, and one eye on the man as he recounted his tale. Frank claimed he and his partner, a woman named Maggie, worked for "Customs Enforcement," which was a nice way of saying he was a fed, and he worked for ICE. They'd been in plain clothes, outside in that ridiculously cold weather doing some sort of surveillance on a warehouse. The place was right on the water, supposedly employing a large group of undocumented Chinese workers. When the collapse came, the warehouse disappeared, revealing a group of about 15 men and women who'd been outside, smoking on a patio. Frank and his partner identified themselves, and everyone just started shooting at each other. The dungeon opened up right in the middle of their firefight. His partner, Maggie, stumbled into the stairwell, and it wouldn't let go of her. So he went in with her. Five of the others, for reasons he said he couldn't fathom, followed them in.

He went on to recount a firefight in the hallway. Of a confrontation with their leader—Rebecca W—who'd shot him three times before he got her right in the heart. He'd thought he was going to die, but he'd healed amazingly fast. He'd looted her body and chased down the last one, only to see the man get eaten by a plant monster, a thing that came out of a giant pod. It was called a vine creeper. I'd seen one of them during the show's premiere. From there Frank found a tutorial guild, his wounds were fully healed, and here he was. He'd been using his gun and the ones he'd looted from the others, but he was now out of ammo.

"That one," he said. "Rebecca. Rebecca Wong. She was the boss of the operation. A human trafficker. A modern-day slave driver. We were days away from taking down the whole operation."

"You poor man," Donut said at the end of his story. Her demeanor toward him had made a complete turn. "I am just devasted about your partner."

He shrugged. "I appreciate that." He went up and grabbed a cookie. He ate it, and the **+9.8 EXP** notification dinged over his head.

"Was this Rebecca the one who killed your partner?" I asked. I watched the notification over the man's head fade away.

"No," he said, shaking his head. The man sat back down. "It was one of her goons, the same guy who got killed by the vine creeper. He shot Maggie." The man lowered his head.

The show had moved to the second half of the program, showing humans who were performing well. A woman dressed in snow gear and what looked like a Valkyrie helmet had an enchanted crossbow that shot firebolts. It showed her plowing through a group of dog-faced goblin things. Gnolls.

"Hey," I said. "Since you looted those guys you killed, I don't suppose you have any pants that might fit me in that bag of yours? Or shoes?"

He paused. "Sure, boss. If you don't mind wearing the clothes of a dead man."

CARL: Donut. Do not say anything out loud. Can you see this?
DONUT: WHAT IS HAPPENING?
CARL: Don't type in all caps. I think Frank is going to try to hurt or incapacitate us. This is important. Do not react. Do not fight back at all. Whatever you do, don't fire a magic missile. Just let it happen. Trust me on this. I'm going to present an opening. I want to entice him into action.
DONUT: WHAT DO YOU MEAN? FRANK IS AN AMERICAN HERO.

CARL: Frank is full of shit. He's lying. I think there might be
    somebody else in here with us, and they are getting ready
    to jump us. I'll explain in a minute. We're going to have to
    run. Get ready.
DONUT: I DO NOT LIKE THIS, CARL.

A pair of khaki pants appeared in his hand. They had an enormous bloodstain down the side of them. He tossed them to me. "These are the biggest pants I have. I don't know if they'll fit you or not. I have a couple pairs of shoes in here, too, but it doesn't say what their sizes are."

"Thanks," I said. I paused, waiting to see if he would toss me a pair of shoes, but he was making a show of pretending to sort through his inventory. He wanted me to try the pants on first, which I noticed right away were much too small. And they were women's pants. I sighed. *Oh well.*

I stood and turned my back. I made motions like I was pulling my kneepads off.

Everything that happened next occurred over the course of less than a second.

I saw the blue dot appear in the bathroom hallway, just as the woman emerged from around the corner. At the same moment, Donut leaped into the air with a panicked yowl as Frank pulled his weapon from his inventory and fired at the cat.

The woman, pistol aimed directly at my head, also fired.

On the television, Lucia Mar, along with her two rottweilers, Cici and Gustavo 3, tore through a group of red demon-like monsters. The girl was like a demon herself, savagely swinging her mace.

Donut landed on the table with the cookies. Her body slid, moving through the plate, which disappeared and reappeared as if it wasn't really there. Her feet scrambled as she plummeted off the edge of the table. She hit the floor and bounced back up, screaming at the top of her lungs. "Carl, Carl! Help!"

"I'm here," I said. "We gotta go now. We have less than two minutes."

She paused, looking back and forth between me and the two frozen crawlers. Both had the word **Naughty** blazing over their head. I recounted my earlier discussion with Mordecai. This was after Donut had eaten the enhanced pet biscuit and while we'd waited for her to transform.

"You said they teleport out of here if she turns into a monster. So monsters can't ever get into safe areas? What if I leave the door open? They won't be able to wander in?"

"Oh, they'll wander in," Mordecai said. "Always close the door. If it's a mob, it'll teleport away the moment it attacks you. But they'll trash the place, too."

"What if Donut doesn't turn into a monster, but she also doesn't recognize me? She sometimes bites people she doesn't recognize. Will she teleport away, then?"

"No. It's different for crawlers. There's no violence and no stealing in the safe rooms. It's a strict, ironclad rule. You get three strikes. The first time, you freeze in place for about 100 seconds while you get an automated lecture on playing nice. The second time it's for an hour. The third time you're stripped of all your gear and teleported into a mob nest."

So when Frank Q and his partner—her name really was Maggie, Maggie My—decided to kill us to take our gear or whatever the hell they were doing, they made the mistake of using a safe area as their point of attack. It obviously was their first—and last—attempt at doing it that way.

"But how did you know?" Donut cried, looking between the two frozen people. They had been frozen the very moment they'd pulled the triggers. The bullets didn't appear to have even left the barrels yet. "Are you psychic? And where did this lady come from? I just don't understand. This is very distressing."

"We don't have time," I said as I added the pants to my inventory. I had a vague notion to pick Frank up, rearrange him so his gun was facing his partner, but I was afraid the system would count that as an act of violence on my part. "We gotta go now."

Before we rushed outside, I took a precious second to examine the attributes of Maggie My.

She was about the same age as Frank, so around 40 years old, athletic. A white woman with closely cropped brown hair. She wore shining metallic pants and boots. She wore a leather jacket similar to my own—though hers had both of their sleeves. She didn't appear to hold any weapons other than her gun.

Crawler #324,116. "Maggie My."
    Level 9.
    Race: Human.
    Class: Not yet assigned.

She had five skulls next to her name.

Between her and Frank, they'd killed eight people. *Eight.* They both had the ability to go completely stealth. I doubted they had been sleeping in the bathroom. They'd likely heard that explosion from earlier and tracked us to the safe room. We'd left a wake of dead rot stickers along the way, a literal path of destruction to this space.

Frank had said people turned translucent when they slept. Was that true? It certainly wasn't true for Donut, but she was also in my party. Maybe they had meant to sneak up on us and kill us in our sleep, but when they realized they couldn't, they'd gone to the bathroom to wait. Maybe the plan was to sneak up on me from behind while I went to the men's room. I didn't know.

We jumped outside, and I plotted a path to the closest main artery. I downed an Iron Skin potion and gave one to Donut, making her drink it. A couple of red dot clusters appeared between here and there. I didn't want to waste time fighting them. The hallway was too thin, the ground too bumpy to use the chopper. Plus, one blast from a rot sticker was likely to turn the powered bicycle into a bomb.

So we ran. I wanted to avoid the mobs if we could. Every mob we left alive was one they'd have to deal with.

"Why are we running?" Donut asked. "We can take them."

"I don't know if we can," I said. "They both have guns. He's level eight, the same as us, and she's level nine. Getting to nine is hard, so she probably has a lot of skills. Besides, I *really* don't want to have one of those skull markers by my name. Even if they have it coming, everyone else we meet won't know that. We will never get anyone to talk to us."

"But if we don't stop them, they'll hurt somebody else."

I stopped dead in the hallway. I looked at the cat. It was a very un-Donut-like thing to say. But worse, it was the truth.

"Goddamnit, Donut," I said. I looked back over my shoulder in the direction of the safe room. They'd be awake already by now, though I suspected—and hoped—they wouldn't just come running.

They probably *were* going to hurt somebody else. If they could find someone. But what could we do?

Donut fired a magic missile, killing a group of the regular level two rats that seemed to infest every corridor regardless of neighborhood. The rats sizzled and fell onto their backs. One of them dropped a poor rat skin and a rat steak.

"Don't take that inventory," I said. "Cancel it out."

Donut huffed but complied. She loved looting corpses. The person to kill a mob had first right to loot for a couple minutes after the battle, but if they canceled out the box, the corpse became fair game.

I had an idea, but I didn't know if it would work. We didn't have time, but I needed to test it. I pulled one of the goblin smoke bombs out of my stash, lit the wick, and then quickly added it to the rat's inventory. It let me do it. Like with most games, it allowed me to add items to the corpse's inventory as if it was a chest. The rat had a grid pattern inventory that looked as if it couldn't hold very much. This was how inventory had been for crawlers last season.

I had to see if the smoke bomb remained lit. They'd said that items didn't retain their momentum, but what about this? Thanks to my level 5 in Explosives Handling, now when I examined incendiary items, I received some extra information:

Goblin Smoke Bomb.
Type: Deflagration.
Effect: Opaque smoke over a 10 meter radius for 3 minutes.
Status: Good. (89/100)
Emits a stinking cloud of billowing multicolor smoke that lasts for three minutes before dispersing. Use to either confuse enemies or as a stage prop at a hair metal concert.

It didn't say the bomb was lit. I pulled the bomb out, and to my relief, the wick still crackled and spat. I quickly added it back to the rat's grid. Everything was the same, but the status had changed to Discharge Imminent. (34/100).

I then examined my pile of goblin dynamite. They were all out of 50, not 100, and all of them were either in Detonation Imminent or Danger. It appeared the danger warning appeared once the status was below 15.

I gingerly removed the most unstable piece of dynamite I had, one that was 10/50 and added it to the rat's inventory without lighting it. I noted, despite me handling the dynamite as carefully as I could, it'd gone down to 9/50. *Jesus.* I was lucky I hadn't blown myself to bits earlier. This next one was at 13/50. I lit it and then quickly added it to the rat's inventory.

If they followed, they'd likely come down this same hall. That guy had picked Rebecca W's corpse clean, including her clothes. People who did that were the type to loot everything. If they came across the rat, hopefully they'd think we'd been in too much of a hurry to stop and loot for ourselves. Rats didn't normally drop stuff other than skin and meat. It was suspicious as fuck. But, maybe . . . maybe we'd get lucky. If Frank did pull the three items out of the rat inventory, it would literally blow up in his hands.

For now, it was the best we could do.

"Okay," I said, nervously looking over my shoulder. I remembered they could go invisible, at least on the map. "Let's go."

We turned, and we kept running for the artery.

"How did you know?" Donut asked as we continued to jog.

"He was lying. He was lying right from the start," I said.

"So he's not a federal agent?" she asked. Her breaths were coming in wheezes, but the hallway was close.

"I don't know," I said. "I think he might be. He talks and acts like a cop. But his whole story was bullshit. That Rebecca woman was a level three. He said they'd gotten into a firefight right away, but that couldn't be true. She had that apple core *in* her inventory. That meant she'd gone to a tutorial guild and gotten her inventory turned on. And then he ate that cookie, and I saw he received 9.8 experience instead of 10, which meant he was in a party with someone. Someone alive. Also, he had his arm draped over the chair, and I could see he was twitching his finger. He was typing into the chat. He hadn't figured out how to use it with just his brain."

Donut stared up at me as we ran.

"How is it you're James Bond when it comes to strangers, but Miss Beatrice could date three different guys at once, and you had no idea?"

"*Three* different guys?"

"Well, you were one of them, so two, I guess. Then again, it's three if you count Angel's owner. Does it count as cheating when it's with another woman? There's so many human nuances I don't understand."

"Of course it counts as cheating," I said. *For fuck's sake.*

"But you were always watching those videos on your iPad with the two women rolling around and cleaning each other. Would it have been cheating if Miss Beatrice let you watch?"

"We're not having this conversation right now, Donut."

We reached the hallway and I pulled the chopper out of my inventory. This would be the first time we would actually drive the thing. I tossed a lump of coal into the hopper and prayed it wouldn't explode on us. As we prepared to leave, the dungeon reverberated with an announcement. It was the daily update.

Hello, Crawlers. Another excellent, exciting day! We are very happy to have you with us, and we hope everyone is having a great time. You're really bringing it, and we at Borant truly appreciate the enthusiasm you're giving to this production.

I have a couple of announcements. First off, we want to assure everyone that we have quashed all the bugs with the new toilets. Both the exploding issue and the, ah, unfortunate suction issue with some of the units have been resolved. There is absolutely no need to be afraid of them. Those of you who have been using the hallways to relieve yourselves, please stop. We don't want to have to start using punitive measures.

A couple additional patch notes . . . We have added support for all of the languages that were missing from our library. So for those of you who are hearing this and finally understanding what I'm saying for the first time . . . welcome. You'll figure the rest out, I'm sure. Also with the languages, we've implemented full cross support for native speech. So now Mandarin speakers will understand English speakers and so forth.

The Feral Rabies debuff is now curable with a health potion or spell. And the contagion is no longer airborne. Sorry about that, New Zealand.

We have removed the Blender Fiend mobs. The mob's difficulty level appears to be too high. Their collective gets stronger each time they, uh, blend, and after working their way through a group of 15,000 crawlers in a single day, we've been forced to take action to prevent a premature extinction event. Rest assured they will be reintroduced on a lower floor. The Street Preacher neighborhood boss has been upgraded to a borough boss. In addition, we have tweaked the strength levels of a few dozen other mobs, too many to mention here. So just be aware of that.

One last note. A lot of crawlers are heading into the stair-
ways prematurely. Again, it's your choice, but it's probably best
for you to get as much experience as you can. And just so you
know for later, we won't feature you on the recap episode if
viewers can't tunnel into your feed. So if you hit the stairs three
or four days before a collapse, you are going to miss out.

That's it for now. Keep up the good work, and kill, kill, kill!

"We didn't get to see the rest of the show," Donut said. "Do you
think we were on it?"

"I doubt it," I said. I eased onto the alligator skull seat. Underneath me, the whole bike rumbled with potential energy. It had
pedals like a bicycle, but it also had a throttle. I had to move the bike
by pumping my legs, but once I reached the speed I wanted, I turned
the throttle, and the bike would lock that speed in place. It was a
strange setup.

The engine built into the chassis was already getting hot. I would
have to spread my legs out to keep from getting burned to hell. I
sighed. I really, really needed pants.

Donut jumped up into her sidecar seat. She started licking her
paw as we zoomed off down the road, trying to put as much distance
between us and that neighborhood as we could.

21

IF FRANK AND MAGGIE FOUND MY TRAP, I DIDN'T RECEIVE A NOTIFI-
cation. The best-case scenario was that they were both dead, and I
didn't get credit for it. Of all the achievements in this game, Crawler
Killer was one I wanted to avoid.

I did not receive any sort of achievement or skill for setting a trap,
and it was a safe bet that'd be a thing here. I took that as a good sign.
Donut and I did, however, receive an achievement for our "fight"
with Frank Q and Maggie My.

> **New Achievement! Bitchmeat!**
> You've been attacked by a fellow crawler in a safe zone, and
> the system has been forced to save your ass. That usually sug-
> gests you're either really annoying, or you snore.
> If this were a prison, you would now be my bitch. Wait . . .
> *Reward*: Bitches don't get rewards.

I laughed. For the first time since we'd entered this ridiculous
game, I laughed at one of the stupid notifications.

The ride was significantly smoother than I anticipated. We got
about three or four miles per lump of coal, and I had an almost endless supply.

We only managed to travel east for a single junction before we hit
a wall, and we were forced to choose between north and south. If the
map in my head was accurate, we'd hit the edge of Lake Washington
above, once again proving that the dungeon didn't truly circle the

planet. We went south, traveling down a rough approximation of the I-5 corridor for a short time before passages that went east and west started reappearing. I strongly suspected we needed to head east and inland before we saw any stairwells. But the problem was directly east was a large mountain range up above, and if the dungeon had been desolate before, it'd be downright abandoned here. Not for another 100 miles.

We decided to resume our trek east anyway, heading farther away from the western edge of the US coastline.

We drove for hours, seeing no sign of people or mobs or stairwells. It was difficult to gauge how fast we were actually moving, but I guessed it was about 20 miles per hour. My **Chopper Pilot** skill rose steadily as I drove. Once I hit level 5, the throttle actually allowed me to increase our speed.

I didn't want to go too fast, but I felt it was important to find a denser area of the labyrinth. From what little I'd seen on the show, I knew there were areas different than this. I had the sense that these giant squares were nothing more than just filler, like the randomly generated terrain at the edge of some maps in open-world games.

As we drove, I made Donut keep her map on full screen so she could better scan the area, looking for points of interest. We saw fewer and fewer training guilds out here, but they were there. The bathrooms continued to be all over the place, and rest areas dotted the maps, too.

My thoughts wandered to my father. If he could only see me now, sitting on this thing, holding my legs out so they wouldn't burn on the side of the glorified moped. He'd laugh, call me a damn fool. He'd been a motorcycle guy. Not a full-time leather-clad biker. He was more of a weekend warrior.

I hadn't talked to or heard from the man in over 12 years. Not since he'd abandoned me that day, leaving me all alone in the world.

Before today, I'd never been on a motorcycle in my life, not that this thing really counted as one. I had a bicycle now that I sometimes rode to work if the weather was good, but I'd never even ridden on a dirt bike, let alone anything more powerful.

We stopped once to use a restroom that appeared just off the main corridor. Once we entered the hallway, we were beset by a group of bipedal, raccoon-headed monsters that were as tall as my knee. These things were called Scat Thugs, and the ones here on the edge of the corridor were all level three. They were about as strong as regular goblins and were armed with needlelike spears. A pair charged me and got skewered by my kneepads. I took all their spears as loot, which were useless to me, but hopefully I'd be able to sell them later.

We used the bathroom—thankfully neither of us exploded—and we headed out on our way.

But the short excursion taught me something important. Those mobs were right there, barely twenty feet from the edge of the never-ending artery. We hadn't seen their dots until we'd stopped the bike and approached the boundary of the alley. The fog of war encroached tighter upon us the faster we were going. That was important to know. We needed a skill or a spell or some sort of special ability that would allow us to navigate better. We were literally driving blind, and I didn't like that. It was only a matter of time before we drove headfirst into a trap.

We decided to go back on the road, heading deeper east. I moved slower.

And then, after several hours, we finally saw something new.

I stopped the chopper, examining the spray-painted sign on the wall.

TWO CROSSROADS EAST, THREE SOUTH. STAIRS + PEOPLE.

It was written in English in red runny spray paint. I ran my hand across it. It didn't come off on my finger, but it had a tacky texture. The paint was only hours old.

"Do you think it's a trap?" Donut asked.

"Maybe," I said.

Now that we'd stopped, I could see several X's on my map indicating mob corpses just down the hallways. We ventured in to get a better look. These were white horned goat things with mouths full of fangs. I examined the first one.

Lootable Corpse. Chilly Goat. Level 4. Killed by Crawler Brandon An with an assist by Crawler Chris Andrews 2.
    Inventory is empty.

I examined all the goats in the area, and I counted 15 different names who had either killed or assisted in the slaying of the mobs. The goats had been sliced, fried with spells, and I saw several broken arrow shafts, though the arrowheads themselves were all gone. Some of the monsters were literally smashed flat, like the person had an enormous hammer.

"I'm pretty sure it's not a trap," I said. "Let's go find them."

The spray-painted notifications continued the closer we got to the area.

Right where the sign told us to go was a T junction. I coasted to a stop. The chopper made a *chug-chug-chug* noise. It would need another lump soon. I was getting good at understanding its sounds and vibrations. My ass was killing me, and my legs ached. On the ground was an arrow pointing left, which was farther east.

Looking at the map, I could see this area was different than any place we'd entered before. The east and west roads didn't continue straight, but they curved away, indicating we'd come to the edge of a massive circle.

I suddenly had an uneasy feeling about what might be at the center of this area.

"I see the stairwell," Donut said. "If you zoom out the map, it's right on the edge of what we can see."

Sure enough. In the area immediately south, and presumably in the center of this giant loop, there appeared to be a stairwell. I hovered over the white square on the map, and it simply read, **Stairwell to Floor Two.**

I didn't see any other blue dots or anything else. Just the empty expanse of the fog of war.

"Look, there's something written on the ground," Donut said, pointing down the left hallway.

After a minute's hesitation, I stored the chopper, and we went toward the sign on foot.

THIS ROAD IS SAFE. WE ARE GATHERED A MILE AND A HALF THIS WAY. DO NOT GO DEEPER INTO THE SPIRAL OR YOU WILL ACTIVATE THE BOROUGH BOSS.

Shit. Mordecai had said the bosses wouldn't be guarding the stairwells until the fourth floor.

"I wonder what's in there," Donut asked, looking at the solid wall to our right.

Just as she said it, the wall rumbled as something rushed past on the other side. It was like we were standing on a train platform. Whatever it was, it was something fast. Something big.

Very, very big.

We walked on foot. After about a quarter mile, a rounded portcullis appeared on our right, leading toward the center of the circle. The crossbeam gate was lifted about halfway up the floor. We'd be able to slip under and go deeper into the loop if we wanted. There appeared to be another ring just inside. The graffiti had called it a spiral. Looking inside, I could see another doorway just down this wide interior hallway. So it was more like a round maze than a spiral.

If we slid under the gate, it would no doubt slide closed and trap us.

"Let's wait a second," I said. "I want to see what it is."

We didn't have to wait long. The creature, whatever it was, rushed by in a flash, too fast for me to get an info box. It rolled like a ball. It was pink, fleshy, and it was the size of the entire hallway. It was like a nightmare *Pac-Man* monster. It made a terrible grunting noise as it rocketed by, shaking the walls. The stench of sewage wafted up as it passed.

"My heavens," Donut said, crinkling her face like I'd tried to feed her vegetables. "This is going to be unpleasant."

22

We passed three more of the rounded entrances before we came across the encampment.

It was a full quarter turn from where we started, at the end of another artery. My heart swelled when I saw the sheer number of people there. There were about forty blue dots gathered at what appeared to be a drawbridge leading into the round maze.

My enthusiasm waned when I saw the manner of people waiting for us.

Almost all of them were still level one. And they were elderly. Not cool-grandpa-dude-at-the-club elderly. But holy-crap-I-love-you-gam-gam-but-how-the-hell-are-you-still-alive elderly. Most of them were in wheelchairs. Those who weren't had walkers. Most were in robes and caps, and piles of blankets littered the hallway. They sat gathered together. Most appeared to be asleep.

Another older woman stood apart from the group. This one was pushing 70, not 100 like the others. She stood stiffly, her black eyes watching us. This woman was wrapped head to toe in an endless amount of scarves, and her skin was like a relief map of a shriveled prune. A red checkered trapper hat with earflaps sat skewed on her head. She leaned on a shopping cart filled to the brim with blankets and other odds and ends, including a plastic pink flamingo that had an arrow stuck in its head.

I remembered the stairs I'd had to descend, and I wondered how they'd managed to get the wheelchairs and shopping cart down here.

I caught sight of a group of younger, more able-bodied crawlers. One of them, a chubby Black guy, saw us approach and waved. He came jogging up.

"Oh thank god," the man said. "Did you see our signs?"

"We did," I said. I examined his properties.

Crawler #12,330,671. "Brandon An."
   Level 6.
   Race: Human.
   Class: Not yet assigned.

He had a single bronze star by his name. The man wore a heavy winter jacket despite the heat. He had a gigantic hammer looped over his shoulder. The weapon was comically big. The round head was almost as wide as the tire on my chopper. It glittered, obviously made of some sort of magical lightweight metal. He didn't appear to have any other armor or gear.

"We?" the man said, frowning as he examined my properties. He took a hesitant step back, as if he was startled. "Is there more than one of you?" He looked down at Donut, and his frown deepened.

For a moment I was afraid that I had received a skull next to my name without realizing. But then I remembered what my real title was. It didn't say my name was Carl. It said I was **Royal Bodyguard Carl**, and Donut was **Grand Champion Best in Dungeon Princess Donut**.

I could only imagine how that looked to someone meeting me for the first time.

Another man approached, this one was **Chris Andrews 2**. He was also level six. The two men were clearly brothers. He was taller and less stocky. Chris wore a metal skullcap but didn't appear to have any weapons.

"Yes, we are *we*," Donut said. "I mean, really. I am right here. Rude."

Chris and Brandon just looked at each other. Then Brandon burst out laughing.

"I'm sorry, man," he said to me. "I didn't realize. I saw your name, and I thought . . ."

"Yeah," I said. "You thought I was a nut. She talks. She also probably has higher stats than anybody else here."

Brandon went to a knee and patted Donut on the head. She looked simultaneously outraged and thrilled that he had touched her. "Well, it's nice to meet you, Princess Donut. I'm sorry if I offended you, pretty girl. I've never met a talking cat before."

"It's quite all right," Donut said, mollified. "Apology accepted."

We walked back toward the group. Despite what I had seen earlier with the goat corpses, it appeared there were only four people here in fighting shape. Both Brandon and Chris were level six. A round Hispanic woman—**Yolanda Martinez 13**—was around 50 years old and only stood about four foot eleven. She was level five and carried a bow and had a quiver hanging over her shoulder. The quiver was so big on her, it almost dragged on the floor. She was in medical scrubs, and she wore a plastic ID on her breast. It read "Meadow Lark. Yolanda. CNA."

The fourth was another woman carrying a longsword. She, too, wore scrubs, though she also wore a magical cloak. Her name was **Imani C**. I guessed the woman weighed about 90 pounds, if that. She looked to be about 20 years old. Her terrified, hollowed-out eyes suggested she had seen some shit.

All four of them had a single bronze star after their names.

Imani also had skulls.

A lot of skulls.

On the interface, it was one big skull followed by two more regular ones. When I hovered over it, it said, **Crawler Killer × 12**.

She was also level 10, the highest we'd seen so far.

DONUT: CARL, IT IS ANOTHER VILE MURDERER.

CARL: I don't think so, not this time. Also, I know you don't have to type in all caps. I've seen you do it before. It makes you sound like you are yelling.

DONUT: I AM YELLING, CARL.

"We are the night staff at an eldercare facility in Wenatchee," Brandon was saying after I introduced myself to the others. Yolanda greeted me with enthusiasm. Imani said nothing. "We had a fire alarm and were forced to go outside because *someone*"—he eyed the woman with the shopping cart—"started a barrel fire outside our building and caught it on fire."

I examined the woman with the shopping cart. She was obviously homeless. *We're all homeless now.* She stood there, looking off into space, gnawing on a blackened fingernail.

Crawler #7,450 "Agatha."
    Level 2.
    Race: Human.
    Class: Not yet assigned.

"Anyway," Brandon said. "We had to evacuate the building, all 250 residents out into the freezing cold right when it happened."

I looked at the group, counting for the first time. There were a total of 38 people here, including the four workers and Agatha.

"There were 250 of you?" I asked, looking the group over.

"Yeah," Brandon said more quietly. "Not everyone came down here. And not everyone who did is still with us."

He went on to explain what happened next.

The fire started and quickly engulfed the outside of their building. Luckily, the fire had been on the side of the cafeteria, in an alley area where Agatha had been camped out. Nobody had been hurt by the blaze itself, but evacuations at elder facilities were always an especially dangerous affair. It was no simple task to get everyone out.

The local police and fire departments had arrived by the dozens. Firefighters assisted with the fire and with handing out blankets to the freezing residents and workers of the facility. They'd been in the process of getting the keys to a nearby elementary school to get everyone out of the cold.

"But how did you get them down the stairs?" I asked.

Brandon looked, again, at Agatha. "The entrance appeared right in the street, literally in the middle of the group. A bunch of folks fell in. There were stairs just like you said. But then Agatha over there pushed her cart right onto the stairs like she was . . . Well, I don't know what the hell she was doing. But the stairs transformed into a ramp. It *wanted* her to come on down. A long, easy ramp. Agatha was the first to voluntarily go down there, cackling like she always does. Hollerin' she'd saved all our lives. The folks who fell in when it opened, we never saw them again." He shuddered. "They weren't there when we got to the bottom."

"Did you go because of the cold?" I asked.

He eyed my naked legs. "We didn't mean to go all the way in, but it was warm in there—you know what I mean? So I pushed a few residents right into the entrance where the ramp wasn't so steep so that hot air was blasting up on them. I figured we could wait there until we knew what we were going to do. Only a few of the cops and paramedics remained after the collapse. They just took off running in all sorts of directions, like they had some place better to go. But some stayed, and they helped me bring the residents into the warmth. It let me do it. We moved several over, but then, after we'd moved about half the residents into the warmth, it just stopped letting me leave. My foot was trapped. My brother wasn't even in the hole, but when he grabbed my hand, it wouldn't let him move, either. And it started hurting after a minute. It only stopped when we moved down the ramp. When we got that twenty-minute warning, when it said anyone lurking in the stairwell wouldn't get out? We just went in. We didn't have a choice."

"What about the cops and paramedics?"

"We had about twenty guys with us, including a couple firemen and cops who decided to go in. Most didn't. We all helped getting the residents inside the hall." He pointed over his shoulder, indicating the artery that led to this quarter of the circle. "It was right there, just around that corner where we came in. Most of these folks haven't moved hardly at all since we got here. We've been bringing them food from a safe room that's about a mile away."

"Where are the cops and firefighters now?" I asked.

He nodded at the circle. "Most went in there when we first found this place. The gates closed. Then about five minutes later, the gates opened up again, and those guys were just gone. Our tutorial guide lady, Mistress Tiatha, she said all borough and city bosses will have stairwells for the first four or five levels. But there will be a bunch of other stairs in random places, too. A couple of us went out searching for them, hoping we could find a stairwell that's easier to get to than this one. This was just a while back." Brandon cast a nervous glance at the elderly patients. He leaned in and whispered, "They're all dead. You can see when they die on the party menu. They all got picked off by something that'd been hunting them one by one. Even Doctor Gracie, and she was a damn MMA fighter. Us four? We're the last of the non-residents left. Us and Agatha."

I turned to regard the large group of elderly patients. Looking upon them gave me a terrible sinking feeling. *They shouldn't be here.* This wasn't going to end well.

Agatha had pulled a blue IKEA bag from her shopping cart. She produced a can of metallic silver spray paint from the bag. She hobbled over to the wall and sprayed a giant circle, then turned it into a happy face. Then she leaned in and sniffed the wall, muttering something to herself the whole time.

"Don't waste the spray paint, Agatha," Brandon called.

"It's mine!" Agatha said, clutching the IKEA bag to herself. "You stole it from me."

"And you stole it from Stan's," Brandon said. "Just . . . just don't waste it, okay?"

"Have you thought about moving all these folks to the safe room?" I asked. "It has to be more comfortable than the hallway."

"It's already full," Brandon said. "It's a damn Waffle House from Alabama. Can you believe that? The place has a capacity of 30 people, and my brother, Chris, has been helping the more coherent, more mobile ones get over there. There's this gnome thing in there that's cooking them food and singing. They all love it." He smiled sadly. "Those folks at the Waffle House. They made a vote, and they decided they're not coming out. They're treating it like a giant party."

"He doesn't talk much, does he?" I asked, indicating Brandon's brother, Chris.

Brandon shook his head while Chris looked at me impassively.

"He's not exactly mute," Brandon said. "But he don't say too much. Growing up, our mom thought he was slow. They put him in a special school because he never spoke. But he's not dumb. He does talk. Think of him as Silent Bob. If he says something, you better listen."

Brandon nodded sagely.

I hesitated. "And her?" I asked, indicating Imani. I watched as she helped a woman to a nearby door. A bathroom. She made the woman open the door herself. The floor outside the bathroom was stained red. I shuddered, remembering the exploding "bug" from the announcements. After the woman was safely delivered to the bathroom, Imani turned and helped a man in a wheelchair take a sip of water. Yolanda also moved amongst the others, talking softly.

Brandon shook his head. "We got attacked once, right after we found that tutorial place. I . . . I don't really want to talk about it, man. But Imani, she had that sword, and several of the residents, we were taking them in groups to Mistress Tiatha. They can't move so quick. It was for the better. Letting those things burn them, that'd been much worse."

I nodded. I had questions, but I knew some things were best left unasked. It wasn't lost on me that her high level was probably a direct result of her having to kill 12 of her former patients. And she'd probably gained a loot box or two.

"These people still can't walk? So the dungeon's fast healing and all those healing spells and such don't work?"

"Oh, it's amazing," Brandon said. "But it's a curse, too. All of these folks have been cured of hundreds of their little ailments. Not a one of them brought any of their medications with them down here, and it's been okay. But at the same time, they ain't getting any younger. Or stronger. And those who've lost memories or cognitive function, that hasn't been fixed. It's like it cured anything that's going to kill them, but it didn't make them better than they were, either."

I sighed, turning my attention to the large rounded entrance to the maze. There was a short bridge, an entrance about three times the size of the smaller portcullis entrances that peppered the way, with a raised giant gate big enough to allow a pair of goblin dozers through side by side. It led to another round courtyard with three exits. The walls shook as the monster sped by, but it didn't appear to enter this courtyard area.

"So, what's the plan?" I asked.

"The original plan was to gather as many people as we could and then storm the maze. We think it's shaped like a spiral. But nobody was coming, so they went looking for other exits. And that didn't work out so well. Now it's just us, and we can't kill that thing. Nobody even knows what it is."

"And then what?" I asked. "Even if we had free passage to the stairs . . ." I let it hang.

"I know, I know," Brandon said. "But I just can't leave them. I was hoping, maybe if we could get them all down to the second level, then we could do the same thing for the third level. And then they'd all get to choose a class and maybe they wouldn't be, you know . . ."

"Useless?" Donut asked.

I nodded. I felt for the guy and the other three. Would I have stayed, continued with my duty? Even when it was so damn hopeless? What a nightmare. I thought I'd had it bad, but these guys . . . The world was over. There was no hope for these poor people they'd been in charge of protecting. This harsh environment wasn't meant for the weak, the frail.

Yet to these four—Brandon, Chris, Yolanda, and Imani—the idea of giving up their duty wasn't even a question.

I spent some time recounting our story, including our clash in the last safe room. I told them of our two encounters with neighborhood bosses.

"I can do something similar with this boss," I said. "I think I can build a bomb that'll go off on its own when the monster hits it. That way we don't have to get locked in there to fight."

"It won't work," Yolanda said, coming up to stand with us. "You know those little doors, the ones that let you see the monster? They're protected somehow. I thought to try to hit it with my bow, but the arrow bounces right off. I poked at it with my finger, and it feels like thick clay. It even glows blue if you touch it. They look like entrances, but they ain't. I think *maybe* you can go in that way if you push yourself really hard, but I wouldn't try it. And I wouldn't be pushing no bomb through that. The only way in is through this big gate here. And the monster doesn't go into that first room. So you can't hurt it without first getting locked in."

"But we don't know for sure," Brandon added. "Once the gate closed, we couldn't see in there at all. We couldn't hear. We couldn't talk using the party chat, not with the ones in there. It was like they'd been cut from the party."

I sighed. We had two choices. We could leave these guys and hope to find another set of stairs somewhere. Or we could fight the borough boss here.

Neither choice was appealing. Whatever that thing was, it would be almost impossible to kill. I remembered that scene from the latest recap episode. It had been forty against one borough boss, and it had slaughtered them. We didn't even know what the hell the monster was.

I looked at the clock. We had 40 hours. Geez. Had it really been that long since we'd run away from Frank and Maggie? There would be another show in 10 hours. We'd done nothing today except travel a hundred miles or so from where we started.

And speaking of Frank and Maggie. I had a terrible realization. "Your people, the ones who died while looking for more stairs. Which direction did they go?"

"Mostly west, toward Seattle. They would've been north of where you were. I remember where we killed the chilly goats. That was the farthest out my brother and I had gone. We separated from the group right around there and headed back here."

"And how long ago did the last one disappear?"

"It was earlier today. Barely five or six hours ago."

I looked down at Donut, thinking. It could've been them, Frank and Maggie. But that would mean they'd gotten to this area before us. That didn't make sense. We were pretty far from where we'd last encountered them. Could there be another group of crawlers killing people off? Or was it a monster? Without finding their bodies, we'd never know.

Behind me, one of the elderly women started sobbing. Another, a man with a back so curved his chin rested against his own chest, scooted forward on his walker and patted her on the back. The hunchbacked man was wearing a veteran's cap. He had been US Army Special Forces once upon a time.

If I'm gonna die, I might as well do it in the pursuit of a worthy cause.

"Are there any other rest areas around here?" I asked. "Ones that aren't full?"

"Yeah, we know of two. One of them doesn't have anything in it except a vending machine that hands out wrapped candies. They taste like piss but give you a +1 boost to your dexterity for ten minutes. The machine only works for you once a day. The next place is further down. It's a Taco Bell from Peru and has full facilities, including coffee." He leaned in. "And beer. Good beer."

"What about the mobs near there?" I asked. "Also, how about training guilds?"

"We've cleared out the next two quadrants. Some of the other guys killed the first neighborhood boss. They said it was like a giant demon man in a suit made of skin. We got the second boss. All of us here were in on that fight. That one was a floating crystal thing, but it shattered when I hit it with my hammer a few times. The next area after that, next to the Taco Bell, is still crawling with monsters.

They're lizard creatures. They jump and bite and poison you. I got hit once, and I thought I was going to die. The poison ran out on its own just before it killed me, and that was only because I kept taking health potions. We didn't want to mess around in that neighborhood after that. But there are a couple training guilds in the area."

"Okay, good," I said. "This is what's going to happen. Donut and I are going to spend the rest of today grinding. If you can manage to pry a pair of those rattle cans from Agatha over there, I'll take them with us. I'm going to try to level up my skills as much as possible. You guys should do the same. Be wary of any other crawlers. Especially ones with the skulls by their names. We're going to watch episode three, get some sleep, and then we're going to come back here. And then all of us—Me, Donut, and you four—are going to go into there, and we're going to fuck that boss up. We're going to get your people down those stairs. Sound like a plan?"

"And how are we going to do that?" a new voice asked. It was Imani, speaking for the first time.

I grinned. "Don't worry. I have an idea."

23

"SO, WHAT'S THIS GRAND IDEA OF YOURS?" DONUT ASKED AS WE walked away. With her new skirtlike crupper combined with the butterfly talisman around her collar, she jingled when we walked. "How are we going to kill that thing?"

"I have no fucking clue," I said. "But we need them to train. It's our only choice. It took us a full day to find this set of stairs, and we are almost out of time. It's better to face the enemy you know than the one you don't."

"We don't know this enemy," Donut said. "Wait, what are you doing?"

I'd come to the first of the spray-painted signs pointing toward the encampment. I took the can of red paint they'd given me, and I sprayed completely over it, covering it up.

"Did you see that Imani's level?" I asked, standing to see if I could still read it. "She was level 10. And that was partially because she'd been forced to kill all those people."

"So? Are you saying if someone else comes, they might kill all the old people? Just to get experience? Oh, Carl, darling. Nobody is quite that evil." Donut paused. "Are they?"

"I don't know," I said. "And I don't want to find out, either."

"But what if a big group of good guys comes through? And they miss it because you covered it up?"

"Look where we are, Donut. We were lucky to find these people. There aren't any big groups of good guys, not in these parts. It's only sharks and minnows. Now come on. Let's find that Taco Bell."

"So which one are we?" Donut asked as we trekked off.

I didn't answer. I couldn't.

Brandon said they'd put dozens of signs up all over the place. As we headed north, I either defaced or changed all the ones I could find. There was no way I'd get to them all, but it made me feel better.

I was busy changing a sign from saying 2 BLOCKS SOUTH to 12 BLOCKS SOUTH when Donut lifted her head, sniffing. "Two more rats around the corner."

A moment later, their dots appeared.

"Your sense of smell is getting better," I said.

"No, I think the rats are getting stinkier," she said.

We'd killed at least 30 rats between here and the encampment. These rats were bigger and fatter than the ones we'd fought earlier. They were all level three. Before we'd left, I'd quietly asked Brandon if they'd looted the corpses of the folks who'd been killed right when they'd entered the dungeon. He'd been horrified at first until I explained that I needed pants and shoes. He'd given me directions. They'd looted the extra wheelchairs, walkers, and canes, but they hadn't touched their clothes. It would've required them to physically remove them. The thought made me ill. It also gave me a new burst of hatred for Frank Q and Maggie My, who had stripped the body of Rebecca W. They'd probably removed the clothes of the other ones they'd killed, too.

When we got to where the elderly folks had died, all that was left were piles of bones and shredded clothes, nothing usable. I picked up the gnawed remains of a slipper, tossing it down with disgust. The rats had devoured everything else, tearing through the corpses like a hurricane. And now the rats in the area were bigger.

We turned the corner and entered a new quadrant. A pair of humanoid creatures with loincloths and crude clubs saw us and hopped in our direction, hissing. These were three-foot-tall lizard monsters, like Brandon had stated, the tallest of them almost as high as my hip. They looked like upright Komodo dragons from the waist up.

Small but muscular. Their legs were long and bent, kangaroo-like and scaly.

Troglodyte Pygmy—Level 2
   Oh, these fuckers. With intelligence just shy of an oft-dropped toddler, the standard troglodyte pygmy warrior would be harmless if it wasn't so damn fast. Or venomous.

Brandon had warned me about their special attack, so I was ready. Donut hit the first with a magic missile while the second leaped right at me, hissing and baring his giant fangs.

I hit it with a right hook, my chain-covered fist smashing its head, changing the creature's trajectory so it splattered against the wall of the tunnel. It exploded like a damn tomato. Donut's target had practically vaporized under her single missile strike. Her *Magic Missile* spell had risen to level five, and she now had the option to choose how many mana points to put into each casting, from three to six. Her intelligence was currently 24, meaning she could fire eight missiles if she kept the power setting at three.

I poked at the burned-out husk of troglodyte with my bare toe. It'd only been a few days, but I barely felt the ground now when I walked. Random rocks still hurt, but not so much as they would've before. "That didn't look like a three-mana missile."

"That was a six," Donut said, sniffing at her handiwork. "They really need to make this less disgusting."

"If it's a level two monster, a three will probably one-shot it," I said. Neither dropped any loot, but I took their clubs.

"If it's about to bite my face off, it's getting a six," said Donut.

We spent the next hour hunting down and killing all the troglodytes we could. The level threes were called Troglodyte Bashers and the level fours were Troglodyte Virtuosos. The bashers were twice as big, making them almost human-sized. They didn't have any other special abilities, and they had more regular legs. The virtuosos had a tongue attack that surprised me at first. They were the same size as the level twos, but they could shoot their tongues almost fifteen feet. The thin, wet tongues stung like a whip, inflicting poison, which was immediately canceled thanks to my nightgaunt cloak.

Donut and I were starting to become adept at fighting as a team. She'd wait for an opening to fire her missiles, and I'd move in to finish them off with a kick or a punch. I could tell just by her stance when—and where—she was going to move. She jumped on my shoulder with ease, using my height to fire on her targets from above. She'd hide behind me, easily slipping between my jacket and cloak, hanging on my back with her claws to avoid a poison attack. Well, any attack really. We didn't level up yet to nine, but we were well on our way. It seemed after level eight, the amount of experience it took to hit the next level was absurdly high. We were plateauing. Even though I couldn't distribute my stat points, my fighting skills were steadily climbing, giving my attacks more and more damage. The difficulty would probably start all over again when we went down a floor.

If we went down a floor.

After killing a Troglodyte Basher, all that was left from one of Donut's missile strikes was the lizard's head rolling about like a lumpy soccer ball. She jumped down and idly batted at it while I caught my breath. With a single swipe, the skull flew across the hallway and shattered into the wall, leaving a crack in the stones.

"You need to practice with your claws," I said, looking at the damage. "My strength is nine, and yours is 18. You are literally twice as strong as I am, and I'm pretty damn strong now. You could probably swipe through steel if you just tried."

"Fighting with one's claws is just so inelegant," she said. "It's not ladylike."

"And shooting lasers out of your eyes is?"

"Oh my, yes. With my *Magic Missile* I don't get blood on me like a common house cat. I don't end up matted and filthy. I can't even imagine it. I'd end up looking like Ferdinand."

"Who the hell is Ferdinand?"

"Nobody you'd know."

I sighed. "Just think about it, okay?"

She didn't answer.

We found the troglodyte boss room after a couple hours of grinding through the hallways. This one was a little differently shaped than the others. The room was a long rectangle with what appeared to be a smaller room at the entrance, meaning I wouldn't be able to pull off my bomb-from-afar method of boss killing. The highest mob in this area was a level four, meaning—hopefully—the boss wouldn't be too strong. Probably a level seven or eight.

It was dangerous, but if we couldn't handle a floor one neighborhood boss by now, we'd have no chance against whatever was guarding those stairs. We decided to go for it.

We hesitantly approached the boss room. The front door to this one was one of those glass automatic sliding doors, though I couldn't see inside. The sign on the door was in English. It said, **OPEN 24 HOURS** and **FITNESS, WEIGHTS, GAINS**.

I grabbed a cigarette and lit it. It was my second-to-last one. I took a deep drag.

We stepped inside.

24

LIKE THE DOOR INDICATED, THIS WAS A HIGH-CEILINGED GYM. THERE was a small receptionist's desk with a turnstile. Signs hung on the wall filled with slogans like **TODAY IS THE DAY YOU GAIN** and **EXCUSES DON'T LOSE CALORIES** and **RELEASE THE BEAST**. The place smelled of sweat and oil and testosterone. From around the corner I could see racks of fitness equipment. While not tiny, the place was much smaller than the last boss room. I didn't dare throw a dynamite stick in here.

A loud, deep grunting filled the gym, followed by the familiar *ching* of metal weights crashing together.

A level two troglodyte hissed at us from the counter, and Donut jumped to my shoulder and slammed him with a missile. He fell over, dead.

"Hey, was that a three power? He didn't explode."

"Yes, it was. I'm conserving my mana."

The automatic door slammed shut behind us, and the well-lit room turned red.

The familiar music started to play as I pushed my way through the turnstile. The boss battle message blared, almost identical to last time. Our mug shots floated into the air, and we were announced as we rounded the corner. Six of the level three Troglodyte Bashers filled the room, working the machines. A trio of the virtuosos stood in the opposite corner.

And then there was the boss.

The monstrosity stood across the room, admiring himself in the mirror as he curled a pair of absurdly large dumbbells. The creature stopped when we entered the room. He dropped the weights. The pair embedded themselves halfway into the floor with a reverberating *crash*. Wood splintered up all around where they fell. The beast slowly turned in our direction, and the world paused the moment his eyes met mine.

Ah, fuck, I thought as the face of the creature zoomed big on my interface.

Versus . . .

   The Juicer!

   Level 9 Neighborhood Boss!

   With a body enhanced by the finest anabolic steroids the dark web has to offer, the Juicer spends his days pushing iron, snapping necks, and crying that his pimple-infested sac is a third the size it once was. Having reached a plateau, rage now fills his enlarged heart. All he ever wanted was to gain, but right now he'll settle on bringing out . . .

The music hit a crescendo with a dun, dun, *dun*!

   . . . the paaaaain!

"The cheese factor on some of these descriptions is just horrifying," Donut muttered. "It's worse than that *Knight Rider* show you love so much."

Once again, this creature was a person from our world, though without the description it wouldn't be quite as obvious. It was like they'd taken a Troglodyte Basher and merged it with a contestant from a bodybuilding contest. And then inflated his muscles well past what a normal body could sustain. He was a couple of inches taller than me. He still had the lizard head, and a scaled body and tail. He wore little black shorts and nothing else, revealing a preposterously muscled physique, covered in tributaries of bulging veins as thick as my finger. The thing was so shredded, he was like a kid in a snowsuit who couldn't put his arms down. His trap muscles made him look as if he had tumors sprouting from the edge of his shoulder to halfway up his scaled head. His thighs were the size of beer kegs, forcing him into a ridiculous wide stance. He waddled when he moved.

"Bro," the monstrosity croaked. "I need a spot, bro." He pulled a round metallic free weight from a rack. The disk was the size of a manhole cover. With a twist of his waist, he threw it right at my head. The giant weight burst into flames as it rocketed toward me.

"Holy fuck!" I cried as I jumped out of the way. Donut leaped in the other direction. The weight crashed into a treadmill and exploded, shattering the mirror behind it.

I activated my scroll of *Confusing Fog* as the other troglodytes descended on me. The effect was immediate. A thick, wet fog filled the room, temporarily blinding me before it faded before my eyes. Water beaded over everything, making the ground slick. I could still see the outline of the cloud in the room, but the opacity of the effect was halved. I knew the troglodytes couldn't see a thing. The scroll didn't say how long the effect lasted, but I suspected it wasn't long. We had to act fast.

The troglodytes, blinded, started running into each other and the scattered gym equipment. The Juicer picked up another weight and chucked it in a random direction. "Bro," he groaned. "Bro, I can't see."

I rushed toward the group of bashers as yet another weight crashed against the squat rack, knocking it on its side with a mighty clang. We'd decided ahead of time that I'd take out the support creatures first if I could while Donut dealt full-strength head shots to the boss. I leaped over a glute machine, punching down into the wide-eyed, confused face of a basher. These guys took at least four or five punches to stay down. My fist burned as I tore through them.

I swept the leg out of the final basher, and he tumbled, hitting his head on the padded chair of a chest press. As I caved in the side of his head with my fist, the fog cleared, just as quickly as it had come.

Damnit. I read my second scroll as I scrambled away from a flaming disk. It smashed into the same chest press, sending flaming hunks of metal in every direction like shrapnel. I cried out as my exposed hip exploded in pain. Blood geysered down my leg. I cast my *Heal* spell just as the fog refilled the chamber. The *Confusing Fog* had lasted barely fifteen or twenty seconds, and I only had one scroll left.

Donut bounced back and forth around the room, launching at the Juicer, who was content to stay where he was and hurl metal at us. The powerful magic missiles were having an obvious effect on the boss monster, but his health bar was still in the green by the time Donut had to drink a mana potion. The Juicer grunted every time the missiles hit his head, followed by a bellow of rage. He'd pick up another weight and toss it in Donut's general direction. She was smart enough to move after each blast. The weights flew through the mist like comets.

In addition to avoiding the attacks by the boss, Donut had to dodge the random tongue lashes from the virtuosos. She tried to keep a machine between herself and the poison-dealing monsters. Only I had the anti-poison resistance, and if she got hit, we'd have a hard time keeping her alive until she'd be allowed to drink an antidote potion.

Both my leg and my hand healed as I launched myself toward the other side of the room at the three virtuosos. One blindly shot his tongue, and it smashed into a chin-up-bar machine next to me. I grasped the tongue with my left hand before it could recede, and the lizard made a strangled cry as it tried to retract but found he couldn't.

He retracted anyway, getting dragged across the room toward me. His large mouth clamped down on my fist. I cried out in pain. I banged the head against the side of a machine, but the body remained firmly attached. Its dozens of sharp teeth were embedded in the bones of my arm. The virtuoso wasn't dead, but he was literally choking on my fist. He seemed just as desperate to get free as I was. His body weighed barely anything, and it flailed desperately as it dangled off my arm.

I reached the other two lizards just as the fog began to clear again. "I'm almost out," Donut cried behind me.

I snap-kicked one in the stomach, and he doubled over. I smashed down with my foot, breaking his neck as I whirled on the third, hitting him with a right cross. I took my left fist, which was still inside the mouth of the first troglodyte, and I pummeled the third to death.

The lizard affixed to me also died during the beating, and his body broke off at the neck with a disgusting *snap*. The teeth remained painfully attached to my left wrist, like I was wearing a bizarre boxing glove made of troglodyte head. Bits of gore and bone still hung from the neck hole. I whirled to face the boss.

The Juicer's health was about two-thirds gone. The entire top half of his body was blackened and scorched. I could no longer see his beady eyes glaring at me.

"Bro," he said. "Not cool. That was my bro." He picked up another weight and flung it at me. I dove out of the way. It hit the wall, shattering. Shrapnel cut into me. Burning little pieces of metal peppered the side of my head. I fell backward over another machine, my ankle getting caught in the wire. I read my final scroll of *Confusing Fog* as I extracted myself. Another weight rocketed toward me, whirring over my head like a buzz saw. It exploded behind me.

More metal chunks cut into me. My health plummeted into the red. I mentally clicked a health potion from my hotlist as I peeled the skull off my wrist. It was like trying to free a boiled egg from its shell. I had to break the head from the jaw to free my hand. The skull clattered to the ground. After I drank the potion, I noted I had a 15-second cooldown before I could drink another. Donut's cooldown was much longer, closer to two minutes. I didn't have time to wonder why we were different.

The fog filled the room, and I rushed at the boss.

This is a terrible idea, I thought as I approached from behind. The monster was bent over, feeling blindly for another weight from the rack. He'd pulled all the weights off of one pole, but there were more right below it. Blinded, he couldn't see what to grab.

I grasped at a barbell that appeared to have about 250 pounds on each side. I grasped the stop and ripped half the weights free, which clattered to the ground near my feet. I held on to the barbell before it could tumble forward off the bench. I brandished the lopsided makeshift weapon like a giant mace. Before, lifting 250 pounds plus the bar would have been next to impossible. I normally benched 230 pounds—which was a respectable amount. With my strength now at nine, I could still feel the weight, but I lifted it easily. It was enough to be awkward and maybe too much to just regularly walk around with. But I knew I could easily swing it, and I did, as hard as I could, at the monster's scaly head.

Crash. My whole body shuddered, as if I'd swung at a solid wall. The boss staggered, falling on his side, dropping the weight he'd managed to pull free. The bar trembled, and the three weights fell off the far end. I smacked him one more time with the much lighter bar, then tossed it. I picked up one of the 100-pound weights at my feet, lifted it over my head in both my hands, and smashed down on the Juicer. I smashed, and I smashed. His health bar slowly descended as he cried out.

"Stop, ow! No, bro! It hurts!"

Just when I thought he was done, about to die, he twisted, his giant arm shot up fast as a snake strike, and it grasped my wrist. It felt as if a steel shackle had wrapped around me. *Oh fuck,* I thought as I dropped the bloody, dripping weight—which bounced off the monstrosity's stomach. He took his other hand and grasped my neck.

"This is gonna hella burn," he said, sitting up. The fog cleared, and his eyes focused on me. Despite being lizard-faced, a row of pustules circled his eyes, like zits that had grown up through the scales. He stank of sweat and burned flesh and Axe body spray. He started to squeeze, and I knew I was dead. My health bar plummeted.

A magic missile slammed into the Juicer's back. This was a weak one, and the monster barely acknowledged it with a grunt.

"Hold on, Carl!" Donut cried. She emerged, flying through the air, claws out like a tiger pouncing on unsuspecting prey. She landed directly on the monster's massive, bulbous shoulder, and she bit down hard on his vein-covered neck as her rear legs scrabbled at his back. Tendrils of green and red tissue went flying, as if she were a potato peeler gone haywire. She bit through one of the veins on his neck, vampire-like. Blood sprayed as if she had struck oil, soaking Donut, who gurgled in response.

The giant hand at my neck went slack, and he slapped backward at Donut. He barely hit her, a glancing blow, but she rocketed off the creature's back as if she'd been shot out of a cannon. She hit the far wall with a sickening *crunch.*

"Donut!" I cried. I scrambled to my feet, wheezing for breath as the monster reached for his shredded back in obvious agonizing pain. Blood sprayed from his neck as if she'd sheared off a water spigot. The blood just kept coming and coming, an impossible amount.

The Juicer looked at me, eyes surprised, as if he hadn't realized I was still alive.

"I'm proud of you, bro," he said. "You fought through the pain."

I hit him with a weak jab, and that's all it took. The boss, whose health was already all but depleted, crumpled onto his back. I smashed his solid head with my foot. The system seemed to release whatever supernatural protection it gave to bones and flesh once the creature was dead, and his head caved in easily under my heel. It felt as if I'd stepped into a rotten watermelon. I didn't pause to look at the carnage. I rushed across the room toward Donut.

She lay in a bloodied heap on the floor, her leg bent in the wrong direction. Her health bar held nothing but the barest sliver of red.

"Donut," I cried, coming to my knees before her. "Goddamnit, Donut. Don't you do this to me."

She gasped, not dead. The cat was entirely soaked in blood. But she was alive! I worriedly watched her health, terrified it might go lower. Sometimes when you were injured, it continued to decrease, just like on the surface.

The **Winner!** graphic appeared on my screen, and the music stopped as I plunged into my inventory. I had to wait 10 frustrating seconds for the bullshit to clear before I could find what I was searching for.

I had a scroll of *Heal Critter.* I read it, but it didn't work on her. The scroll evaporated from my menu with an error message. **No Valid Target Available. You just wasted a valuable scroll, dumbass.**

I couldn't cast my *Heal* spell on her, even if I did have enough Mana points, which I didn't. Instead, I pulled a healing potion out of my inventory and uncorked it, ready to pour it into her mouth.

I paused. She'd taken a mana potion just a few minutes earlier. She had a much longer potion countdown than I did. It probably had something to do with our constitution levels. I couldn't examine her and tell where that countdown was, if it had run out or not. Would it hurt her if I tried to feed the potion to her early? I didn't know. Any damage now would surely kill her.

I quickly pulled a second healing potion and decided to test it on myself. Using the quick slots, it wouldn't allow me to take a second potion, but surely the game couldn't stop me from doing it manually.

I downed one health potion, which brought my health back up. This was my first time actually physically drinking one. It tasted oddly like kiwi juice. The bottle disappeared with a *poof.* The fifteen-second timer appeared, and I drank the second potion before the timer was done.

You have been poisoned!
   Poison effect nullified.

"Goddamnit," I growled. I leaned over Donut, rubbing her soft fur. "Stay with me," I said.

Crack! The cat murmured in pain as her broken leg magically set itself. The sliver of health grew longer. She was healing. Getting better.

I sighed, relief washing over me. She would heal on her own, but it was going to take a while. I'd wait another five minutes before I risked giving her the potion, which would ease her pain.

"Carl. Carl, is that you?" Donut asked after a minute, lifting her head pitifully. "Did we get it?"

"We got it, Donut," I said. "*You* got it. Don't move. Just rest for a minute. You saved my life."

"I have been grievously injured in battle," she said. "In saving you, I have made the ultimate sacrifice. I can feel my life fading away, Carl. I'm circling that last bend into the drain. This is the end. I used my claws like you said, and I have perished as a result. Miss Beatrice is going to be most displeased with you." She coughed twice, two coughs that sounded suspiciously fake. "Tell her I fought bravely. Tell her I fought to the end. Find Ferdinand, tell him I loved him. I loved him ever since I first saw him."

Her health suddenly rocketed back up on its own. She'd taken one of her own health potions. I sighed, relieved.

"The light, I think I see the light," she croaked as I sat back and crossed my arms. Her eyes were clenched shut in mock pain. "This mortal coil is shed."

"Oh, get up," I said, looking about the room. "Help me loot all this crap."

25

AFTER SNAGGING THE NEIGHBORHOOD MAP, I SPENT SOME TIME grabbing all the weight equipment I could carry. There was a lot of it. Free weights and dumbbells littered the room. I took them all. I grabbed multiple weight benches, which weighed nothing once I removed the bars. I broke down a door I hadn't noticed earlier, and within were several mats and heavy medicine balls and various pieces of broken gym equipment along with some wrenches and other tools. All into the inventory, including the broken door. I then took everything off the office counter on the receptionist's desk, including a laptop computer with a dead battery, and a cabinet filled with paper files.

"Why are you even bothering?" Donut asked, having fully recovered. She frantically attempted to clean the blood off of herself. She was caked. She needed a shower and a brushing. The brushing part was going to be a problem.

"If we can lift it, then we take it," I said. "It only takes a second. The system is really good about categorizing it all. For some things, like that cabinet, it's faster to pick the whole thing up and add everything into the inventory than it is to search it. For example"—I held out my hand, and a half-full bottle of Johnnie Walker Black appeared—"this was hidden in that cabinet somewhere. The inventory system lets me keep it all together, and it lets me take things out of it, too. It's great once you figure out how to work it. We don't know what will be useful and when, so if it's not bolted to the ground, it's going into the bag."

Our next stop was a nearby training guild. Thanks to the boss being a higher level than expected, we both hit level nine. The wide expanse of experience needed to hit level ten spread before us. We also both had piles of loot boxes to open.

"Three stars, I see," Mordecai said as we entered the training guild. He paused, his eyes going glossy for a moment. "You took out a level nine boss on your own? Most impressive!"

"Yeah, it was a dumb idea," I said. "Not knowing what we're going to face really sucks. It's hard to prepare for fights when you're going in blind." I sat heavily in the chair while Donut leaped for the fireplace and paused her manic cleaning to open her boxes.

The rat creature nodded. "Let me examine the fight notes, and I can tell you what you can improve upon."

He grunted after a moment. "Okay, a couple things are clear. First off, brilliant move killing the goblin boss. Those guys are tough, but they aren't as hard as that thing you just fought. That's a new one to me." He shook his head. "The Juicer."

"I think it was somebody from our world mixed up with one of those troglodytes," I said. "He wasn't as lucid as the Hoarder lady had been. They'd done something to him to make him say all that dumb shit. The bosses are caricatures, exaggerated stereotypes. It's like they're being controlled by an AI, but their consciousness is still rattling around in there, too. It's really bizarre."

Mordecai nodded. "It's what they do. Right now across the universe, every eye is focused on Earth. Programs about your culture are reaching all the corners of the galaxy. The bosses are a part of that. It's like this every season. Anyway, let's look at your performance. When you hit it with that heavy weight, you did the same amount of damage as you would've with your fist. You need to understand how powerful your bare-knuckle skill has become. It's just as good right now as any unenchanted weapon you may find. I understand it's not convenient sometimes, but I recommend sticking with the bare-hand attack. Also, you wasted those *Confusing Fog* scrolls. Next time, have the party member with the highest intelligence read any scrolls if you can. Your intelligence of three made it so the fog only lasted fifteen seconds. Princess Donut's intelligence level would've resulted in the fog lasting for 120 seconds per scroll."

"Damn," I said. "Also, is that why she can't take potions so often? Because her constitution is low?"

"Yes," Mordecai said. "That shred attack of hers is very powerful, but it's useless until she gains more armor and more health. You're lucky she hadn't broken her neck. Picking a class or a race with a high base constitution will help, but not much. She'll need to load up on items that enhance it, and those tend to be less common."

I looked at Donut, who was hissing with rage at the piles of torches that kept appearing in front of her. She'd received yet another spell book in the Bronze Boss Box, but she hadn't read it yet. Most everything else appeared to be the same old crap with a couple exceptions. She got a bracelet from a Silver Adventurer Box she'd received for finally dealing melee damage. The bracelet added +2 to her dexterity stat, bringing it to 12. She equipped it, and it wrapped snuggly around her front leg.

She also received a dozen *Heal* scrolls from a Silver Survivor's Box. That one was rewarded to her because she'd ended a boss battle with less than 5% of her health. The scrolls were good to have because there was no countdown between reading each one, and even better yet, we could use the scrolls on each other.

She looked up at us. "I am already one of god's most perfect creatures, so I won't be changing race when the opportunity arises. I was born a cat, and I will die a cat. In fact, I'm going to have to insist that Carl choose a cat race as well."

"I am not going to change into a cat," I said. "In fact, I've been thinking about it, and I decided I'm going to stick with human."

Donut did her approximation of a shrug and glowed as she read the magical tome.

"Did you at least read the description first?" I asked. "What was it?"

Mordecai nodded. "That's a good one. *Puddle Jumper.*"

"What does it do?" I asked.

"She can teleport herself and up to three others to somewhere else that is within her line of sight. It will be especially useful if you come across rivers of lava or other impassable locations. Higher levels of the spell allow her to go further. If she manages to hit level 15 with the spell, it works almost as well as *Teleport*, one of the most powerful, most important spells to have in this dungeon. It costs 20 mana to cast and has a ten-second delay and a five-*hour* cooldown. It's not good as a combat spell with that long of a delay, but it's still great to have."

"What we really need is the ability to heal each other better," I said.

"Yes. Yes, you do," Mordecai said. "There are a lot of methods out there. Those twelve *Heal* scrolls are good, and I suspect you're about to get a few more. But for now, I would avoid letting Donut use her melee attacks unless it's absolutely necessary. Her strength stat is phenomenal for this floor. But it'll start to catch up to her later. She was at strength 18 during that fight. By way of comparison, the Juicer had a strength of 25. She's in the wrong body to properly utilize that stat for hand-to-hand combat. Plus her health is simply too low. For now." He nodded at the cat, who had resumed her hopeless self-grooming. "And you, little one. Your Dodge skill is level four. Keep working on it. Once it hits five, it'll be much easier for you."

"Look," I said, "the real reason we're here is because we've only found one set of stairs down, but there's a problem."

Mordecai's eyes widened as I told him about the others and the borough boss.

"The solution is simple," he said. "Skip the boss and keep searching for another set of stairs. They're out there, and most aren't guarded."

"We drove for a day straight before we found this one," I said. "I'm really worried this is our only chance. Do you know what type of monster that is? Do you have any tips?"

"If I did know what it was, I wouldn't be allowed to tell you. I have a very specific, rigorous set of rules I must follow, especially when it comes to bosses. Come back here after the fight, and I'll happily sit down with you and analyze the battle and tell you all the boss's stats. But if I tell you about the boss ahead of time, it's considered cheating. You don't want to be caught cheating. I *can* tell you that it's madness to face a borough boss with only six crawlers."

I sighed. All of this talk about future levels and choosing a race and class was a waste of time. None of that was going to matter if we didn't manage to make it past the first damn floor.

"Is there *anything* you can tell me?"

Mordecai thought for a moment. "Tell me, what does that Juicer boss have in common with that bad llama mob you fought earlier?"

I shrugged. "They're both drug addicts?"

"No, not that. How did you kill the llama?"

"I throat-punched him, and it made his head melt off."

Mordecai nodded. "And the Juicer? What attack, do you suppose, took him down?"

"It was a combination of several things, but probably when Donut bit his neck and tapped directly into his bloodstream." I laughed as Donut glowered at me. She still looked as if she'd tried to reenact that final scene from *Carrie*.

"That's exactly right," Mordecai said. "Most of these creatures have a weakness. The throat for the llamas, the high-pressure vein for the boss. Sometimes it's obvious, sometimes it's not. The Hoarder, for example. I can now tell you her weakness was the bugs coming out of her mouth. If you'd killed one before it had fully emerged, the next cockroach in line wouldn't have been able to get out. It would've choked and killed her."

"I never really thought of it that way," I said.

"Look for a vulnerability, and once you find it, exploit it. You haven't yet walked into a boss battle completely blind like you say. There have been clues every time. There will always be clues. Look for them."

There will always be clues. What did we know about this borough boss?

I thought about that as I sat down and examined my new achievements and boxes.

In addition to the boss box, it was mostly the standard stuff. My bare-knuckle and other fighting skills all ticked up to six, including my Smush skill. My Iron Punch rose to five. I received random achievements for riding the chopper for more than five hours. Another for having killed more than a 100 wandering monsters in the maze. I'd received a Bronze Survivor's Box for having less than 10% health when the boss died. I received five more of the *Heal* scrolls for that one, leaving us with 17 of them. Most of the other prizes were the standard Bronze or Silver Adventurer Boxes. Potions, bandages, biscuits. I did receive a random cowboy hat, which I tossed into my inventory.

I also was awarded an interesting achievement:

New achievement! Two Chicks at the Same Time.
You killed two mobs at once using only their own bodies against each other. On a brutality scale of *Bambi* to *Martyrs*, that is a solid Seven.
Reward: You've received a Gold Brawler Box!

I also received another Gold Looter Box for storing more than 10 tons' worth of crap in my storage.

The boss box contained a pile of ninja stars.

Enchanted Shuriken of Bloodlust, (X 100)
Small, low-damage throwing stars. These bad boys aren't anything special upon first glance. They're the same black stars you wannabe ninjas purchased at the knife shop and the swap meet when you were kids. The same throwing stars you'd drill into the drywall of your room until your mom caught you and took them away. And while these shuriken don't have the ability to turn you into a ninja, nor do they have the capacity to make your mom stop drinking, they are enchanted with a Bloodlust

enhancement. For every monster you damage with a shuriken from this set, the damage against that monster type rises by 8%.

I looked at Mordecai. "When it says the damage increases by 8%, does it mean 8% from the original amount, or 8% compounded? That's a big deal after a while."

"Huh, I don't know," Mordecai said. "Hang on." His eyes went glossy as he presumably entered some sort of tutorial-guide-only help menu.

"Good news. It's compounded," he said after a minute. "So each hit will be 8% higher than the previous amount. The bad news is, the stars are very fragile."

That sounded pretty awesome at first, but I suspected it wasn't that great of an enchantment. It'd take a long time to power them up. I'd have to do a ton of throwing to make them worthwhile. I only had 100 of them. I'd have to collect them back each time. And if they broke a lot, then I might only get one chance to really use them.

The Gold Looter Box contained yet another skill potion. It was once again a Determine Value skill tonic. I drank it, leveling the skill up to two. I couldn't see a difference in the menu. I suspected I'd need three more before it became really useful.

The brawler box contained the best item of the lot. After my shirt and cloak, it was easily the greatest loot I'd won so far in the dungeon. It was exactly the type of weapon I'd been hoping for.

Enchanted War Gauntlet of the Exalted Grull. (Right-Handed)
   +3 Strength (In Fist Mode Only).
   +1 Dexterity.
   +2 Skill Levels to Iron Punch.
   +1 Skill Level to Powerful Strike.
   2% chance to Stun enemy upon a successful hit.
   Item is a wrist bracer that transforms into a spiked war gauntlet made of orcish steel when the hand is shaped into a

fist or wields a hilted weapon for more than two seconds at a time. This item on its own does not negate the bare-knuckle skill bonus.

Warning: If you use this weapon to strike adherents of the war god Grull, you have a 1.5% chance to transfigure your target into the deity himself. Trust me on this. You don't want to do that.

A bigger, redder WARNING. Remove this item before you jerk off.

"Hey, Mordecai," I said as I removed the chain and slipped the charcoal-colored bracer over my wrist. "How can I tell if someone worships Grull?"

He grunted. "Equine-class creatures worship him. So if it's a horse or a centaur, or a tikbalang, then he might worship Grull. Creatures like that bad llama might also pray to him, but not until after the third floor. The biggest tell is that they smear blue makeup all over themselves and won't stop talking about wenches and dying gloriously in battle." Mordecai paused. He looked up nervously, as if not sure he should say this next part. "And, just so you know, Grull isn't a real god. There are no real gods in this game."

"Does that really make a difference?" I asked.

Mordecai was suddenly solemn, and I didn't know why. He looked at me, intense. "You said you worry that some of these bosses and mobs are like you, here against their will." He pointed downward, indicating the lower levels. "That's not always going to be the case. *Especially* later on. Remember that. There are no gods here. Just those who pay for the privilege."

"Okay," I said, trying to make sense of what he was desperately attempting to tell me.

"What the goodness is a tikbalang?" Donut asked, pausing in her cleaning. "It sounds like some sort of disease a sailor would get."

"Do you know what a horse is?" Mordecai asked, looking up. He seemed relieved for the question.

"Of course."

"They're like that. But meaner."

I closed my fist. Two seconds ticked by, I felt a haptic buzz all up my arm, and with a *whoosh*, my hand turned into a spiked hunk of metal. I had to clench my fist really tight to make it work, which was good. The last thing I needed was this thing appearing when I didn't want it to. I examined the malevolent-looking gauntlet. There was nothing ornate about it. It was black, angular with multiple gleaming spikes. A tool, nothing more. It felt heavy on my hand, but not too heavy. No more breaking fingers when I punched something. I felt the extra strength ripple through me. I released my fist, and the gauntlet vanished in a puff of smoke that smelled of burned hair.

"Awesome," I said.

26

"ARE YOU READY?" I ASKED BRANDON AS WE POISED AT THE EN-
trance to the borough boss chamber.

"No," he said, smiling sadly. He clutched onto his massive war
hammer for a moment. It disappeared into his inventory. The giant
weapon could only get in the way during the first part of the plan.
Donut perched on my shoulder while the others crowded behind us.

We didn't have time left for any more training, any more preparation. It was now or never.

The third episode of *Dungeon Crawler World* hadn't offered any
additional insight. Donut and I had sat in the Taco Bell watching it
on the screen while the proprietor, another Bopca Protector named
Sebastian, sat next to us and brushed Donut's hair with one of his
own brushes, which he'd gifted to her after her third shower. Her
insane charisma of 41 caused the level 21 NPC to practically fall in
love with her the moment we entered the safe zone. I sipped on a
delicious Peruvian beer and picked at my T-bone steak as we watched
crawlers by the dozens get slaughtered while the host breathlessly
described the action.

The second half of the program had zeroed in on five different
groups of adventurers, including that woman with the magical crossbow and Lucia Mar with her two rottweilers. The other three groups
were larger, including one that comprised 150 African soldiers armed
with AK-47s. All of these groups, if the show was to be believed,
were just moonwalking their way through the dungeon. All of them
had found stairwells down already and were camping near them,

waiting for the clock to tick to exactly six hours before they descended.

Much to Donut's dismay, we were once again snubbed by the program. I didn't care. I was much more occupied with that number. I couldn't get it out of my head.

2,552,085.

From thirteen million to this in just under four days. A cataclysm. Every single one of those numbers was a person, someone who had lived, breathed, hoped, laughed. And they were just gone. The announcement hadn't offered any additional insight, either. Another, more stern warning about using the hallways as a bathroom. A litany of changes regarding spells and power levels of mobs, none of which affected us. After sleeping for a few hours, we headed back to the encampment, and I related my dubious off-the-cuff plan to the group of crawlers who had all appeared shocked that we'd actually returned.

"Here we go," I said now, stepping across the drawbridge and through the giant archway.

Brandon, Chris, Yolanda, and Imani followed. We hesitantly entered the round courtyard to the spiral maze.

"No, Agatha, don't!" I heard a voice behind me. It was Yolanda yelling at the woman with the shopping cart, who'd wheeled up behind us.

The woman didn't listen to Yolanda and pushed her way into the entrance hall, cackling with delight. "You're not doing this without ol' Agatha."

"We don't have room for you, Agatha!" Yolanda yelled. "Get back!"

"Crazy bat," Brandon said. "You're gonna get us all killed."

"I think that roly-poly is the one that's gonna get us all killed," Agatha said.

"Shut up. Everybody, shut up," Imani said, raising her hand. "Listen for the monster."

"Don't worry," I said. "It's going to announce itself at any moment."

The gate behind us slammed shut as music rose. Metal bars magically appeared, locking us in.

This was different music than usual. Faster, more frenetic. An EDM beat mixed by a DJ hopped up on Adderall. A deep bass reverberated off the ground.

The lights flickered, then went dark. A moment later, they came back on, filling the area with the purple hue of a black light. Neon lights appeared on the ceiling. Lasers ripped across the hallways, flashing in beat with the music. We'd stepped into a rave. The sound of rock scraping filled the room, louder than the song. I turned in a circle, trying to find the source.

It was the walls of the courtyard, I realized. They were sinking into the ground, leaving us exposed.

B-B-B-Boss Battle!

The voice was distorted, even louder than last time.

You have discovered the lair of a Borough Boss!
      Ladies and Gentlemen, it is time for the main event! Are you ready? Can you feel it coming? I SAID, ARE YOU READY?
      I want you to put your hands together.
      Aaaand here. We. Gooooo!

I grimaced as I waited for the walls of the round courtyard to finish sinking into the Earth.

I turned to Brandon. "Get ready." I had to shout the words.

The man nodded. Sweat beaded on his forehead. Behind, the three others spread out. Chris and short Yolanda both looked absolutely terrified. Imani clutched her sword in two hands, looking grim. Agatha stood there, seemingly oblivious, scratching a hair between her two bulbous eyes.

Our seven mug shots appeared floating in the air, one by one. I
noted we were in three groups. The **Royal Court of Princess Donut.**
Meadow Lark. And Agatha was just **Crawler Agatha.** The giant **Versus**
slammed into place. The metallic word was in a silver font instead
of a bronze one this time. The words burst into flames, and even
though this was supposedly virtual text, I felt a blast of heat.

And that's when we saw it.

With the wall fully retracted, a hallway spread before us, like we
were standing on the landing before a tunnel in a subway, but without the drop. The round tunnel was about as wide as a single-lane
freeway, about fifteen feet tall. The creature roared by right in front
of us, startlingly fast, moving from right to left. It was massive, made
of flesh, rolling like a pinball. It stank of sewage and rotten meat. It
grunted and squealed, a high-pitched, angry pig noise. The flesh was
pink, rippling, covered in eyes and random hairs and tusks. But there
was something else there, too. Random flaps of black and white cloth
were embedded in the flesh, mixed in with swaths of red sequined
fabric.

"What in the holy hell is that?" Brandon shouted. "It looks like
there are . . ."

The world froze.

The

    Ball

    of

    Swine!

    Level 15 Borough Boss!

    Also known as the Pork Chop Express, the Ball of Swine is
one of the rarest, most deadly battle formations of the Tuskling.
Encompassing at least 30 Tuskling knights and their ladyloves,
a Ball formation requires a specific set of circumstances to cre-
ate. Combine a gathering of Tuskling aristocracy, add an alcohol-
fueled, sexually charged orgy of war lust, and sometimes, just
sometimes, the wild, ancient battle magic that permeates their

war-torn world casts the spell, forming the ball. The Tusklings, the ruling class of the Orcish Supremacy, shape into an inseparable sphere that rolls onto the countryside. The ball of pork won't stop its night of terror until it has crushed the poor, the weak, and the lesser citizens under its unstoppable weight.

Plucked directly from a Tuskling High Caucus moments after it formed, this particular ball has been transferred here to this dungeon for your entertainment, ladies and gentlemen. The magic of the ball won't allow them to stop until every last drop of crawler blood is squeezed right out of their human bodies!

The world unfroze, and the ball continued its trajectory, rolling away down the path. Ahead of me, more walls moved and shifted, grinding loudly. The walls and entranceways were creating new paths, guiding the massive ball in our direction.

"Wow," Donut said from my shoulder. "I'm feeling really ignored right now. Why is it always human this, human that? Why can't it be 'blood is squeezed out of their human and feline bodies'?"

Looking to my left and right, I could see what was about to happen. With the lowering of the walls, a new path opened up, and we were on it. The heavy, pounding music was deliberate. We could no longer feel the oncoming train of the giant pig ball. At its current speed, it would circle around onto us in a minute, maybe less.

"Move!" I cried.

"Where?" Brandon called.

"Away from here," I said.

I pulled the first of several spike strips from my inventory and dropped it on the ground before rushing forward. We moved toward the long, wide path the ball had just rocketed over. A moment later, the ball rushed past again, right where we'd been standing, missing Agatha and her shopping cart by inches. The woman cackled with joy as the squealing wind blew up the flaps on her hat.

In the brief moment it passed by, I caught sight of a tuskling face jutting from the center side of the ball, spinning like an ornamental car rim. The orc creature was large and meaty from what I could tell. It held a tusked, wild boar of a face that was twice as wide as a person's. The face had four tusks. Two long, curved tusks and a second pair farther back, crossed in front of its ugly face. This one was female, I guessed. Purple eyeshadow ran from the top of its bulbous black stare. Her crossed tusks were pierced in multiple places. She also appeared to have a giant purple flower on her head, but the flower was pressed into the pink flesh of the ball, completely flattened. Her mouth was open in a constant angry squeal.

Above the monstrosity appeared a health bar. It was fully green, but the spike strip had damaged it for at least a single point. That was good.

A wall rose into the air, blocking us from going back the direction we'd just come.

Our plan hadn't anticipated that the walls were going to change. Looking at the ground, I could see a groove had formed onto the stone, multiple concentric circles leading toward the center of the small arena. Some of the grooves led directly into walls.

Amongst the grooves, dozens of long, straight lines crisscrossed the ground at right angles. This was where the walls would go up and down. We needed to find a flat area wide enough for our redoubt. The deeper we went, the closer to the stairs, the more quickly the pig ball would circle around.

"Look for solid hunks of ground. Big ones with no grooves!" I called as I threw a second spike strip onto the ground. "And go!"

An entranceway to the next ring appeared about ten feet behind us. "Move!" I cried. We rushed for the small gate, Agatha going in first. A hunk of stone started rising from the ground as I rushed through, stumbling.

"There!" Imani called, pointing to a large square on the ground through a second doorway, yet another circle deeper. It was like a gap in the path, designed to encompass two circles at once.

"Go!" I cried, rushing forward and dropping a third and a fourth strip. Despite the heavy bass, I felt the ball hurtle past on the other side of the wall. High-pitched squealing rocketed away like the whine of a race car. *It's getting faster.*

We rushed to the center of the square. This chunk of the floor was like a railroad switch, a place where the ball could change paths. The space was about 15 feet by 15 feet with no crevices. Perfect.

"It's coming from this way," I said, pointing right. "I think it needs two loops to get here. Let's do this. Just like we practiced. Go!" I pointed at Agatha. "You, sit your ass down on the ground in the middle, and don't move."

"I ain't leaving my . . . Hey!" Agatha cried as I grasped the heavy cart from both sides and lifted it into the air, wasting a few precious seconds to put it into my inventory.

"Thief!" she cried. "Thief!"

"Agatha, he'll give it back. Sit down!" Yolanda cried as she started pulling her V-shaped braces from her inventory.

I ignored the screaming crazy woman as I pulled the heavy goblin table from my own inventory and placed it on its side. All around me, the others went to work. We'd been practicing this for hours. We'd gotten it down to less than 20 seconds for the main structure, and another 20 to put it all together. Hopefully that was enough time.

It had taken us almost five hours to build the pieces of the redoubt, or, as Brandon called it, "The Speed Bump." Brandon and his brother weren't nurses at the facility. They were the maintenance guys, and these dudes knew what they were doing. They didn't normally work after hours, but they'd been there that night, pushing overtime, trying to fix an oven that was on the fritz before the morning staff showed up to make breakfast. I had described my idea. I spread out a bunch of the looted goblin tools for them, explained exactly what I wanted to do, and we went straight to work.

We created a portable modular fortress. Consisting of tables, weight equipment, and loads of other odds and ends, the angled, four-foot-high structure looked like a lopsided tortoiseshell when it was completed.

We didn't have any sort of welding equipment, but the goblins had hand-cranked drills and large toothed bolts designed to screw into the holes the drills created. They also had these small half-moon saws that cut through steel with alarming ease. We removed the legs from the workshop tables, then bolted new ones on, utilizing the load-bearing legs from the weight equipment. The tables were designed to sit solidly at a low angle when we put them on their side. After, we bolted weight benches onto the sides of the tables, like attaching shutters to the edges of a doorframe.

Both Brandon and Imani had received items that gave them boosts to their strength, and they each had two sections of wall to place. The pieces were large and unwieldy, and heavy as shit, but when placed down in the correct order—Imani, then Brandon, then Imani, then me with the largest piece, and then finally Brandon—the multiple pieces slid together, bolts moving into precisely placed holes. Brandon and I moved to the roof—made of the crossbars of weight racks—while Chris and Imani twisted massive fist-sized butterfly bolts, affixing the pieces together. Yolanda pulled the rest of the angled braces out of her inventory, sliding them into place one after another, moving in a circle around the circumference of the pentagon-ish defense.

"This is just like something they'd do on that show, *The A-Team*," Donut had exclaimed when we'd practiced this earlier. "Or maybe *MacGyver*. The real MacGyver with the hair and the stargate. Not that abysmal remake."

"I liked that show," Chris had said as he worked. It was the first and only time I had heard him speak.

"Which one? *The A-Team* or *MacGyver*?" Donut asked. "Or do you mean the remake? Please tell me you don't mean the remake."

Chris never answered.

Once the top was bolted into place, Brandon, Imani, and I moved to the last, crucial part. The braces for the roof: five heavy-duty barbell poles designed to hold more than a thousand pounds of weight each. I discovered if I held my hand in just the correct place and called the heavy pole from inventory, it wedged itself perfectly between the roof and ground, solid as a concrete pillar.

Our mini fortress had a usable area of about ten by ten feet, and we had to move about on our hands and knees. It was tight when it was just the six of us, but with the addition of Agatha, who continued to wail about her damn shopping cart, we could barely move without slamming into each other. And because she'd joined us, we didn't have room to place the final, center pole.

I looked worriedly at that center cross section of the roof just as Donut exclaimed, "Here it comes!"

If this boss had any sort of fire or lightning or acid attack, we were absolutely fucked. So far it seemed each boss only had one main attack, and this one's was pretty obvious. It rolled right the fuck over you.

My kneepads had an attribute that canceled out momentum-based attacks. But if my experience with video games was any indication, one couldn't count on that sort of thing when it came to bosses. Plus there was no way I was going to test it.

Once, as a kid, I was riding down a country road with my mom and dad. They'd been fighting, as usual, and I'd climbed into the very back of the SUV, as far back as I could get. I'd oftentimes do this, staring out the rear window as the world whipped by, pretending like I was in the cockpit of a spaceship. On this day a large yellow truck was behind us. It was one of those box trucks, a Penske, something people rented to move.

It happened so fast. One moment, I was staring up at the guy, who was getting so close to my dad's ass that I had to crane my neck up to see him, and then the truck was just stopped, pulling away from us, the top peeled off like a sardine can. We'd gone under a bridge, and the truck was too tall. As I watched, the sides of the truck fell away, spilling furniture and boxes all over the road with a resounding *crash*! The main cab of the truck tilted violently to its side, broken away from the rest of the body. My dad heard the accident, looked up into the rearview mirror, muttered, "That's a shame," and just kept driving as my mom yelled at him to stop. He didn't.

That's what I was hoping would happen here. This massive ball of flesh filled the hallway, from the ground to the ceiling. My forward section of the redoubt was wider, giving a more gradual angle, just enough to wedge the ball between us and the ceiling nice and tight.

Like Mordecai had suggested, I needed to look at the clues. Those strange entrances dotting the side of the arena were there for a reason. It was so we could catch a glimpse of the monster. All I could see was that it was big, round, fast, and shoved tightly into the tunnel.

My first idea was to build a solid wall, but as we observed the ball from one of the many portcullis entrances, the track forced the monster directly into a 90-degree angle. It bounced right off, barely losing speed as it turned away. *There will always be clues.*

It never lost momentum. It just kept going and going. So we needed to stop it somehow, and we needed to be in a position to do something about it once it did. I was hoping it'd hit our structure and get wedged in good. From there, Imani would stab, Donut would shoot missiles, Chris would cast his spells, and the rest of us would jab our makeshift ninja-star-tipped spears up into the boss until its health ran out.

Most of the goblin tables were made of thick, hefty steel, which was why they were so damn heavy. The wide table we used for the front of the redoubt also had a pitted wooden covering. Brandon, Chris, and I had spent a good five minutes throwing fifty of my ninja shuriken deep into the wood, adding black spikes to the ramp. Spikes that would hopefully damage the boss each time they pierced its flesh. Unfortunately, only about 20 of the stars remained unbroken.

That part had been Brandon's idea. I'd shown him the shuriken and allowed him to read the description.

"These things are way more powerful than you realize," he'd said, voice filled with awe. "Do the math. Compounding damage means if you poke something 200 times, it's like literally millions of points of damage."

"I don't do math," I said. "But I do know we ain't poking anything 200 times with these things. Look." I pulled a single star out. I'd tested it earlier to see if I had any sort of ninja skill. It'd received a single chip, and the red enchantment had faded away. Mordecai wasn't kidding when he said these things were fragile. They were clearly meant to only be used once, tempering their value.

Despite their fragility, we'd used several of the stars to create the spike strips, nothing more than a pair of stars placed between two pieces of bolted-together wood. They'd survive one or two stabbings before breaking. The strips wouldn't be stopping the monster by themselves, but each time it rolled over one, the amount of damage inflicted on the boss would increase by 8%.

"Brace," I cried, grasping onto the wall as the monster barreled toward us, impossibly fast.

Crash!

The entire structure shuddered and slid with a horrifying *screech*. All four of the ceiling braces popped out of place and went flying. One bounced hard off Yolanda, throwing her over. The terrible stench filled the now-dark chamber. An unending high-pitched squealing filled the air.

We'd done it.

The ceiling sagged, bending ominously as dark squares of flesh pushed through the empty spaces of the lattice pattern. The ceiling was going to break. We were going to be crushed. The ball had managed to squeeze itself between the top of the tunnel and our fortress, the massive pressure pushing down against our defense.

"Stab!" I cried as the stick appeared in my hand. It was half of a chin-up bar with a goblin clamp at the end, clutched onto a tied-together cluster of three stars. I hoped they'd be less likely to break if bunched together. I jabbed upward, poking the flesh. It felt as if I was doing nothing. Next to me, Imani struggled to get her long-sword angled and through the holes in the ceiling. She was pushing her sword all the way in and pulling out, over and over. Pigs squealed, blood rained. The music quickened. To my left, bolts popped from holes, shooting off like bullets. One clobbered Agatha, who didn't appear to notice despite a well of blood that appeared. She was still screaming something about her shopping cart. Above, the pressure grew. I stabbed, and I stabbed.

And then, just as the top collapsed, I pierced upward and there was a mighty *Pop!* like a balloon.

Tuxedoed male and female tusklings in glittering formal gowns rained down upon us as our ill-fated fortress collapsed. The lattice-patterned ceiling broke into pieces, the metal clanging and bending where it was bolted together. My hobbled-together spear was caught in one of the ceiling's holes. It ripped out of my hands as I was violently crushed onto the ground. I arched my back, protecting Donut under my body. Squeals and screams and hollering filled the hall as my minimap turned into a mass of red dots.

A fat, heavy orc crashed into me, and we both rolled, tangled in pieces of ceiling. Donut yowled and leaped away. The ninja-star-covered tabletop lay broken to my right. A handful of stars still glowed red, and the creature rolled onto them, squealing with pain. I pulled myself to my feet just as Donut leaped onto my shoulder. She was screaming something incoherent, shooting magic missiles point-blank at the tusklings, who rocketed backward with each hit.

I stepped on the squealing tuskling, smushing him deeper into the shuriken-covered wood. His health bar dropped, slowly at first and then just plummeted away as the exponential damage bonus kicked in.

Half of the creatures were already dead.

I caught eyes with the next closest tuskling, a male in a tuxedo.

He was unarmed and completely disoriented. He held what appeared to be a wine flute in his hand that was miraculously unbroken and still full of alcohol. The creatures were odd, much shorter than I had anticipated. They had large, wide bodies and torsos one and a half times as bulky as a regular human. Their large warthog heads sat too close to their shoulders, making them look neckless. But from the waist down, their bodies were comically short. The beasts only stood about four and a half feet tall. I quickly examined his properties as the tottering creature pulled the wine flute to his mouth.

Tuskling Knight. Level 4.

When it comes to the Tuskling, their titles are about as accurate as their dating website photos. The once-mighty warriors conquered the Orcish Supremacy hundreds of years ago, defeating all the other clans. They are now shells of the mighty warriors they once were. The honorarium "Knight" roughly translates to "Overweight, alcoholic bureaucrat who spends his days making new laws to oppress the poor and his nights drinking and getting pegged." Knights and their slightly more dangerous female counterparts, Tuskling courtesans, are only worthy adversaries when they come together to form an ancient Tuskling battle formation known as a "Ball of Swine."

I formed a fist.

"On my back," I called to Donut. She was out of magic missiles, and she'd already taken a mana potion. She dove under my cloak, hanging on to the back of my jacket like a backpack. She'd pop up when she'd regenerated enough mana to cast another missile over my shoulder.

I pulled my arm back and punched the fat tuxedoed knight with all of my strength. The pig man's health was already in the red, and his face caved in under the crushing blow of the spiked gauntlet. He dropped, still clutching onto his glass of wine. Half of his snout remained attached to my fist.

Miraculously, I didn't feel a thing. I only felt the impact in my arm. Not my hand.

"*Yes,*" I said, whirling on my next opponent as I shook the gore free. A female. A courtesan. The men were all level four, and the women were all level five. This one was slightly taller and fatter than the others. She wore a glittering red gown with multiple leather straps looped over and around her like a vest. It was like some sort of weird BDSM getup. She, too, was looking around, dazed, and screaming in confusion. It seemed they had no memories of their time in the pig ball. They were victims, just as all the other bosses had been.

But their dots were red, time was running out, and they weren't human. I took a step forward, and I swung. The punch knocked her health down halfway. She hit the ground with an *oof,* raising her arms to block the blows. I kicked at her savagely, screaming, maybe crying. I kicked and I kicked until her health bar went away.

Behind the woman, Imani was also screaming, swinging her sword as tears streamed down her face. She stood over the prone form of Yolanda, whose health bar was alarmingly low. Brandon had retrieved his giant maul, which glittered with lightning when he swung it. Chris twirled an ethereal magic spear. The spear was a spell he could cast. It lasted for five minutes.

Agatha hadn't moved, but she stood once the walls fell away. Blood gushed down the side of her head, her eyes wide as she watched the action. She clutched her hands together.

All of the internal walls had retracted once we'd popped the swine ball. We'd gone from a tight hallway to a wide-open field. The purple-hued arena spread around us, the size of an entire quadrant. The music still beat, and colorful lasers shot through the space like we were in a massive 1980s-themed roller rink. The roof rose the closer it got to the center. A bright light shone at the very center of the dome. The stairs. A red force field surrounded the stairwell.

I knew exactly what had to be done to get that force field to drop.

There were more of the tusklings than there were of us, but they were shocked and confused, having been transported from their own world to this place.

They were weaponless, they were untrained, and they were slaughtered.

27

THE LAST TUSKLING TO FALL WAS DIFFERENT THAN THE OTHERS. She was a level eight, a "Tuskling Dominatrix." She fell after being crushed under Brandon's hammer.

The music stopped, and the lights returned to normal. The world froze. The **Winner!** notification appeared. Behind me, Chris fell to his knees, and he hung his head low. We just looked at each other, nobody saying anything. Imani fed Yolanda a health potion, and the woman sat up, wobbling, holding the side of her head. Agatha shuffled toward me, shaking her fist. Half of the woman's head was caked in blood, and she didn't seem to notice.

"Give it back!" she cried.

"Here," I said. I pulled the shopping cart into existence a foot off the ground, and it crashed down loudly.

"Hey," she cried. She clutched an IKEA bag off the top and peered inside, as if afraid I'd stolen something. She poked suspiciously at the pink flamingo at the end of her cart.

"You know, you can put all of this into your own inventory," I said. "You don't need to wheel it around."

"She hasn't gone through the tutorial," Yolanda said. The small woman, who still had blood all over her own face, pulled out a cloth and cleaned off Agatha's. "She doesn't have an inventory yet."

That didn't surprise me. What did surprise me was that Agatha was level two, not one. How had she done that? She wasn't in the Meadow Lark party. That meant she must have killed a mob. I wondered what the story was there. Actually, no, I realized, looking at

Agatha now. She'd hit level four, thanks to the boss. She hadn't done anything, but she'd been in the room, and that counted for something at least. Donut and I were both now level 10. Halfway to 11. We'd received a ton of experience, more than I'd expected. Imani *was* level 11 now. Chris and Brandon had skipped level seven altogether and were level eight. Yolanda had jumped from five to level six.

I didn't even want to think about how all that experience was distributed. It seemed there were a dozen different calculators running all at once to figure it out. It gave me a headache.

"We need to find whatever the boss dropped," I said.

"It's over there," Donut said. "The dominatrix lady has it. I already got mine."

For the first time, I looked about, taking stock of the damage we'd dealt. All of us had managed to survive relatively unscathed, but this section of the room and everyone in it looked like someone had spilled a giant can of SpaghettiOs on us from above. The crushed and disemboweled tuskling bodies lay everywhere, mixed in with the shattered pieces of our fortress.

"That didn't go as expected," Brandon said. He shook his hand, spraying blood everywhere.

"We're alive," I said as I reached down to loot the persistent item from the tuskling's corpse.

The AI seemed to be doing a whispery David Attenborough impersonation as he read the description of the item:

Borough Field Guide.

Ahh, look at you. The intrepid explorer. Alone. Lost. *Afraid.*

But there is no reason to be frightened. Not today, not now. Not when the trusty field guide has added monster types to this area of the map. Now when you gaze upon the unknown, that fear is somewhat lessened. Instead of delving into the strange, mysterious dark, being devoured by an unseen horror, you will now know exactly what it is as it chews upon your tasty innards.

I blinked at the description; then I pulled up my minimap, zooming it out. Sure enough, now the individual quadrants were outlined. Most of my screen was filled with the large arena, but the very edge of a few adjacent quadrants ringed the exterior of the map. I mentally hovered over one to the far southeast, in an area none of us had ventured into. The fog of war obscured the hallways themselves, but when I hovered over it, a tooltip popped up.

Mobs Level 2–5. Axebeak.

That would be extremely useful, but like with the neighborhood map, the area was limited. Plus one had to actually get to the center and kill the boss to get the information. I wasn't certain exactly how big a "borough" really was in this game, though I suspected the area shrank the lower one went.

"Hey, are you kids doing okay?" a voice called. It echoed in the large chamber. I turned to see an elderly man edging his way into the room with his walker. The walker made a *click, click, click* each time he pushed his way farther into the chamber. "We heard a loud noise, and the gate disappeared! Oh my, it smells something awful in here."

"Randall, don't come in here!" Yolanda called, jogging toward the man.

I turned my attention back to the carnage. I gazed at the hoofed feet of the tusklings and sighed. They had no shoes, and their legs were much too short. I picked up a loose tuxedo jacket. It was like a tent, and it was covered with blood. It smelled like hot diarrhea. I put it into my inventory.

Brandon came to stand next to me. The guy looked shell-shocked.

"It's weird, isn't it?" I asked, indicating the carnage. "They're from another world. They're aliens, right? But they're wearing tuxedos. Tuxedos are from Earth, not wherever they're from. I don't get it."

"I asked our guildmaster, Mistress Tiatha, the same thing," Brandon said. He reached down to pick something up from the floor. It was a sharp tooth. "One of the mobs we had to fight early on was little fire-breathing monkeys wearing lederhosen. You know what I'm talking about? That weird German-pantsuit-shorts things with the hats. They look like waiters at an Oktoberfest tent?"

"Yeah, I know what you mean," I said.

"Well, anyway. She said the Synd . . ." He paused, looking at the ceiling dubiously. "The big guys, they not only seeded our world with the people millions of years ago, but they keep people here the whole time. Sometimes they're actual humans, but from other worlds. And these guys were steering culture. Inventing stuff, writing books and songs that already existed. She said every world comes out with their own unique culture and language, but some things are universal."

"But why?" I asked. "What do they get out of it? It seems like so much effort."

Brandon shrugged. "I don't know. Maybe they think we'll integrate better if we already have some sort of common ground, but I don't know. We probably won't ever know. We only see what they let us."

I looted the corpses of the tusklings I'd killed myself. There was some jewelry that wasn't enchanted including a ruby necklace that seemed pretty valuable according to my inventory list. I took that weird leather thing from the woman. The system labeled it as a **Pig Harness**. There wasn't any other loot in my pile. I saw Imani holding what appeared to be an enormous strap-on dildo with two fingers. She dropped it on the floor with a look of disgust. Donut hopped over and took it into her own inventory.

She looked up at me. "Everything, right?"

I nodded. "Everything."

I salvaged all the ninja stars I could find and all the remaining pieces of the redoubt. I had a new tab in my inventory labeled **Worthless Garbage**.

I also spent a few minutes surreptitiously looking around the arena for the remains of the party that had gone before us. Their X's didn't appear on the map, just as they hadn't with the elderly folk Imani had killed. I didn't know why. There was probably a tight time limit on that sort of thing, but I didn't know for certain. This game had so many damn rules, I couldn't wrap my head around it.

Finally, Donut and I approached the stairwell. The force field was gone. The timer was at five hours and counting.

I looked back over my shoulder at the others. Brandon was talking quietly with his brother while Yolanda and Imani had started bringing the others into the large room. Chris jogged off as I watched. I knew exactly where he was going. He was headed toward that safe room. He'd tell the 30 folks waiting that they could leave if they wanted to.

"What do you want to do?" I quietly asked Donut.

"Whatever do you mean?"

"We're going to go down those stairs, and it's going to be a whole new floor with new challenges. We can either stick with these guys, or we can keep doing our own thing."

Donut looked up, her large yellow eyes boring into me.

"Oh, Carl. How is it I know what you're going to do before you do?" she asked.

I looked at the gathering group of elderly folks, and I nodded. *Shit.*

"Goddamnit, Donut," I said. She was right. Of course. What was the point of living if I couldn't live with myself?

I reached into my pocket and I pulled out my last cigarette. I looked at it for a long moment. I popped it into my mouth, and I lit it. It tasted like ash.

"I suggest we do what we've been doing," Donut said. "It doesn't have to be one or the other option. We set up a place for them to remain safe, and then you and I go out and do our own thing. We can keep our own party and set up a group chat with the others. I know how to do it now. When we find the next set of stairs down, we go get them and bring them with us."

I grinned down at the cat. "I knew there was a good kitty in there somewhere."

She bristled. "If it were up to me, I'd leave them all. But I know you're a softy. Besides, if we get them down to that third level, we'll need someone with thumbs if you're going to turn into a cat."

"I'm not turning myself into a cat," I said. "I couldn't even if I want to anyway. Mordecai said so." I dropped the cigarette, unfinished. I ground it out on the floor. I went to a knee and patted her. She let me.

"By the way," I asked as I stroked the cat, "I've been meaning to ask you. Who's Ferdinand?"

Donut pulled away at that, her tail swishing. "I have no idea whatever you're talking about. Whoever that is, he sounds like someone awful. Wait . . . where's Agatha?"

I looked about for the woman. I didn't see her. Had she gone outside? I turned toward the stairs, and I noticed they weren't stairs at all, but a long ramp. *Shit. The woman is going to get herself killed.*

"OKAY, HERE'S THE PLAN," I SAID TO BRANDON LATER, AFTER WE finished examining the stairwell. "We're going to go down there and make sure the area is clear for you and your people. Do you need our help with your people?"

"No," Brandon said. "We got it. You don't want to go and open your boxes first?"

"I do," I said, "but the closest place to do it is pretty far, and I don't want to tempt fate. We'll go down and try to find the closest safe room. Our guy said they're just as easy to find on the second floor as the first. Once we do, we'll carve a safe path to it."

"Okay, then," Brandon said. He held out his hand. "Thank you. I mean that." I shook it. He then went to his knee and scratched Donut. "You, too, Princess Donut."

"Of course, sweetheart," she said, pushing her head against his hand.

"Oh," Brandon said, "and try to find Agatha if you can. She's a crazy asshole, but she's our crazy asshole."

I nodded. We turned and headed toward the stairs. I looked at Donut. "You ready?"

She flipped her tail, and I followed her down the ramp.

AT THE BOTTOM OF THE STAIRS-TURNED-RAMP WAS A DOOR AL-most identical to the one we'd used to enter the dungeon. I stared at the giant carving of the fish man. *Go fuck yourself,* I thought as I put my hand against the door. I pushed.

But instead of the gate opening like last time, there was a flash of light and a moment of disorienting nausea, followed by a quick feeling of falling.

And then suddenly Donut and I were standing in a plush room staring at a strange round door. All of my status bars had disap-peared. I turned in a circle, bewildered. There was a couch that ap-peared to be made of blue crushed velvet. I stood upon a soft, thick carpet, also blue. There was a strange sense of motion to the room, and I immediately knew we were on a boat. I could tell right away from experience that this vessel was large, but not huge. Maybe 100 feet. At the far end of the room was a bar with an honest-to-goodness fruit basket sitting on it. Sitting next to the basket was a stemmed bowl filled with what seemed to be cat food. Instinctively, I made a fist, and my gauntlet appeared. Only partially relieved, I unsummoned my weapon.

"What the fuck is this?" I asked.

But the second the words came out of my mouth, I knew exactly what this was.

Donut was literally hopping up and down, her tail ramrod straight. "Carl, Carl! It's happening! It's really happening!"

Just as my addled brain was coming to terms with our sudden change of scenery, the door irised open. A woman wearing a simple black dress stepped in, clutching onto a tablet. She was human, but clearly not from Earth. She was absurdly thin. Not anorexic. She just seemed more *squished* than a regular human. She stood about five foot five, so a normal height, but her head was only about three-quarters as wide as it should be, making her appear almost elf-like, but without the prerequisite pointed ears. She seemed to be about my age, and her features were Asian, but with long blond hair she kept in a tight bun.

"Hello, Carl and Your Majesty Princess Donut," she said, speaking in Syndicate Standard. Her voice was light and musical. Almost cartoonish. "My name is Lexis. I am an associate producer for the program, *Dungeon Crawler After Hours with Odette.* Congratulations on that last battle, and congratulations on making it down to the second floor. Odette would love to interview you two, on air, regarding your progress so far."

Donut squealed with pleasure.

PART TWO

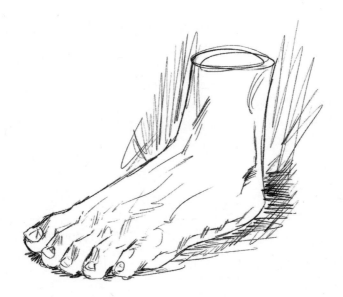

28

"OKAY," LEXIS SAID AS I SAT DOWN ON THE COUCH, MY HEAD SPIN-
ning. I was still covered in blood, and I suddenly felt very, very dirty.
"We'll be ready for you in about twenty minutes. Please relax and
avail yourselves of the complimentary treats." She indicated the bar.
"Okay?"

"Okay," Donut said.

I still couldn't believe it. Actually, I could believe it. Five nights
ago I'd gone to bed, and everything I'd been worried about was so
stupid, so petty, so . . . small. We were about to be interviewed on a
program that would be seen by *trillions* of people.

"A couple of things," Lexis continued, talking fast. "I know this
is probably disorienting to you, being your first interview. Right
now, you are standing in what is called a production trailer. It is lo-
cated on the surface of your planet. You are still technically in the
game even though you can't use your menus. Like safe rooms, production trailers have their own rules, too many to discuss now." She
reached forward and touched my shoulder. She felt hollow, almost
weightless. Like a bird. "I am really here right now with you. However, my engineer and I are the only other people here. When you
walk through that door"—she pointed over her shoulder, indicating
the oval-shaped entrance that opened and closed like a camera
shutter—"you're going to walk onto a studio set. From what I understand, this setup should be very familiar to your culture. This studio,
including Odette and the entire audience, is not really there. The
couch is there, but everything else is virtual. They are filming from

a location very far away. I'm supposed to tell you it is similar to the holodeck from your television series *Star Trek*. However you won't be able to touch anything. Any other guests, even fellow crawlers, will also be holo, at least for this interview. You are the only crawlers in this particular production trailer. I will tell you when it's time, and you will walk onto the set. You will wave, and you will proceed directly to the couch next to the desk, Your Majesty sitting closer to Odette. Do not approach the audience, or you will run into a wall that you can't see. That room is not as big as it appears. Questions?"

I just stared at the woman. I hadn't felt this out of my element since the moment the dungeon first opened.

"Makeup?" Donut asked.

"Not for this interview, Your Majesty," Lexis said. "The audience will have just watched a highlights reel of your time in the dungeon followed by the entirety of that last boss fight. It will appear as if you walked straight from the fight to the stage."

"Got it," Donut said. "So we address her as 'Odette'?"

"Correct."

"Live or taped?"

"It's taped, though it will be tunneled in just a few short hours."

"What's the tone of the show? Is it more editorial or more fluff? What works better with your audience? Do you want us to be serious and more technical, or should I just let Carl be Carl?"

Donut was asking these questions as if she'd been doing this her whole life.

A smile tugged at the corner of Lexis's mouth. "This is a private production about the crawl. It won't be censored. The more entertaining you are, the better it will play."

"Got it," Donut said.

"Hold up a second," I said. "What do you mean by 'private production'?"

Lexis turned to me. "The main program, *Dungeon Crawler World: Earth*, is owned by the Syndicate government, and this season it is produced by the Mu . . . the Borant Corporation. Syndicate rules allow for private production companies to produce their own programs as long as they pay for the production themselves and pay an advertising stipend. This particular show, *Dungeon Crawler After Hours with Odette*, will tunnel immediately after the main program. It is produced by the Titan Conglomerate with production assistance by over a dozen participating independent systems. It is the largest, most tunneled private program in existence. The host, Odette, is the most beloved interviewer and program host in the history of the galaxy. So try to make a good impression."

"Wonderful," I said, leaning back. "Just wonderful."

Next to me, Donut was shaking with excitement. Literally shaking.

"Anything else we should know?" Donut asked.

"Nope," Lexis said. "Just be yourselves, have fun with the questions, and you'll be fine."

"Thank you, Lexis," Donut said. "That'll be all."

"Great," Lexis said. She hit a button on her tablet, turned, and strode out of the room.

I looked at the cat sitting next to me, and I wondered, not for the first time, if this was all a dream. An hour and a half earlier I'd been certain I was about to die, and now I was aboard some sort of yacht from another planet, ready to be interviewed on an intergalactic talk show.

"Okay," Donut said the moment Lexis left the room. She started to frantically clean herself. "Let me do all the talking unless Odette asks a question directly of you. I just can't believe it. I am so excited!"

"Just be careful, okay?" I said. I stood, moving toward the odd door. It did not open on its own. There were no windows, but there was a small door by the bar. I pushed it open, revealing a bathroom with a litter box. Above the toilet was a round porthole about the size of a dinner plate. I stood upon the toilet, straining on my tiptoes to peer outside. It was dark, and I couldn't see a thing except the glint of the moon off relatively calm water. Stars shone in the night sky. I felt an unexpected longing at the sight of the stars. I put my hand against the window to see if I could push it open. Whatever this was, it wasn't glass. There didn't appear to be a way of escape. I wondered what would happen if I formed my gauntlet and punched the window as hard as I could.

Probably nothing. And even if we did escape, then what? We were in the middle of the ocean in the middle of winter, and I still didn't have pants.

"Careful of what?" Donut asked from the other room.

"These people aren't our friends," I said, coming back into the room. I took a banana from the fruit basket, peeled it, and took a bite. "Don't forget that."

I attempted to put the rest of the fruit and the basket into my inventory, but my menus weren't working at all.

There was no garbage can in the room. An oversight. I tossed the peel on the counter.

"Do you want this cat food?" I asked, sniffing it.

"Are you crazy?" Donut said. "And get it all over my face?"

There was a little bag sitting behind the bowl of wet cat food. Purrfect Cat Treats. They had done their research. I picked up the bag and shook it. Donut was on the counter a half a second later. "Okay, but just one."

I took an apple and bit down as Donut ate her fifth treat. The apple suddenly reminded me of the dead, naked form of Rebecca W. I put it back in the basket, no longer hungry.

"Carl," Donut said as she crunched down on another treat. "Out there with all the punching and the grunting and the disgusting, exploding goblins. That is your world." She made a motion with her paw, indicating this room. "This is mine. I know this might be difficult for you to understand, but I have been doing this my entire life. Every cat show I have ever done is an interview. I was bred for this. Let me do my thing."

"You didn't talk before," I said. "And having a judge stick her finger up your ass is not the same thing as being interviewed for a television show."

"I have never had anybody ever stick anything up there, thank you very much. Really, Carl. Don't be so crude. This is why I'm to do the talking."

"Okay, you two," Lexis said, coming into the room. "Let's go."

"Don't be surly. You can be surly sometimes," Donut whispered as we lined up outside the door.

A small *ping* emanated from Lexis's tablet. The door irised open.

"Go," Lexis said, putting her hand on my back, pushing. "Smile and wave. Smile and wave!"

I was propelled out of the room, Donut walking in front of me with her tail swishing back and forth as we moved from the small room onto a giant, brightly lit set.

I was momentarily blinded as we stepped out. And even though we hadn't really moved off the surface, I was briefly overwhelmed. *I am seeing something from another world. Holy shit.*

I heard the audience before I saw them. They were going *berserk*. Hoots, hollers, and animallike trills filled the room, shaking the floor. I realized, belatedly, that I had stopped. Donut, seeing I had stopped, also paused, but she made it look like it was on purpose. She circled, sat down halfway between the door and the couch, and she rolled on her side, hopping up onto her feet, and swishing her tail. Her armored skirt poofed out with a little jingle as she hopped. The cheers got louder.

I used the moment to look about the room. It was just as Lexis had described. It was a black stage with a space-themed nebula background. The colorful spinning cloud of blue-and-red space dust and the dots of distant stars filled the back wall. Odette's desk was, well, a desk. It sat next to a couch identical to the one in the waiting room. "The greenroom," Donut had called it, even though it was blue. The set could've been from any Earth talk show, with a couple of glaring differences.

There were no visible cameras. The lights seemed to come out of nowhere, appearing and disappearing without any sort of physical source.

The audience was mostly in shadow. It was a large room, with seats and something else—viewing pods of some sort—stretching up in a stadium pattern. I watched as some of the audience members vanished, flickered, and reappeared. The crowd was a shadowy sea of aliens of all types. Humans, pig-headed orcs similar to the ones we'd just killed, and eagle-headed creatures like Mordecai's true form. Bug-eyed, expressionless gray aliens. Tentacled things. Dozens of others, too many to take in. The viewing pods were filled with murky water, and I caught sight of what might've been a kua-tin, though much thinner than the image in the door carving.

And then there was Odette.

Looking upon the woman, it was difficult for my brain to put it all together. I kept thinking, *What the fuck? What the fucking fuck?* over and over. Part crab, part praying mantis, part centerfold for *Juggz* magazine's "Freaks of Nature" issue. I just stared, not able to tell if I was looking at one creature. Or two. Or five.

But then she moved, and something clicked in my brain, allowing it all to come together.

Odette was a naked crab-taur wearing a bug mask.

The lower body of the woman was entirely crab. Black and red with a lumpy shell and multiple chitinous legs. The shape and makeup of the shell were that of a king crab, but the size of a brown bear. Her body seemed completely separate from the rest of her form. The legs crowded one another, unable to tuck themselves underneath the desk. The legs seemed to twitch on their own accord. Malevolent, ready to strike. Her triangular bug head was black with mirrored compound eyes the size of footballs. Twin antennae spread from her head with a span over at least six feet, as wide as the crab body.

But the oddest part of this woman was her torso.

Her naked ebony body, from her stomach to her neck was that of a plus-sized human model who had bribed a third-world plastic surgeon into enhancing her breasts well beyond anything that could ever be considered natural. Or sexy. Or anything other than *What the fuck?* The colossal breasts sat atop the table like a pair of pigs suckling against their mother. Her nipples faced downward, her areolas absurdly oversized, even on the massive breasts, each the size of a DirecTV satellite dish.

There was no conceivable way, even as big as she was, that her body could sustain those ginormous breasts without her back breaking like a twig.

Jesus. No wonder this show is so damn popular.

Donut looked up at me, her yellow eyes pleading for me to move.

I took a deep breath, plastered a smile on my face, and I waved. Then I walked toward the couch.

Odette calmed the crowd as we settled down. She waved her humanlike arms at everyone to be quiet. She had long fake nails that curved like claws. They were painted blue, matching the couch. Her body moved oddly, rising up and down as the crab body readjusted itself. She raised herself up as we sat, making it so her chest didn't block the audience's view of her praying mantis head.

They'd placed a large pillow on the seat so Donut could sit atop it. The cat jumped up and sat straight.

"Welcome, welcome," Odette said, her voice surprisingly feminine, though she sounded older than I expected. "Your Majesty, it is a pleasure to have you here."

"Thank you so much, Odette," Donut said. "The pleasure is all ours. Carl and I have both been looking forward to meeting you. When I first heard about you, I couldn't stop thinking, *I really want to get on that couch and meet her.*" Donut turned to face the crowd. Her voice had gone up in pitch, sounding nothing like her regular speaking voice. "And meet all of you guys. I daresay, what a great-looking audience. I'd much rather be here than with those filthy goblins. How's everybody doing tonight?"

The couch vibrated with the sound of the crowd's pleasure.

"You enjoying the show?" Donut asked.

Again, screams.

"Now, let me ask you something," Odette said. She turned and leaned in. Her massive breasts barely sloshed over, as if she had some sort of accordion system connecting her chest with the boobs. "So you might not realize this, but we've been watching you two from the beginning. You might not be getting any love on the official program, but you two are quite the sensation. We are so excited to have you on the show tonight. But something that people want to know is about your title, Princess Donut. So you are Earth royalty?"

No. No, no, no, I thought. *Don't.*

"Why, yes, I am, Odette," Donut said. "Now, you have to understand, Earth has a ruling class. The humans." She glanced sideways at the crowd and lifted her paw. "Thumbs. It's all about the thumbs." The crowd laughed. "But amongst cats, which is what I am, we have what's called an elective monarchy. But it's really just a beauty contest. My full name is 'GC, BWR, NW Princess Donut the Queen Anne Chonk.' I wouldn't think of boring you guys with all of my titles." She leaned toward the audience and stage-whispered, "GC stands for 'Grand Champion.'"

I realized I was staring at Donut as if she'd just sprouted a corn dog from her forehead. I had to consciously make an effort to close my mouth. *An elective monarchy?* Where the hell did that come from? Who was this cat, and what had she done with Donut?

Odette nodded. I could not read any sort of expression on her bug face. "And you've won this beauty contest?"

Donut flipped her tail, and I swear to god the cat fucking winked. She looked right into the middle of the crowd and asked, her voice seductive. "What do you think?"

The crowd roared.

"I love it. You two are so adorable. I'm so happy to have you here with us." Her bug gaze focused on me.

Ah shit.

"So, Carl, before you came on, I promised my audience I'd get you to say it."

I looked at her blankly.

"Say what?" I asked.

"You know," Odette said. She waved her hand as if she was trying to coax it out of me. "Your catchphrase."

This is not real life. This can't be real life. "I have no idea what you're talking about."

Odette turned toward the audience. "He doesn't know what I'm talking about." She laughed. They laughed. "I'll tell you what. I'll give you a hint."

A screen appeared, floating in midair in front of me. It was me and Donut, from above. It was a scene from early on. We were peering into an alleyway, and a moment later I leaped back as a blob of lava rocketed out toward us. I screamed, "Goddamnit, Donut!" The scene changed. I was being attacked by a pair of cockroaches while Donut watched from a pile of garbage. "Goddamnit, Donut!" I screamed. The scenes kept changing, over and over, each time ending with me saying the same thing. I'd said it at least fifteen times.

Odette cocked her head at me. "Figure it out yet?"

I sighed inwardly, doing my best not to let my dismay show. "Goddamnit, Donut," I said.

Boisterous cheers followed.

"Now let's go back to one of those clips we just watched," Odette said. "I was hoping to get some insights from you guys."

"Of course," Donut said.

That scene with the cockroaches reappeared. I heard my voice call out, "A little help here!"

It was the final moments of our battle with the Hoarder. My stomach dropped, watching that scene from above. The camera focused on my own face. I was stricken with how scared I looked. The blasting music from the fight was gone. The giant woman was gagging and sobbing, and the visceral sounds shook my bones.

"She's almost dead. You can kill them when you kill her!" Donut cried on the video.

The clip ended, and the audience was screaming with laughter.

"Now, Carl," Odette said. Her breasts made a slight sloshing noise on the desk. "What're you thinking here, when Donut wasn't helping you?"

"It happened so fast," I said. "I wasn't thinking anything."

"And you, Donut? You saw him there, surrounded. You're stronger than him." Odette waved her hand, and our stats appeared floating in the air over us. "Wow. A lot stronger than him."

"Yet here we are," Donut said. "Carl handled it like the champion he is. And besides, darling, if he was in real trouble, I would've certainly helped. Like I did with that juicy boss we faced." She looked at me. "What was his name? Juicy? Juiced? The Juice? Now *that* was a fight, wasn't it?"

The crowd roared their approval.

We talked for about five more minutes. Odette would ask a question about something that happened. Donut would answer. She had the crowd eating out of her paws. Odette asked me about my pants. They showed Donut asking if there was a reward for worst dressed in the dungeon, and it showed me standing there, looking pitiful in my kneepads. The words "**WORST DRESSED**" appeared floating over me. I pretended to laugh.

"So, what's next for you two? Do you intend on staying with team Meadow Lark?" Odette asked.

"That's the plan for now," Donut said. "It depends on what we find on the next floor." She flicked her tail a few times. "But I want to tell you something, Odette." She stood on the chair, facing the audience. "I promise all of you. You guys are going to want to follow me and Carl. You're going to want to favorite us. Because whatever it is we face, we're not just going to kill them."

"No?" Odette asked, amused.

"Oh no. We are going to kill them big. We are going to kill them with *style*."

Thirty seconds later, and the audience was still screaming.

Odette had to shout over her own crowd. "We are out of time, but thank you so much, Carl and Her Royal Majesty Princess Donut! Good luck to you two! I will see you all next time!"

The throng continued to go berserk. She'd stolen that line from Mordecai. "Kill them with style? Really?" I whispered.

But Donut didn't answer. She hadn't heard me. She stood on the edge of the pillow, standing like that damn lion from the *Lion King*, her chest heaving with pride as she looked back into the holographic mass of adoring fans. Her eyes sparkled. I suddenly had a feeling of dread. That look. That hunger. That was dangerous. She'd had but a single taste, but I could already tell. She was addicted to this. To the crowd. To the cheers. It was going to be a problem.

"Goddamnit, Donut," I muttered.

29

THE LIGHTS OF THE STUDIO FLIPPED ALL THE WAY ON, AND THE audience snapped away. The studio remained, but the bleachers were just gone. Odette remained behind the desk.

"Great show, everyone," Odette said, looking up at the ceiling. There wasn't anybody else in the room that I could see. She looked over our shoulders. "Give us five, Plexis. Watch the packets and ping me if one of those AIs sticks their nose in here. I want to talk to our guests for a minute without anybody snooping."

I turned to see Lexis standing at the door that led back into the greenroom. "Yes, ma'am," Lexis said, backing into the other room. The door closed.

Odette looked down at Donut. "I do that, too. Pretend to not really remember someone's name. You should see them preen when I suddenly do remember. You, Donut, are a natural. Great job. We had that Lucia Mar and her two mongrels onstage before you, and that little psychopath does not know how to work a crowd. One of her dogs mauled my producer. It's a nightmare. God, I gotta get out of this thing. Give me a moment."

I watched in horror as the alien reached up and removed her own head. But it wasn't a head after all. The praying mantis skull was actually a helmet. It pulled away to reveal a human woman, approximately sixty years old. Her eyes were just a little wide for her face to pass as someone from Earth. A moment later, the woman's crab body skittered back, and the chest with the enormous breasts remained attached to the desk. Her whole torso peeled away, revealing a dark shirt. She wore a necklace with a heart on it. If it weren't for the crab body and the eyes, she'd look like any other human.

"What the hell?" I said, looking at her. "Is the body fake, too?"

"Everything you see is fake," Odette said. "This is show business."

There was a loud crack, and I watched, fascinated, as she pulled herself from the crab body using her two arms. The crab collapsed with a clatter, like it had just died, its legs curled in on themselves.

Odette did not have any legs. Her body stopped right at her stomach. A flat disk zipped up from under the desk. She pulled herself onto the platform, and she floated in midair, able to control her movement. The legless human zoomed around the desk and came to hover in front of the couch. Her magical wheelchair emanated a slight buzzing sound.

"Much better," she said, sighing. "People think it's the same crab each time, but it's not. We keep a whole nest of the things out on the ranch, and we have to kill a new one each time I go on camera. We don't advertise that, lest we raise the ire of one of the many animal and mob rights protest groups."

"Of all the things to dress up as," I asked, still looking at the bizarre pair of bodiless breasts sitting on the table. "Why . . . that? I couldn't even tell what that is."

"Oh, you will," she said. "That entire getup was my armor when I was like you. It was what I was wearing when I reached the stairwell for the thirteenth floor. It's how people know me."

"How was that boob thing armor?"

"Young man," Odette said. "This gear you have now, this loot? It's nothing compared to what's coming."

"Mordecai . . . our trainer guy. He said only one person ever made it to the thirteenth floor, and it was a dude. He died," I said.

"That's true," Odette said. "I never went down the stairs. I'd struck a deal. That's a long story, and it's not for today. But I'm glad you brought up Mordecai. That's who I actually want to talk to you about. I know this is his last crawl. I'd like for you to tell him to seek me out when this is all over."

"Mordecai? How do you know each other?" Donut asked. "Were you on the same season?"

"They couldn't have been," I said. "Odette is human, and Mordecai is a bird guy. They're from different planets."

"They're called skyfowl," Odette said. "And my season was long before Mordecai's. I was his trainer. In fact, that's how I found you. I keep an eye on him, and I watched you guys as you stumbled into his guild room."

"His trainer? Wow," I said. "That must've been a really long time ago."

"It was," Odette said. "So, can I count on you?"

I shrugged. "Sure, we'll tell him."

She nodded. "Thank you. Now, I'm going to give you guys some advice. Don't talk about this out loud once you go back. The mudskippers won't like it."

"Mudskippers?" I said. "You mean Bor . . ." I paused, looking at the ceiling.

"They can't hear you in here. But don't say that phrase in the dungeon. Mudskipper. They attempted to get it listed as hate speech by the Syndicate a couple cycles back. Hardly anyone called them that until they made a big deal about it. But yes, that's what I mean. The kua-tin. Borant. Nobody likes the kua-tin, at least not their system of government. Borant is a different story. Some of those folks are okay. All they want is to put on a good show. I'm sure they were incensed when they were forced into this early release."

I looked at Donut. "We won't say anything," I said.

"Good. First thing. You're going to step onto that second floor, and in a day or so, you're going to find your social numbers have gone meteoric. Those people are following *you*, Carl and Donut. So when you go down to the third floor, you"—she pointed at Donut—"need to stay as a cute, cuddly cat. They'll tempt you with some very powerful creature races. Going viral early is both a blessing and a curse. People are in love with Donut the cat. Not Donut the saber-toothed void leopard. Don't change your race, whatever you do. I've seen it happen dozens of times. They change, and their numbers plummet. It's why nobody sponsors a crawler earlier than the fourth floor now."

"I wouldn't even consider it," Donut said.

"That's my girl," Odette said.

"And me?" I asked.

She shrugged. "People are used to seeing humans, so it's not as crucial for you to stay the same. As long as it's not *too* different. If she stays that tiny little thing, she's going to need to be protected. Mordecai will be the one to lead you through the process of picking a race and class. There'll be a lot of information. He won't be allowed to steer you, at least not overtly, but if I taught him anything, it's how to help you decide for yourself. I don't know what's going to be on the table—it's different every season. Listen for his clues. He knows what he's doing. He's going to do his best to guide you."

"Okay," I said. "Thanks."

"Also," she added, "if you want pants, you should probably stop bitching about not having them."

"So, it's like I suspected," I said. "The loot boxes aren't really random."

"Of course not," said Odette. "It's even written into the rules. Look at me." She floated back, holding out her arms. "I lost my legs to a Fiend Scythe on the eleventh floor. I was all but dead. I dragged myself to a safe room, opened my boxes, and I received this"—she poked a black belt around her waist, just above the line where her legs were gone—"in a *gold* box. This is a legendary item, at least. It allows me to attach body parts of other monsters to myself. I had to drag myself back out there and kill that crab first, but I took its body as my legs. And I continued on my way."

"Your legs don't grow back?" Donut asked.

"No," Odette said. "Not if they're completely severed off. But that's not the point. People were watching me. I had five sponsors, a record at the time. Me dying alone in a safe room was not good for anyone involved. They didn't care if I lived or died, as long as that death was glorious. So they gave me the perfect item to compel me to get my ass back out there and at least try. Yes, this is a game. Yes, there are controls in place to make it fair. Sort of. But more importantly, this is a for-profit venture in the entertainment industry. And if you staying alive means more profits, then you'll find your loot to be a lot more convenient. But if the AI senses screwing you over will make the show more interesting, you better believe it'll fuck you right in the ass at the worst possible moment. Don't ever forget that. You can't count on anybody but yourselves."

"So, no more complaining," I said. "At least not out loud."

"Not when it's funny for you to not have pants." She turned to Donut. "Or when someone hisses every time they get another torch in one of their boxes."

Donut swished her tail angrily. "I have 230 torches in my inventory. It's absolutely ridiculous."

"One last piece of advice," Odette said. "Never trust someone unless you know what they're getting out of it. Never trust someone if their motivations aren't clear. Mordecai, for example. He won't tell you this, but the season doesn't count against his indentureship unless one of his crawlers makes it to the fourth floor."

"So if we don't make it, he's stuck until next season?" I asked.

"He's stuck until the next *Borant-sponsored* season, which'll be at least another seven or eight seasons after this one. And with the political environment as it is, a lot of people aren't certain Borant will be around that long. All indentureship contracts get frozen during a bankruptcy-seizure action."

"Wait, what?" I asked.

She waved her hand. "That's not something you need to worry yourselves over. Concentrate on the crawl."

Donut jumped down from the couch and ran to the far wall. She stopped about halfway across the room, her face smushing against an invisible barrier. It appeared the studio went deeper than it really did. She put her feet up on the invisible wall, making it look as if she was standing on two feet. "Carl, look," she said. "This room is quite odd."

"Remember what Lexis said?" I called out to her. "We're not really in the studio. That's the far end of the boat. Be careful."

I turned back to Odette. "Whatever you guys did to her is wearing off," I said.

The woman nodded. She didn't even deny it. She was also watching the cat pounce around the end of the room. "In many ways, she's still a child. It's part of the reason why so many are enchanted with her. It works well in the dungeon. But for interviews, sometimes they need a little nudge."

I bit my lip. I didn't know if I should be angry or not. "What did you do?"

She shrugged. "It's nothing insidious. It was in her cat treats. It's temporary. It increased her wisdom and a few confidence stats by a point and a half. Not much. It makes for a better interview. It's no different than drinking a glass of strong wine."

"I thought wisdom wasn't a stat anymore," I said.

"Oh, honey. Everything is a stat. Just because you can't see it doesn't mean it's not really there. But you're more right than you realize. None of these top-tier stats you see are real. Not truly. A higher intelligence doesn't mean you're smarter. It means you have more mana points. It means you can remember things better. It's really a mishmash of a hundred other stats all combined."

Donut came back, her tail swishing. "This room is much smaller than it looks."

"So how about you, Odette? What are your motivations?" I asked as I stood from the couch. It was time to go. "For helping us, I mean. You said not to trust anyone until you know what their motivations are."

The older woman smiled. "My audience loves you. The longer you stay alive, the more money I make. And there is nothing I love in this universe more than money. Now get back in there and try not to die."

30

DUNGEON FLOOR 2.

Views: 0
Followers: 0
Favorites: 0

"THERE'S NOBODY ON MY LIST," DONUT SAID. "I DON'T HAVE ANY followers yet."

We'd been on the second floor for about five seconds. Thankfully, Brandon and his crew hadn't come down yet. We still had two hours until the collapse, and I suspected they were waiting to see if Chris could convince the thirty folks holed up in that Waffle House to come down. I wouldn't expect to see the first ones emerge for another hour.

"I don't think it gets turned on until after the recap episode," I said. "And Mordecai said it updates slow anyway." Tonight's episode coincided with the closing of the first floor. I was hoping we could find a safe room before then.

The episode was usually a little more than an hour long, and after that, Odette's show would air. And if that show was as popular as they'd implied, the views would start rolling in. I knew, deep down, that this was probably a good thing. The more fans, the better chances we had. But I still had a terrible, ominous feeling that all this attention was a mistake. There was something to be said about being anonymous. Quietly efficient. That wasn't going to happen, not here, not when I had Donut with me.

Looking about, this second floor was set up similarly to the first, but instead of emerging at the end of a main hallway, I could see that we were in the middle of a quadrant. The floors here were white. The lichen on the wall had an orangish tint to it. The walls, instead of stone, were made of cinder block. I punched the wall with my gauntlet to see if it would break. A large crack appeared, but it wouldn't break further, like it was magically protected. I punched another nearby block, and the same thing happened. It cracked easily, but it didn't break more than that.

"Well, this is boring. How are we supposed to set the intergalactic internet on fire when the second floor is the same as the first floor?" Donut asked.

"Mordecai had said that would be the case. It's not until the third or fourth floor where things start to get weird."

"Hopefully the monsters will be more exciting," Donut said.

"They'll be similar. Just a little harder."

"Look, look," Donut said. "When you zoom out the map, top right corner. Northeast."

I did, and immediately saw what she was looking at. The icon sat in the midst of the fog, but there it was. An overwhelming sense of relief washed over me. I didn't see any safe rooms or tutorial guilds yet, but at least we had this.

Stairwell to Floor Three.

"Let's work our way toward there and see about clearing that quadrant out," I said. "Keep an eye open for safe rooms."

I saw the X on the map the moment we turned the corner. My heart leaped, afraid that this was going to be the corpse of Agatha. But it was a smaller X. One of a mob.

I hovered over the spot, and it read, **Corpse—Level 2 Brindle Grub.**

"Level two. That's good. I wonder if Agatha killed it," I said. We wouldn't be able to tell until we were closer. A few more steps, and a pair of red dots appeared in the same hallway, between us and the body. They seemed to also be moving toward the corpse.

"Okay, be careful," I whispered. I peeked around the corner.

There the mobs were, a pair of fuzzy, cat-sized monsters with no legs. Bugs with similar black-and-brown coloring to Donut. These were large, fat worms. They didn't appear to be moving too quickly, also level two. They were the same type of creature as the corpse.

Brindle Grub. Level 2.

Have you ever found a dead, bloated, and decomposing body? Have ya poked it with a stick just to see what would wiggle out? Perhaps rubbed it with your bare foot? You know you've wanted to. Well, wonder no more. Here on the second floor, rats are yesterday's news. Brindle Grubs are now all the rage, and janitor duty falls unto them. The more monsters you kill in an area, the more the grubs eat. The more the grubs eat, the bigger they get. Once you start finding them in the pupa stage, you best move on. Grubs are easy to kill. Their older siblings are not.

"You take the left one. I'll get the second," I said as Donut jumped to my shoulder.

We strode around the corner. Donut blasted the first one with a full-power magic missile, and the thing exploded, leaving nothing but a white mess of goo. They had the same sort of squishy innards as the Scatterer bugs from the first floor.

"Get ready with a *Heal* scroll in case their blood is acid or something," I said.

I formed a fist, rushing up. The second grub was making a pitiful squeaking noise, trying to get away at a turtle's pace. I smashed down with my gauntlet. It was like punching pudding. A toddler could kill these things.

The bug goo didn't appear to be toxic. The bugs didn't offer any discernible experience, either. These seemed to be much less dangerous than the rats. I wondered what sort of monster they turned into.

We moved to examine the smushed remains of the third corpse. It was as I suspected.

Lootable Corpse. Brindle Grub. Level 2. Killed by Crawler Agatha.
Vial of Brindle Grub Hemolymph (Alchemy Material).

It looked as if she'd run over the thing with her shopping cart. It took about ten minutes before a corpse became lootable by other crawlers, and that was the only indication of how long ago this had been. Her head start was several hours by now thanks to our interlude on the surface. I took the vial.

Donut jumped down and sniffed at the corpse. She made a disgusted face. "Repulsive. I see a couple more red dots one hallway over."

I looked at my map, and the red dots weren't there. A blink, and then they appeared. I'd been noticing that recently, that Donut could sense active monsters a few moments before I could. I suspected it had something to do with her race, but I wasn't certain. These dots were moving quickly down the adjacent hallway.

"Those aren't grubs. If the bugs are like the rats, then we haven't yet met the mobs of this quadrant." I took my foot, and I smashed down on the remains of the corpse that Agatha had killed. I smashed and crushed, smearing the innards all over the place until the X disappeared on the map.

"Carl," Donut said, looking between me and the splattered remains. "Are you quite all right?"

"Did you read that description of the grubs?" I said as I wiped my foot on a cinder block. I could barely feel the bottom of my soles. The sides of my foot were still as sensitive as ever. "We can't just leave corpses lying around. Even their own corpses. Not in this part of the dungeon. From now on, we do our best to leave as little behind as possible."

She crinkled her nose. "I don't feel as if that's an efficient use of our time. My people aren't going to enjoy watching me desecrate the dead. This is just revolting. I'd much rather you not do this."

"Your people aren't going to enjoy watching you get killed by whatever these things grow up to be."

We continued down the hall, turning a junction, then another, angling toward the other red dots. These guys were moving in what looked like a patrol pattern. I suspected if we continued farther in that direction we'd find their base and the neighborhood boss. That wasn't something I wanted to tackle just yet.

"Let's go get these things already. It's taking much too long," Donut said, hopping up and down. With her collar charm and crupper, she sounded like a bell.

"Goddamnit, Donut," I said. "You're a cat. You need to work on your stealth."

The creatures paused; then they both stopped in the hallway and started moving quickly in our direction.

"See?" I said. "We need to see what the mobs are before we force confrontations."

I stepped out, waiting for them to round the corner. Donut returned to my shoulder.

She was starting to reply to me, but she squealed in anger the moment the mobs appeared. She dug her paws painfully into my shoulder as she tensed. She fired off two rapid-succession missiles. Both of the creatures hit the ground, their health moving into the red. Barely. They got up and continued toward us, snarling and snapping.

And barking.

The AI approximated a terrible Australian accent.

Danger Dingo. Level 5.

 These aren't the cute, cuddly, baby-eating puppies from the land down under. No, mate. The Danger Dingo features a stronger body, sharper teeth, and a penchant for black metal bands such as Dimmu Borgir and Satyricon. Where there are dingoes, their Kobold riders and slave masters usually aren't far behind.

"*Die!*" Donut screamed, shooting two more missiles. Both of the monsters fell over, dead and steaming. She'd used 24 of her 26 mana points in seconds. She sat on my shoulder, breathing heavily.

"So," I said, looking down at the corpses, which continued their forward trajectory, sliding to a stop at our feet. "Not a fan of dogs, are we?" These guys didn't look much like regular dingoes. First off, they were huge, about the size of mastiffs. They each had a fur pattern on their faces that looked like heavy metal corpse paint. Their fangs were absurdly long and sharp, giving them an almost prehistoric look. Both dropped Poor Dingo Pelts, which Donut looted.

One of them also dropped something we hadn't seen yet. A pair of gold coins. Donut snatched them away before I could examine the money's properties.

"I must admit, I did get a little carried away there," Donut said. With a swipe of her claw, she ripped the dingo's head right off. She kicked it, and the head exploded against the wall. Once again, the corpses on this level were significantly more fragile once they died. I watched as she gingerly and matter-of-factly tore the corpses to shreds, careful not to get any gore on herself. She kept saying, "Ew, ew, gross, ew," as she did it. She wasn't quite successful keeping the blood off of her, and by the time she was done, both her forward legs were soaked red.

"What happened to not wanting to desecrate a corpse?"

"Cocker spaniels deserve to have their corpses desecrated."

"Those aren't . . ." I stopped myself. I wasn't going to argue with her. She knew perfectly well these weren't cocker spaniels. She was just playing for the camera.

"Let's back out of this area for now." I indicated the curved hallway. I could see a few larger rooms ahead, and I suspected we'd be knee-deep in dingoes and kobolds if we went farther.

As we approached the main hallway, I didn't see any further signs of the dingo mobs, but we did find a couple more dead grubs. And plenty more living ones. The things were everywhere, and we had to kill them by the dozens.

"There's a safe room," Donut said. "It's right off the hallway."

I looked, and she was right. It was in the wrong direction from the stairwell, but it was close.

We headed that way, edging into another quadrant. This one was filled with floating brains with tentacles tangling under them. They looked like jellyfish. They were called "Mind Horrors," and were all level four. They used something called a psionic attack. Donut wasn't affected at all by them, but I was. I could feel them before I saw them, their presence causing an almost debilitating headache. But they were physically weak, and they moved slowly, like little minia-ture blimps. I could punch them out of the sky before their mental attacks lowered my health more than a few points. Their brain-shaped bodies had the consistency of a jam-filled kickball. They bounced when they hit the ground, sometimes splattering.

I didn't want to go farther into this neighborhood, but we cleared the way to the safe room.

The room, unfortunately, wasn't one of the restaurants with a Bopca Protector, though the chamber itself was much bigger than any other safe room I'd seen. It appeared to be some sort of storm shelter. The signs on the doors for the restrooms were in French. The television screens were attached to the walls on one end of the cav-ernous room. About fifty dusty cots were pushed up against another wall. There was no food, no cookies, no vending machines. Just bath-rooms, showers, and sinks.

But there was something I'd never seen before. A mailbox attached to a pole in the ground near the wall with the televisions. It was a stan-dard black mailbox with a little red flag, the kind someone out in the suburbs would have in front of their house. I immediately moved to the box and tried to open the little door, but I received an error message.

Why would someone send you mail?

"Weird," I said.

The number of boxes and achievements we'd received was less than usual, but I still had quite a few. Several of my battle stats had also ticked up. I sat down on one of the cots and examined my achievements as Donut did the same.

New achievement! Borough Boss!

So, you've stumbled into the chamber of the second-weakest type of boss. If you survive this, it means you are in the top 5% of all crawlers. Too bad only the top .25% make it past the next tier.

Reward: Yeah, no.

New achievement! Bully and a Thief!

You've stolen property from a fellow crawler who is a lower level than you. What's next, tough guy? Kicking puppies?

Reward: You've received a Bronze Asshole's Box.

That one confused me for a moment until I realized I'd gotten it for taking Agatha's shopping cart.

New achievement! Battlefield Construction!

You built a structure and deployed it in battle. And your mother thought you were wasting your life away while you spent all those hours eating Doritos and playing *Minecraft*. If only she could see you now. Too bad she's probably dead.

Reward: You've received a Silver Mechanic's Box!

For this next one, the AI once again used his sexy voice. I cringed.

New achievement! This Little Piggy Went to Market!

Oh yeah, baby. You have killed more than five opponents during boss battles using your bare feet. You are making Daddy very, very happy.

Reward: You've received a Platinum Shoebox.

"What the fuck, dude?" I muttered at the ceiling. I shuddered. I eyed Donut, who was already opening her boxes. I wasn't going to tell her about this one. Still, a platinum box? That almost made it worth it. Almost. I couldn't wait to see what was in the "random" loot box.

A few more achievements popped up, all concerning us defeating the boss. Killing a borough boss. Killing a borough boss with a mixed group. Killing a borough boss in under 10 minutes. Killing a borough boss with more than 10 minions. None of the achievements offered any good loot except the Silver Boss Box. After that, there was only one achievement left:

New achievement! You Found Stairs!
You have found a stairwell down to the next floor. They say the cream rises to the top. So what does that say about you?
Reward: This barely qualifies as an achievement. Your reward is that you're alive to read this.

Next, I moved to loot boxes. The items appeared one by one, rapidly appearing and disappearing into my virtual bag. I went into my inventory, selected the **New** tab, and inspected the items one at a time.

The asshole box bestowed five gold pieces and three little pieces of paper. **Drink Ticket [× 3]—Desperado Club.** When I examined the little red paper, all it said was **Redeem at the Desperado Club for a free "drink."** I stared dubiously at the quotation marks around "drink."

The Silver Mechanic's Box contained a really interesting item. A tool. I pulled it out of my inventory and examined it. It looked like a silver oversized lollipop with a button on the handle.

The Goo-Inator 3000.
This is a shaping tool. May only be used at a workbench. Assists in shaping materials into something else. You might want to keep the business end away from your face.

That sounded pretty cool, but I wouldn't be able to use it until I bought a personal space, which I couldn't do until the fourth floor. For now it would have to sit in my inventory and wait.

Next up was the prize from the Silver Boss Box. I'd received 100 gold coins and a potion.

Cheat Code Potion
   Warning: This item has a short shelf life.
   This item will expire shortly after it was generated. In other words, this isn't something you can hoard. Don't be a wuss. Drink it now.
   Causes one recently used combat or magic-themed skill to increase by three. Choice is random and permanent.

A red flashing timer appeared at the bottom of the description. It was down to 17 minutes and counting. *Shit.* I added it to my hotlist and drank.

I felt a crackling sensation in my mouth, like I'd just downed a whole packet of Pop Rocks.

Your Pugilism Skill has been increased by 3! Your Pugilism Skill is now level 10.

Damn. I had a pile of bonuses now, all relating to unarmed combat. With the combination of my Iron Punch and Powerful Strike skills, plus my unarmed combat bonus and my Pugilism skill, my fists packed just as much damage as Brandon's lightning maul. I knew the skill levels would come more slowly now, but I could probably punch a steel beam and put a dent in it.

At the same time, I knew my progress wasn't anything special. Not compared to some of the others from the last recap episode. That Lucia Mar kid was completely decked out in magical gear. She had an obvious dexterity bonus. The kid was running on walls and doing flips and shit already, splattering monsters with her mace. The crossbow woman with the Valkyrie helmet was also crazy strong, likely twice as powerful as me. I'd watched in awe as she picked up a bear-sized, slobbering tentacle monster and threw it into the air, shooting it twice with her repeating crossbow before it exploded.

They were giving us these incredible upgrades, but I also knew the monsters were going to keep pace with our progress. And while I felt overpowered, a part of me feared I was actually falling behind.

I had one last item to examine. *"Goddamnit,"* I muttered under my breath. I pulled it into my hand and examined its properties. It was a little black folder with a zipper. I zipped it open, revealing multiple miniature tools.

Enchanted Pedicure Kit of the Sylph.

This kit contains 12 essential items for proper foot care.

The magical enhancements of this item may only be imbued within a Safe or Personal Space.

Warning: All of these enhancements require you to remain barefoot.

Why? Because you know why.

From a pumice stone to a cuticle pusher, this personal hygiene kit will keep your feet both luscious and in perfect fighting shape. Nightly care of your feet and toenails will result in the following bonuses:

+15% damage to barefoot attacks for 30 hours.

+3 to the Smush skill for 30 hours.

+Unbreakable buff (feet only) for 30 hours. This buff keeps your pretty little metatarsals nice and unbroken.

+Celestially Nimble and Tidy buff (feet only) for 30 hours. Not only will your tootsies look nice, bright, and shiny, but any traps set off by footfalls will now prompt an alarm and have a 5-second delay before being triggered.

I sighed. That very last buff was a great prize. Other than the goblin dozer, we hadn't dealt with any traps yet. Mordecai had mentioned them, but I didn't know when they would start showing up.

We were going to need more than just a five-second warning, but this was better than nothing.

I looked at the kit dubiously before shoving it back into the inventory. I had no idea what most of those little metal items did. Would I have to use all of them to turn the enhancements on? How long would it take? Beatrice could literally spend hours in the bathroom poking, prodding, and plucking at herself. Donut usually sat on the counter in the bathroom with her, meowing for attention. Which meant Donut had watched her do it a number of times. I was going to have to ask the cat if she knew how to use the items. Shit.

I watched as Donut trotted over to the mailbox, leaped so she was standing on top of it, and then sat down as the front of the box opened up on its own. A tome floated out and hovered before her. It vanished as she added it to her inventory.

"What the hell was that?" I asked.

She poofed her chest out. "Thanks to that boss box, I am now a member of the Dungeon Book of the Floor Club. I get one spell book per level, which is mailed to me."

"What? Really? That's way better than what I received. What book did you get?"

Instead of answering me, her body flashed with light. She'd read the book, giving herself the spell.

"Ew," she said after a moment. "What an awful spell. We really need to save these book things instead of wasting them."

"Goddamnit, Do—" I caught myself. "You know this. You have to read the description before applying it to yourself. What is the spell? What does it do?"

I couldn't examine her spells, so I had to rely on what she told me. I knew she had four spells, not including this new one. She had the *Heal* spell everyone started with, *Torch*, *Magic Missile*, and *Puddle Jumper*, which she'd only tried once. She also had a tome of *Minion Army* she couldn't yet read, and I had that tome of *Wisp Armor*.

"It's called *Second Chance*. It costs 10 mana to cast. I can raise a monster from the dead. It has to be a lower level than me. They will fight for us for as many minutes as the spell's level. The level is one, so it'll only last for a minute."

"Holy crap," I said. "That's badass. It's a necromancy spell!"

"It's disgusting," Donut said. She shuddered. "The dead are gross enough. It's much worse when they're moving around. It probably groans and stuff, too. You know how I feel about groaning."

I had a quick memory of being slashed at once while Bea and I were getting busy. It wasn't very funny at the time, but we'd laughed about it later. Donut had gotten banned from the bedroom during sexy time after that. She'd howl at the door, and we'd have to put music on to drown her out.

"Whatever happened to killing them with style?" I said, trying not to laugh.

"One doesn't have to resort to gore-themed violence in order to be stylish."

"Yeah," I said. "But imagine raising one of those dingoes back from the dead and using it to kill another dingo. And then raising that one, too. You'd be like the Lucia Mar kid with her two dogs, but yours will be zombie dogs."

Her eyes got huge. "This is the best spell ever."

31

BRANDON AND CREW WERE STILL BRINGING PEOPLE INTO THE SAFE room as the next episode premiered.

Right when the show started, the timer finally ran out. The world rumbled, and the ground under my feet shook. The shaking lasted but a second. I stopped and gazed at the number on the television screen. It flashed, going from just over two million to 1,292,526.

More people had made it down to the next level than I expected. Still, those numbers. Those goddamned numbers. I wished we didn't have to look at them. In that brief moment, as I helped push a woman—her name was Elle McGibbons—in a wheelchair into the storm shelter, over 700,000 people died. A third of the remaining crawlers. The first floor had claimed a little more than 10 million people.

"Thank you, honey," the woman said as I rolled her to the others. "Can you put *Divorce Court* on the television? My Barry used to watch that show. It reminds me of him."

"I don't think that show is on anymore, Mrs. McGibbons," I said.

"That's okay," she said.

Above the number with the remaining crawlers, the countdown to level collapse blinked a few times, then reset. Six days and counting.

"Six days?" Brandon said, coming to stand beside me. "Mistress Tiatha had said it would be ten."

"Yeah, our guy said the same thing," I said. "At least we know where the stairs are this time."

As the scenes of carnage played out on the television—they were showing a man and a woman running from a three-headed baboon—I took stock of the room.

We'd only gained six more residents from the Waffle House safe room, meaning 24 of them had elected to stay behind. I thought about that for a moment. *Good for them,* I decided. They'd gained a measure of control in those last few moments. They went out on their own terms. Brandon said they'd all been singing when he'd last seen them.

Agatha remained missing. Chris sat in the corner, his head low. He might've been crying. I wanted to give the man space. Imani and Yolanda worked their way around the residents. Yolanda helped them to the bathrooms while Imani handed out crawler biscuits.

Donut paced the floor in front of the television screen, waiting for the second half of the program. We wouldn't be able to watch Odette's show, and we still didn't know if we'd get any airtime on the main program.

"After everyone sleeps, I was hoping to get your help with something," Brandon said.

I already knew what he was going to ask.

"You're going to send them all down the stairs to the third floor early."

"Yes," he said. "They can't train, so there's no point in keeping them here."

"What about you?" I asked. "Your levels need work."

He shook his head. "We talked about it. All of us are going to go down. We'll take our chances on the third floor. We don't want to risk getting separated."

On the screen, a woman screamed as her arm was bitten off by a monster that looked like an eggplant with teeth.

"We'll scout the way and clear it out for you," I said.

"Thank you," Brandon said.

"Did you get anything good in your boss box?" I asked. He now had a bright silver star next to his name in the interface, along with the rest of us.

He grinned. "I got a magic boomerang. Chris got some book-of-the-club thing. Imani doesn't tell us what she gets, and Yolanda received a new type of quiver."

"There's something I've been wanting to ask you about Agatha," I said.

"Everyone, quiet! Quiet!" Donut called. "It's time for the good part!"

The screen focused on that group of men from Africa. Their party name was "Le Mouvement." They'd gone from 150 to about 80 after some internal strife. Several of the members sported skulls by their avatars now.

The show had helpfully added a graphic showing how much ammunition they had left. The 80 men were down to under 500 rounds. Hopefully they were training themselves in other weapon types.

Lucia Mar and her dogs obliterated a nest of brown shaggy monsters before descending the stairs. I knew right afterward she'd been whisked away to appear on Odette's show. She'd been onstage just before us, where one of her dogs had attacked a producer. The woman with the Valkyrie helmet had teamed up with a group of three more women. They worked together to kill a yeti borough boss thing before using the stairs to descend.

And just like that, there we were.

Beside me, Donut gasped as we appeared. We were on-screen for less than 15 seconds. The program was playing scenes from multiple groups of crawlers, rapid-fire, all of them fighting bosses or running toward the stairs as the timer ran down. I knew some of these scenes must have played out just thirty minutes earlier.

It showed us huddled underneath the redoubt as Donut screamed, "Here it comes!"

The view changed to the Ball of Swine rolling up the ramp,

getting stuck. It moved back inside our miniature fort as the brace broke and smashed Yolanda in the head. It showed the ball break apart, and then it cut to Donut screaming as she fired magic missiles point-blank into the tusklings. It ended with Imani making a sour face as she dropped the strap-on dildo on the floor.

All of our mug shots appeared. A moment later, the show moved onto another group.

"They didn't put Agatha's picture on the screen," Yolanda said. "Does that mean she's dead?"

"I think that's exactly what it means," I said, my voice grim. There was no way the crazy old woman could survive down here on her own. Nobody had said it out loud yet, but we were all thinking it.

"Wait," Chris said. Brandon's brother had a deeper voice, and it surprised me when he spoke. This was only the second time I'd heard him speak. "There's more to it. She was edited out of the scene. She was next to me under the speed bump, but she wasn't there when they showed it."

"Oh yeah," Brandon said. "Weird."

"What does that mean?" Yolanda asked.

"Who the hell knows?" I said.

Donut was ignoring all of this as she hopped up and down. "Two shows in one day, Carl. Two shows! Maybe there is more, too. Do you think we're on more shows?"

I sighed. "Donut. You need to stop obsessing over this. It's dangerous. It's going to get us killed."

"I'm not obsessing," she said. "What makes you think I've been obsessing?"

"People like you because of what you've been doing," I said. "If you start playing for the camera, they're going to like you less. And if you die, you won't be remembered at all. So try not to think about it."

"I don't know what you're talking about, Carl," she said.

The show wrapped up. And a moment later, the announcement rattled through the storm shelter.

Hello, Crawlers.

Welcome to the second floor. Congratulations to all of you. We have just under 1.3 million crawlers still in the game. That number is slightly lower than our projections, so we are speeding up the second-floor timer to the minimum legally allowed by the rules. You have six days to find a staircase down. Once again, we urge you all to wait until the last possible moment to descend.

As soon as this announcement ends, you will find that follows and favorites will be turned on for our viewers. The numbers will populate slowly on your interface, so don't be too disappointed if you don't see anything just yet.

We have improved how patronage works this season. This is a major change, so please pay attention.

All crawlers are now limited to three patrons, and all three spots will be up for auction for one day immediately upon the induction of the fourth floor, then fifth, then sixth floors, respectively. Your benefactors may so choose to transfer their patronage to other parties at their own discretion starting on the seventh floor.

All patronage spots will become available at a bid of one credit, meaning this season virtually all living crawlers will have patrons.

But be warned. Any bids the patron pays *above* the standard patronage fee will be reflected in loot box discounts for that patron. Any funds *below* the fee will be reflected in additional costs to that patron for loot boxes. In other words, the more your patron pays for you, the more and higher-quality benefactor boxes you may receive. The higher your social numbers, the better your chances at receiving the best loot. Your tutorial

guide should have more details and will help you if you have any
additional questions.

Finally, we must say we are disappointed in the disrespect
we are being shown regarding the bathrooms. As of this moment, if any human-born crawler intentionally urinates or defe-
cates anywhere outside a designated bathroom area, they will
be immediately and swiftly penalized in the form of a Rage Elemental plucked from the 13th floor. This elemental will kill them
and everyone in their party before they can get their pants
back up.

That's it for tonight. Have fun out there, and remember to
kill, kill, kill!

Brandon turned to Yolanda. "You better tell Jack not to pee in
the hallways anymore."

Yolanda had gone pale. I hadn't even realized that this was a
problem. Jack was one of the guys who used a walker, not a wheelchair. He wore a Cincinnati Bengals hat and was always poking at
the female residents, saying, "You still alive, Marybeth?" None of
them were named Marybeth.

"I have a few adult pads left. I'll make sure he puts one on,"
Yolanda said.

"Their reasoning for speeding it up doesn't make any sense,"
Imani said.

I nodded, agreeing. "If anything, it seems like they're trying to
get rid of us faster."

"Carl, Carl! I have a follower! My first follower!" Donut cried.
"Another! A view! I have a view!"

"Yeah," I said. "You know that viewer is watching you right now.
So maybe you should stop acting crazy. We talked about this."

Donut stiffened, her eyes going wide. "You're right," she said. She
sat down and licked her paw, suddenly looking nonchalant. "That
was quite the battle today, don't you think, Carl?"

She said this in a weird, stilted I'm-trying-to-act-casual-but-I'm-not-very-good-at-it voice.

I sighed, and it took everything not to say my catchphrase out loud. *She's going to get used to it. It's new, so you gotta give her time.* After Odette's show finished airing, I knew those numbers were going to skyrocket.

This was going to be a long night.

32

AS WE APPROACHED THE QUADRANT WITH THE STAIRWELL, WE could now see that there was a tutorial guild and another safe room just beyond the stairs. The plan was to probe the monsters, see how difficult they were. If it was something we could handle, we'd clear them out. Once we found the boss room, we'd make a judgment call on how to proceed. After that, we'd escort team Meadow Lark into the stairwell.

We'd gone to sleep and woken up with our social numbers in the stratosphere. Donut's views and follows were about equal with my own, but her favorites were twice as high. It made sense. Mordecai had said people only got a limited number of favorites to use, and Donut was the more entertaining member of our duo. I was okay with that.

I tried not to think about it. We had important work to do today. Even Donut, thankfully, began to pay attention to the task at hand as we saw the first few red dots appear on our map. She'd been saying some motivational bullshit about seizing the day and fighting for the honor of our elders, but I think even she realized she was being annoying. A couple followers had ticked away, and you'd have thought that someone had stabbed her in the face with the way she'd reacted.

The dots were just off the main thoroughfare. The main arteries on this floor weren't as wide as they'd been one floor up, and the ground was less even. Within the actual quadrants, we had to watch our step. The concrete floor was cracked and splintered. Little sharp rocks were everywhere.

I kicked a rock away. Below, my shiny toes glittered. I'd tried to get Donut to show me how to use the pedicure kit, and she'd laughed at me. It was Imani, of all people, who'd sat down with me. The stoic nurse pulled the tools out one at a time, matter-of-factly explaining how they worked.

The buffs all activated after about fifteen minutes of work. I didn't need to use all the items. I just had to make a show of it. But now my feet glittered, and while the sensation wasn't any different than it had been before, I could sense the unbreakable aspect of my foot bones. I knew if I dropped a boulder on my toes, they wouldn't splinter. It'd still hurt, but they'd remain intact and unscarred and as pretty as ever for the psychotic AI.

I peered around the corner at the monsters. There were three of them sitting in a wide room lit by torches. They sat in a circle, playing dice. They were small troll-like humanoids with oversized heads. Each had a hook nose, ruddy cheeks, and a mouth with only a few teeth. They wore tattered green overalls covered in patches. Each had Pilgrim-style buckled shoes. Much too small for me.

If it wasn't for their mottled skin and curly black hair, I'd think they were a type of goblin. All three of them had runny noses. They coughed and sneezed and snorted and rubbed their sleeves with their arms as they played their game.

All three of them had slingshots on their laps. Ranged weapons. I didn't like ranged weapons.

Unvaccinated Clurichaun Rev-Up Consultant—Level 3
　　If you hear banjo music, run.
　　Clurichauns are distant hillbilly relatives of the Leprechauns. And while the Leprechauns are said to guard vast piles of gold, the only thing Clurichauns might hoard are Polaroids of their own sisters sitting on the can and questionable business

schemes. This particular sect is of the unvaccinated variety.
Don't let them sneeze on you.

WARNING: This is a fairy-class mob. Mobs of this class inflict
20% more damage against you due to your Goblin Pass.

I eased back around the corner.

"Man, I really wish we could figure out a way to turn their dots white. Then we could use your Charm skill."

"Do they have wings? My butterfly-collar charm causes winged fairies to like me."

"I don't think they do," I said.

"Maybe if we capture one, we can talk to it," Donut said.

"I'd say that's a good idea," I said. "But not with these guys. We need to kill them from a distance. They're toxic. I'm pretty sure they inflict something like your sepsis debuff on us. Let's try hitting them with three magic missiles, super quick. Do a four power for each one and see what happens. If they don't go down, hit them again."

Donut nodded and jumped to my shoulder. "Ready," she said, all business.

We popped around the corner. *Thwap, thwap, thwap.*

Donut struck each one with a head shot. They didn't even know what hit them. They died where they sat.

"How many mana points do you have left?"

"Fourteen," Donut said.

"Do you want to try your new *Second Chance* spell? It costs ten, right?"

I didn't have to ask her twice. Donut's whole body glowed a neon purple. A moment later, one of the clurichauns twitched. It glowed purple, matching Donut's hue. It stumbled to its feet and just stood there, its scorched and blown-in head listing to the side. A moan emanated from its wet, snotty mouth. On my shoulder, Donut shuddered. A one-minute timer hovered over the undead creature. A clear liquid oozed out of the hole in its head. It moaned again, this time louder.

Undead Minion of Crawler Princess Donut—Unvaccinated Clurichaun Consultant—Level 1

It continued to sway, not moving from that spot.

"This is most unpleasant," Donut said. She made a sound like she
was going to retch. "I do not like this, Carl."

"I wonder if they'll always be level one," I said, fascinated. "Can
you control it?"

"I don't know," Donut said hesitantly. "I don't have any sort of
controls." She made a kind of uncomfortable whimpering noise,
something I'd never heard from her before. "You," she said, calling
to the zombie. It didn't seem to react. "Rip up the dead bodies of
your friends."

It swayed there for another moment. The countdown was down
to 25 seconds. Then it went to its knees and started taking apart one
of his companions. It reached into the stomach and just yanked a line
of intestines out like a magician pulling streamers from a hat. They
just kept coming and coming. The zombie groaned with an almost
sexual pleasure. I felt a twinge of sickness gurgle in my own stomach.

"Yeah, that's really gross," I said.

The zombie clattered over, dead once again a few short seconds
later. It'd left its job unfinished.

I eyed the remains dubiously. I knew we needed to destroy the
corpses, but there were only so many ways the game could warn me
that these guys were toxic. I didn't even know if getting close enough
to loot them was a good idea.

Before I could protest, Donut jumped down and looted them
anyway. As a quadruped, she could pull the loose non-slotted items
like the slingshots and the dice into her own inventory without actually touching them as long as they weren't too heavy or too far
away. I had to physically pick them up, which meant getting close to
the contaminated bodies.

"Each of them has a clay jug of something called toilet-grade
moonshine," Donut said.

"They're like the llamas," I said. "They probably sell the stuff to the other mobs."

We decided to forgo destroying the corpses for now. We'd angle back on our way out and kill any grubs skulking around the area. I contemplated just blowing the bodies up, but that seemed like a waste of perfectly good explosives. I could probably concoct something that would burn them. I had gallons and gallons of flammable liquid. Their moonshine would probably work, too. But it would take some thinking and trial and error. I really needed to get my hands on something like a poleax I could use to chop things up from afar.

"Did they have any slingshot ammo on them?" I asked as we crept deeper into the hallway.

"Yeah. They have little bags of rocks," Donut said.

"Give me one of the slingshots and a couple bags. I want to try it out."

It look me about three seconds to realize I wasn't going to be a deadly wielder of the slingshot anytime soon. But I was going to practice. I needed some sort of ranged weapon, one a bit more subtle than my usual stick of dynamite. As a kid, I'd had a slingshot, and I'd been pretty good with it. I used to set toy cars up on the edge of the fence and try to hit them.

The memory suddenly turned sour. I remembered my dad finding my slingshot. He and his friends had played with it, breaking the band. He'd promised he'd get me a new one. He never did.

For the next hour we cleared out all of the clurichauns along the outer ring of the quadrant. And by we, I mean Donut. So far, all we found were the level three version. After each skirmish, Donut would raise one of them from the dead, and I would practice hitting him with the slingshot.

The weapon did hardly any damage at all, though I was getting good at consistently hitting the monsters in the head. My Slingshot skill eventually rose to three, but it didn't want to budge past that.

Donut's skill in the *Second Chance* spell also rose to level three.

The zombies weren't any more powerful, but the monsters now hung around for three minutes instead of one.

Donut looted something unusual from one of the bodies. A pamphlet entitled **Rev-Up. Make Money. Be Your Own Boss. Move to the Next Floor Down**. It didn't appear to be magical. It was just a regular trifold pamphlet.

"Let me see it," I said. The colorful front showed a group of three laughing female clurichauns holding jugs of the moonshine. Several little phrases covered the pamphlet, written in Syndicate Standard. Things like "You're the Boss Now" and "Your own hours" and "It's not a pyramid!" and "Safe!*"

Inside the pamphlet was a wall of text of mostly gibberish about the benefits of becoming a "Rev-Up Moonshine Consultant." On the right was a picture of a pyramid with "It's not a pyramid!" written all over it.

The bottom of the brochure stated, "See Krakaren or one of her downline consultants and learn how you can Rev-Up your life today!" On the back page it read, "Coming soon! Rev-Up Smoothies! Portable! Delicious! Invigorating!" The entire line was crossed out with "Discontinued" written under it.

"Do you think we can become consultants?" Donut asked after she spent an inordinate amount of time reading the pamphlet. "It says as business owners we gain power over ourselves and can seize our own destinies."

"That doesn't even mean anything," I said. "They're just making fun of pyramid schemes. You remember when Bea wanted to start selling those leggings? It's like that." The closet in Donut's trophy room had been filled with boxes of the things. Donut had gotten into one of the boxes and peed in it. I smiled, remembering. Bea had raged at the poor cat.

"It's not a pyramid, though. It says so right here."

"Come on," I said. "These things are hostile toward us, so it wouldn't work anyway. I think these pamphlets are for other mobs on this floor, not crawlers. Besides, we can just kill them and take it all for ourselves."

Donut put the pamphlet away. "Yeah, that does seem easier. We won't have to pay our upline or make the initial seed investment when we do it that way."

As we finished our circle of the outer ring of the quadrant, I was forced to kill one of the clurichauns with a punch to the head. Donut missed a shot, and the little monster came running right at me, impossibly fast. It didn't bother with its slingshot, opting to grapple. It gurgled, sounding pug-like, clawing at me with little pocked hands. I formed a fist, but it happened too fast. My gauntlet took two seconds to form, which was a long time when one was having to react. My first bare-knuckle hit stunned it. I hit it a second time, this time with the gauntlet, and the monster went flying, his head caved in. When I opened my hand, my fingers were covered with a lime green oily residue.

Warning: You've been infected with the Taint.

"Fuck."

A blinking five-minute timer appeared. In a panic, I pulled up my health screen to see what that was.

The Taint.

    Having the Taint is like having the giggles. Or like having the time of your life. But instead of it being a good thing, you are balancing on the precipice of death. You may not heal your health using any method while you are inflicted with the Taint.

Receiving the debuff scared the ever-loving crap out of me. I could deal with poison and several other attacks thanks to my armor, but we had no protection against this type of assault. Our *Heal* spells, potions, and scrolls didn't help. We needed something to ward off stuff like this. In those five seconds before I could read the description, I was genuinely scared I had received something that was going to kill me.

On its own, the debuff wasn't a big deal. I simply had to wait it out. I suspected it was part of a one-two punch. They first inflicted you with the Taint; then they hit you with something else that seeped your health away. If that was the case, it didn't matter if these guys were only level three. They were dangerous.

"We're not fucking around with these guys anymore," I said. "Let me think a minute."

We'd collected 25 jugs of the moonshine. Donut gave me one, and I examined the large clay container.

Rev-Up Toilet-Grade Moonshine
  Type: Accelerant.
  Effect: Highly flammable liquid. Explosive fumes.
  Status: Will not activate until introduced to flame.
  At 180 proof, this moonshine will take the hair off your chest and then put it back on. The Rev-Up version is distilled using two types of sugars: the slime trails left behind by the passage of the Brindle Grub, and a secretive proprietary source. Created exclusively on the dungeon's second floor by the Rev-Up company, jugs of this concoction are highly sought after by the drinking establishments that populate the third, sixth, ninth, twelfth, fifteenth, and eighteenth floors. Drinking a swig (defined as 1.5 ounces) of this "potion" will immediately cause you to gain the Shit-Faced debuff, has a 50% chance to render you Blind for a period of 30 hours, a 5% chance to immediately kill you, and a 45% chance to permanently raise a random stat by two points.

"It does say they're valuable," Donut said. "Do you think we can really sell them if we don't become consultants?"

"That's what it sounds like," I said. "Other than that tiara of yours, this is the first time we've really seen anything that clues us in about the deeper floors."

Donut indicated the tattoo of the dagger on my neck. "The

Desperado Club," she said. "Maybe it'll be on the next floor. I bet they'll buy them all from us because we're members of the club! We'll be rich!"

"Maybe," I said. "We'll see if we have any jugs left when we're done."

"What do you mean?" Donut asked. "What are we doing with them?"

I grinned. "I don't suppose you have any extra torches?"

———

CARL'S JUG O' BOOM

Type: Incendiary Tossable.

Effect: When lit and tossed, results in a small explosion, followed by burning splash damage over a wide area. Flames will burn for 15 seconds per level of attacker's level of Incendiary Device Handling.

Status: Inert until torch is activated.

Created by an unstable pantsless man who talks to a cat, Carl's Jug O' Boom takes the bigger-is-better approach when it comes to hobgoblin fire bottles. Burns hotter, bigger, and faster than your normal Molotov cocktail. The use of a standard torch instead of a cloth wick makes these devices much more stable. Just don't drop it once it's lit, lest you find yourself doing a Joan of Arc impersonation.

I received a host of achievements after I finished the bottle. I read the description again and sighed.

"Carl, look, they named it after you!"

"Yeah, Donut. I see that," I said.

"Do you think everybody will see it like that?"

"I don't know. I hope not," I said.

My Incendiary Device Handling skill had jumped up to five immediately upon the construction of the "device." All I had done was opened up the jug, poured a splash or two out until it was about three-quarters full, added a couple ounces of goblin oil from my inventory, and then stuck a torch in the hole. The short, tapered torch fit perfectly into the mouth of the jug, sealing it like a cork. It was almost like it had been made for it.

We tested one just to see if it would actually work. The clay moonshine jugs seemed pretty solid, and I was afraid they wouldn't break. The bottles had "Rev-Up" written on the side of them.

The cool thing about torches was that I could just look at them and mentally select "**Activate**," and they would start burning. No lighter required.

I lit the torch, grasped the jug by the little round handle, and tossed it high in the air, arcing it toward a group of three dead clurichauns.

Whoosh! The jug shattered easily. The explosion itself was insignificant, but the angry flames splashed like water over a wide area, crackling and hissing angrily, glowing blue. We had to step back.

"Wow!" Donut cried, hopping up and down. "Would you look at that!"

The flames reached the ceiling, and we had to step farther out of the room due to the heat. When it finally died out a minute and fifteen seconds later, all that remained in the room were blackened crumbly husks of bodies and ash.

"Well, that's pretty damn cool," I said.

We sat down and made ten more of the devices. After the fire, the room smelled oddly of whiskey and toast. Most of the jugs were already about three-quarters full, which was good. I didn't have to waste any of the moonshine.

Out of curiosity, I examined the jugs in my inventory and compared their value to my other explosive devices. The jugs were pretty high on the list, just above the smoke bombs.

The full unaltered jugs of moonshine were more valuable, however. In fact, they were near the top of my list, just above the engineer's table I still had, the only intact table I had left after our construction of the redoubt.

These things were much less dangerous—to me at least—than the sticks of goblin dynamite. But they were a little *too* good. We lost the ability to loot the corpses when they burned away, meaning we lost our ability to get more jugs. We moved toward the staircase. We decided to incinerate every other room, which would keep our jug supply stable. We continued our pattern of Donut raising the dead and me practicing with the slingshot, which slowed our progress but gave us some much-needed training. My Slingshot skill remained constant. However, I received a few other skills, including Aiming and Steady Hand. Donut's skill in *Second Chance* ticked up to level four.

We finally came across a new type of mob just outside of the boss room, which was thankfully separate from the stairwell. This room was big and, like the goblin workshop, filled with dozens of the little assholes. There wasn't any sort of giant machinery, but a tube ran along the ceiling from the far boss chamber to the center of the room, curving down into what looked like a filthy aluminum bathtub. There were piles of the bottles, both empty and full in the room. The snot-covered level threes were taking the jugs and tipping them into the tub to fill them up. At the far end of the room was a doorway guarded by a pair of small floating creatures. These weren't clurichauns, but small, fat fairies who buzzed about with a pair of hummingbird wings. They looked like miniature winged soccer moms. I peered around the corner and examined their properties.

Laminak Rev-Up Consultant Elite—Level 6

   The second tier of the Rev-Up empire, these Laminak consultants don't need to speak to a manager. They *are* the managers. They run their business with brutal efficiency. It is said if one of their underlings falls behind on their sales quotas, they punish them by requiring them to take a sip of their own product. Those that survive are repurposed as workers for the filling room or, worse, as still engineers, working directly under Krakaren herself.

These mobs do not have any special abilities other than immunity to most health-seeping attacks. Having survived years
drinking their own product, it is said their essence is especially
valuable, prized as a shield against disease.

In a dusty corner of the room stood what appeared to be a pair of
child-sized stationary bikes, the kind gyms used for their spinning
classes. There was some sort of goblin-style pulley system attached
to it, but I couldn't tell what was going on from here. A banner hung
from the ceiling in the same corner, but it was only attached by one
end, and it dangled vertically, forgotten. The banner read, "Rev-Up
Smoothies! Invigorating!"

"Okay," I said. "We need to kill everyone in the room, but if we
want to keep those jugs and that moonshine, we can't blow them up
or burn them out. Plus it sounds like we can get something good
from the corpses of the laminak things."

"Goodness me," Donut said. "How can we do that?"

We peeked again around the corner, keeping low.

"Do you think you can jump over there?" I asked, pointing at the
far wall with the two fairies. "Using your spell, I mean."

"Oh, yes. Definitely."

I nodded. "Good. Here's the plan."

33

THE TWO BIGGEST PROBLEMS WITH DONUT'S *PUDDLE JUMPER* SPELL were the cooldown and the mana cost. Once cast, she couldn't do it again for five hours, which meant once she was in that room, she couldn't teleport out.

Secondly, it cost 20 mana points. She only had 26 mana, and while she had plenty of mana restoration potions, she still had that awful two-minute cooldown between potions. Her points were restoring themselves more and more quickly, but it was still too slow to count on it for combat. She was going to be woefully underpowered, so if something went wrong—and something always went wrong—the only thing she had going for herself was her speed.

We decided I would stay behind during this part of the assault. With my extra fairy aggro, we weren't certain what would happen if we both showed ourselves. The plan was simple, but it made me nervous, mostly because I didn't have any control. This was my idea, but the cat was doing all the heavy lifting.

"If you get in trouble, I'll toss a smoke bomb," I said. "Just jump and run, okay?"

Donut nodded. She was putting on a brave face, but I could tell she was also anxious.

"Okay, let's do this," she said.

We moved back to the corner, peering around the edge. Donut cast her spell, which had a ten-second countdown. She flashed, her form starting to fade until she disappeared with a loud, wet *pop*.

She reappeared at the far end of the room, right between the two laminak fairies. She started rapidly speaking with them as all the clurichauns in the room jumped to their feet and turned to attack.

The soccer mom fairies were winged; therefore Donut had the ability to turn their dots white, removing their hostility. The problem was that only two of them were the airborne-type fairies. The other 40 or so were not. We were hoping Donut could talk to the two fairies, using her charm like she did with the goblins. The fairies would then tell their subordinates not to attack Donut.

From my side of the room, I could see that the two fairies had, thankfully, fallen under Donut's charm. I couldn't hear what they were saying, but like the goblins, they'd been turned right away.

One of the fairies yelled at the clurichauns, speaking in Syndicate Standard. "Get back to work!" she called. "This is a client, not an enemy." The dozens of monsters looked at each other and reluctantly returned to their stations, but all of them kept their eyes on Donut, all grumbling and looking uneasy.

DONUT: CARL, THEIR DOTS AREN'T TURNING WHITE, ONLY THE
    TWO FAIRIES.
CARL: Okay, we planned for this. Don't wait. Go for plan B.
DONUT: IT IS CALLED PLAN PIED PIPER, NOT PLAN B.
CARL: Goddamnit, Donut. Just be careful.

Despite her charisma being an outstanding 43, we still didn't know how well this whole charm thing worked. It was clear she wasn't some sort of walking mind-control goddess, at least not with monsters that were programmed to dislike her. As with everything else, there was more to it, a hidden balance I couldn't see. It worked great with white dots, but getting the dots white was still a mystery.

But that was okay. We'd prepared for this contingency. Instead of talking them into giving us all the moonshine, we had plan B. Plan Pied Piper.

Donut confidently stepped into the room, walking in my direction. She kept a wide distance from the toxic clurichauns, but she headed toward me. The two fairies followed. Sparkles trailed in the air as they bobbed up and down.

"It's just horrible," Donut was saying. "It's like someone came in and slaughtered them all. I, for one, was devastated. At first I thought it was one of those filthy crawlers, but then I saw one of those dogs with the painted faces. The dingoes."

"The kobolds?" one of the fairies said, sounding perplexed. "Why would the kobolds attack us? We get along fine with the kobolds."

"Come. Come see," Donut said. She looked about the room. "All of you should come."

"They need to stay and work," the fairy said. The pudgy fairy swept her hair out of her eyes. Both of them wore an inverted bob haircut. The one doing the speaking wore what looked like a pantsuit made out of leaves. The other was in a dress made of the same materials.

Donut stopped and looked directly at the fairy. "No, they should come, too. All of them."

"Everybody come on! We're taking a break!" the fairy said.

"A . . . a what?" one of the clurichauns asked.

"Just come, the princess wants to show us something."

I pulled away from the corner and rushed down to the next chamber. In the center were three dead clurichauns. We hadn't firebombed this room, though one of them had been zombiefied. I moved into the next hall down, just outside of the room. Like with most of these rooms, the entranceway was a small room of its own, like a foyer with a raised rounded ceiling. A pair of brindle grubs was in the hall farther down, inching their way toward the corpses. *Jesus,* I thought. These things were everywhere. I rushed over and stomped them both down and returned to the foyer. I waited for Donut to Pied Piper the group into the chamber.

CARL: Donut, I am in place.

DONUT: WE ARE COMING.

"Look at this, just look," Donut was saying a minute later as she strode into the room. She gave the dead monsters a wide berth, walking into the chamber. "Come, everybody, gather around. Take a look."

I could hear them crowding into the room as I leaned against the wall, hidden behind the entrance to the next hallway down. I pulled two boom jugs from my inventory and held one in each hand.

"This was not a dingo attack," one of the fairies was saying. "One of them has been hit with necromancy magic."

"No, no, come look at this, Caroline," Donut said. "It's in the hallway over here. Tell your workers to stay here. Uh, it'll be good for them to look at what happens to those who don't, uh, work hard or something."

"Okay," the fairy said. She started shouting orders at the crowd of grumbling clurichauns.

A moment later Donut and the two fairies floated into the dark foyer, moving past me. Donut stopped just as the two fairies noticed me standing there.

"What's this?" the pantsuit fairy said, floating away with surprise. She was smaller than I realized, no bigger than a crow. The laminak looked just like a miniature 40-something woman. She carried no weapons.

"Carl, I'd like you to meet Caroline and Max. It's okay, ladies. Carl needs to show you something."

They were looking down at the pair of jugs in my hands.

"Where did you get this?" the other fairy asked. "And what did you do to our product?"

I grinned. "Let me show you." I mentally clicked **Activate** on both the torches, stepped to the side to the room's entrance, and I tossed both jugs in at the group of 40 monsters stupidly staring back at us.

The hands of the pantsuit fairy started glowing red just as Donut leaped into the air and snagged the laminak like she was catching a bird. The cat's crupper jingled and poofed out like a skirt as she fell.

Donut clasped the fairy between two claws as she chomped down. She shook her head, breaking the fairy's neck.

The second fairy zipped up to the ceiling of the entrance hall, lightning fast, out of reach, screaming as I swiped at her, trying to catch her in the air. *Damnit.* I wanted to kill them without hurting their fragile little bodies.

"Not fair," the fairy screamed. The air crackled with her passage. She sounded desperate, on the verge of tears. "Not fair! We were going to move down to the third floor." Her hands also glowed red, and she fired a magic missile right at me.

It hit me square in the chest, and I flew backward, slamming onto my back, sliding a few feet into the room with the raging inferno. A note flashed. **Warning: Damage Enhanced.** It felt as if I'd been kicked by a damn horse. My vision flashed red, this time a health warning. I felt broken bones in my chest just as the searing heat threatened to catch my hair on fire. I clicked a healing potion as I scrambled to my feet. My chest crackled as it mended itself. I pulled myself back into the hall, out of the raging heat, the breath still knocked out of me.

The plan, plan B at least, had gone off without a hitch until now. The fairy remained up on the ceiling, screaming down at Donut, shooting magic missiles down at the cat, who was doing a much better job at dodging them.

After a moment, the fairy seemed to run out of mana. She continued to scream down at us. She was trapped as long as Donut and I each guarded one of the doors to the foyer.

"You can jump that high, can't you?" I muttered.

"Probably," Donut said, out of breath. "Or I can hit her with *Magic Missile.* I have much better aim than she does. I can hit her with a three power, and it probably won't hurt her body too much. She's level six, after all."

"Missile her if she runs," I said, pulling the slingshot out of my inventory.

It took ten shots before I hit her. The rock caught her in the wing, and she dropped a few feet before recovering. Her health barely went down. She was a quick little fucker. She kept screaming for someone named Damien to come help.

Damien never came.

"She's going to regenerate her mana before you get her," Donut said. "Hurry up, or I'm going to do it."

I aimed and fired, trying to anticipate where she was going to be. The rock clipped her in the wing again, and she cried out in pain, dropping again.

Donut leaped into the air and caught her before she could recover. They hit the ground with a *crunch*.

"Honestly, Carl," Donut said, spitting the dead fairy onto the ground next to the other one. "Must I do all the work?"

"I'm training," I said. I indicated the room behind me, where I'd received experience for killing 40 monsters all at once. "Besides, I just hit level 11."

"Me, too, actually," Donut said.

My Slingshot skill remained at three, but my Aiming skill went up to four.

Both of the fairies dropped 25 gold pieces, and each had five brochures in their inventory.

The description said their "essence" was valuable, but the only thing that remained was their bodies.

Laminak Rev-Up Consultant Elite Corpse (Alchemy Material).

"Damnit," I said. I'd been hoping they would just drop potions, something to protect us against the Taint disease.

Donut didn't want the corpses in her inventory, so I took them both. When I pulled them in, their bodies disappeared, but their clothes and wings remained on the ground. I took those, too.

"We didn't get a good potion, but that was still pretty awesome," Donut said as we headed back toward the filling room. "My first solo mission. I bet I'd be fine crawling this dungeon all by myself."

I nodded. Still, I couldn't help but feel like an asshole. The feeling wasn't as bad as I'd felt after the whole thing with the goblin babies, but there was something inherently distasteful about using Donut's charm ability to kill things. Yes, these were monsters that wouldn't hesitate about killing us. But like with the goblins, once Donut turned them neutral, we saw a part of their personalities one didn't normally see with monsters.

We were going to move down to the third floor. Jesus. Her voice had been filled with such longing, such despair.

I remembered what Mordecai had said, that the mobs in deeper levels weren't going to be as sympathetic. I really hoped so. I needed to remember who the real enemies were. The Syndicate. Borant. The kua-tin. I felt bad about killing monsters who were nothing more than pawns, but the fact was we needed to get as strong as we could. It was us or them.

"You're not going to break me," I whispered. It'd become a mantra.

"What?" Donut asked.

"Nothing," I said.

We walked into the large room. I went to work grabbing all the empty and full jugs I could. I grabbed another two tables, including one called an "Alchemy workstation." By the time we were done, we had 80 empty jugs and another 60 full ones.

I decided against filling the empty jugs with the moonshine from the tub. The metal container was bolted to the ground, so I couldn't take the whole thing, and I feared just touching the liquid would have some sort of nasty effect, like blinding me. Or worse.

The liquid continued to drip in from the next room over.

The door to the boss chamber looked like the entrance to some sort of community center. It had "Live, Laugh, Love" written on the top of the door in little cutout wooden letters. Under that was a schedule of events. The next event scheduled was for noon on the day after the collapse. It read, "Good news, everyone! Little Breannlyne has the chicken pox! Potluck Pox party here at noon. No peanuts. Let's get that immunity!"

"I think we should probably just leave this boss alone," I said. "There might be more kids in there. And if there's a moonshine still, it'll probably blow up just as easy as that goblin engine. We only have one hobgoblin detonator left, and I don't want to waste it if we don't have to. If we just toss dynamite or a boom jar in there, we might not get away in time. I bet the explosion will be big. It's not worth it to just go in there and fight face-to-face, not when we don't have a real defense against that Taint debuff. We don't know how many of those things there will be."

I was afraid Donut was going to protest, but she didn't.

We moved to the corner of the room. I pulled the "Rev-Up Smoothies! Invigorating!" banner off the wall. It was made of a cotton-like cloth. I put it in my inventory as I moved to investigate the two stationary bicycles.

A pulley ran from the tire to a small, flat platform welded onto the front of the bike. A little black segmented wheel, no bigger than a half-dollar coin, sat in the middle of the platform. Weird.

I noticed a pair of dust-covered wooden boxes tucked away in the corner. I picked one up, and the top slid off. I examined the contents. It was filled with empty clinking glass containers with screw-on lids. The box held twelve of them. Also shoved into the box was another, similar black lid with little blades on it.

I examined the little lid using the tooltips.

"Oh," I said. "I see. It's a blender. A bicycle-powered blender. It looks like it hasn't been used at all." I pulled one of the glass tubes out and unscrewed the cover. I could screw the bladed cover onto the glass and pop the whole thing onto the platform. If I turned the pedals on the small bike, it'd turn the blades, supposedly blending whatever was in the glass. Then I could flip it over, remove the bladed cover, and replace it with the original top, leaving me with a glass bottle of whatever I decided to blend.

Like a smoothie.

We had something similar, though not bicycle-powered, in our apartment.

I peeked in the second box, and this one only held six glasses instead of twelve. The bladed part of the blender was missing. A sheet of paper sat in the box, and I pulled it free.

Rev-Up Immunity Smoothie Recipe.

"Holy crap," I said. The recipe only required two items. "No wonder they discontinued this. Gross."

"What, what?" Donut asked.

"This is all game setup," I said as I started putting all the items into my inventory. One of the bikes was bolted to the ground, but the second wasn't. I picked it up and pulled it in. "You're supposed to find this and make the recipe. If you make the smoothie, you'll have immunity from the Taint debuff and something called the Vigorous Measles. And then you'll have the proper protection to fight the boss." I swallowed. "It's really gross, though. I don't want to go in there. I think we should just take these . . ."

I never finished the sentence.

The door to the boss room blasted open. A pair of pink tentacles, each at least fifteen feet long, reached out, swaying into the room. A terrible earsplitting screech filled the air, followed by a second screech. Then a third and a fourth.

Each octopus-like tentacle was covered with mouths. Dozens of them. Each mouth was wide, big around as a Frisbee, but human-shaped with bright red human lips. There were no eyes or other facial features. Just a cacophony of screaming voices saying nothing. Just screaming.

Familiar music started to play, barely discernible under the constant shrieks.

At the far end of the chamber where we'd walked in, bars dropped down, locking up the room.

"What the hell?" I cried, backing against the wall. "This isn't a boss chamber!"

A new achievement appeared, and it announced itself before I could wave it into the folder.

New Achievement! Wait, Bosses Can Leave Their Rooms?
     Welcome to the second floor, bitches.
     Reward: This shit plays great on the recap episode. If you scream loud enough, maybe you'll make the show.

34

Krakaren Clone!

Level 10 Neighborhood Boss!

First off, this isn't *the* Krakaren. This is *a* Krakaren. For every one that is killed, Krakaren Prime births two more.

Part of a collective mind intent upon destroying any semblance of scientific progress in the universe, the Krakaren is the only communal brain entity in the galaxy who actually gets stupider as time moves on. Consisting of multiple shrieking tentacles, members of the Krakaren cooperative spend their days birthing their disease-laden minions, creating and selling harmful products, attempting to debate scientific experts, and proselytizing to the weak minded, all in an attempt to . . . Well, nobody knows what the hell their end goal is.

Even Eris, Goddess of Chaos, doesn't want anything to do with these crazy assholes.

The moment the description ended, a portion of wall above the door broke open, and a third tentacle burst into the room from the next chamber over, swinging blindly about.

"Carl, Carl, what are we going to do?" Donut cried, pushing herself into the corner. "It's huge!"

The first two tentacles retracted, and a pair of clurichaun consultants came out of the door, looking wildly about.

"Shit," I said. "Keep them away! I need to make a goddamned smoothie!"

"What about the tentacles?" Donut cried.

I eyed the tentacle sweeping about the ceiling of the room. It kept smashing into the pipe that led to the tub of moonshine.

"Don't attack the boss yet. I don't think it can see. Focus on those guys." I pulled a glass smoothie container into my right hand. I pulled a jug of unaltered moonshine from my inventory into my left. Donut leaped onto my shoulder and shot a pair of magic missiles, nailing both of the clurichauns, who dropped dead at the doorway. A third hesitantly peeked out, looking for us. Donut got him right in the head, and he also collapsed.

I pulled the cork with my teeth, and I filled the smoothie container a third of the way with the moonshine. Thankfully it had a little line on the glass. I didn't know how exact this had to be.

Directly above us, the cinder block wall broke apart, showering us with rock. A tentacle burst forth, screaming. It scrabbled, swinging at nothing, swaying just feet over our heads.

Above, the mouths dripped with goo. I jumped out of the way as snot splashed near me. Moonshine sloshed out of the glass, and I had to pour a little more in.

Jesus fuck. I tossed the jug toward the entrance, and it shattered, splashing moonshine. A moment later, another tentacle once again burst from the door hole, sending the three dead clurichauns flying.

I pulled the corpse of the laminak from my inventory. I held the limp, naked, wingless body in my hand. It was still warm. Her little dead eyes stared up in her final shock at having been snatched out of the air by Donut. The sensation was odd, like holding an anatomically correct doll of a pudgy middle-aged woman. I didn't have time to think about it.

I shoved her, headfirst, into the glass container. Her shoulders were a little too wide to fit, so I had to push. The shoulders cracked, and I used my finger to ram her all the way in there, like trying to stuff a Cornish game hen into a thermos. I produced the blender top with the blades, and I had to push hard to get it to screw into place.

"Carl, what in god's name are you doing?"

"It's the recipe," I cried. I screwed the container onto the blender platform. It attached with a *click*. I sat atop the much-too-small bicycle, my knees as high as my chest. I prayed the bike wouldn't break. I prayed my spiked kneepads wouldn't activate, impaling my own chin.

I recited the recipe out loud. "You fill a third of the glass container with moonshine, add one corpse of a laminak fairy, blend until pink, drink warm or chilled. Each smoothie contains ten doses."

"If you think I'm going to drink that . . ."

Across the room, yet another tentacle appeared, this one on the ground. The next tentacle to break through would be right here. I spun my legs. The bike protested at first, but it quickly gained steam, spinning like a regular blender. Within the little glass container, the dead fairy stared back at me, spinning until she was sucked away, the concoction first green, then red, and then pink. After a moment, it started to sparkle.

I pulled the glass bottle off the top just as another two clurichauns entered the chamber, squeezing past the single tentacle that still reached about the room. The tentacle wrapped around the metallic tub and squeezed. It crumpled like a beer can.

Above, a glob of snot fell, splashing off my head and oozing onto my face.

You have been inflicted with the Taint.

"Damnit!" *I really need to start sticking my hood up.*

"Run," I said. "Toward the back of the room."

Behind us, the wall exploded, sending the lone bike flying. It shattered into pieces when it hit the floor.

As I ran, I examined the smoothie in my hand.

Rev-Up Immunity Smoothie.

   One part moonshine, and one part fairy, this smoothie offers 10 doses for the price of one! Each sip of this delicious concoction imbues the following effects:

Temporary immunity to all health-seeping conditions and debuffs.

Temporary protection against all communicable diseases.

Inflicts the Buzzed debuff. (Plus 3 Charisma. Minus 1 Dexterity. Plus Shaky Cam debuff. Plus Truth Serum debuff.)

I didn't have time to think about it. I took a sip.

It tasted as if I'd taken a drink directly from the diseased asshole
of an incontinent skunk. It took all of my strength not to vomit.

"Stick it in your hotlist and drink," I cried, shoving it at Donut
as we reached the end of the room. It disappeared from my hand. She
didn't argue. She glowed as the potion took hold.

A pair of icons flashed, indicating my immunity. The Taint debuff didn't go away, however, which meant I couldn't heal myself.
But at least now I couldn't be inflicted with the death measles or
whatever it was called.

"Death measles," I heard myself say as I ran. "Now *that's* funny."

It wasn't funny. I laughed again. *What the hell is wrong with . . .*

"Ow," I cried as a rock bounced off my head. My health flashed,
my bar moving farther down than it should've. I'd been hit with a
damn slingshot, and the damage was enhanced because of my stupid
goblin tattoo.

I was woozy, and I realized it was the Buzzed debuff. *Whoa.* I had
to consciously keep myself from falling over. If this was Buzzed, I'd
hate to see what the Shit-Faced debuff felt like.

I pulled an angled, still-intact section of the redoubt from my
inventory, putting the shield up as we reached the back corner of the
room. Five tentacles smashed about, and a pair of clurichauns rushed
at us, both of them shooting rocks that pinged off the steel table.

"What's your mana?" I asked.

"Sixteen," Donut cried, her voice slurred. She popped up and fired
a missile at a clurichaun. She hit him in the shoulder, but he still
went down. "Now twelve. Die, motherfucker! Die!"

I barely had time to parse that Donut was also drunk as a

screaming tentacle smashed against the table, rocketing us both against the back wall. My health, already in the red, moved farther down. The monster didn't seem to realize what it hit. I watched as it grasped on the last standing clurichaun, wrapping around him. The mouths stopped screaming, all revealing long, sharp teeth as they pulled the shrieking monster back into the boss room, chewing. It returned a moment later, blood dripping from the mouths, which resumed their caterwaul.

Four more clurichauns rushed into the room. Another tentacle emerged, pushing through yet another hole in the wall.

This tentacle was different. Instead of mouths, it was covered in hundreds of tiny little orifices. The longer, thinner arm reached into the room and made a *psst, psst* noise, like a spray bottle. A fine green mist filled the chamber.

You've been infected with the Vigorous Measles!
Infection negated due to immunity!

"Don't fire any more missiles," I said. My head swam.

"If we die, I want you to know that I love you, Carl," Donut said. "I don't love you as much as I love Miss Beatrice, because she's, you know, she's my person. Or as much as I love Ferdinand. But I love you."

"Focus, Donut," I said. I tried not to let what she'd said sting. But it did. Who the fuck was Ferdinand anyway? *Bea was giving you up, Donut. She was giving you up, trading you in for a younger model.* But I didn't say it. Not out loud. Now was not the time for that conversation. Never was the time for that conversation, not anymore. But especially not now. Not when Bea was fucking dead.

"See that clurichaun there," I said, pointing a shaking hand. "Raise him from the dead."

Two of the clurichauns running at us cried out as they were picked up and crushed by their own boss.

I leaped up, stumbling away as yet another tentacle reached for me. I ducked, and it sailed past.

I was suddenly on the ground. When I'd ducked, I just kept going down. I pulled myself up and kept running.

I formed a fist, and I rushed at the two remaining monsters. I kicked one, who went flying, and then I drunkenly swung at another, connecting with his giant head with a right hook. I pulled back, an ear attached to my spike. I dropped to the ground as a tentacle swooped over my head.

Ahead of me, a clurichaun zombie rose up, groaning.

"Tell him to hold this over his head and run into the boss chamber," I cried. I pulled a boom jug from my inventory as the zombie stood there, swaying, looking at me. For good measure I pulled the most stable stick of dynamite I had and shoved it down his overalls. *Probably a bad idea*, I thought right after I did it.

Oh well.

The zombie grabbed the jug on Donut's instruction and held it over his head, like that guy holding the boom box in that *Say Anything* movie. I lit the torch and sent him on his way. He turned toward the doorway, which was currently empty, and he ran. He barely missed being swept away by another tentacle, and he reached the door just as a seventh tentacle broke through the wall and five more clurichauns emerged, who all stared, unmoving, at the zombie rushing right at them. They moved out of the way, uncomprehending what was happening.

I turned in the opposite direction and ran toward our small shield. I dove behind it, barely dodging another tentacle that swooped right over my head. As I jumped behind the metal shield, Donut yelled, "I thought you said the explosion was going to be too big to use it in here!"

I looked at my health, already perilously low. Donut didn't have a scratch on her. I pulled the alchemy table out of my inventory, putting it directly over us, placing us within a clamshell. I felt as if I was going to vomit. My head continued to swim.

"It probably is," I said. "And I'm probably about to die, but I think you'll be okay."

"Carl, no," Donut said. "No!"

"It's okay," I said. "Go back to Brandon. They'll watch over you." I wrapped myself around the cat.

"I don't want to do this without you," Donut cried. "Carl, I lied before. I won't be fine on my own. I need you. No, no!"

I couldn't answer her before the explosion came.

35

I WASN'T DEAD.

I was deaf. I was blind. I was in a fuck ton of pain. I couldn't feel my legs.

But I wasn't dead.

I gasped for air. My health indicator blinked, the lowest it had ever been. My eardrums had been blown out. My entire face felt burned, my eyes included. The pain was overwhelming, like hundreds of claws pulling at me from different directions at once. They were still pulling, ripping pieces of me away.

The Taint still had a minute left before it would run out. I wasn't out of danger yet. I could feel Donut standing on top of me. I could feel the vibration of her voice. She was shouting, pawing at me desperately.

"If you're saying something to me, I can't hear you," I said, shouting the words.

DONUT: YOU HAVE TO STAND UP. THE ROOM IS ON FIRE. WE KILLED THE BOSS. THE DOOR IS OPEN, BUT THE FIRE IS GETTING CLOSER. HURRY.

"I can't. I think my legs are broken. I can't feel them." I pulled up my health UI, looking at the damage to my body. The entire pie chart was blinking red, all except my feet. My health was at 6% and still ticking downward. I was bleeding internally. I had third-degree burns on my face. My legs were broken where the table had smashed into them.

A moment later, I felt myself moving through the debris. I realized it was Donut dragging me by my cloak, pulling me from the room. My whole body screamed with pain. A blinking message warned I was about to pass out.

> DONUT: CARL, YOU NEED TO WORK ON YOUR CARDIO. YOU ARE MUCH HEAVIER THAN YOU LOOK.

"Ten seconds before you can heal me. Get scroll ready," I croaked as darkness descended.

I AWAKENED, MY BODY SCREAMING. I FELT EVERYTHING INSIDE OF me repair itself. Donut had used one of the *Heal* scrolls, possibly at the last possible second. I jammed down on my healing spell also, which sped up the process. I felt my hearing return, my sight restored. The burn on my face smoothed out.

I didn't move for several moments, sitting there, staring up at the ceiling of the hallway.

"You saved me again," I said to the cat, who sat next to me, desperately cleaning herself. I still didn't dare move, not trusting the bones in my body not to break again.

"That's what I do," she said.

> DONUT: I DON'T WANT TO SAY THIS OUT LOUD, BUT OUR VIEWS WENT WAY UP. ISN'T IT GREAT?

I groaned, rolling onto my side. My one-armed jacket was now scorched to hell. My cloak and other magical items didn't have a scratch on them. I looked down at my toes, and they sparkled.

"I think I was saved by that damn pedicure kit," I said. "The table should have severed my feet right at the ankles. Instead it bounced off and broke my legs. I would've bled out."

The fire in the expanded boss chamber eventually died off, leaving nothing but melted slag. We wandered in.

The alchemy table I'd used as the top part of our shield was undamaged. The other table, the redoubt piece that I'd used here as a shield, was now shattered and scorched.

"Huh, weird," I said. I touched the alchemy workshop table, and it was cool to the touch. I pulled it back into my inventory. I had two such tables now, designed to be placed inside of personal spaces. This one and the engineer's table. It seemed they were indestructible.

This was a bug. A bug I could exploit. I couldn't say anything about it, though. Not out loud. Had the table's invulnerability saved us? I was going to need to pay attention to the nightly list of patch notes to make sure they didn't fix this one. In the meantime, I'd use it to our advantage.

The ductwork on the ceiling hung in tatters, a few pieces still clinging to the chamber by braces. The severed skeletal remains of tentacles lay scattered. The ground was hot to the touch. Donut jumped to my shoulder.

"Let's get the neighborhood map," I said, hesitantly moving toward the main boss chamber. I cringed, afraid we'd find more dead babies.

I shouldered past the long, crumbling skeleton bones to behold the lair of Krakaren.

"It smells like that time you tried microwaving Fancy Feast," Donut said.

"I was drunk," I said. "And you ate that shit right up."

More tattered ductwork filled the room. There had been banners on the wall, but I could no longer read them. I didn't see anything that could be construed as baby skeletons, which was a relief. Dozens of clurichauns had been in here along with a few splatters that might've been laminak fairies.

The mechanical remains of a moonshine still sat in the corner, like I suspected, but it appeared the machine was much smaller than I had guessed it might be. It was probably why I was still alive. I'd assumed the thing to be huge. And explosive.

The remnants of copper tubes snaked from the machine to the main dead body of the Krakaren monster. She'd been huge, twenty feet tall at least, an immobile octopus-like creature. Her stinking dead body leaned against the back wall as we stared at it. Half of her head was burned away, but it seemed she had a beaked mouth and a group of eyes. Black streaks ran down the massive corpse, like running mascara. She stank of rotting seafood.

They'd taken some sort of cosmic octopus creature and combined it with your average suburban anti-vax, let-me-talk-to-your-manager mom. At least that was my impression. The door on the outside of the room, this whole ridiculous storyline with the MLM moonshine certainly made it seem that way.

But there was more to it, too. I suspected the Krakaren "collective" or whatever they called it was a real thing. Sort of. This whole time it had seemed they were just combining absurd stereotypes from Earth with random monsters just to fuck with us. It came to me now as I stared up at this thing that they were doing the opposite. After all, this was all really for the benefit of the audience, not us. They were taking something familiar to the viewers, like these interstellar dumbass octopus monsters, and combining them with an Earth analog in an effort to both teach the watchers about Earth culture and to lampoon interstellar cultures and creatures they felt deserving of scorn. Kind of like the way cartoonists would sometimes personify rats and snakes as scumbags. Or foxes as shady used-car dealers.

Or Persian cats as princesses.

A massive cage filled half the room, still intact. The creatures within had mostly burned to slag, but I could see that it had been filled to the brim with brindle grubs. They were all dead.

"We never got to see the boss up close," Donut said as I moved near enough to loot the neighborhood map.

"Something tells me this isn't the last time we'll see this one," I said as the twists and turns of the neighborhood populated onto my interface. "Ah, fuck."

"What?" Donut asked.

"Look at the map," I said.

At least 50 red dots filled the area. All of them slow-moving. Brindle grubs. It was like they could sense a battle, and they converged on an area. Killing them wasn't a problem. They didn't fight back. I could literally run over them and kill an entire hallway of them in seconds. But that was a lot of them. A whole lot.

I planned out the path to the tutorial guild. It wasn't far. Just a few hundred meters away.

"Let's go talk to Mordecai," I said.

"THAT BITCH REALLY SAID THAT?" MORDECAI SAID, OUTRAGED, AF-ter I told him about Odette's offer. "She wants me to seek *her* out? I would rather spend another 2,000 years in this room than exist in the same solar system as her. I'd rather meet a woman, sire children, and then devour those children than have anything to do with her again."

"So that's a no, then?" Donut asked.

Mordecai was no longer a Rat Hooligan. He'd shapeshifted into a much larger, hairier, and obsidian creature called a Bugaboo. He was like a bear with no neck, with enormous owlish eyes and comically skinny legs. His long arms were also absurdly thin compared to the rest of the seven-foot-tall creature. He looked terrifying and cartoonish at the same time. I'd almost punched him right in the face when we first entered the room. It took a solid ten seconds for me to realize that this was still Mordecai.

I examined his properties now.

Mordecai—Bugaboo. Level 50.
    Guildmaster of this guildhall.

This is a Non-Combatant NPC.

You know that creepy, unkempt guy who lives on the corner? He doesn't seem to have a job. Has a van. Hangs out at the park with a pair of binoculars? Yeah, you get the idea. Solitary monstrosities that never settle in a single place, Bugaboos may be found anywhere on the dungeon's lower floors, often lying in wait for crawlers to pass by so they can jump out and . . . do things to them. They'll tell you they just want to cuddle. That's probably a lie.

"That's quite the monster they chose for you," I said.

Mordecai nodded. "These guys are pretty depraved. They have them on the first and second floors, but the third floor will be filled with them. Don't wander near alleys at night."

"At night?" I asked.

Mordecai waved. "I can't tell you about that." I looked up at him, but he winked at me. I understood.

"So, Odette," I asked. "You don't like her? Is there something we need to be worried about?"

Mordecai took a long, deep breath. "Odette cares about Odette. She is smart, she is cunning, and she is more self-centered than that thing at the center of the galaxy. But her current gig, it is perfect for her. She can be very useful and helpful to you. Until you're not."

It's funny, that's pretty much the exact same thing she'd said about the game's AI. I didn't say that out loud.

"If she invites us back on the show, should we go?" I asked.

Mordecai grunted. "Oh, you should go. Her program is one of the few I would recommend. Not that they'd give you much of a choice. Speaking of shows, there's someone who wants to speak with you. I've been asked to ping her once you showed up here. She'll arrive in about ten or fifteen minutes."

"Another show?" Donut asked. She'd just started combing through her achievements and boxes. She didn't seem to have gotten anything noteworthy except one item. Her boss box contained an

Enchanted Fur Brush of the Ecclesiastic that worked in a similar fashion to my pedicure kit. As long as someone brushed her for ten minutes every night, she'd receive an extra two points to her constitution for 30 hours. It was better than nothing, but even with the buff, her constitution was only four.

"She'll explain who she is when she gets here," Mordecai said. He leaned forward and whispered in my ear, "Do not upset this woman. She has a lot of power over your fate."

I swallowed. I had a feeling this wasn't going to be a good thing.

"I have several questions," I said, settling into the chair.

Mordecai settled uncomfortably across from me. Before, the chairs had been too big for him. Now they were too small. "Let's hear it."

"You said it'd probably be ten days, but it's six," I said.

"Is that a question?" Mordecai asked. He shrugged. "This is the first time I've ever seen it lower than the maximum. The minimum is one day longer. They gave a reason in the last announcement. That's all I can say about that." Mordecai lifted his eyes, looking up at the ceiling.

"Can viewers see us in this room?" I asked.

"Yes," Mordecai said. "Like I said before, the only place they can't follow is in restrooms. They can only hear or see you, however. Not me. Only those with press credentials can see or hear me. Those like Odette. Most people know this and only watch if you have a good loot box to open."

Shit. I hadn't thought about that. Before, Mordecai had been more forthright, but we also hadn't been under a crazy amount of scrutiny, either. Getting straight answers out of him was now going to be more difficult.

"Do you know who Damien is?"

Mordecai looked as if I'd just slapped him. "Who told you that name?" he hissed. "Did Odette tell you about him?"

"Whoa," I said, holding up my hands. "Not Odette. It was a mob. A fairy. She called for him just before we killed her."

Mordecai relaxed. "Those damn fairies. They're always getting themselves in trouble. Damien is a location manager. Each 'City' area has one. There are only three for this floor. He is my manager's manager. You're not supposed to see or know about him. I'm only allowed to tell you about this sort of stuff if you ask directly."

We spent some time talking about the borough boss fight and the last fight with Krakaren. I asked him what her weakness was, and he smiled, telling me he wasn't allowed to say, which really told me my theory was correct. It wasn't the last we'd see of that particular boss.

I asked him about Agatha, about them editing her out of the boss battle. He waved it off. "They probably didn't want to confuse the narrative." Again, I could sense there was more there. I tried not to let my frustration show.

I told him my theory about how they were combining real aliens with Earth stereotypes.

Mordecai looked equally frustrated. He paused, as if thinking hard. "That's mostly correct. Again, it's not really something I can discuss. But this isn't exactly some big secret, either. Some of these monsters are made by AI, some are simply the actual creatures from their world—the tusklings and the Ball of Swine, for example. And some, like you've deduced, are created by a team of writers. Like with anything that's been put together by a team, what you end up with can vary wildly. Those llamas, for example. They are unique to your planet, and I don't recall anything in your culture that suggests they should be anthropomorphized as drug-dealing gangbangers. Someone just thought it'd be an interesting combo. Not everything will be social commentary."

"It's usually just stupid," I muttered.

"It's entertainment," Mordecai said, once again reminding me of something Odette said. There was a much deeper story there, between those two. I wondered if I'd ever learn.

"Also, I've been meaning to ask you about this tattoo on my neck," I said. "The Desperado Club."

"Nope," Mordecai said. "Off-limits. You'll learn about the third floors soon enough. Sorry. Now, you better open your boxes before Zev gets here. Once she's here, the cameras *will* turn off. Cameras will always turn off when kua-tin are around."

Shit. "Okay," I said, opening up my folder.

My IED and Explosives Handling and several other explosives-based skills had leaped to seven thanks to my creation of the Carl's Jug O' Boom. I also received a pretty strange achievement:

New achievement! *Dungeonpreneur.*

You have invented a stackable weapon, device, or potion. You will be memorialized for eternity with your name in the *Dungeon Codex*. Just don't let it go to your head, Elon.

Reward: For every kill made with this device by other crawlers, you will receive a single gold coin. If you survive the dungeon, you will continue to receive this benefit—even during future seasons—at the current gold-to-credit exchange rate for the remainder of your natural life. Our lawyers made us put that last part in, but between you and me, we both know you're going to die, and we're going to keep using your hard work for our own benefit.

Interesting. It was too bad nobody else would ever use these things. The main ingredient—the jug of moonshine—was probably pretty rare. And those jugs were more valuable when they were left unaltered.

I received a bunch of the usual stuff plus a couple hundred gold coins, bringing our hoard to just over 1,000 coins. I went over it all. More potions and torches and biscuits. I had enough food now to feed an army for a month straight. I received a couple goblin boxes and took in more dynamite, smoke bombs, and lighters. I received a Bronze Crowd Control Box and added two scrolls of *Confusing Fog*. This time, I would give them both to Donut.

I opened the boss box.

Don't say anything. Don't say anything out loud.
I couldn't help it. I looked up at the ceiling.
"Really? Fucking really?"
Behind me, Mordecai laughed, but a moment later he added, "Whoa, that's actually a really good prize."
It was a white pair of boxers covered in little red hearts.
"Goddamnit," I muttered as I examined them.

Enchanted BigBoi Boxers.

Have you ever read an *Incredible Hulk* comic and thought to yourself, *Everything rips off of his body except his pants? No way.* Well, spoiler alert. You're not wrong. Size-altering and were-creatures, such as the BigBoi, are required to wear enchanted, self-sizing items lest they wish to turn the dungeon into a nudist colony when they transform. That means everything they wear requires an enchantment. Everything, including their naughty little undies.

+2 to Constitution.

Wearer may cast a level 15 *Protective Shell* once every 30 hours.

"Don't look," I said, and I pulled my scorched and threadbare boxers off and slipped the new ones on. The old ones fell apart in my hands. The first thing I did was open the spell menu, find *Protective Shell*, and move it to my hotlist.

Protective Shell.

Picture yourself in high school. Now picture all the girls who would never get anywhere near you. It's kind of like that, but on purpose.

Cost: This is an item-based spell. This spell does not require mana to cast. If you unequip the associated item, you will lose access to this spell. The cooldown will not reset.

Target: A 3-meter radius sphere centered around the right hand of caster + 50 centimeters of radius per level of Intelligence. [Current Radius: 4.5 meters.]

Duration: 5 seconds + 1 second per level of spell. [Current Duration: 20 seconds.] Requires 30-hour cooldown.

A favorite of frontline tanks and castle guards, the expensive and rare *Protective Shell* spell shields the caster and anyone within the sphere from a mob's physical presence or physical attacks. This spell does not protect against magic or against non-corporeal entities. Unlike the more popular *Shield* spell, this spell does not move with you. This spell's area of effect remains static once cast, unimpeded by your physical surroundings. So if you use this spell only when you really, really need it, you're probably only delaying the inevitable by a few seconds.

"I had that spell during my crawl," Mordecai said. "It saved me more than once. It has a fantastic secondary effect. Since the spell doesn't move once cast, you can . . ."

Warning: You may not wield your weapons while in the presence of Admins. Any attempted violence against an Admin will result in your immediate execution.

The stern message came out of nowhere, and it was spoken in a different voice than any one I'd heard before. Like with the boss battles, it wasn't voiced in my head, but over an unseen loudspeaker.

Donut immediately jumped to my shoulder.

There was a loud *pop*, and a new creature appeared in the room, standing in a puddle right in front of me.

A kua-tin.

36

ALL OF MY MENUS DISAPPEARED. MY ENTIRE HUD SNAPPED OFF. IT was just like it had been when we'd been transported up to the production boat floating on the surface.

I just stared at the person, uncomprehending for several seconds. *Are you kidding me with this shit?*

It was a kua-tin. A female kua-tin. An actual representative from the Borant Corporation. I remembered the massive carving of the fish creature on the doors, and I compared it to this beast. Before, I'd seen similar sea creatures in the audience at the taping of Odette's show. I now knew that those were *not* kua-tin. Those people were very different. And while the gigantic relief carvings on the doors did an adequate job of portraying the aquatic race's features, it left one important detail out.

This kua-tin stood about two feet tall. She was barely tall enough to reach my knee. I examined the woman's properties.

Zev—Borant Corporation Assistant Communications Representative.
This is a Dungeon Admin.

That was it. No additional information, no snarky AI talking about mudskippers.

It took me several moments to take in her outfit.

Zev looked like an astronaut from a 1950s sci-fi comic. She wore a round glass helmet filled with water. A pair of tubes snaked from the back of the helmet to a bulky backpack. The water bubbled like she was in a portable fish tank. The rest of her humanoid fish body was hidden inside of a white mesh space suit. The whole getup was half space age, half old-school deep-diving suit.

"Good evening, ma'am," Mordecai said, standing straight.

"Hello, Mordecai," the fish woman said, her voice amplified through a little speaker on her outfit. "It's nice to finally meet you face-to-face."

There was something about the woman that suddenly made Mordecai visibly relax, but I couldn't tell what it was. There might have been an exchange I couldn't hear. I just didn't know. Even Donut seemed to notice. The cat kept looking back and forth between the tiny fish and the large guildmaster.

"Ma'am, I must say. I haven't seen one of these water suits in centuries," Mordecai said, walking around the woman. "Most kua-tin wear rebreathers around their necks. You can barely see them."

"I've been assured the armor of this device is second to none. If one of my fellow employees wishes to enter this godsforsaken place without any proper armor, then that is on them."

"Ma'am, I don't want to sound rude. But can you move in that thing?" Mordecai asked.

"No," she admitted. "Not really. If you must know, this is my first foray into a dungeon, and I wanted to be safe."

"So you're really here," I said. I resisted the urge to reach down and tap on the glass.

"Yes," she said, looking up at me. "Other corporations may utilize holos for their training guilds and admins, but Borant prefers a more fins-on approach."

"You know you're in no danger while you're in a safe room," Mordecai said. "The mobs know not to attack you. And the AI negates all attacks inside of safe areas. Unless you're planning on going for a stroll, ma'am, I wouldn't worry about it."

"Yeah, well, tell that to those twelve workers in Site Prep. Did you see this morning's update? They were swallowed whole! Or that human admin who didn't realize the no-urinating-in-the-dungeon rule applied to everyone. They said all that was left was splatter on the floor."

I had no idea what was going on with this exchange, but Zev seemed to realize she was talking in front of a pair of crawlers. She returned her gaze up at us.

"Anyway, I wanted to do a meet and greet with you two," Zev said. "This will only take a quick crutch of your time."

"I don't know what that means, but go ahead," I said.

"My name is Zev, and I work within the Borant Corporation's communications department. I am a liaison between Borant and privately owned and operated programs who wish to ren . . . borrow crawlers for their shows. We have identified several individuals and teams who have gained early popularity. As is probably no surprise to you, you two are on that list."

On my shoulder, I felt Donut's claws sink deep into me. The cat was shuddering with pleasure.

"We've already been on one show," I said. *"Dungeon Crawler After Hours with Odette."*

"Yes," she said. "I am aware. Certain production companies are allowed to pluck crawlers away between stairwells. But if they want to transport crawlers to their sets at any other time, after boss battles for example, they must arrange it through our office. Usually these requests are granted automatically, but once crawlers reach a certain level of notoriety, the number of requests can become a bit overwhelming. We generally don't want our crawlers to leave the game more than twice a floor. As you've already received over two dozen interview requests from this most recent boss battle alone, you have automatically been entered into the Crawler Assisted Outreach Program. In other words, you've been assigned a PR agent. Me."

"You're our agent? Our PR agent? You get us gigs?" Donut asked, voice full of wonder.

"That's right," Zev said. "From now on, all interview and panel requests will filter through me. I have opened up a special chat channel so I can send you messages through your interface." Zev looked about distastefully. "Also, they make me come down here and talk to you directly after interviews for a debriefing."

"This is absolutely fabulous," Donut said. "Can we provide advance riders? Like with makeup and greenroom requirements?"

"How about a more important question," I asked. "Can we refuse interviews? Last time we didn't have much of a choice."

She nodded. "I will always ask you before whisking you away. But"—she leaned in, and her entire outfit creaked ominously—"Odette has already contracted with our office. She gets first right of refusal for each floor opening. You're already locked into those interviews, and as long as you keep your numbers up, you will go on her show. That means I'll try to schedule one additional interview for each floor down. You can refuse what show you go on, but I'm afraid you'll be obligated to pick something. We might move to three interviews for the lower floors depending on how it's going and whether or not the party keeps insisting on accelerating the game. And if you survive, of course. But whatever happens, I promise I will do my best to get you quality gigs."

"What about now?" Donut asked. "Do you have something for us now?"

"Yes," she said. "There are a few options, but for this first one, I went ahead and chose a program for you. It's a little less serious than Odette's show, but it will hit a demographic that you aren't yet trending in. Plus it's a roundtable-style discussion, and in this program all crawlers get a parting gift. Sometimes it's a joke, but it's usually something useful."

"A gift?" Donut said. "Carl, we get a gift!"

"Wait, are we doing this *now*?" I asked.

"No," Zev said. "I'll ping you when it's time. It'll be at minus six plus one full."

"Minus what?" I said. I felt a sudden, unexpected wave of rage at the fish woman. It came out of nowhere, and I didn't know what set it off. *She's just a goddamned pawn like everyone else. It's not her fault.*

Still, I couldn't help it. She was a kua-tin. The enemy. The *real* enemy. And I couldn't do anything about it. *Take a deep breath.* "We don't understand your time reference."

She sighed. "Six hours before the next recap episode. Not the one tonight, but the next one. So, in about forty hours. Since you'll be doing your Odette interviews between floors, I figured it'd be best to schedule your second appearance right in the middle of the floor's timer. It'll keep interest up. Also, you should try to line up a major boss battle right as the floor closes like you did last time. That really worked in your favor."

That rage, which I thought I had successfully held back, bubbled up and out. "Goddamnit. God-fucking-damnit," I said. Mordecai raised his hands in alarm, rapidly shaking them, trying to get me to stop. I didn't care. "We are, quite literally, fighting for our lives here. We are not willing participants, and I am getting sick of pretending we are. We are going on these *fucking* interviews not because we want to, but because we have to." The fish looked up at me through her helmet, eyes wide. "Zev, ma'am, whatever the hell I'm supposed to call you so you don't send a lightning bolt up my ass, I don't want to get in trouble with you or Borant or the Syndicate or whoever else is running this bullshit. I am doing what you have asked. I am killing monsters, trying to level up, trying to survive. I will smile, and I will joke, and I will put a proper face on when I go on these shows. But fuck. You have already taken everything from us. Do not ask us to give more than what we have. We are not going to fight or survive on your schedule."

I sat there, my chest heaving, glaring down at the fish. The world seemed frozen. Mordecai looked terrified. Donut, who remained on my shoulder, butted her head against the side of my own. She purred, a deep, silent rumbling. Her reaction surprised me.

But not as much as Zev's reaction.

"Look," she said, after a moment. "I know. Okay? Nobody in this room is an idiot." She pointed at Mordecai. "The moment I appeared, he was terrified of me. Once he saw I wasn't wearing a party badge, he relaxed. When I'm done here, I go back down to the production headquarters, and I will have to face my boss, who *is* a member of the party. If I do or say the wrong thing, my entire family will be wiped from the universe. You're going to go out there and face mobs who know people like you are prowling the halls, trying to find and kill them. They, the sapient ones? They live in constant fear of you guys. We are all parts of the same, inexorable machine. All of us are afraid. Yes, your place in this really sucks. It's not fair. You know it. I know it. The cat knows it. But believe it or not, I am on your side. The better you do, the longer you survive, the better *I* do. So when I tell you that you should do something, you best listen because I know what I'm talking about."

Nobody moved or said anything for several seconds. We just stood there, looking at one another.

"This is just like that scene in season three of *Gossip Girl* when Chuck and Blair break up over the hotel," Donut said.

I turned to regard the cat on my shoulder, and I burst out laughing. I couldn't help it. It wasn't funny. I'd never watched that damn show. Yet I laughed, and I had a hard time stopping.

"No, it's not," Mordecai said a moment later. "How do you even get that from this?"

Zev turned her fish gaze to my cat, then Mordecai. "I can't believe it. You two have watched *Gossip Girl*? Nobody on my team has watched *anything*, except that old show *COPS* and *Judge Judy*. We've been stuck here for 15 solars with nothing for entertainment but Earth-based programs, and I've had nobody to talk to about them."

"Oh, honey," Donut said, jumping down from my shoulder to sit next to the fish. "I have seen everything. Season five, the car accident?"

"No, stop, you're going to make me cry," Zev said, waving her fish arms. I thought, *Fish can cry?* They started rapidly talking with one another about the show. Bea used to sit up and rewatch the series over and over again. She'd clutch onto Donut and sob every time.

"That was dangerous," Mordecai whispered to me as Donut and

Zev continued to talk. "She's about as low-level as you can get and still be an admin, but you need to control your temper. She has the power to end you. All kua-tin are dangerous, party members or not."

"What the hell is the party?" I asked, also whispering. We both took a few steps back. He was right about my temper. I rarely lost it. But that didn't matter right now. This was a rare opportunity, the ability to talk to Mordecai with nobody else listening.

"It's a political party. They're called the Bloom. Now everyone just calls it the party. Ultranationalism. The closest thing you have in your history is maybe Axis Japan with a good splash of Nazi Germany thrown in, but even that's not quite right," he said. "When I signed my indentureship contract, the Bloom represented less than 15% of the votes. Now they control the whole kua-tin system government. They've run it into the ground. The whole system is bankrupt. They've recently started requiring all kua-tin to wear a badge indicating if they're members or not."

"Jesus," I said.

"Listen carefully," Mordecai said, looking nervously down at Zev. "We don't have time to get into the details, but Borant is being forced by their own government to end the game as quickly as possible. You need to be especially careful not to upset them."

"I don't understand," I said, alarm rising. "I thought they started it early to stave off a bankruptcy seizure action or whatever. That's what Odette implied. Wouldn't they want to keep it running as long as possible?"

He nodded. "That's what everyone thought at first. They're doing a cash grab with the new patron system, but they don't get that money, or any money, from the advertising or the tourism funds or elite monster sponsorship or anything else until the season is over. They need that cash as soon as possible. But they also first need to raise enough. Their whole system is balancing on a wire. They need the game to be entertaining and profitable, but they also need it to finish much more quickly than usual. The committee has already issued a warning, putting Borant on notice over the 'bugs' that keep occurring, like the issue with the bathrooms and the overpowered mobs. One too many violations, and Borant could lose everything. There are protections in place, plus there is pushback within the company itself. But the kua-tin government is working extra hard to get you killed."

"That's just wonderful," I said. Zev looked up at me, as if surprised I was still in the room. Mordecai saw this and took a few steps away.

"I think it's time for us to get back out there," I said to Donut. "We need to finish clearing this quadrant out, and then we need to escort team Meadow Lark to the stairs. I want to get it done before the next recap episode."

"We will talk more later," Donut said to Zev.

"Or we can talk over chat!" Zev said. The fish's demeanor had completely changed. "Tell me you've watched *Riverdale*."

Donut gasped.

"Nope," I said, reaching down to scoop the cat up. "You two will talk all night."

"Wait one crutch. I have to leave before you can," Zev said as I put my hand on the door handle to the dungeon. "It's the rules. I'll ping you regarding the next interview." And without further fanfare, she disappeared with a *pop*. Water splashed over my feet as she disappeared.

"There's more I want to discuss," I said to Mordecai. All of our menus snapped back on, the HUD flickering like a booting-up computer. I pulled at the door. "But it is getting late. We'll be . . ." I trailed off as I glanced at the minimap. Why had the map changed color?

The door opened all the way, and a waist-high pile of grubs fell into the room.

37

MORDECAI SHRIEKED IN RAGE. "OUT! OUT OF MY ROOM!" HE KICKED at the monsters, punting them like oversized footballs out into the hallway.

"Gah," I cried, jumping back. "Why aren't they teleporting away?"

"They won't until they attack," he said. "Not on their own, at least." He was scooping them up by the armfuls, tossing them back out into the hall. But it was useless. For every two he tossed out, four more got in. Eventually he gave up and slammed the door, trapping several dozen in the room. He waved his hand, and they all disappeared. He wiped his hands on his fur. "There."

There were hundreds of them in the hallway. Thousands of them. I just stared, dumbfounded. They kept coming and coming.

They're following us, I realized. Where the hell were they coming from, though? Up until now, it had seemed all the dungeon's monsters were pre-seeded. Once we killed all the monsters in an area, that was it. The area was safe. These guys were being spawned somewhere nearby. They had to be.

I leaned against the door and zoomed out the map to view the whole neighborhood. Thousands more of them were crawling their way toward us. They seemed to be coming from the south, from a direction we hadn't yet explored. The hallway with the stairs wasn't yet infested. But it would be soon.

"What the hell is this?" I asked Mordecai.

"I've never seen anything like this, not on the second floor,"

Mordecai said. His eyes had gone glossy, which I recognized as him searching through his special menu. "Yup, as I suspected." He looked at me, his shaggy face looking grim. "They're being spawned."

"Yeah, no shit," I said.

"Every floor has a waste disposal system," he continued. "So far you've seen rats and the grubs. The more dead bodies they eat, the stronger they get. It'll be something different the next floor down. They're supposed to home in on corpses, but if none are nearby, they'll hunt crawlers. That's what they're doing. These guys don't attack, but they'll still swarm at ya."

"But why are there so many of them?"

"It looks like the system is spawning anywhere between one to 15 of them when a corpse is created. It usually doesn't do that unless there aren't any janitor mobs nearby. You killed a lot of mobs in that last battle, so here they are."

"We didn't kill *that* many! Plus, we've been destroying the corpses."

"They probably had a couple hundred grubs in that cage in the boss room," Mordecai said. He paused. "Yes, there were 750 of them. All fried. Plus you killed another 85 clurichauns between grinding away and the boss battle. Destroying the corpses only keeps them from leveling up. It doesn't stop them from being generated. You, my friends, have been set up. You've fallen into a trap. Good news is they're easy to kill. The bad news is these little buggers don't give any experience. At least not the level two ones."

"Wait," I said. "This even works on themselves? So for every grub we step on, 15 more will appear?"

"Sort of," he said. "There's a per-quadrant limit. If you kill all 5,000 of the grubs out there, 75,000 aren't going to appear."

"Do you know what the limit is?" I asked, looking at the map. The entire area blinked red, centered on us.

"Uh, yeah," he said. "You've already hit it. It's 5,000."

Fucking hell. "Is it like this everywhere? Across the whole dungeon?"

"It looks like it," Mordecai said. "It's to keep people from camping out in one area for too long. As long as you keep moving, it shouldn't be an issue."

CARL: Brandon, can you see this?

We'd set up the chat, but we hadn't really used it yet.

BRANDON AN: Loud and clear. You guys doing okay?
CARL: We have an issue. It's not a huge deal yet, but it will be
     soon. Let's get your folks moving toward the stairs now.
     We'll meet you in the hallway outside this quadrant.
BRANDON AN: 10-4. We're on our way. Wait until you see what
     we built.

They were barely three-quarters of a mile away, but with that crowd, it'd take a couple hours at least for them to get set up.

"Come on, Donut," I said. "We need to carve a hole back to the other team. At least these bastards are all the level two grubs."

Even Donut cringed the moment I said that out loud.

WE STARTED BY TOSSING FIREBOMBS IN THE HALLS, THEN MOVING forward, but after a while I realized it was just a waste of good moonshine. The level twos by themselves were literally harmless. I could pick one up and put it on my lap, and it didn't do anything. They were large with scary-looking mandibles, but they didn't bite or attack or anything. They just sort of squeaked and wriggled. And for every one we killed, we were just generating another. Plus, if we didn't properly destroy the body, we were increasing the chance of getting these guys to level up.

The problem was they were so thick in some places, it was impossible not to step on them with my bare feet, crunching them down. I tried my best to avoid them, but for every one I killed, I smeared down with my foot, crunching until the X went away on the map. The moment it died, its friends all turned on it, taking bites from its body. Even when I completely destroyed it, they continued to chew and lap up the remains. I took that as an ominous sign.

If I had to step on more than two or three grubs in a hallway, I tossed a boom jug in behind us. Better safe than sorry.

"This is taking forever," Donut complained from my shoulder.

"We're almost there," I said, pushing a grub away with my foot. This last hallway was mostly clear. Only forty or so of them. Brandon and crew were making record time, he said. They were almost at the rendezvous.

Once we hit the main hallway, we were all going straight to the stairwell. I plotted a path starting a few alleyways north, so we only needed to get them through a pair of grub-infested intersections. As long as we moved relatively quickly, this would work.

And once they were down the stairs, we'd carve our way north, punching back into the neighborhood with the danger dingoes and kobolds. From there we'd head back to the safe room, watch the evening's show, sleep, and then hop on the chopper and spend the rest of the time grinding away in different neighborhoods until it was time to hit the stairs. Hopefully we'd find a different exit, but if not, we'd come back and firebomb our way to the stairwell here.

DONUT: CARL, PEOPLE ARE GETTING BORED WITH THIS! MY
FOLLOWERS HAVEN'T GONE UP IN FIVE MINUTES.
CARL: For fuck's sake, Donut. Don't worry. I'm sure something
awful is going to happen any second.

We exited out into the main hallway. The moment we did, the grubs behind us seemed to lose interest in following. They just stopped, settling down. It was creepy as hell.

I saw the wall of blue dots coming down the hallway. It looked as if it was all of them, so we went jogging toward them. I stopped and laughed the moment I saw the parade.

Imani and Chris were both wearing leather straps across their chests that I recognized as pig harnesses from the tuskling courtesans. They strained as they pulled all of the others behind them.

They'd built a parade float. That's what it looked like. They'd taken the wheels from multiple wheelchairs that no longer had owners and affixed them to long pieces of wood. I had no idea where the wooden platforms had come from, but I knew Imani and Chris both were as obsessive about looting everything as I was. Using some of the goblin tools, they'd cobbled together the contraption.

Looking more closely, it was more like a train or a set of roller-coaster cars. There were a total of 39 people being pulled, most of them sitting upon their own chairs, which sat locked in place, two by two. The ones who normally used walkers sat cross-legged on the boards, watching wide-eyed as they were pulled along. The giant centipede was ten cars long, and each section held four people. The individual cars were attached to one another by a set of glowing metal chains. The same chain attached Chris and Imani to the rest of the train. It seemed it was one chain running from Chris through all the cars and back up to Imani, about 300 feet long.

"It's more maneuverable than it looks," Brandon said, jogging up. "We made it from the safe room to the hallway easily. Chris says once they get going, he barely feels the weight. The only problem is that the cars are too wide to fit through the safe room doors, so we have to stage it all in the hallway. There were a lot of those grubs, but we ran right over them."

"Where'd you get that chain?"

"Imani had a scroll called *Yog's Special Chain* or something like that. She just got it from some gold box. I don't know what for. She could pick any length up to something crazy, like 1,000 feet. It's light as a feather, but the chain only lasts for 30 hours. This whole thing was her idea, though Chris designed it. He even added ramps so they can get on and off easily."

"Hey, you have an extra star by your name," I said.

He nodded. "You know the Mind Horrors? The floating brain

things? Yolanda, Chris, and I went to clear them out. I remembered what you said about needing to train, so I figured we better. Yolanda would shoot them from down the hallway, deflating them before they could hurt us. The boss room was this abandoned warehouse thing. The boss was a giant blimp. We took it out pretty easily thanks to Yolanda. That's also where we got all this wood."

"Did it come out of its room?" I gave him a quick recap of what had happened with Krakaren.

"Christ, dude. Our boss battle was much easier. It never left his lair."

They were lucky to be alive, but I was glad they'd spent the time training themselves. Yolanda was now level nine, equal with both the brothers. Imani was still level 11, and she didn't have the extra bronze star.

"Imani didn't go with you?" I asked.

"No," Brandon said. "Someone had to stay with the residents."

"Any sign of Agatha?" I asked.

"Not a one," he said. "But with these grubs, I'm not surprised. They devour everything. We saw a few level threes on our way up here."

"Yeah, we need to get moving," I said. I pointed to an alleyway. "Guys, down that way," I called to Imani and Chris. They nodded and turned.

"I see a safe room down that way. What's in there?" Brandon asked.

"I don't know," I said. "We haven't checked that one out yet."

This hallway was only a few meters from the edge of the quadrant. It bordered the one with the kobolds, whom we hadn't yet seen. I kept a wary eye out for dingoes. Some of the residents clapped their hands with delight as we turned into the hallway. Mrs. McGibbons, the one who earlier wanted to watch *Divorce Court*, looked down at me as they passed. She was on the very last train car, this one only carrying three riders. She was the only one on the platform in a wheelchair. The other two were men with walkers, both sitting down.

The name over the woman said **Crawler #12,330,800.** "**Elle McGib.**"

"Hi, Carl," she said.

"Hi, Mrs. McGibbons. You remembered my name today," I said, moving to walk alongside the train.

"This reminds me of the tunnel of love," she said. "Back in my time, my Barry and I used to always go to the carnival. We'd eat the cotton candy and throw darts at the balloons. We'd go in the tunnel of love. Back then it was a boat. I'd let him touch my boobs, but only on the outside of my sweater."

I laughed.

"I loved my Barry, but he wasn't the prettiest man to look at. If you were in the tunnel of love with me, I'd have let you do more than touch them on the outside of my clothes."

"Uh," I said. "Thank you?" I couldn't think of a better response. The old woman cackled. Behind her, Yolanda barked with laughter.

"You've been hit on twice now," Donut said. "Once by a meth-addled goblin shaman and once by Abraham Lincoln's grandmother. I can't wait to see who you attract next. Five gold coins says it's some sort of bog witch with a beard."

Yolanda had told me earlier that this woman was 99 years old. I looked up at her. Ninety-nine years. She'd lived an entire life. Had a husband, whom she'd clearly loved. It seemed obscene that she'd be here in this place. I thought of the others who'd spent their final hours in a safe room, singing. *We should have made them all stay. This isn't a kindness, keeping them safe.*

Donut jumped from my shoulder and landed on the woman's lap. The cat's crupper and butterfly talisman jingled when she landed.

"Oh, hello, pretty kitty," the woman said. She started petting the cat. Donut purred loudly.

"Bring that pussy over here," one of the men said. He laughed lewdly. The man seemed even older than Mrs. McGibbons. He wore a Bengals hat too small for his bulbous head.

"Don't be crude, Jack," Yolanda said.

I moved forward to walk alongside Brandon, Chris, and Imani, keeping my eye on the map. Yolanda kept up the rear, walking with her bow at the ready. "We're taking a left two intersections down, right past that safe room. We'll have to cross through an infested area, but I'll firebomb it."

The mass of red dots was already starting to shift toward us. Thankfully they were painfully slow. I could take a nap before they'd reach this hall.

"Carl, thank you," Brandon said. "You are helping us to your own detriment. You are a good man."

I smiled. "If we get to the point where we don't help each other anymore, that's when we stop being human." I felt something catch in my throat, and I coughed.

> **ZEV (ADMIN):** Carl, that was great. Can you say that for me again, but this time, don't cough.

I stopped dead. My neck tingled with goose bumps. I knew we were being watched and followed, but having someone actually comment in my mind was one of the most unnerving sensations I'd ever felt.

> **CARL:** Are you kidding me with this? No, I'm not going to say it again. Have you been watching this whole time?
>
> **ZEV (ADMIN):** You and my other clients. This save-the-elderly storyline is playing great with most viewers. That said, about 20% of the focus group thinks you're wasting time and being stupid. "Deadweight," I think was the term some of them have used. But most of them understand what you're doing. Donut is right, however. It's a little dry. Maybe you can . . . Oh shit, oh fuck. Carl, Donut. Run. Run to the safe room now.

"No, Jack, Jack, no!" Yolanda called.

I turned to see Jack, Cincinnati Bengals hat sitting cockeyed on his head. He'd stood to his full height, using the wheelchair with Mrs. McGibbons and Donut as a brace. His pants were down to his ankles, dick out pissing directly on the wall.

38

THE NEXT SEVERAL SECONDS SEEMED TO HAPPEN IN SLOW MOTION. Donut was the first to react. She jumped up, claws out, as if she meant to decapitate the elderly man. She pulled back at the last moment, instead pushing off his shoulder and sailing through the air, flying until she landed three platforms down.

Yolanda also reacted, just a fraction of a moment behind Donut. She didn't pull her attack. An arrow sprouted from the side of Jack's skull, pinning the hat to his head. She'd been forced to shoot him, but it didn't matter. She'd reacted too late. The now-dead man fell off the trailer and to the ground, still pissing in death. The curved pee stain on the dungeon wall started to sizzle and boil. Smoke rose directly from the point of contact. I realized I was running, running *toward* the back of the train. Behind me, Brandon shouted. The safe room was only a hundred feet away. Chris and Imani were already picking up speed. The second man on the last car, Randall, went flying off the train as it lurched forward. He hit the ground with a loud, painful *crunch*, his walker flying over his head just as the monster appeared.

"Holy fuck!" I cried. "Donut, run!" I continued to sprint toward the thing.

Purple-and-black smoke kept hissing and spitting from the wet stain on the wall. The monster coalesced, coming into existence ten feet behind Yolanda and Randall, just above the prone form of the now-dead Jack. Yolanda hit the monster with two arrows, and the shafts just shattered against the smoke. It didn't even form a health bar, indicating she'd done no damage whatsoever.

The thing was fifteen feet tall and just as wide, made of fulminating, sizzling black-and-purple smoke. It had six legs, each gleaming with obsidian claws the size of rakes. The claws seemed to be the only corporeal parts of its body. The legs were all the same, but the two forward claws were longer, fingerlike with extra joints. A flickering horned skull sat amongst the smoky mass, its eyes made of glowing red fire that poured smoke. It was the skull of some sort of animal, maybe a colossal badger, but with curved goatlike horns. It roared, and the ground shook.

Rage Elemental—Level 93.
    The first recorded summoning of a Rage Elemental, blah, blah, blah. If you are reading this, you likely don't give a shit about the monster's (rather interesting and tragic) history. You're probably running. It's not going to matter. The almost-indestructible Rage Elemental is said to only dissipate after it has claimed 666 souls.
    In other words, you are fucked. Absolutely bite-the-pillow fucked.

A magic missile bounced off the monster's head, and a health bar appeared for a half second before disappearing. *It's self-healing.*

I came skidding to a stop as the train rocketed past me. Donut landed on my shoulder. She was screaming something about not running unless I ran, too. Yolanda stood over the fallen form of Randall. The creature was still growing, the last of the black-and-purple mist twirling around it.

"Fog!" I yelled. Donut, who had read my mind, activated her scroll of *Confusing Fog* at the same moment.

The monstrosity finished forming just as the wall of fog billowed into the hallway. The creature fell to all six legs. The monster spun toward us, impossibly fast, its movements cleaving through the cloud like a boat cutting through waves. It ripped at the dead form of Jack, and the man's body shredded. It leaped forward, clawing at Yolanda and Randall.

I never got to know Yolanda Martinez as much as I would've liked to.

But I didn't have to know her very well to know who she was. I knew she was a quiet, sweet woman who'd been a nurse her entire life. She'd worked sixty hours a week for years to pay for her son to go to college. Her husband had owned a landscaping company. At only four feet eleven, the woman had a presence much bigger than her stature suggested. There was a warmth about her, something I'd never felt as a kid. Just being in her presence imparted a feeling of longing in me, something difficult to describe. Like I wished I could relive my childhood, but this time, I'd have her as my mother, and she would have never, ever left me.

When the apocalypse came for Yolanda, she didn't once waver in her dedication to her patients. She was quick to laugh, quick to smile.

And even though Yolanda Martinez was just as terrified as the rest of us, she stood her ground against a force she couldn't possibly hold back.

She lived her entire life as a hero. She died as one, too.

One moment they were there; the next they were gone. Through the still-developing cloud of *Confusing Fog*, the monster's claws ripped forward, cutting through the nurse and the elderly man as if they weren't even there. Yolanda's body disintegrated in a red cloud of ribbonlike flesh like she was a knitted sweater that had been unraveled all at once.

The monster didn't even break stride; it came for us despite the fog. It swung a mighty claw just as I smashed down on *Protective Shell*.

The monster flew back, as if it was a charging dog that had reached the end of its leash. The transparent glowing semicircle shell spread around me, completely filling this section of the hallway, floor to ceiling.

The rage elemental hissed and squealed with fury as it went flying back, skidding. It jumped up, charging again. Its badger head made it through the shield, but the moment its giant claws touched the force field, it rebounded yet again. It seemed the sharp tips of the monster's claws couldn't make it through the protection.

"Holy shit!" I cried. I hadn't expected that to work. "Run!" Donut leaped off my shoulder as I turned and rushed toward the others, who were struggling to get everyone into the safe room. The individual cars were too wide for the entrance. Imani and Chris were bodily pulling people off their chairs and tossing them into the open door.

The round shield remained firmly in place, and I felt an odd *pop* in my ears as we left its area of effect. The spell was only going to last 20 seconds, and I'd already wasted five of them being dumbfounded.

About halfway to the door, the ground disappeared underneath me. At least that's what I thought had happened, at first. I fell, but I fell upward, crashing into the ceiling. A few feet in front of me, Donut flipped in midair, deftly landing upside down.

In front of me, the very last train car flew upward, and the remaining resident—Mrs. McGibbons—cried out as she also slammed up into the top of the hallway, wheelchair crashing upon her like she'd been dumped face-first down into a hole.

My shoulder crunched, but I slammed a health potion before the pain could hit me.

Gravity had been reversed. The elemental had cast the spell, but it hadn't reached all the way to the safe room door. That last platform, connected by Imani's magic chain, remained attached to the rest of the cars, and it dangled upward, having dislodged its only remaining rider.

I didn't look back. I pulled myself to my feet and kept running, but now I was upside-down, running on the ceiling of the hallway. We rushed toward the crumpled form of Mrs. McGibbons, who groaned and rolled onto her back, feebly pushing the wheelchair off herself. It rolled a few feet forward and reached the edge of the spell's effect. It clattered to the ground. She opened her eyes, and upon seeing that she was now stuck to the roof of the hallway, she started to cry out in fear. Her health was deep in the red.

"I got you," I said, picking her up. I pulled her over my shoulder like a sack.

Ahead of me, Chris and Imani were ushering the last of the residents into the room. I could see Brandon just inside the door, moving them out of the way. Imani was screaming Yolanda's name.

Donut took a step toward the door, and she plummeted off the ceiling, also having reached the edge of the spell's effect. She, once again, landed easily.

"Be careful, Carl!" she called up to me.

"Get the wheelchairs. Then get inside!" I cried as I pulled a health potion and shoved it in Mrs. McGibbon's hand. "Drink this."

I anticipated where the line of gravity was, and I tried a desperate flip maneuver in an attempt not to be upside down when I fell. It didn't work. I shielded the crying woman's body as I landed, once again, in a painful heap on the ground right next to the wooden platform. I groaned and smashed down on my own *Heal* spell.

Behind me, the rage elemental roared as the spell dissipated. It rocketed down the hall at us, claws raking up stones as it ran. It ran on its four back legs and reached forward with its two forward arms, which somehow made the beast seem even more horrifying.

"*Shit.*" I scrambled to my feet. Donut hit it with another magic missile before turning and bolting toward the door. Chris and Imani pulled their last resident in.

I ran. The ground shook as if a locomotive was bearing down on me. Ten feet. Five feet. One foot.

I jumped at the door, banging into the frame and ricocheting inside just as the monstrosity's forward claws swiped at me, missing by millimeters. It squealed in frustration, continuing its forward momentum as it slid down the hallway.

I had a quick sense of déjà vu, of the goblin murder dozer also missing me by inches.

I handed Mrs. McGibbons to Brandon, pulled a boom jug, and returned to the hallway. I lit it and tossed it at the backside of the still-turning elemental before I jumped back into the room and slammed the door.

We could hear the monster's screams through the thick walls. It made a sound that was part pain, part rage, part the end of the fucking world. I knew there was no way I could've really hurt it, but I felt a wave of satisfaction at that horrific, penetrating sound.

A moment later, the door pulsed, creaking worryingly as the elemental attempted to get in. It screamed and thrashed and pounded, throwing itself against the impenetrable door with all its might.

"Jesus," I muttered, reaching down to grab my legs. I closed my eyes, unable to get the sight of Yolanda and Randall out of my head. "Jesus," I repeated, out of breath.

I turned to survey the room. We stood in what appeared to be a dusty, no-way-they-passed-the-health-inspection chicken restaurant. **BIG SHOT CHICKEN**, the sign said. I'd never heard of it. A Bopca Protector stood behind the counter, looking distastefully at the large crowd.

Mrs. McGibbons hadn't taken the potion I'd given her, but she still clutched it in her hand. I watched as Brandon helped her drink it down. She continued to cry as her health rose.

Most of the residents were on the ground, weeping for help. They'd been savagely tossed into the room. Imani, tears on her cheeks, was helping them one by one to the booths so they could sit and recover, administering healing potions to those who needed them. Donut had saved several wheelchairs, but there was no way we had enough now. Chris, his head low, turned to also help. Donut jumped to my shoulder, and her whole body was shaking.

"Fucking Jack," Brandon said, growling the words. "He knew. We explained it to him."

Zev's message echoed in my head. This was a mistake. Helping these people. *All we are doing is hindering our own training and delaying their inevitable deaths.* It would've been kinder to have left them on the first floor rather than subject them to this terror.

I looked up at the screens.

Time to Recap Episode: 1 hour, 40 minutes.
  Time to Level Collapse: 4 days, 20 hours.
  Remaining Crawlers: 1,033,992.

"You saved me," Mrs. McGibbons said, sitting up on the floor. Ninety-nine years old. I didn't think I'd ever met anyone that old before. Not a human, at least. "Thank you. Thank you so much."

I smiled weakly. "Of course," I said.

"Jack was always an ass," she continued. She made a clucking noise. "Poor Yolanda. She was such a good kid. And Randall. Dumb as a pigeon, that one. But he deserved better than that. At least it was quick."

"Do you think it's gonna leave?" Donut asked.

Behind me, the door continued to smash and rock under the onslaught of the screaming rage elemental.

39

Views: 212 Billion
Followers: 4.4 Billion
Favorites: 793 Million

THE RECAP EPISODE STARTED WITH A CLOSE-UP SHOT OF JACK'S
purple, veined, and uncircumcised dick, huge on the screen. The
headline screamed, "Trapped! Meadow Lark and The Royal Court of
Princess Donut in Peril!"

"Wow," Donut said. "Yours isn't nearly that big. Or oily-looking.
And it doesn't have that hat thing."

If looks could kill, the glare Imani shot at the cat would've ripped
her in two.

"Goddamnit, Donut," I muttered before realizing I'd said it.
"Not now."

The screen showed, in slow motion, Jack pulling it out, turning
to the wall, and peeing. It switched to Yolanda's horrified face, then
Donut leaping for him, claws out. It showed the arrow piercing him
right in the temple, the player-killer skull icon slowly starting to
form over Yolanda's head, and then the man falling from the
platform.

"I can't watch this," Imani said, getting up and turning away.

A "See what happens next!" appeared on the screen. Then the
show started. As promised, it was a compilation of people getting
surprised by bosses leaving their rooms. I noted two different scenes
with Krakaren bosses. The shots kept coming and coming of people
getting slaughtered.

I eased back in the chair and took a bite of fried chicken. A part of me registered that the food was downright delicious, but I could barely taste it. Donut sat at the table being lovingly groomed with her new brush by the Bopca Protector. The constitution buff had activated many minutes earlier, but she demanded he keep brushing.

This safe room, like the first one we'd visited, had 20 rooms for rent. They were still free on the second level. People slept in all twenty of them.

Outside, the rage elemental continued to scream and smash at the door. It hadn't let up, not for one second. The thing seemed to have an endless supply of energy.

I already had a plan on how to deal with it. I'd discussed it over chat with Donut. I'd have to wait at least a full Syndicate standard day—another 28 hours—before we'd be able to do it. That was how long the cooldown for my *Protective Shell* spell was.

The problem was, this plan required us to abandon team Meadow Lark. Not just the elderly folks. All of them. I sighed, unable to concentrate on the show.

Zev disappeared off the chat after the skirmish in the hallway. Donut, who'd apparently been chatting with her non-stop, was worried about the kua-tin. I didn't care. I was dreading our obligation to go on this talk show. We'd have to go on the show before we left here.

A wave of grubs descended upon us. I didn't know what was going to happen once they reached the hall with the rage elemental. I was hoping perhaps they'd distract the creature, cause it to wander off. I suspected we wouldn't get that lucky, but I had hope. Looking at the map, I guessed we'd find out just as the show ended.

Donut and I both received a pair of achievements after our fight with the rage elemental.

New achievement! What Goes Up . . .
    You have been struck with and survived the dreaded *Reverse Gravity* Spell. Well, you fared better than Albert II, the first Earth mammal to reach space alive. He was a rhesus monkey, in

case you're wondering. He went up just fine. He didn't stick the landing.

 Reward: You can now tell people you're more durable than a monkey named Albert.

New achievement! Like a Moth to the Flame.

You attacked and caused damage to a mob that is more than 75 levels above your own. The fact that you're reading this suggests you're the luckiest fucker in the dungeon. Just remember, luck goes both ways, like your mom.

Reward: You've received a Platinum Lucky Bastard Box!

Both of us received a similar item in the platinum box. It was a lottery scratch-off ticket, just like any scratcher ticket one could buy at a gas station or a liquor store. The tickets themselves were different. Donut's was red and green and had a small graphic of a troll-like creature throwing gold coins in the air. It was called **Dungeon Gold Rush**. She had six spots to scratch off. She immediately moved to scratch it, but received an error message telling her she couldn't use the ticket in a safe room. I made her hand it over so I could read the description.

Dungeon Gold Rush!

Scratch off one spot, and depending on the symbol revealed, your next attack against a mob will have varying effects! Guaranteed laughs! One-hour cooldown between scratches.

I flipped the little cardboard ticket over, and it revealed about twenty different symbols. Most of the results were good, like **Mob drops 5,000 coins** or **Damage against Mob is doubled**. But a few of the symbols offered some not-so-good choices. Like **Mob splits in two**. Or **Mob is invulnerable for 30 seconds**.

"Yeah, don't use this," I said. "Not until we talk about it some.

The last thing we need is you scratching off a symbol that'll quadruple the next mob's strength."

The cat sighed. "Or I can scratch off a symbol, and I will get 5,000 coins, Carl. Why must you always be so pessimistic?"

"Donut. Like it said, luck goes both ways. We'll talk about it later."

"Fine," she said. I placed the ticket in front of her, and she huffed as it disappeared into her inventory. "What does yours do?"

My ticket was the same size, but it only had five spots to scratch off. It was red on one side and pink on the other. A small cartoon dragon sat in the corner holding a spoon. The dragon's tongue was out, licking its lips. I read the description.

Fireball or Custard?

Scratch off a spot in the midst of battle, and this zany ticket casts a spell at the closest red-tagged mob! Each spot has a 50-50 chance. Will it cast a level 15 Fireball? Will it cast a glob of delicious, healing Strawberry Custard? Who knows! Either way, the results will be a hoot! Thirty-minute cooldown between scratches.

"I love custard!" Donut cried after I showed her the ticket. She looked up at the Bopca Protector, whose name was Qwist. "Get me custard."

"Yes, Princess. Right away, Princess. What flavor?" the Bopca asked.

Donut had finished the custard by the time the show premiered. She'd chosen strawberry, turned her nose up at it, and gone with vanilla. We watched now as the disaster-porno half of the show ended and the next part started. It was nothing new. The African warriors had finally run out of ammo. Several were using their AK-47s as clubs, but a few now had bows and arrows or swords. Lucia Mar was tearing her way through the dungeon. She had four player-killer skulls by her name now, but they didn't show why or how that had happened.

Interestingly, I noticed for the first time that neither of her rottweilers had any skulls or stars by their names. It was because they were pets, I realized. Donut had originally been listed as a pet, but she'd transformed into a crawler early on. Weird.

The crossbow-firing Valkyrie woman and her ever-growing crowd of female warriors were also killing their way through the dungeon. They'd named their group Brynhild's Daughters. The woman's name was Hekla, and the announcer gave a short history of her home country of Iceland. The AI was throwing loot at her to emphasize the Nordic shieldmaiden persona she was forming, including a ridiculous glittering breastplate that seemed more apt for the cover of a harem fantasy novel than appropriate dungeon armor.

"She's amazing," Donut whispered. "We should hook up with her group."

"Something tells me I wouldn't be too welcome," I said.

The show ended with a short description of the issues with the bathrooms and some bullshit explanation why they had been forced to implement the rage elemental trap.

"Yeah, because piss is worse than blood and guts and whatever that is that comes out of the grubs," I said.

It replayed the scene from the beginning of the episode with Jack whipping it out. It continued, showing Yolanda's death in gruesome slow-motion detail. It showed me flying up to the ceiling, then hopping to my feet and running upside down, *Matrix*-style. Then me picking Mrs. McGibbons up and making it into the room with a millisecond to spare. I jumped out of the room brandishing the boom jug.

The show paused, showing the recipe of the Carl's Jug O' Boom. My mug shot appeared briefly with **Added to the** *Dungeon Codex* stamped over it.

The scene resumed, showing me tossing the jug at the back of the monster before slamming the door. Its health plummeted almost

25%. The six-legged black-badger-skull thing screamed, momentarily stunned by the attack. It took a good ten seconds before it recovered, jumping up and resuming its attack against the door. It shrieked in earsplitting fury as it healed itself. The healing moved much more slowly, I noted, thanks to the napalm-like effect of the boom jug.

It ended with Donut saying, "Do you think it's gonna leave?"

The show snapped off, and nobody said anything.

"He really did have a weird-looking dick," Chris said after a moment.

Imani walked up to him, wrapped her arms against the large man, and started laughing and crying at the same time.

Hello, Crawlers,

Short message today. The dungeon is humming along nicely. Thanks again for your support. We have a lot of interest already in the new patron-bidding program. So please keep up the good work!

We have a few changes to announce.

If you've watched the recap episode that just aired, you can see our penalties regarding the bathrooms have been a rousing success. The penalties will remain in place for the remainder of this floor, but I'm happy to announce they will be removed upon the collapse of this floor. Thank you, everyone, for your cooperation.

The Satan's Lil' Hedgehogs mob has been removed and placed on a deeper floor. Their armor-piercing quill attack has been deemed too strong for this floor by the System AI. Apologies to all those affected. We've had a few complaints about the proliferation of the grub mobs. This is not a bug and is by design.

Finally, due to the abundance of crawlers camping in safe rooms upon the collapse of the first floor, we've been forced to make a difficult decision. From now on, all safe rooms and safe areas will close one hour prior to floor collapse. Any crawler

who is in a designated safe area will be teleported to just outside that area at one hour prior.

   As always, kill, kill, kill!

On the message board, a new timer appeared, just below the **Time
to Level Collapse** timer.

   Time to Safe Room Closure. It was one hour faster than the level
timer.

   I met eyes with Brandon, who looked stricken. At that moment
I knew he'd been thinking the same thing as me: that it was time to
just give it up.

   DONUT: Our views! Carl, our views!

Outside, the door stopped bashing itself in. It was oddly quiet. I
looked up at the minimap. The mass of grubs had reached the
hallway, and the elemental finally noticed them. It left the door and
tore through them as I watched. It followed the line of red dots
around the corner and disappeared down the hallway. I had a moment to think, *Shit, we should've been ready to run*, but it was over in
less than a minute. The thousands of red dots were just gone.

   The description stated the elemental dissipated after it claimed
666 souls, whatever that meant. I was hoping that the grubs counted
toward that number.

   They didn't.

   The elemental returned to the door, thrashing and smashing,
trying to get back in.

   If we had run, it would have followed us. Even if we'd used the
chopper, there was no way we'd have gotten away. Not unless we'd
split up and gone in different directions. And even then, it probably
would've gotten us.

   The map seemed to flicker for a moment, and a long line of X's
appeared where the grubs had all died. Already more red dots appeared, moving toward their fallen brothers and sisters.

On the map, near the stairs, just a quarter mile away, a group of fifteen red dots sat. I hadn't noticed them before. I hovered over the icons.

Grub—Pupa Stage.

A counter, currently at just under 10 hours, was ticking away next to their names.

I remembered the scene from the recap episode. The level 93 mob, after sliding down the hall, had been hurt by my boom jug. It'd taken almost a quarter of its life away before it healed itself.

Then I remembered something else. It was something Rory the shamanka, the one with all the piercings on her face, had told us. I hadn't thought much about it at the time. I looked down at Donut.

CARL: The plan has changed. We can't wait for my shield to cool down.

"Come on, Donut," I said out loud, pushing a table away in the corner of the restaurant. We were going to need a lot of space.

"What're you doing?" Brandon asked, standing from his table.

I pulled a bunch of items from my inventory, piling them on the floor. The round free weights clanged loudly as they hit the tiles.

"I need your help," I said.

40

WE STILL HAD SOME CANS OF AGATHA'S SPRAY PAINT, AND I PAINTED "Mother of All Bombs" on the side of the contraption.

It took us about five hours to finish building the launcher. Brandon pointed out MOAB actually stood for "Massive Ordnance Air Blast," but his brother said, "Don't be that guy."

"It doesn't matter," Brandon said. "The name is still wrong. When they say 'Mother of all bombs,' they mean one giant bomb. Not whatever this thing is. You should call it the Bomb Chicken or something."

"It's too late," I said, indicating the spray paint. "I've already named it. Besides, I like the name. It's a play on words."

"Well, I'm going to call it the Bomb Chicken whether you like it or not," Brandon declared.

I'd discovered something interesting while building the device. This should've been obvious earlier, but it hadn't even occurred to me. In the safe room, all of my sticks of dynamite were harmless. I could pull them out, and under status they had **Inert While in Safe Room**, followed by a parenthesis stating their real status. Their status still ticked down while being handled, and I didn't want to tempt fate enough to find out what would happen when that status reached zero, but I was relatively certain they wouldn't blow.

Brandon stepped back now, admiring our work.

"Do you really think this is going to kill it?" he asked, suddenly serious.

"Not a chance," I said. "That thing is level 93. It ain't going to like this too much, but there's no way it'll be enough. The babies will slow it down, though."

Brandon gave me a sour look. "If it's not going to kill it, then why are we doing this?"

"It's all part of the plan," I said.

"Wait. What, exactly, is the plan?" he asked. He waved at my contraption. "I thought this was the plan."

"Like I said, it's part of it, but it's not all of it. I can't tell you the rest," I said, pointing up at the ceiling, which had become the universal gesture for *The assholes are listening.*

Since this scheme involved using a dungeon exploit, I wanted to keep it in my head. Even Donut didn't know the full extent. Mordecai told us that the viewers couldn't see our private chats, but Borant and the dungeon AI could. I didn't want to risk them changing the rules on us at the last second.

Because that would really suck. Not that I'd live long enough to complain about it.

We needed to get safely into the hallway. So the first component of this insane scheme was also one of the most terrifying parts.

My first suggestion was to wait for the grubs to regroup and get close enough for the rage elemental to go hunting them again. But the grubs were painfully slow, and more and more of them were hitting the pupa stage, meaning they were no longer moving around.

Imani came up with a bold solution. "Why don't we just open the damn door?" she said.

This was hours ago, right when we started building the MOAB.

We all looked at each other. I immediately grasped what she was saying. The idea was horrifying, but she was right. We were in a safe room. Mobs would teleport away. Not far away, according to Mordecai, but they would still be ejected.

"Well, shit," I said, putting down my goblin riveter. "Maybe we don't need to build this thing at all."

So we tested it. We moved everyone to the other side of the restaurant, near the entrance to the sleeping chambers. I didn't know

340 of MATT DINNIMAN

what was trembling more, me or the door. If we were wrong about this . . .

I walked up, and I hesitantly reached for the exit. The moment I turned the handle, the door burst inward, and a giant claw raked at me, coming at my face as I flew back into the room.

Thwum. The sound of the monster teleporting away was odd, like that of an electrical generator turning on.

"Holy crap, that worked," I said, sitting up. My eyes searched the map, looking for it. I didn't see it anywhere.

But a moment later, my relief turned to dread as I saw the dot rocketing toward us. It'd come from the main hallway. "Shit, it's really booking it. It remembers where we are."

"Keep the door open," Imani said. "See if the dungeon sends it farther away this time. Or if it learns."

It was maybe 90 seconds before it entered our hallway again. It killed any grubs it passed, but it seemed to ignore the ones in the pupa stage. It roared and shrieked, came to the door, and once again tried to swipe at me.

Again, it teleported away. This time it came from another hallway down, but it appeared to have still been teleported out into the main hallway. We tried it several times. Each time, the elemental took anywhere from 75 to 120 seconds to return. It was clear the monster was unintelligent, nothing more than the single-minded embodiment of rage. We eventually closed the door, not wanting to create any more grub corpses.

I sighed, going back to work on the MOAB.

Now, hours later, it was finally time to put my idea to the test. I was less confident about this than I was with the whole portable-fortress idea. That time I knew we faced a mob meant to be killed. This was different. This was something meant as a punitive action, a punishment. It wasn't meant to be fair, to be survivable.

The chopper hummed merrily away, aimed directly at the exit to the chamber. With Donut's sidecar, it was too big to get through the door. We'd been forced to remove it. Instead, we added the newly built bike trailer, affixing the tall MOAB to it and adding the equally tall seat for Donut behind the launcher. She'd have to duck in order for us to leave the room. She sat there now, facing backward, a look of grim determination on her fuzzy face, like a tail gunner in a WWII bomber.

"I think I like Bomb Chicken better, too," Donut announced.

"Too late," I said. I nodded at Imani, who stood at the door, ready to pull it open.

"Okay," she said. "I'll count down from three."

DONUT: EVERYONE IN THE UNIVERSE IS WATCHING THIS. I JUST HIT ONE TRILLION VIEWS, CARL. ONE TRILLION.

"Focus, Donut," I said, not bothering to use the chat.

"One!" Imani yanked the door open. The massive, terrifying rage elemental lunged and, as always, teleported away. The space where it had occupied shimmered, crackling like superheated air.

I pushed hard on the pedals of the bike, and we rushed into the hallway. Everything out here was blackened and turned to ash. It smelled like burning garbage, reminding me of the Hoarder's chamber. There was no sign of the train cars or the remaining wheelchairs and walkers that had been abandoned. The only thing that had survived was the 300-foot-long length of glittering magical chain, which I had grabbed earlier.

Behind me, Imani slammed the door. I pedaled down the hall, turning the throttle. The trailer was built using broken hunks of wood, and the spare chopper wheels we'd looted from the goblins. I could barely feel its weight. It squeaked loudly, but it didn't bounce under the press of the MOAB. We passed the nearby intersection and furiously increased speed until we reached the next one down, another two hundred meters away. We angled ourselves so we faced this new hallway, and we waited.

"Here it comes," Donut said a moment later. The dot appeared, and the elemental rushed down the distant hall, moving like an Earth-destroying meteor sent from the heavens.

"As soon as it rounds the curve, we go," I said. We had to make sure it saw us. If it stopped at the door again, we'd have to loop around to gain its attention, using the closer hallway. I didn't want to do that. The fewer corners we had to take with this trailer, the better.

Far down the hallway, a little more than a quarter of a mile away, it appeared, running full tilt.

I didn't have to worry about whether or not it was going to see us. It saw. The horned badger skull skidded to a stop, looking in our direction. It shrieked with indignation and resumed its gallop, headed straight at us.

Holy shit, that thing is fast. I pumped my legs.

"Go! Go!" Donut cried. Thanks to my Chopper Pilot skill and the help of the throttle, we could reach top speed in seconds. It still felt as if we weren't moving at all. The bike could go about 25 miles per hour before it got too hot. The elemental was like a cheetah. Unimpeded, it would run us down in seconds.

We hurtled down the hallway. "Fire the first baby!" I cried.

Brandon was correct that the title MOAB was misleading.

The apparatus wasn't a bomb at all, but a device designed to launch bombs. Multiple types of bombs.

"It's the bombs' mother," I'd said. "Get it? And we can name the bombs its babies."

None of them had been impressed.

"You need to stick to punching things and blowing them up," Donut had said. "Leave the creative to me."

The device wasn't complicated, but it had to be precisely built, especially here with the bumpy hallways. It was little more than a curved, ski-jump-like ramp made from a pair of spare-part chopper wheel wells, with a pair of half-pipe channels at the end to keep the "babies" steady, and tiny shock-absorbing front-wheelchair coasters for the very end of the ramp, keeping the end of the conduit inches from the ground.

As a kid, I'd had something similar for my Matchbox cars. You dropped the cars into the top, and gravity took care of the rest. They'd plummet down the waterslide-like ramp, gaining speed, hitting the ground at full throttle. If you built the ramp correctly, especially the part at the end, the cars would ease onto the flat surface, still accelerating by the time they were halfway across the room.

It'd taken us several hours to get this correct. We had very little space to test this in, but thanks to the know-how from Brandon and Chris, I was confident that the babies would work as intended.

We knew this monster had at least two attacks. The claws and the *Reverse Gravity* spell. We also knew that the *Gravity* spell had a somewhat limited range. So in order to get to our destination, we needed to keep the elemental far away long enough to get there.

"Bombs away!" Donut cried. She pulled the wheeled, back-heavy bomb from her inventory. It fit perfectly into the grooves, and she gave it a nudge. It rocketed down the ramp, hit the ground with a bump, and continued straight. From our perspective, it zoomed away. It didn't rear up like I had feared.

"Brandon, you beautiful son of a bitch!" I yelled as I watched the first bomb roll away over my shoulder.

I'd wanted to put the weight in the front, but Brandon had insisted that was a mistake, that the bombs would flip. Instead, he'd drawn with his finger on the table, explaining how to weigh them down. He'd then gone off on some Isaac Newton math bullshit. He'd said the babies wouldn't go as far back as they would've if I'd been sitting still. He talked about some *MythBusters* episode where they shot a soccer ball out the back of a moving car, and the ball had dropped straight to the ground. I told him I didn't care as long as the bombs were far away from the chopper when they went off.

After several frustrating failed attempts to automate the launching process, we'd come up with a solution. Once Donut was seated at the correct height, she could pull the "babies" out of her inventory, and they'd emerge right on the platform. Each bomb was the size of a snowboard, but it was shaped and weighted like a champion pinewood derby car. Wheels had suddenly become a precious commodity, but we had something almost as good: free weights. A lot of free weights of different sizes. When tightened and greased properly, they became very effective wheels.

This first baby—"Baby Uno"—was different than the others. It was heavier and bigger. It contained three boom jugs, a clay jug filled with nothing but goblin oil, and a small jar of gunpowder. The last of my hobgoblin pus sat in the middle of the bomb, and I held the magical trigger into my hand now, waiting for Donut's signal.

We had four types of babies: baby uno, boom jar babies, shredder babies, and, finally, oh shit babies.

The oh shit babies consisted of two boom jars with a full-sized gunpowder satchel wrapped in dynamite. Those remained in my own inventory, too dangerous for Donut to touch. They were a last resort, and I prayed we wouldn't have to use them here.

I watched the red dot stream down the hallway, approaching the corner. Far behind us, the heavy bomb coasted to a stop.

"Hang on," I cried, and I jammed on the detonator. There was a maddening five-second delay. I turned my attention forward. "Oh fuck."

We hit the first intersection, filled with the grub pupae, a dozen of them. "What the hell, man?" I cried, dodging the giant mounds. I wasn't expecting them to be this damn big. Donut cried out as the trailer bumped ominously. Each mound was about the size of a human standing erect. Red and yellow lights flashed underneath the wet, pulsating sacs.

"Drop the bola!" I yelled.

We had two levers next to Donut's chair. The red one and the black one. We'd originally designed these as bomb launchers before we gave up, deciding to just use the more stable inventory system. But we'd still built two chambers on either side of the MOAB. Donut pulled the black lever, and the bottom of the chamber slid away.

Imani's chain, with heavy weights at either end, dropped away, snaking through the chamber. The monster, hopefully, would get its legs tangled in the thin unbreakable link. It probably would only impede it for a second or two, but every second counted.

Behind us, the bomb detonated with a ripping, screaming roar. Dust cascaded off the ceiling. It had blown a half second too late, hitting the monster in the back. I didn't dare look behind me, but I could see on the map it had propelled the monster halfway down the hall, even closer to us. The red dot of the elemental rolled to a stop.

"Drop the boom babies," I cried. This next hall was filled with grubs, mostly level threes, which I hadn't yet fought. These were larger, about twice as big as the regular grubs. They had long, pointed tails that they whipped ineffectively up at us as we passed. The level threes were too big to just run over with the chopper, and I had to dodge them.

Cow-Tailed Brindle Grub. Level 3.
    The final form before they hit the pupa stage, the Cow-Tailed Brindle Grub is finally able to defend itself, kind of like the way a toddler holding a plastic baseball bat is able to defend himself.

"The cars are going to hit the grubs," Donut cried. "They're in the way!"

"Do it anyway," I yelled, increasing speed. Below me, the chopper became dangerously hot.

"Bombs away," Donut cried. I heard the distinctive clack of the bomb's wheels locking in place. The torch sizzled as Donut activated it, and it rolled away down the launcher ramp.

Sure enough, the wheeled bomb hit a group of grubs and flipped, crashing and then detonating. A wave of heat washed over me, but I didn't take any damage. We were going fast enough. Barely. The entire hallway lit with blue flames.

"Yes!" Donut cried. "Burn, baby, burn!"

Farther behind, the elemental resumed its pursuit. It stopped yet again a moment later. It'd been ensnared by the chain. The monster roared in anger, shaking the very foundation of the world.

"Away," Donut called, dropping another boom baby. Then another. Then a third. We continued to carpet-bomb the hallway behind us. If the jugs didn't ignite on their own, Donut hit them with a low-powered magic missile once we were far away enough. She only had to do that a couple times. Most of the cars hit grubs and flipped.

"Whoa!" Donut yelled.

The whole back of the trailer flew up into the air, almost knocking me from my seat. But it crashed down a moment later. A just-launched boom baby flew into the ceiling and exploded.

The elemental had cast its spell, but we'd been too far away. Behind us, the top of the chamber erupted in flames. My head and back burned, and I took a small amount of damage. Donut cried out in pain. She healed herself a moment later with her spell.

"Hold on," I cried. We were almost there, but I had a sharp left coming up. I could see this hallway was filled with more of the pupae. "Like we talked about! Drop a shredder, wait a second, then do another boom."

We screeched around the corner, the trailer skidding. I had to jerk around a set of pupae rising like stalagmites. We'd only made a few of the gunpowder babies, but I'd made them for this part of the stretch. I had no idea if this would work, but I figured it couldn't hurt.

Donut released the gunpowder and shrapnel-filled bomb. "The shredders." For these, we used a long length of wick. I had to light wicks using a lighter, but thanks to Donut's quadruped status, the system allowed her to light them the same way she lit torches, with a mental click. She launched the massive shrapnel grenade. The long wick trailed sparks, like the tail of a rat. The baby crashed into one of the pupa mounds and fell on its side. A moment later, it blew, ripping the pupa to shreds.

I hazarded a glance over my shoulder, just long enough to see several human-sized, hornet-like creatures vomit out of the sacs. The uncooked monsters hit the ground and started convulsing.

I was hoping if I injured the chrysalis sacs, the monsters would come out, and the elemental would waste a valuable second or two ripping them to shreds.

We filled the last stretch of hallway with moonshine and fire. The elemental seemed to be moving more cautiously, but it continued to follow. Ahead, the stairwell materialized.

A warning appeared, blinking ominously just below the handlebars.

Goblin Copper Chopper—Boiler Breach Imminent.

"Goddamnit," I growled. I'd pushed it too hard. We had 15 seconds. I tried to remember which of the valves to turn to release the pressure. I couldn't.

"Fuck it," I said, increasing the speed.

"I thought we were going to the other safe room!" Donut cried. "We're not going down the stairs, are we?"

We entered the large round room. The stairwell loomed before us, a hole in the ground with a bright light shining directly up into the air. All around us, pupae pulsed, most of them ringing the walls. There were dozens of them now. All had timers over their heads, some of them only at a few hours.

The actual stairs faced the wrong direction, but that was okay. There was no railing or barrier. This was nothing but a hole in the ground, as wide as one of the tunnels, just like it had been on the surface.

"Oil slick! Then jump," I cried.

"Jump? Are you crazy!"

"Goddamnit, Donut. Do it!"

She pulled the red lever, and the bottom of the second chamber fell away. Champagne-colored oil sprayed onto the floor.

"Jump," I cried. Donut and I both leaped from the fast-moving vehicle. It continued its forward trajectory, spilling oil onto the rocky ground, plummeting into the deep stairway hole. The chopper disappeared from view. It crunched, followed by a relatively small explosion. Black smoke billowed into the air.

"What did you do that for?" Donut yelled as we both scrambled to our feet.

"Get your *Puddle Jumper* spell ready," I said. I pointed behind us, at the far end of the distant hallway, the opposite direction we'd come. Mordecai's guild room was just around the corner from there. "Send us there. Cast it when I tell you."

"Okay," she said, her voice filled with uncertainty. "Don't forget, it's ten seconds!"

The elemental had, indeed, stopped to eviscerate the hornet creatures in the hall, giving me just enough time to think about how much of a crazy asshole I was. *The stairs are right there. We can just go down and be safe. If this doesn't work, you are dead.*

I stood right at the edge of the hole.

"Cast now!" I cried.

Why not? I thought, and I pulled one of the oh shit babies from my inventory and gently placed it down on the ground in front of us. It sat there like a giant skateboard. Two boom jars, gunpowder, and a ring of dynamite.

Nine seconds.

"It's coming!" Donut screamed, her voice more terrified than I ever heard. She leaped to my shoulder.

Eight seconds.

In front of us, the rage elemental emerged from the billowing smoke of the hall. It was a beast from hell, huge. Terrifying. A length of chain was still attached to its back leg. To my surprise, the monster's health was in the red. Barely in the red, but it had been more hurt than I expected. It saw us, and it paused.

Five seconds.

It bellowed, long and hard.

I looked up, for the first time, and I realized the ceiling of this chamber, like the borough boss room on the floor above, was very, very high. If it cast *Reverse Gravity* now . . .

Three seconds.

It charged.

Two seconds.

"Stay with me," I said.

It passed the threshold of the room, and the moment its six legs hit the floor, it started to slide on the oil slick. It barely seemed to notice. It roared as it rocketed toward us, forward fingers ready to slash. I remembered what it did to Yolanda, unraveling her.

We disappeared, reappearing about 500 feet away, down the hall. A horrific, indignant shriek filled the dungeon, followed by the distinctive whoosh of a big-ass explosion. I hit the ground and covered Donut, but it was okay. The bomb was deep in the hole when it went off, and we were far away.

A moment passed. I watched the minimap, looking for signs that the monster had survived.

The dot was gone. Absolute silence followed. My stomach heaved, an aftereffect of the sudden teleportation.

Relief washed over me. I sat down right there on the floor. My heart, which had been oddly calm throughout, was now a jackhammer. My arms felt numb, tingling with the overdose of adrenaline. My entire body trembled.

A moment later, Donut cried in outrage, "We didn't get any experience! Carl, you broke the game!"

"We didn't get any experience because we're not the ones who killed it."

"What?" Donut said. "I don't understand."

I remembered what Rory, the goblin shamanka, had told us. It'd only been a few days ago, but it felt like a lifetime. *If we climb down the stairs, we die. You get halfway down, and your body just dissolves. I've seen it myself.*

Mordecai had said something similar once, too. Mobs who dared to attempt to descend didn't teleport away. They died. We'd tricked the monster into the hole. Once it was in there, the dungeon followed its own rules, and it dissolved the elemental.

Unfortunately, the system didn't look too kindly on what we'd done. We hadn't been awarded experience for the kill. I'd received a couple achievements, but not many.

But that was okay. We were still alive. I took in the mass of red grub dots and X's littering the map. I felt as if I'd been awake for two days straight. I groaned, pulling myself to my feet. We still had a lot of work to do.

CARL: Brandon. Get your people to the stairs. Do it now. The way is safe, but it won't be for long.

41

I STILL HAD PLENTY OF MOONSHINE LEFT, AND DONUT AND I SPENT the hour torching all the pupae in the large room. I looked up at the map. There was no way we could get to them all. We were going to have to hightail it out of here.

With the unfortunate destruction of the chopper, our travel options were now limited. I had enough crap in my massive inventory to probably build another one, but I didn't know what I was doing with the boiler part of the mechanism. Hopefully we could find another set of goblins to help us. Or better yet, find something more reliable.

About forty minutes after we killed the elemental, the tattered remains of Meadow Lark entered the chamber. Brandon, Chris, and Imani had built a second, less elegant transportation system. There were 36 residents left, and they were piled into three separate shopping-cart-like contraptions built with chopper wheels and hunks of wood. Chris and Imani pushed the two larger "people buckets" as Brandon called them. This time, both of them strained with the effort. Brandon, whose strength was nowhere near the others', also awkwardly pushed a group of six people into the room.

"We didn't need your directions," Brandon said. "There's a long trail of scorched hallway that leads directly to this hole." He paused.

"There are a lot of those chrysalis things out there. You sure you don't just want to come with us?"

"I'm sure," I said. I looked into the smoking hole. "Do me a favor, though, and pick up anything you find down there. There probably isn't much left."

He nodded. I reached out to shake his hand, and he pulled me into a hug. "You two take care of yourselves, okay?"

I grinned. "You do the same."

I said my goodbyes to Chris and Imani. I found Donut on the lap of Mrs. McGibbons, purring away.

"Barry?" she asked as I walked up. "Barry, where are we?"

"We're in the dungeon, Mrs. McGibbons. It's me, Carl. You're going down to the next floor."

She looked at me, her eyes registering confusion. Once again, I felt a wave of doubt wash over me. Was this the right thing? What else could we do?

"The dungeon?" she asked. "Like a sex thing?"

"I don't know if I'm ever going to see you again," I said, kneeling down. She sat in the people bucket, looking about, eyes wide. "I wanted to say goodbye."

She reached up and touched my cheek. At that moment, she looked every day of her 99 years. Her hands were worryingly cold. "We should have had children, Barry. I wish I hadn't talked you into working so hard."

I grasped her hand. "It's okay. It's going to be okay." I remembered my mom saying the same thing to me the day she had left. It had been a lie then, and it was a lie now.

"I think I've had too much to drink," she said. "Or I'm having another one of those acid flashbacks. This cat keeps talking to me."

I smiled. "Goodbye, Mrs. McGibbons."

───────

IMANI WAS THE LAST TO GO DOWN THE RAMP. IT'D GONE QUICKLY. She waved, unsmiling at us. I waved back, and we turned away.

"Do you think we'll ever see them again?" Donut asked.

"I don't know," I said.

We angled toward the quadrant with the kobolds, killing all the grubs and burning all the pupae we passed. Earlier, I had noted a safe room deep in the kobold quadrant, along the back side of the area. We would grind our way toward it and try to get a nap before we had to do this next interview.

Hopefully the hornet monsters, when they hatched, would remain in their area.

KOBOLD RIDER—LEVEL 5

Here's an interesting fact. The DNA of a kobold and the DNA of a chihuahua are almost identical. That should tell you almost everything you need to know about these yappy little assholes.

Small, angry, think they are bigger than they really are, there is nothing more terrifying than a pack of these little bastards charging at you across the battlefield, at least in their own minds. But don't underestimate them, either. They are fearless, they are intelligent, and they bite first, ask questions later.

Their mounts, the Danger Dingoes, should probably worry you.

The last time I'd played *Dungeons and Dragons* had been aboard the USCGC *Stratton*. I remembered kobolds as little lizard-like monsters. In the game I'd played, the dungeon master had them as minions of a small dragon. Here, they were different. They, indeed, looked like goddamned armored chihuahuas. They were about the same size as the barking little dogs, but they stood upright and wore chain mail armor that seemed to be made out of beer can tabs. Each wore tiny metal caps with a spike on them.

Most of them were armed with long, angry-looking spears with feathers hanging off the end. They wielded them like lances.

"Dogs riding dogs," Donut spat as the pair of danger-dingo-riding kobolds charged at us. "I've had nightmares like this." She hissed and fired a pair of magic missiles, hitting the mounts. The level five dingoes stumbled, rolling forward. I formed a fist as the two kobold riders went flying. The first one crunched onto the ground, breaking his neck. The second bounced up, yapping, teeth frothing. It charged at me. I punched it, and it splattered against the wall. The things were more solid than they looked.

I fell back as one of the dingoes lunged at me. This one had a **Septic** debuff blinking over its head. This monster's snarl and bark were deeper, more terrifying than that of its rider. Their white face paint made them appear even more frightening. Donut leaped onto the back of the dingo, ripping with her rear claws as she hopped high into the air and fired a third magic missile at the still-recovering second mount, killing it. The dingo on top of me shuddered, then fell over dead. Stinking blood and gore washed over me as I pushed it off.

Donut landed deftly next to me and started licking her paw.

"That was pretty slick," I said, brushing myself off. My entire front was soaked in gore. "You're getting a lot better at that."

"I think I have a bonus to damage against canine creatures," she said. "That reminds me: I saw something weird earlier, and I forgot to tell you about it. It was a new tab that said 'Racial benefits,' but it was only there for a second. It blinked and disappeared."

"That *is* weird," I said. Instinctively, I pulled up my own menu, and I didn't have anything like that.

The safe room was just around the corner. After we obliterated the kobold and dingo corpses, we headed toward it. This was another one of the non-manned rooms. The room appeared to have once been some sort of industrial kitchen, but with all the appliances removed except a large walk-in freezer that still was in working order. We inspected the giant refrigerator, but it was empty.

A stainless steel counter stood underneath the set of screens, and on the counter was a plain metallic toaster surrounded by a pile of crumbs. It didn't seem to be plugged into anything, but I couldn't lift it up, either. Up on the screen it read, **Free Mana Toast! One per Crawler!**

I pressed down the little handle, and a moment later it popped up. A burned triangle of toast jumped out, landing on the counter. I picked it up and smelled it. I examined its properties.

Mana Toast.
This is toast.
It refills your mana. That's it. Nothing more. Fuck you.

"Well, that was unnecessary," I muttered. I gave my piece to Donut, who tucked them both away into her inventory.

The room also contained a drinking fountain, a couple chairs and cots, and a set of bathrooms. As had become our custom, we checked both of the bathrooms out. They were empty, but someone had clearly been here before us. The toilet paper had all been taken, and the shampoo dispenser in the women's shower had been emptied. The floor was wet, like someone had recently taken a shower.

MUKTA (ADMIN): Crawlers Carl and Princess Donut. You are to be transported to your interview in ten minutes. Prepare yourselves.

Mukta?

DONUT: WHO ARE YOU? WHERE IS ZEV?
MUKTA (ADMIN): Your Outreach Associate has been put in a time-out. She will return to you tomorrow. I am her substitute until then.

I glanced up at the clock. We had eight hours until the next episode. That wasn't right.

CARL: We weren't supposed to go for another couple hours.
MUKTA (ADMIN): Administrator Zev had you scheduled on a program called *Dungeon Crawl Tactics*. I have overridden

her decision and picked a better program for you. This one
is paying a higher fee. Do not worry. It is similar to the
other one. It is still roundtable-style. Close enough at least.
They still offer gifts to the participants.

CARL: We were promised the right to refuse interviews. I don't
want to go on this one.

MUKTA (ADMIN): You seem to be under the impression that you
have a say in this, Crawler.

DONUT: WHAT DID ZEV DO? WHY IS SHE IN A TIME-OUT?

The message clicked away, and the chat disappeared from our log.
There was no way to respond or initiate a new message.

"Carl, I'm not ready!" A brush appeared in front of her. "Brush
me, quick!"

The front of my jacket was still covered in dingo gore. I moved
to the bathroom to clean myself off the best I could. "I'll get to you
in a minute."

"I don't like this," I said a few minutes later as I brushed a knot
out of Donut's fur. This was my first time doing this since we'd come
to the dungeon. I had a quick memory of Bea teaching me how to
properly brush the cat. The first time I'd ever done it, Donut had
yowled and tried to disembowel me. Bea and I had fallen over ourselves laughing at the indignant look on the cat's face. It had taken
months before she'd sit still and let me do it.

We only had a couple minutes, and I spent it looking at the handful of achievements I'd received from our rage elemental gambit.
Donut actually had several more than I did, all of them bomb-
themed ones I'd already received. She didn't waste time opening the
associated boxes just yet, instead opting to use her precious few minutes cleaning herself.

Most of my own bomb-themed skills moved up to level nine. I
now had a handful of mechanic and construction-themed skills as
well. I received two achievements of note:

New achievement! Grease Monkey!

Don't get ahead of yourself, Dale. You built and deployed a wheeled device. When the primitive humans in Mesopotamia made the first wheel, they probably thought they were hot shit, too. It still took them another 5,000 years after that to invent the toilet.

Reward: You've received a Silver Mechanic's Box!

New achievement! You Call That a Trap?

A mob has been injured because of something you purposely left lying around the dungeon. From scattered Legos to spiked pits to buckets of flesh-devouring Skinner Ants to dimensional rifts that instantly boil all the blood in one's body, the art of trap making has a celebrated and storied history in the annals of *Dungeon Crawler World*.

So if you're going to do it, you better do it right. Whatever it was that gave you this achievement, it was probably something stupid. This will help you make the next trap more . . . exciting.

Remember: If you don't make it titillating, we will.

Reward: You've received a Gold Sapper's Box!

I was a bit confused about what, specifically, gave me the trap achievement. I knew Donut had received this one, too. I guessed it was from either dropping the chain or the oil slick. Probably not the bombs, which were placed in another category.

The mechanic's box gave me a tool called a Gorgon Marital Aid. It was shaped like a spatula. "What the hell is this?" I muttered, pulling up its properties.

Gorgon Marital Aid.

A favorite amongst intergalactic porn stars, this is a hardening and de-hardening tool. May only be used at a workbench. Assists in fusing joints or creating varying degrees of plasticity in otherwise rigid materials without affecting material strength.

That seemed like a pretty useful tool. I put it in my inventory next to my goo-inator 3000.

The sapper's box contained two items. A sapper's table that practically knocked me over when it appeared. It was a table just like my engineering and alchemy tables. The description noted that explosive items or traps created at the table didn't lose stability or couldn't be prematurely set off.

The second item in the box was a trap-building item. There were ten of them, and each one was nothing more than a tiny black box the size of a dime with a long length of wire attached.

Proximity Trigger.

Trigger Warning! Traumatizing content! Using a Sapper's Table, the highly valuable Proximity Trigger may be attached to any non-static trap. Allows for the establishment of activation conditions, including countdowns, mob-type triggers, etc.

Sure enough, the moment I put the item in my inventory, it placed itself near the top of the list in terms of value, right behind that ridiculous Fireball or Custard lottery ticket. And I now had ten of them.

After all of that, my level was still stuck at 11. It was near the edge of 12, but it had barely budged since the fight with Krakaren. The plan was, for now, to kill off the kobolds and then move out of the area. I was hoping to be at least level 13 by the time we hit the stairs.

MUKTA (ADMIN): Transferring now.

Before I even had the chance to finish my thought, we disappeared and reappeared.

Donut, who had been sitting on a chair, reappeared two feet in the air. She yowled in surprise and fell. Her metallic crupper clinked onto the boat's deck. The ground roiled. As always, my HUD snapped off.

We were on another boat, one much smaller than the last one. There were no windows and no doors. There were no features at all other than a pair of chairs that sat cramped together at one end of the room. The place was about the size of a large walk-in closet. I could reach up and touch the ceiling, which seemed to be made of plastic. The room smelled of salt water and was about 20 degrees cooler than the dungeon.

A floating Frisbee thing descended from the low ceiling. The jet-black metallic disk hummed. A single blue light flashed on the edge. It spoke in a soothing female robotic voice.

"My name is Mexx-55. You are in a rental trailer owned and operated by Senegal Production Systems, Unlimited. This trailer is used by multiple tunnel productions related to the crawl. For this session, use of these facilities has been leased by the program *Death Watch Extreme Dungeon Mayhem*. Sit in the provided chairs and keep your limbs to your side while the table generates. The holo will commence in 60 seconds."

"No greenroom?" Donut said, looking around, outraged. "No snacks?"

"Please sit down," Mexx-55 repeated.

"What's the host's name?" Donut asked.

"The Maestro," Mexx-55 said. Her previously emotionless voice hinted an air of distaste.

"*Death Watch Extreme Dungeon Mayhem?*" I muttered, moving to the chair. The moment we sat, Donut's seat rose up. A table formed out of the wall, grinding in place in front of us. It was only about two feet wide. "That's the stupidest name I've ever heard."

"Yeah, wait until you see the show," Mexx-55 said before rising up into the ceiling.

42

"I'M GOING TO VOMIT," DONUT SAID AS THE FLOOR HEAVED. "I'M GO-ing to puke on television, Carl."

"You'll get used to it," I said. "I think when the holo starts, it stabilizes. Just breathe."

"I don't like puking. I don't want to puke!"

I laughed. "Really? I seem to recall you had a thing for vomiting on my pillow."

"That was different. I did that on purpose."

"I knew it! I fucking knew it."

Donut made a gagging noise. "The last place didn't bounce around this much."

"The seas were calmer, and it was a bigger boat," I said. "Breathe."

The dark, heaving room flickered, and the lights turned on, revealing an audience. They had no reaction to our sudden appearance, and I suspected we weren't yet visible to them. The sensation of movement was suddenly much more muted. It was still there, but the holo had some sort of compensation effect.

I looked about the suddenly bigger room. A table floated before us, much larger than the actual table in the trailer. This table curved, shaped like a smile. We sat in the second and third seats. To our left was a larger, more ornate chair. It was made of dark wood with what appeared to be red velvet cushions. The armrests were made of pig skulls. Four more plain empty chairs appeared to our right, curving along the table.

I looked over my shoulder, and the backdrop was an elephant-like monster with three spike-covered trunks. The animation swung its head back and forth in a loop with the word "Extreme" exploding over and over in the midst of the image.

The crowd suddenly started screaming and cheering. I snapped my attention forward, but I couldn't see what they were hollering at. Their attention was to my left. I realized the show had started, and the host had appeared, but for whatever reason, we couldn't see him or her yet. This was a different setup to Odette's show. I suspected we'd just magically appear when it was our turn.

This went on for several minutes. The crowd started chanting something. It took me a moment to understand what they were saying. "Die, die, die," they seemed to be repeating. They were watching a video, I realized, their attention focused on the main screen, which for me still showed the elephant graphic. They burst into screams of pleasure as whatever it was they were watching died. "Glurp, glurp!" they screamed. "Glurp, glurp!"

I spent a few moments examining the crowd, who continued to laugh and cheer. The audience's makeup was fairly similar to Odette's crowd, with a glaring difference that made my stomach sink.

"Oh fuck," I grumbled when I finally saw it.

I focused on a group of humans sitting in the second row, hooting and screaming and laughing boisterously. There was a cruel air to their laughter. It was almost a tangible thing, like a black malevolent cloud that embraced the presence of the entire audience. I was reminded of that day when my dad and his friends broke my slingshot. They'd been firing rocks at squirrels, laughing in a similar way.

These humans in the second row were all male, and they were all about twelve or thirteen years old. It seemed the entire audience consisted of young, pre- and early teen, males. One of them was wearing a red shirt that said "GLURP!" on it.

"Glurp, glurp!" the audience yelled. "Glurp, glurp!"

"Donut," I said, talking quickly. "This crowd is going to be a lot different than the last one. They're all kids. I don't think they're the happy, cartoon-watching kind, either."

"Carl, we've gone over this," Donut said. "You sit there and look angry, and I do the talking. Remember?"

To our left, the host suddenly appeared. There was no warning. He showed up in midsentence. A floating note appeared in front of me. **ON AIR SOON. BE READY.**

". . . know you little cunts are gonna love today's surprise panelists! Your Maestro had to bang some slimy mudskipper tail to pull this one off. But nothing is too good for Maestro's piglets! Suck it! Suck it good, piglets!"

"Glurp, glurp!" the audience screamed. "Glurp, glurp!"

The host—the Maestro—was an orc. A huge, muscular orc.

He looked a lot like a tuskling, but it was clear this was a different type of the same species. The tusklings were dwarf versions of these guys. Tuskling skin was bright pink, piglike. The Maestro's flesh was darker, covered in black bristly hair. He reminded me of a wild boar. His left tusk was completely gold. He stood about six and a half feet tall, built like a tank. A line of earrings circled his left ear. He wore a hot pink silken shirt, buttoned halfway up, revealing a hairy, well-muscled chest covered in gold chains. I couldn't tell for certain, but I had the distinct impression he was only in his early twenties.

I hated him instantly.

To my right now sat two humans, two men about my age. Both of them were Asian. Their ragged, bewildered look pegged them as fellow crawlers. One of them noticed us and pointed, talking quickly to his companion. I couldn't hear what they were saying, but it seemed like they recognized us. I waved, and they waved back, both of them bowing rapidly.

They turned and also waved at the empty chairs to their right. There was someone there, but we couldn't see who it was.

"So we have six guests today. Two stupid, lame guests. Two VIP surprise guests, and then two more surprise guests for our VIPs. Our VIPs today are so hot, we are—for the very first time—coming to you live! That is how hard I am working for you. We'll start with the lame guests. Watch this shit, piglets."

A screen appeared in front of us. It showed a party of four crawlers running from a group of ten Troglodyte Bashers. The lizard monsters were armed with spiked clubs. The crawler group consisted of the two guys sitting next to us, a woman, and a third male. Only the male who wasn't here appeared to be armed. He held a long, odd sword with teeth on it like a saw. None of them wore any sort of armor. They turned the corner and stopped dead.

I felt sick to my stomach, seeing what they faced. Just around the bend was a familiar sight. Five grub pupae sat blocking their retreat. The middle sac was in the midst of ripping open. A massive hornet burst forth and buzzed into the air. The only resemblance it bore to the brindle grub was the top half of its bug face. The monster consisted of a huge hornet-like body with a pair of arms with grasping clawed fingers. It looked at the four crawlers and spat. A glob of white goo shot out and hit the male with the sword. It splattered directly on the man's face. He screamed, falling to the ground, dropping the sword. The glob was like acid. It sizzled and crackled. His pain-filled screeches continued as the troglodytes stopped at the corner, boxing them all in. The other pupae started to pulsate and tear as four more hornets appeared. The woman reached down to pick up the sword. The world on the screen froze.

At first I thought they'd simply paused the scene, but then the two men disappeared. When they vanished, there was a puff of air, and the sword blew a foot away, clattering loudly. Everything else, including the mobs, remained frozen.

The crowd burst into a mix of applause and jeers. The two men next to us were now visible to the audience.

"You know what time it is, piglets?" the Maestro shouted.

"Death Watch! Death Watch!" the crowd screamed.

"Okay, so we got two crawlers here. Their full names are quite the snout full, and does it really matter?" Laughter followed. "The fellow with the acne scars is Li Jun and the bald fucker we'll just call Zhang. Say hello, meat."

It took the two men a moment to realize the Maestro was talking to them.

"Hello," Li Jun said. "I don't understand what is happening."

"Okay, so let me catch you up since you're too stupid to figure it out. You're on Death Watch, a segment of my show. That means we just plucked you away from certain death. You're welcome. Before, your plight was hopeless. Now you have a chance to survive. But we'll get to that in a second."

The Maestro waved up at the screen. "You all have been hit with a *Time Freeze* spell, and it will run out just as this episode ends. We have a little game we'd like you to play to give you the opportunity to live past the next few seconds. Yeah?"

"Okay," Li Jun said, exchanging a look with his companion. "What do we need to do?"

"Death Watch! Death Watch!" the crowd chanted.

"We're going to show you a series of scenes, and you have to guess if the crawler survives or not. But before we begin, I want to know a little about you guys." The Maestro waved his hand; the stats of the two men appeared floating over both of them. Both were level seven. They each had a single bronze star over their heads. Both had a strength of eight, meaning they'd received some sort of enhancement. Also of note was Zhang's constitution, which was at 15, making it one point higher than my own.

"Li Jun," the Maestro said, "did you know your three companions before the game started?"

The poor man seemed terrified and bewildered. "Yes. Yes, sir. We all work together in a warehouse. All except my sister, Li Na."

"So that doll up on the screen there, the one reaching for the sword. She's your sister?"

"Yes, sir."

The orc nodded thoughtfully. "Would you do anything to save her?"

"Death Watch! Death Watch!" the crowd screamed.

"What do you mean?" the man asked.

The Maestro ignored him. He turned to Zhang. "And you, Zhang. What do you think about Li Na?"

"What do I think about her? She's my best friend's sister. She's like my own sister."

"And what about your fourth companion? The guy who just got his face spooged on by that Brindled Vespa? He's your friend, too?"

"Yes," Zhang said after a moment. The bald man's eyes were fixed on the frozen scene. "He's our manager."

"The big boss man, huh?" the Maestro said. "So, if you were forced to choose between saving him and saving Li Na, you'd pick the girl, right?"

Zhang just looked at the orc, refusing to answer.

"That's okay, buddy. You might not have to choose. We're going to play a game. This is how it works. We're going to show you four scenes, and we want you to guess if the crawler is going to live or die through the encounter. If you guess correctly, you will receive a teleport point. When we're done, for every point you have, you can spend it to save yourselves or one of your companions. The recipient of each teleport point will be immediately transferred to the closest safe room. If you decide to throw a point at ol' spooge-face, he will be healed, so don't worry about that. Ready? Good, let's go."

The scene showed a woman running from a giant beaver thing holding a battle-axe.

"Fuck this," I said, and I stood from my chair.

"Carl, where are you going?" Donut asked.

"Come on, Donut. This is beyond the pale. Fuck this guy." The table was blocking my exit. I climbed up on it, feeling forward for where the real table ended. I reached it, and hopped down, my legs piercing through the illusion.

A moment later the lights of the chamber snapped back on, and the holo dispersed. Mexx-55 emerged, floating down from her spot on the ceiling. But when she spoke, the voice was different. This was a gruff male voice. Also an orc if I had to guess.

"Get back in your seat, Crawler," the voice said. "You're scheduled to be on-screen after this segment. This show is being tunneled live. We do not have time for tantrums."

"Go fuck yourself," I said.

"Carl, you're going to get us in trouble," Donut said.

"You are ordered to sit," the voice said. "We have paid the appearance fee, and you will participate in the program. If you refuse, we are authorized to drop you into this ocean, drowning you both."

"Bullshit," I said. "You're not Borant, and you're not the Syndicate. There's no way they'd authorize that. We are not participating in this cruelty."

Nothing happened for several moments. Donut jumped up to my shoulder. "You're gonna get us in trouble," she said again, this time more quietly.

"Crawler Carl, this is Administrator Mukta," a new voice said. "You are required to take your seat, or there will be consequences."

"I'll go on as many shows as you want, but we're not doing this one," I said.

"Carl, we will discuss this when you are done. If you do not participate, we *will* accelerate you. There are plenty of other crawlers to show on our program. This is not a bluff."

Deep breath, I thought. *You will not break me. You will not fucking break me.*

"Can that other guy hear me right now?" I asked.

A pause. "No, he cannot," Mukta said.

"As long as I don't talk shit about you guys, will there be consequences for what I say? As long as I participate, I mean?"

Another pause, and this one was longer than before. "They have paid for your appearance. Nothing else."

"All right," I said. "Tell him we want on the show. Now. Before this Death Watch segment ends." Without waiting for an answer, I returned to my seat. The table once again pushed itself out, and the holo resumed.

"Carl, what are you doing?" Donut asked as she settled back in place.

"I'm the one who talks this time," I said.

The studio re-formed. The crowd was screaming and laughing. On the screen, a dead man convulsed on the ground as a group of baby-faced winged fairies splashed about in his corpse like it was a kiddie pool.

"Sorry, it looks like you got that one wrong, too. You have two teleport points," the Maestro said. "I need a decision."

Neither of the men said anything.

The Maestro leaned forward in his ornate chair. He smiled wickedly. "I need a decision, or nobody gets saved."

"Then nobody gets saved," Li Jun said. He looked at Zhang. "We die together."

"Aw, isn't that fucking sweet?" the Maestro said. "Very well, if that's what you want. Piglets, should we give them what they want?"

"Death Watch! Death Watch!"

"No, wait," Zhang said. "Save Li Jun and Li Na."

"No," Li Jun said. He reached out and put his hand on his friend's shoulder. "We stand together."

A sour look passed across the Maestro's face. He said something, but it was muted. He paused, then nodded. A moment passed, and the cruel smile reappeared on his face.

"We're going to do something a little different, piglets. Our VIP guests have been watching backstage, and it seems like they have something to say."

The crowd screamed its approval.

ON AIR IN TEN SECONDS.

The Maestro was playing this off like this was his idea. "Okay, piglets, my next two guests do not need any introduction. The last you probably saw of these two, they were stuck in a room with a bunch of old fucks. Are they going to escape? Spoiler alert: They just got out. We were going to show what these crazy assholes did to get free, but since they want to suck on it so bad, we're going to bring them on early."

"Glurp, glurp! Glurp, glurp!"

YOU ARE NOW ON AIR.

The studio became brighter, and the crowd went berserk. Donut made a show of licking her paw, looking aloof.

"Crawler Carl and *Princess* Donut," the Maestro said. He drew out the word "Princess," and it dripped with sarcasm. "Piglets, you probably don't know this. These two just broke a record for the most watched second-floor battle in the history of *Dungeon Crawler World*. If it were me, I would've killed every last one of those geriatric sandbags and reaped the experience, but you know how it is with humans." He looked down at Donut. "And cats, apparently. All that effort, and what did they get? No experience, no real loot." He shrugged. "But you can't argue with results. Carl and Donut, say hello to my piglets."

"We want in on the game," I said, not bothering to greet the crowd. "We want to play Death Watch, too."

The Maestro laughed, an uncertain timbre to it. "That's not how it works, Carl. I knew you were a crazy mother—"

"They have two points. Let's use them to transfer me and Donut to that spot." I looked at the crowd. "Wouldn't that be cool?"

The crowd roared. "Death Watch! Death Watch!"

It took a moment for the large orc to recover. "People talk about how stupid you are, Carl. But I never realized you were this stupid. If you're feeling suicidal, then . . ."

I leaned in, pointing my finger. "No, you listen to me, pork boy. If you're going to fuck with people like this, then at least make it fair. They played your game, and they won two points. You said they can use those two points to transfer people away. I don't see why it can't be used to transfer people in, either."

The crowd seemed to love this idea.

"It doesn't work that way," the Maestro repeated. "You're not part of the game. It's against the rules."

"Yeah, fuck the rules." I looked at the crowd. "I think we should tell the rules to suck it. What do you think?"

"Glurp, glurp! Glurp, glurp!"

The Maestro did *not* like his audience glurping for someone else. I recognized that look on his face, of fulminating under-the-surface rage. I felt a deep satisfaction at that. I didn't know if this was a good idea or an incredibly dumb one, but I felt the urge to keep poking at him.

The truth was, I didn't really want to be transferred to this battle, likely halfway across the world. I felt for these guys, and I wanted to help them. But if helping Brandon and crew taught me anything, it was that I needed to balance it out. There was a difference between giving aid and sacrificing yourself for people you didn't even know. Still, this felt like the right thing. I knew my argument was nonsensical. I also knew how this sort of crowd thought. This Maestro guy was the worst kind of a bully. A bully with an audience. I had to do something. For the moment I didn't have a plan other than pissing him off as much as I could.

I looked over at the two empty chairs to the right of Zhang and Li Jun. A thought struck me. What had he said? *Two more surprise guests for our VIPs.* So it was somebody we knew. I had a sudden, strong suspicion who it was. If I was right, then I knew I could push the Maestro even further. He had a plan. A cruel plan, and going down this path was doing nothing but distracting from the narrative he was attempting to build. That meant the more I pushed, the more it would piss him off, and the more desperate he'd get to steer the conversation back on track.

On television shows and in kids' books, they always repeated the bullies-will-back-down-when-stood-up-to mantra. That was utter horseshit. It always has been. That only worked when the one standing up to the bully was stronger than them. The Maestro and I were not on equal footing. But my short confrontation in the production trailer taught me something important. I didn't need to be stronger than him. Donut and I were something better. We were expensive.

I had a hunch that they'd spent a lot of money to get me and Donut on this show, maybe even overextended themselves. We were popular, and Donut had proven herself a reliable guest. The fact they were using a shitty rental trailer and didn't have their own suggested this production ran on the same sort of shoestring budget most You-Tube shows had.

The Maestro, seething, said, "You dumb shit. These guys were dead! I saved them. I'm giving them a second chance. Maybe I *will* transfer you into that fight. How would you like that? And we'll transfer the other four out, so you have no backup at all. Your ridiculous luck wouldn't save you then. I don't think you've fought a Brindled Vespa yet. In a second, there'll be five of them in that hallway. You'll be utterly fucked."

I smiled. "You're too much of a pussy to do it. I dare you."

"Death Watch! Death Watch!"

The Maestro looked so angry I thought he might actually cry. I suspected—and hoped—he *couldn't* do it. If I knew one thing about Borant, it was that they nickel-and-dimed everything. This Death Watch segment probably cost a lot of money, and that was with regular, low-view crawlers. There was no way they'd be able to send one of the game's highest-value streams into danger like that.

When people became red-zone angry, they were, in general, unpredictable. That wasn't true with bullies. I knew this from experience. It was the opposite with bullies. I knew exactly what was about to happen.

I turned to Li Jun and Zhang, who sat next to me, mouths agape. I quickly whispered, "Grab your sister and the other guy and run toward the troglodytes and through them. Leave the sword. The lizards are really dumb and slow, and their attention is on the hornets. You'll only have a few seconds."

"But," Li Jun said, "you wanted to trade places. . . ."

The Maestro growled, "You don't tell me what to do on my own show, meat." He slammed down on a button on his table, and the two men to my right vanished.

The words "Death Watch Extreme!" appeared on the giant display. The two men appeared back in the scene in the hallway, caught between the hornets and the troglodytes. For a moment, everything remained frozen except the two men.

Zhang reacted first, shouting, "Grab your sister!" as he reached down to pick up the fallen third man.

Just as he moved to pick him up, the scene unfroze. The sister stumbled as the sword she was grabbing for was suddenly several feet away. Li Jun grasped her wrist and pointed. "Run!" he cried. The three of them scrambled directly at the crowd of troglodytes, who stood like turkeys, watching the hornets.

The monsters—Brindled Vespas he'd called them—didn't care who their victims were. Multiple globs of white spit shot out, splashing into the lizards, who in turn raised their clubs and charged at the bugs.

Both groups of monsters ignored the four humans, who managed to slip away and out into the hall. The scene ended with Zhang forcing a healing potion into the mouth of their companion before they slipped into a safe room. The video snapped off to a mix of jeers and scattered applause. The audience's reaction was subdued, as if they weren't sure how to respond.

I looked up at the Maestro, a huge smile on my face.

"Glurp on that, motherfucker," I said.

43

"UH, LET'S NOW WATCH HOW OUR TWO GUESTS ESCAPED THAT SAFE room," the Maestro said after the audience's laughter died down.

The stage went dark as the screen replayed our desperate escape from the rage elemental. It showed the scene from the point of view of the hallway, with the chopper bursting out of the room, screeching around the corner, Donut sitting high on the contraption. The audience roared their approval. Next to us, the Maestro screamed and ranted at some unseen producer. It was all muted. The large orc seemed to be out of breath and enraged.

"Carl, you scare me when you get that angry," Donut whispered.

I reached over and scratched her head. "I'm sorry," I said. "I'm not really as mad as I look. I'm just trying to make *him* angry."

"It worked. Now he hates us. I don't like people hating us. Our followers are going to go down."

I grunted. "Yeah, I don't think you need to worry about that. Look, Donut. The show isn't over yet. See those two chairs over there. I think it's—"

"Do you think it's Miss Beatrice?" Donut asked. "Maybe her and her boyfriend?" She gasped. "Or maybe it's Miss Beatrice and Ferdinand."

"No, Donut," I said. "It's not going to be Bea and whoever the hell—"

"Listen here, pukes," the Maestro said, interrupting. He smiled big, but his words held no mirth. He'd calmed himself, probably after getting some advice from his producer. The audience continued to watch the recap of our escape, oohing and aahing at the explosions. They couldn't hear this exchange. "This is my fucking show. You need to learn your place."

"You were never a crawler, were you?" I asked.

He seemed genuinely offended by the question. He laughed with derision. "You savages are all the same. I come from a civilized system. My family has a long history with the dungeon. We were there when the Syndicate *created* the crawl. We are of gods and royalty." He indicated the tiara on Donut's head. "If you pukes make it to the ninth floor, you'll learn all about what my family can do."

I looked at Donut's small jeweled tiara, trying to remember the exact description. I hadn't thought about it for several days. The tooltip system didn't work here, but I recalled part of it. It's what gave her the ability to imbue the Septic debuff. Because she'd put it on, she'd become a royal member of the "Blood Sultanate." We could only get off the ninth floor if all other members of that family were killed, including the Sultan himself. I had no idea what any of that meant.

I remembered what Mordecai had said. *That . . . that will be a challenge. You can always leave the party. That crown is on her head, not yours.*

"Your family?" I asked. "Wait, are you guys part of the Blood Sultanate?"

He laughed again. "Do I look like a fucking Naga to you?" He sat straighter. "My family's Skull Clan has been victorious six times out of the last ten Faction Wars. Top three every time. The pitiful Blood Sultanate is almost always the first of the nine to get eliminated. You idiots have been dead since the moment she put on that crown."

I tried to ignore the pit of dread that had formed in my gut. "What about you? Are *you* going to be on the ninth floor?"

On the screen, Donut and I stood at the edge of the hole to the next floor down. The camera was positioned from the POV of the rage elemental. We looked tiny standing there, a trail of black smoke rising behind us. The entire crowd held its breath as the monstrosity charged.

"I will be there. I was of age last season, but the stupid Squim Conglomerate always plays Battle Royale, which doesn't have a Faction Wars or Celestial Ascendancy segment. But I will be there this year. I'm on my way to your stupid planet right now." He pounded his chest like he was a gorilla. "I will be War Leader Maestro of the Skull Clan."

I nodded. It always astounded me how easy it was to get assholes to talk, as long as they were talking about themselves. "So, if you're in the dungeon, what happens if you get hurt? Do you guys really die?"

He scoffed. "You think you could actually . . ."

The crowd went absolutely apeshit as the scene ended, and the lights snapped back on. Donut stood on her hind legs and raised her two front paws in the air. "That's how it's done!" she yelled. "Next time, we'll kill that thing ourselves and send pictures to his mama! We'll tell her to . . . What was it, Carl?"

"Suck it," I said.

"Glurp, glurp! Glurp, glurp!" the audience cried.

The Maestro was back to his sneering, condescending self. His unseen producer was smart enough to explain that having a tantrum during a live program would make this spiral even further out of his control. I sighed. Whatever happened next, it wasn't going to be pleasant. Might as well get it over with.

The Maestro waved for the crowd to quiet down. They eventually did.

"So that's how you did it. You used the dungeon's rules to save yourselves."

I shrugged. "That thing was level 93. We weren't gonna kill it."

The Maestro grinned. "Nobody, not even me, can say you don't have the balls of a Taurin. But a lot of my piglets seem to think you have had it too easy. Some say you've been stumbling your way through the dungeon, only surviving because you're the AI's pet.

That happens from time to time: The dungeon turns a crawler into its bitch." He reached over and scratched at his hairy chest. His fingernails were disgusting.

He continued. "I have two surprise guests for our VIPs. You have any guesses who they might be, meat?"

I put my hand on Donut before she could say anything out loud. The last thing we needed right now was to give the Maestro ammunition to mock her.

"Can they see us now?" I asked, turning to look at the empty chairs.

"They've been watching this whole time," the Maestro said. "And man, they do not like you."

It didn't take a rocket scientist to figure out who this was. Other than Brandon and crew, we'd only come across one other group of crawlers. I'd been thinking *maybe* it was Rory and Lorelai, the goblin shamankas. I didn't know if bringing mobs out of the dungeon was a thing. But I remembered that Zhang and Li Jun had waved at them, and I doubted they'd have reacted like that toward a pair of scary-looking goblins.

"Hi, Frank Q. Hi, Maggie My," I said. "I see you didn't find the present I left for you. That's too bad."

The Maestro smiled huge, and for a terrifying moment, I thought I had guessed incorrectly. *Could it possibly be Beatrice? No,* I decided. *No fucking way.*

"Watch this, piglets," he said. "Let's see if they're right."

The video started and I relaxed. It was a recap of Frank and Maggie's journey so far. I watched as the two player killers stumbled into the dungeon. But, curiously, they had someone else with them. A teenage girl. It showed them coming into a tutorial guild. We watched as their guide—one of those floating brain Mind Horrors— sat the three of them down and told them the only way to survive was to kill other crawlers. The guide had a deep, rumbly voice, unlike anything I'd heard before. It was terrifying. The teenager wept as the guide explained what had to be done. Maggie clutched onto the girl, hugging her tightly.

The scene switched to the girl on the ground, injured and crying. We hadn't seen what had happened. It looked as if she'd maybe been hit with a glob of bad llama lava. Frank was also injured, convulsing nearby as blood pooled around them. The woman, Maggie, sobbed as she went to her knees in front of the girl.

"Mom," the girl said. "It hurts."

"I know, baby," Maggie said. She reached down, and to my utter astonishment, she wrapped her hands around the girl's throat. She choked her own daughter until she died. When it was done, Maggie leaned against the dungeon wall and wailed.

"What the hell?" I asked, astounded. I turned to the empty chairs. "You didn't have to do that. She wasn't dead. She would've recovered."

The recap continued. We were being shown these scenes out of order. This was now something from before the daughter's death. We watched Frank and Maggie and the daughter come across a much larger group. This group included Rebecca W and several other men. Frank and Maggie introduced themselves as a married couple, and the teenager was their daughter, Yvette. They waited until the others' backs were turned, and Frank and Maggie ambushed them. They pulled their guns and shot them all. Yvette cried for them to stop. Rebecca and another man fled, and Frank chased them. It showed the man running directly into some plant mob thing I'd never seen before, and Frank finally tracking Rebecca down, cornering her in the quadrant with the Scatterer bugs. The screen split, showing Yvette screaming while Maggie tried to calm her. One of the other men they'd shot wasn't dead. Maggie put a gun in Yvette's hand, told her to shoot the man to get the experience. The girl refused.

As I expected, Frank's entire backstory was complete made-up bullshit. I still didn't know if they were cops or not. I suspected they were. Either way, Rebecca W hadn't been some sort of human trafficker. She'd been someone like me. Afraid and, at the end, alone. She'd been betrayed and hunted down by a fellow human. I thought of the woman's naked, stripped-bare body. I shook my head in disgust.

The two had received multiple loot boxes from being player killers, including a ring that gave Maggie an area-of-effect stealth ability and a potion that imbued Frank with the ability to track down nearby crawlers.

I noted that Maggie's stealth ability worked like my *Protective Shell*. It cast in a static semicircle area. It didn't move with them. That was good to know.

I watched as they hunted several other crawlers, most of them people wandering about on their own. Most of them appeared to have been homeless, some elderly. All of them were afraid. All of them had been so happy to see someone else before they were murdered. Yvette was in some of these scenes. She wasn't in others. The girl never participated in the killings.

"The best part is coming up," the Maestro announced.

The video, finally, showed a much-abridged version of Donut and me coming across Frank Q in the safe room and of them attacking us, of them getting frozen. It showed me putting the dynamite in the rat corpse.

But then I saw something unexpected. My heart sank the moment I realized what was happening.

"Mom?" Yvette asked, coming out of the bathroom. The girl stopped in horror upon seeing both of her parents frozen in the safe room.

Oh. Oh no, I thought. She'd been there. Yvette had been there the whole time. She'd been hiding with her mother under the stealth field.

I see you didn't find the present I left for you. Now I knew why the Maestro had smiled so big when I said that.

I held my breath as the two murderers and their daughter approached the rat corpse. Maggie yelled at Frank not to loot it. He did it anyway. If I remembered correctly, we'd left five items in its inventory: a hunk of rat steak, a skin, a lit smoke bomb, a lit stick of dynamite, and an unlit, unstable stick. Frank only pulled out one item.

The lit dynamite stick. He dropped it in surprise, and all three turned to run. A moment passed, and the dynamite went off. Shrapnel blasted the three crawlers. Yvette went down, and so did Frank. A hunk of dislodged rock sheared the man's hand right off.

A llama hadn't given those horrible injuries to the teenage girl.

I had.

The scene ended, the lights switched on, and Maggie and Frank emerged to our right.

Donut hissed. The crowd's response was mixed. Half cheers, half insults and screams, as if they weren't sure whose side they were supposed to be on. I spent the moment observing the two crawlers. Frank was missing his right hand. But that wasn't all that had changed about him. The man had a hollowed-out 1,000-yard stare. He looked as if he'd aged ten years in just a few days. *Do I look like that?* His missing hand wasn't a rounded healed stump like one would expect. It was a straight cut, like he was a mannequin whose hand had been removed.

The woman, Maggie, glared directly at me.

I returned her stare. "You didn't have to kill her," I said when the audience finally silenced. "Why did you do that? To get the experience? She would've healed. Your own daughter? Jesus fuck, lady."

"You don't know," she said to me, spitting the words. "You don't know anything. You didn't get the whole story."

"She wasn't dead yet," I repeated. "She would've healed."

"Fuck you," Maggie said. "You don't know what we've had to do to survive."

"Survive? Your daughter is dead. But it's okay, because you got credit for the kill. I'm sure she'd be so fucking proud," I said.

Maggie leaped from her chair, pulling a black dagger that glowed with a purple halo. She lunged at me.

I didn't flinch. Her jab passed harmlessly through my throat. The dagger dropped away as Maggie cried out in pain, clutching her hand. She'd likely just stabbed the invisible wall of their production trailer.

"Children, children," the Maestro said, plainly enjoying this. He was back on familiar ground. "Clearly you guys have a beef with one another."

Frank whispered something to Maggie, who returned to her chair. He tried to put an arm on her shoulder. She pushed him away.

"As far as I'm concerned, any business I've had with these two has already been transacted," I said. I turned toward Frank and met the man's eyes. The man had changed significantly since the last time we'd seen each other. He looked away and down. "I'm sorry about what happened to your kid. But fuck you. Fuck both of you. She deserved better. We all would've been stronger together. Your game guide is a piece of shit."

Maggie growled. "I am going to find you, and I am going to watch you die. You and the fucking cat."

"Oooooh," the crowd said, like we were on an episode of the god-damned *Jerry Springer Show*.

"Don't bring me into this," Donut said, raising a paw in defense. "I'm not the one who went all danger dingo on my own kid."

The crowd screamed with laughter. I had to hand it to her. Donut was oftentimes caught off guard, but she was highly adaptable. She knew how to read a crowd—that was for sure. But as much as I disliked these two assholes, they weren't the real enemy. We needed to end this. This bullshit didn't serve any of us.

I turned to the Maestro. "Congratulations. You've reunited us. We all know how she feels about the matter. I've said my piece. If that's all, we'll be going now."

"No, no, why so quick to leave?" For the next several minutes, the Maestro attempted to ask us leading questions. *So why did you kill your own daughter? Carl, how does it feel to know you're partially responsible for the death of another human?* Maggie said nothing but "Fuck you." Frank hadn't said a word this whole time. Donut would only talk directly to the audience, and I just grunted responses.

It was obvious that the orc wasn't good at asking interview

questions, especially with a group of hostile guests. The crowd grew restless.

Donut started making wisecracks. The Maestro tried to ask her something, and she just ignored him. She looked directly at the audience and said, "I once watched a cocker spaniel lick her own butthole for thirty minutes straight. That was more insightful than that question."

Eventually, the Maestro threw his large hands in the air and gave up. The orc had a panicked look to him. He knew this entire episode had been a dumpster fire from the start. But then the orc's eyes sparkled with one last glimmer of hope. I braced myself for whatever bullshit was coming.

"Well, I have parting gifts for each of the teams," he said. "Are you piglets excited to see what we got for the crawlers?"

The crowd responded half-heartedly. A few of the audience members had already flickered and disappeared from the stream, leaving empty spaces in the crowd.

"Hopefully it's a door so we can get back to the dungeon," Donut muttered. The audience laughed. But she wasn't fooling me. The cat was shaking with pleasure. Even now, Donut couldn't contain herself. That damn cat loved her presents.

"Let's give our VIPs their gift first, shall we?"

A box appeared in front of me. This was a literal cardboard box. I hesitantly reached forward, and it was really there.

"This is just a present for Carl. Sorry about that, Donut," the Maestro said. He leaned forward expectantly. I could feel Donut deflate next to me. I realized I'd been stroking her back without thinking about it. "Carl, I know this is something you want really bad. We paid a lot of money to make sure you have the very best."

I opened the box. *You asshole.* I had to laugh. It was a perfectly chosen gift to troll me. I probably would've laughed even if we'd been on another show.

"Carl. You have boots now!" Donut said.

It was a brand-new pair of Bates zip-up tactical boots. They were identical to the service boots I wore on active duty. I picked one up. Sure enough, they were in my size.

"We even got you socks," the Maestro said. "They're in the box!"

"Thanks!" I said, pulling the box onto my lap. "These will be really comfortable when I'm in a safe room!" I put the lid back on. There was no way I was going to wear these things.

Now that my soles had fully acclimated, me wearing shoes would put me at a massive disadvantage. I had several buffs and skills that only worked if I was barefoot, and the orc knew it. The gift was just him being a dick. He was expecting me to react, to rant and rave. He should've known by now that wasn't the sort of bait that would snag me. The audience barely reacted at all. They either didn't understand the intended troll or didn't care.

"I love them," I added. I tapped the top of the box, smiling. "I hope they weren't too expensive."

The Maestro took a deep breath and gave me his best fuck-you glare. He turned to Frank and Maggie. "And now, you two. Frank has a skill called Find Crawler, which shows you any crawlers within five square kilometers." The Maestro waved his hand. "I don't think that is good enough." A potion appeared in front of them. Maggie snatched it up, looking at it. "That there is a Legendary Skill Potion, taken from my clan's own stock. Either of you drink that fucker down, and it will upgrade your Find Crawler skill to level 15." He turned to look at me, smiling again. "That means you can put in any crawler's name, and it'll tell you exactly where they are, no matter how far."

"Wait, can I drink this? Frank is the one with the skill," Maggie asked.

"Oh yeah," he said. "That'll take you all the way to the top level of 20 if you have the right class. But if you take it now, it'll take you up to 15 no problem."

I sighed. "So, are we done here?"

The Maestro seemed to be at a loss for words, pissed his gifts hadn't gone over well with the audience. "Uh, thanks to my piglets.

You know the Maestro takes care of you fuckers. You know what to do!"

The audience lukewarmly glurp-glurped.

"Well, we probably won't be coming back on this show, pork boy," I said, standing up. Donut jumped to my shoulder and waved vigorously at the audience. "But I imagine we'll see each other again soon enough. I look forward to kicking your ass all over again on the ninth floor. That is, if you're not too much of a puss to face me."

Now that. That garnered a reaction from the crowd.

As the show ended, and the crowd cheered, finally happy to have something to holler about, I turned my attention to the two crawlers sitting next to us. Frank continued to stare straight down, a shell of a man. Maggie clutched the skill potion to her chest, staring at me.

For the first time, the woman smiled.

44

"I DON'T UNDERSTAND WHY SHE KILLED HER DAUGHTER," DONUT said after we returned to the safe room. She immediately started opening the loot boxes from the earlier battle. She received nothing new except two "Trap Modules" from her Gold Sapper's Box. One was called a Spike Module and the other an Alarm Module. These were ready-to-go traps, no tinkering required. We could upgrade and reconfigure them, but it required the use of our sapper's table, which wouldn't happen until the fourth floor.

Despite Mukta's warning that we'd have a discussion after the show, there was no sign of the admin. The program ended, and we'd immediately transported back to the room. I still clutched the shoebox in my hands. I sighed and put it all in my inventory. I pulled out my pedicure kit and started to work on my feet as Donut continued to talk, rapid-fire. She'd been like this after the last interview, too. She got some sort of adrenaline rush from being on camera, even when the show was a disaster. "She had a pretty name. Yvette. I like that name. Did you see? She didn't want to kill people. But then her mom killed her. It's really sad. But I'm also kind of relieved—you know what I mean? Since her mom killed her, that means you didn't kill her. It would've been an accident, but still . . ."

"Aren't you tired?" I asked. I was exhausted. I rubbed the bottom of my foot with the little stone thing. I could just feel the AI watching me. The recap show would air in a few hours, and I wanted to get some sleep before that. Afterward, we needed to head out.

Donut plopped herself on my shoulder, settling in to sleep after I finished with my feet.

"He was kind of a jerk, huh? The orc guy, I mean. But do you remember what he said? We broke the record."

"Yes, Donut," I said. I closed my eyes.

"Carl?"

"What, Donut?" I said, trying not to let the exasperation sound in my voice.

"I heard what he said to you—about the ninth floor, I mean."

"Don't let that idiot bother you."

"No, not the orc. I mean Mordecai. When he told you that you should leave me when we get to that floor. I heard him."

"Let's worry about getting to the third floor before we even think about something as far away as the ninth. We don't even know what the hell that is all about."

"Okay," she said, her voice small. She finally settled next to me, and she was asleep before I was.

I SLEPT THROUGH THE FIRST PART OF THE RECAP EPISODE. I AWAK-ened to find Donut sitting on the chair, her attention on the screen. She looked back at me. "They haven't mentioned us yet. But they showed those guys from Africa, Le Mouvement. They found a city boss. It was a just a see-through blob the size of a house! It killed all of them. There was one guy on the outside of where they were locked in, and now he's all alone. Everyone died except him. They showed him sitting on the ground just crying for like a minute straight. The blob looked like it was made of Jell-O. They couldn't figure out how to hurt it. I bet fire would've worked. They didn't have much room to run around, though. The boss room was a series of tubes, like a sewer system."

"Christ," I said, looking up at the screen. It now showed Lucia Mar smashing a Brindled Vespa into pieces with her mace. She had some sort of personal magical shield I'd never noticed before. The hornet spat at her, and the white glob hit the shield, sizzling and floating in the air a good two inches from the side of her head.

"No wonder," I grumbled.

The last ten minutes of the show were dedicated to our escape. The recap was almost identical to the one they'd showed on the Maestro's show, but with added music and better production values. They showed close-up freeze frames of the MOAB and spinning 3D renderings of the individual bombs.

It showed the rage elemental tumbling into the hole, and the oh shit baby exploding right next to it. We watched as the monster's health bar plummeted, almost hit zero, and then the monster dissolved.

Experience Denied slammed onto the screen.

"Hey, that wasn't fair," Donut cried. "We would've killed it if it hadn't dissolved!"

"Maybe," I said. I was suspicious about how easy it was to do damage to the elemental, considering its high level. Either my bombs were overpowered, or the monster was especially weak for its level.

I suspected there was something else we were missing. The monster probably split in two or blew up on death or something equally horrible. It was almost as if the game was daring us to summon another one and to try to kill it fair and square this time. We'd probably rocket up a dozen levels if we managed it. I could already think of a dozen ways to summon one and have something waiting for it, something that'd kill it for sure. Once you knew how the monster worked, it wasn't so difficult. It *had* to be a trap.

The show ended with Imani pausing at the scorched entrance to the third floor. She looked up into the air and raised a middle finger before going inside.

The show ended, and I suddenly felt very alone. The feeling came out of nowhere. I thought of that last member of Le Mouvement being locked outside the boss area, only to find everyone he knew was just gone. What a nightmare.

I looked up at the ticker. **990,303.**

We'd gone below one million, and I hadn't noticed. For every person that ticked away, I felt I was losing a part of myself, a part of my humanity. I thought of what Donut had said before we'd fallen asleep, and of the unspoken question she had asked and of the answer I hadn't given her.

The announcement came, and even though I knew it was coming, the sudden booming voice surprised me.

Hello, Crawlers,

Keep up the good work. Everything is running smoothly. Now that we've reached the halfway point of the level, game guides are now able to instruct you upon some of the intricacies re-garding the third floor and how the race- and class-selection process works. Be sure to visit your game guide prior to de-scending in order to make the transition more smooth.

Effective immediately, any non-sapient mobs who happen upon a stairwell will not be disintegrated. Yes, we all just watched that rule get exploited on the recap episode. It was very clever and very exciting. But it's not going to happen again.

The System AI has determined the proliferation of the Brin-dled Vespas is too aggressive, and we have halved the number of these mobs currently in the dungeon. In addition, the damage from their spitting-acid attack has been adjusted down. Slightly. Please note, new Brindle Grubs will continue to generate upon the creation of a corpse, but each one now only has a 50% chance to proceed to the pupa stage.

That's it for now. Now go out there and kill, kill, kill!

The moment the announcement ended, a message popped up.

Admin Notice. A new tab is available in your interface.

I blinked. That was unexpected. I opened up my interface, and indeed, there was a new section. **ACCOUNTS**. I clicked on it.

There was only one item:

Creator's Fee. Carl's Jug O' Boom. Royalty: 1 Gold Coin per Kill. Current kills: 4.

There was a button. **Cash Out Now.** Below that was a very small line that I could barely read. There was no way to zoom in. I had to squint to read it.

Count updates once daily. Two gold coins plus 25% Deposit fee, rounded up, deducted upon cash out. Funds not deposited are subject to forfeiture upon death.

"Twenty-five percent!" I said. "Highway robbery." If I cashed out now, I'd only receive a single gold coin. If I'd had five coins, I'd still only receive one coin because they rounded the fee up.

"What?" Donut asked.

I waved my hand. "It's nothing. I'll explain later. Let's get going."

"Are we running? Is that what we're doing? Hiding from Frank Q and Maggie My?"

"No," I said. "That was my first instinct, but now that I've slept on it, I've changed my mind. That woman is hell-bent on hunting us down, and we're going to have to deal with it sooner rather than later. I don't know if they're coming now or not. I'd much rather be ready for her than have her sneak up behind us."

"But how can we do that? They can track us and go invisible, and we can't do either of those."

"Her invisibility is not nearly as powerful as I first thought. We'll need to take out the local neighborhood boss and get that map. It'll make our lives much easier. . . ."

Warning: You may not wield your weapons while in the presence of Admins. Any attempted violence against an Admin will result in your immediate execution.

"Shit," I said, looking up at the ceiling. "Mukta is coming."

Pop! Water splashed over my feet, and a familiar armored kua-tin appeared. My interface snapped off.

"Zev!" Donut cried. "Where were you! I was worried."

"Hello, Carl, hello, Princess Donut. I'm here for your show debriefing."

"Are you okay?" Donut asked.

"Yes, thank you," Zev said. "I was censured by the system AI. I was given a suspension because the system determined that I had cheated by warning you of the rage elemental before it appeared. My representative appealed the decision on my behalf, and upon further review, it was determined that you'd noticed the man urinating simultaneously with my exclamation, so the censure was removed from my record." She sighed, filling her mask with bubbles. "But even though my record is technically clean, it's not really. Once the AI notices you, it's difficult to get it to un-notice you, so I have to be extra careful from now on."

"Are we in trouble?" Donut asked. "That orc guy was really mean to Carl."

"No," Zev said. "It was improper for you to attempt to disengage from the interview, but the Borant Corporation wishes to commend you for showing proper respect to the organization. They're actually quite pleased with you right now."

"Commend us?" I said. "Really?" *Proper respect?* The thought of giving respect to anything Borant did made me sick. Anyone who mistook fear for respect was a fool.

"The politics regarding all of this is too complicated to even begin to explain. However, that particular production, while technically private, is owned and operated by a prince of a faction that is allied with another faction that is at odds with the Borant system. All of it would make your head spin if I were to explain it to you."

"If you don't like those guys, then why did you let them interview us? That show is awful, Zev. It's . . ." *It's almost as cruel as the game itself,* I almost said. "It's abusive."

She nodded. "And I would like to apologize. Mukta should never have booked it. The show I had scheduled also caters to the younger crowd, but it would be a discussion regarding specific tactics you use in the dungeon. They do it in a creative, silly way. But to answer your question, Borant is not allowed to discriminate against Syndicate-member production companies. Especially when said companies are tied to production sponsors. This is monitored very closely by the AI. Anything to do with money is watched carefully, especially this season."

"So that Maestro asshole is a prince?" I asked. "No wonder he's such a cheesedick. I didn't realize he was royalty. I assumed the show didn't have very much money."

"He *is* a prince," Zev said. "But that production is owned by his older brother, Crown Prince Stalwart. I think their father gives them a small stipend to make the show, probably to keep them busy."

I thought of that voice that had threatened us when we'd attempted to bail. If that was him, he seemed just as much of a douche as his younger brother. "Prince Stalwart? That name is almost as bad as 'the Maestro.'"

"They're orcs. Everything they do is mawkish."

I had no idea what the word "mawkish" meant, but I assumed it translated to "cheesy." "So these guys are different than the tusklings? I know they are obviously a different race, but I thought the tusklings were the rulers of all the orcs."

"The tusklings are the rulers of the Orcish Supremacy. Stalwart and the Maestro are princes of the Skull Empire. That's a whole different system. If the Orcish Supremacy is a child with a lemonade stand, the Skull Empire is the Walmart Corporation. It's one of the largest and oldest Syndicate governments."

"Yeah, he'd said something about creating the crawl." I glanced down at Donut. "He also talked a bit about the ninth floor. How he's going to be there."

"Sorry, I can't really discuss that yet. Mordecai is now authorized to tell you about the third floor, but that's it."

"Is there anything you can tell us?" I asked.

She looked pained. "What I can say is that every three floors are the same setting. Sort of. The third, sixth, ninth, and so forth are all linked in a way that will later become clear."

I thought about what Mordecai had whispered to me earlier, that Borant was trying to end the game as soon as possible.

"What if all the crawlers die before the ninth floor even starts?"

"That probably isn't going to happen," she said. "It's starting to look like we'll get there much faster than usual, but we've never had a full player extinction before the ninth floor. It happens *on* the ninth floor a lot, but not before it. Again, I can't tell you much, but those floors . . . three, six, nine, twelve, fifteen, and eighteen, all come into existence at the same time. *You* can only visit them in context with the rest of the crawl, but that doesn't mean they're not being utilized. Whatever happens on the ninth and twelfth floors happens with or without the crawlers. It's a game within the game where you are not the main focus. At least not until you get there. Sorry, that's all I can say."

"Okay," I said. "I was just wondering. I'm not going to worry about it until we get there, I guess."

"That's the spirit! Now we need to talk about the next couple of days. I was just brainstorming with my team, and we agree that you two need to concentrate on building up your character. You're already in a good position, but a couple extra levels would really help you out. Now that the Meadow Lark storyline is completed, we can wait a day or two before really focusing on the next story arc."

"Story arc?" I said. "Really?"

"How is this thing with Maggie and Frank going over?" Donut asked.

Zev waved dismissively. "It has potential, but it's already tired. Those two have a good amount of followers, especially after last night, but not many people think they're going to survive long enough for that Maggie lady to make good on her threat. She's not very charismatic, and she's acting more and more irrationally. This gripe you have with Prince Maestro is getting much more attention, especially with that Pork Boy Snick that just showed up. Two hours old, and it's already trending all over the social media tunnels. But like we've already discussed, that whole story won't bear fruit until much later. We feel you can get away with coasting for a few days until you hit the next floor down, but once you do hit the Over City, you really need to focus on something compelling. Just train, and try not to be too boring. Maybe take out a boss or two. And don't pick anything weird during race selection."

"Back up," I said. "What the hell is a 'Pork Boy Snick'?"

She chuckled nervously. "Yeah, I need to tell you about this. So, you have . . . had . . . a similar phenomenon on Earth. Are you familiar with the concept of fan fiction?"

"Wait, what's that?" Donut asked.

Zev whirled on Donut. "Oh my gods, Donut. You would love it. There was this whole website, and it was filled with stories about *Gossip Girl*. But it was written by people like you and me. Actual fans, not the writers. So the stories aren't real. Or canon, they called it. But some were great! I tried writing one once, but it didn't get many views."

"That sounds like the greatest thing in the world," Donut said. "You can make it so the show never ends! Wait. People are writing stories about *us*? Me and Carl?"

"Yeah, so a snick is kind of like fan fiction, but it's a video. So it's like a fan fiction movie. You can experience the scene from any of the characters' points of view, or you can just watch it. This particular video is short, and a little . . . What is the word? Um, explicit."

"What was in the video?" Donut asked. "What do you mean by explicit? Was I in it?"

"No," Zev said. "Just Carl. Carl and the Maestro. And let's just say Carl has the upper hand during the scene."

"Uh," I said. I tried to think of something to say, but I couldn't think of anything. "Who made it?"

"So, that's the interesting part. It's a bit of a mystery. It showed up just a few hours after your interview. Nobody knows where it came from. But it went very viral, very fast. The quality is flawless. In fact, it came out so fast, some people think it's real. It's not . . . right?"

"Are you asking me if I fucked the orc?"

"Wait, it's a sex tape? With Carl and the Maestro?" Donut said. She practically fell off her chair, laughing. "And I thought it was going to be a bog witch that finally stole his heart."

"It *is* a little funny," Zev said. "But the Skull Empire probably isn't going to find it amusing. They haven't reacted yet, at least not officially. They're not known for their measured responses to insults."

"Is it an insult, though?" I asked. "I'm not gay, but does it matter? The tusklings seem to be very open with, you know, weird stuff. Do people really care?"

"It's not that," Zev said. "You're right. Most wouldn't care. But this is a prince of the Skull Empire. And that video is both graphic and humiliating. You two . . . say things to each other."

"Can we watch it?" Donut asked. "I want to watch it!"

"That sort of thing has to happen all the time," I said. "That prince is such a cockwomble, I can't imagine the intergalactic internet isn't filled with stuff like that."

"Oh, it is. This is different. The quality is so good, and it is just everywhere right now. Everyone is calling the Prince 'Pork Boy' and, uh, 'Carl's Naughty Little Piggie.' You have to watch the video. Anyway, if the Skull Empire demands people stop calling him that, it's going to be just like the mudskipper thing all over again. In the past hour, your appearance fee has doubled. You're now equal with Lucia Mar. The fact this has happened at the expense of the Skull Empire has made the party very happy with you."

"Oh shit," I said, any sense of amusement fleeing. "The last thing we need is some giant sponsor gunning for us. Any interview we do, they're just going to ask me about it, and I can tell you right now, there's nothing I'm willing to say to make those assholes hate me less."

"There's no such thing as bad publicity," Zev said. "Borant's official stance on this is that as long as you do not disparage the company, the party, or the Syndicate itself, any opinion you air about other governments will not be met with any sort of punitive action. Besides, there's not much the other governments can do to you. Not until the sixth floor. Or if they spring for a deity sponsorship this season. But anyway, don't worry about anything happening outside your floor. That's my job. Now I gotta get going. Your next scheduled appearance is on Odette's show. In the meantime, I'll be available on chat. Bye to both of you."

A moment later, she popped away, splashing water all over the floor.

"I'm glad she's okay," Donut said. "I feel bad we got her in trouble."

I barely heard her. I couldn't stop thinking about the video. This Skull Empire government had to know how much of an asshole that prince was. Plus they couldn't blame me for something I didn't make, could they?

My HUD snapped back on. The first thing I noticed was that my followers had increased significantly in the past hour. With the combination of the recap episode and this stupid video, that feeling of loneliness I'd felt earlier was all but gone. I now felt like a bug under a microscope. I wondered how many people *really* thought that the snick was real. I always wondered that about conspiracy theorists. I always suspected most of them were just trolling. Surely the real number couldn't be very many.

"Carl, darling. I can't believe you hooked up with that guy," Donut said loudly. She pushed at the door, heading out of the room. "He sure squealed a lot, though." Her laughter trailed off into the hallway.

"Goddamnit, Donut," I said.

45

FINDING THE BOSS CHAMBER OF THE KOBOLDS WAS EASY.

Heavy, thrumming metal music blasted through the halls. It was a cacophony of sound with growling, deep vocals and guitars that were almost seizure-like. I couldn't tell if the vocalist was singing in English, or if he was even human at all. The words sounded like deeply distorted barking. Considering the enemies of this quadrant, I wouldn't be surprised if the singer was a kobold or a dingo.

We followed the sound, which grew louder and louder until it was physically painful. Donut and I couldn't talk to one another, and we had to rely on the chat to communicate. We killed a half dozen kobolds and an equal number of dingoes along the way, plus a handful of the brindle grubs. Both of us hit level 12 by the time we approached the source.

> DONUT: THIS MUSIC IS MAKING MY HEAD HURT. WHY CAN'T THEY PLAY SOMETHING GOOD? LIKE OASIS.
> CARL: Oasis? Where did you get that from? Even Bea didn't listen to Oasis.
> DONUT: NO, MISS BEATRICE LIKES COUNTRY MUSIC. THAT'S JUST AS BAD AS THIS.
> CARL: Yeah, that should've been my first warning.
> DONUT: THERE IS THE BOSS CHAMBER.

The outer kobold boss chamber was set up as a giant dog kennel. The text on the walls was in Portuguese, indicating the place had been some sort of municipal dog pound. It was a group of three long hallways flanked by cages. There was a secondary main chamber with a door at the end of the middle hallway, but we already knew from experience that whatever the boss was going to be, it would likely come out of that second room. That second door was huge, like the double doors of a barn. An ominous sign.

Most of the cages were empty, but not all of them. Each row had four or five locked pens with danger dingoes within. I didn't see any signs of the kobolds. A handful of cages also contained the X's of dead monsters. Here, in this context, the large dingoes looked especially doglike, and I suddenly felt an uneasy sympathy for them. The monsters didn't bark or attack the cages as we passed by them. They sat there, curled up, looking pitiful.

Their dots, however, remained red on the minimap.

DONUT: SHOULD WE KILL THEM? WE SHOULD PROBABLY KILL
   THEM.

It would be easy, free experience. And I knew once that boss chamber opened, these doors would likely also open. But it felt wrong. I remembered Mordecai's advice regarding the boss rooms. *There will always be clues.*

CARL: Hang on. Not yet. Let's try to figure out what's going on
   here.

I stopped at one of the cages. The dingo was on its side, breathing heavily, its back turned.

"Hey, buddy, you doing okay?" I said, yelling the words. I couldn't even hear my own voice.

The dingo looked up, turning its head toward me. He was missing an eye, a recent injury. His white face paint mixed red with blood. Then I noticed the injuries on his side, a mixture of old scars and new ones around his flank and along the side of his neck.

The song ended. A moment later, a new one started, just as loud and heavy. But in that brief moment of silence, I heard something coming from the main boss chamber.

Cheering.

I knew, then, what this was.

Goddamnit, I thought. I hated this place. I hated it so damn much. I looked up at the boss room door.

I searched my inventory. I didn't have any scrolls of *Heal Critter* left, but I did have a ton of pet biscuits. Donut still ate them despite being classified as a regular crawler. But unless we were locked in the dungeon for fifty years, we'd never run out of the food. I took a single biscuit from my inventory and tossed it into the cage.

DONUT: CARL, WHAT ARE YOU DOING? THAT IS MY FOOD.

CARL: I'm trying something. Let's see what happens.

DONUT: THIS IS A BETRAYAL MOST FOUL.

CARL: You know the viewers can't see this chat. Don't be such a drama queen.

The dingo painfully pulled himself up, sniffed at the food, and he ate the tiny biscuit. He sat back down and turned his back.

The dot on the minimap blinked and turned white.

Yes.

We repeated the process for all the other dingoes in the cages. There was a total of fourteen of them. Most of them were in similar shape to the first one.

Three cages also contained dead danger dingoes. I debated whether or not to have Donut raise them from the dead prior to the battle, but there didn't seem to be a way to open the cages. Donut's ten-mana *Second Chance* spell was now level five. Instead of reanimating the corpses for five minutes, once she hit level five, they now remained animated for ten minutes, which was usually long enough to finish out a battle. She could now apparently resurrect monsters up to five levels higher than herself.

She currently had a pool of 28 mana points. She had two pieces of mana toast and a pile of mana restoration potions, though with her two-minute cooldown between potions, their use in battle became negligible. So we decided to wait and see what we faced first.

My plan wasn't too exciting, but it was safe. The door to the main chamber didn't seem to be opening, at least not yet, so we were going to use our tried-and-true method of firebomb and run.

But just as I pulled a boom jug out of my inventory, our luck ran out.

The music abruptly stopped. My ears rang, feeling heavy in my head. Within the chamber, the cheering ceased. The double barn doors started to open. Behind us, the door to the secondary chamber slammed shut. Above, new, more familiar music started to play.

Boss Battle!

That's right! You have discovered another lair of a Neighborhood Boss!

Put your game faces on, ladies and gentlemen! *Aaaand* **Here. We. Go!**

"Shit," I said, scrambling toward the barn doors. As I ran, I had a brief moment to marvel at how much I'd changed in the past week. My original instinct would've been to hide. Instead, I ran toward the danger.

I lit the torch on the jug, and I tossed it directly at the still-opening doors. Just as the jug took flight, the doors flew all the way open, revealing a mass of about 40 kobolds emerging from the room, cheering and chanting. I did not see any boss at all.

The world froze with the jug in midair. It hung like a comet. The group of kobolds was just starting to look up at the object in the air, rocketing toward them, their eyes registering surprise.

My eyes focused on the kobold in the center of the congregation. He still appeared to be one of the level five kobold riders, but he was much better dressed. He wore what appeared to be a fur coat made out of dingo fur and he wore spiked boots, making him a head taller than the others. In his hands he held a small metal-reinforced cage, about the size of a shoebox. His hands were frozen in the act of pulling open the enclosure, the little entrance pointed directly at us like a gun barrel.

Uh-oh, I thought.

Our mug shots splattered into view, and the **Versus** stamped onto the image.

Ralph

　Frenzied Gerbil

　Level 11 Neighborhood Boss!

　Before we send you off to certain death, it's time for a short history lesson.

　When the Black Death swept through 14th-century Europe, killing upwards of 200 million people and forever altering the course of human history, one of the original culprits of the epidemic was said to be the black rat, carrying plague-infested fleas into population centers to wreak their destruction.

　This is, in fact, not true. The true perpetrator was actually the Asian great gerbil, who took advantage of the warmer climate to travel the Silk Road and bring the disease into Europe.

　This is only important to know because Ralph, champion pit fighter of the kobold training grounds, lives his life in a perpetual state of rage. Why? Because he feels that human death toll of 200 million is much too low, and he will do everything in his power to triple that number.

　Starting with you.

　The only survivor of a family of gerbils left to starve by a child who'd grown bored with the pets, Ralph had to commit unspeakable acts of cannibalism in order to endure.

　Part Earth rodent, part the embodiment of death, Frenzied Gerbils are regular mobs one might encounter on the fifth or seventh floors. But Ralph here is special. He has dedicated his existence to fighting and training in hopes that one day he might exact his revenge against the humans he so despises.

He is fast, he is angry, and by the time you're done reading this, he's already halfway to your jugular.

You might want to duck.

The moment the extra-long description ended, the world unfroze, and chaos erupted all around us.

I threw my body to the ground just as the furry, squealing rodent sailed over my head. He'd shot out of the carrier so fast I hadn't even seen him.

At the same moment, the boom jug exploded in the midst of the kobolds, evaporating most of them instantly, including Ralph's owner, the pimped-out kobold.

The fist-sized ball of fur screamed with rage as he landed harmlessly down the long hallway. Donut jumped to my shoulder and shot a magic missile at the tiny monster, and she scored a direct hit. It flew farther back, sliding and tumbling. A health bar appeared, indicating she'd taken maybe 15% of its health away.

"Good shot," I cried.

The tiny boss looked mostly like a regular gerbil with the exception of its mouth, which defied logic and physics. Its ravening jaw appeared normal when closed, but when the tiny, absurdly cute creature screamed, its mouth opened huge, just as wide as the dingoes it fought in the arena. It squealed angrily now, and its mouth burst open, obscuring the small creature attached to it. This was a round, frothing set of gnashing teeth big enough for me to stick my entire head within.

"All righty, then," I said, standing to my full height as the creature snarled at us and prepared to charge again.

"Carl, I can't help but think this boss has been placed here for a very specific purpose," Donut said. She shot at it again with a magic missile, but this one missed. The gerbil squealed and jumped back.

"What do you mean?" I asked.

Most of the kobolds were dead, but a few at the edges of the blast had survived. One kobold, trailing blood, dragged itself to the wall and pressed a button recessed against the wall near the barn doors. A deep rumbling filled the chamber as the cages all started to open.

"Bad idea, buddy," I called to the kobold.

The dingoes emerged from their cages. Their dots on the minimap remained white. They slunk low, growling. Most of them were still injured, in obvious pain. But whatever spell had kept them under the control of their kobold slave masters had been broken by a simple act of kindness.

One of the dingoes—that first one we'd fed—leaped out and pounced right onto Ralph. It happened quick, lightning fast. The one-eyed dingo swallowed the rodent whole in a swift, snapping gulp. Just like that, and the boss was gone.

Behind us, the remaining kobolds fell back as the other dingoes turned on their former masters, dropping upon them and ripping them apart savagely. The kobolds weren't armed, and there weren't many of them. The barking, snarling dingoes finished them off in seconds.

If we hadn't turned the dingoes on our side, this would've been a much more difficult battle. That had been the "trick" of this particular boss room. I silently thanked Mordecai for his advice. As unfair as this world was, it was still a game. There were puzzles and hidden paths to survival, and we needed to continue to keep our eyes open.

"Well, that was quite easy," Donut said. "And a little anticlimactic, if I must say so." She looked back at the first dingo, the one who'd eaten the boss. "I guess I was wrong."

I looked about the room. The kobolds were all dead. From the main boss chamber, the sound of multiple unknown creatures started to howl and trill and yip. These weren't particularly loud or menacing sounds, and I could barely hear them over the background music. None of them sounded like dingoes. Now that the smoke was clearing, I could see within the boss chamber. Like I expected, it was a small fighting arena. More cages circled the distant walls. I couldn't see the contents from this distance, but it was a mix of red and white dots. I suspected if we hadn't killed the kobolds so quickly, one of them would've likely run back in and opened those cages as well.

The boss music still played, and the realization startled me. "This isn't over yet," I said. "We're missing something." I formed a fist, preparing for an attack. "And what did you mean? What were you wrong about?"

The other dingoes all slinked away. Some bared their teeth at us as they passed, but in a submissive gesture, not an angry one. This close, the massive 200-pound dingoes were even more terrifying to behold. While they all wore the white face paint, none wore it exactly the same. They congregated at the end of the chamber by the locked door. They scratched at the exit, like dogs wanting to go outside.

The one-eyed dingo who'd eaten Ralph continued to stand where he'd swallowed the miniature boss. He seemed frozen in place. The creature looked at us and started to whine.

Donut looked pointedly at my foot. "It's a small rodent. Your feet are all nice and shiny. As Miss Beatrice used to say, 'Time to pay the Daddy tax.'"

"Wait, what? Under what circumstances would she say that?"

At that moment, the dingo's head exploded.

The creature looked at us, cocked its head to the side, and then *boom*. Red-and-white gore splattered everywhere. The still-alive gerbil burst forth, flying directly at my throat. It was halfway across the room before the poor headless dingo hit the ground. The tiny furry rocket squealed.

I'd been ready. I Mike Tysoned it with all my strength. The gerbil bounced off the floor with a sickening *crunch*, sliding until it hit the edge of a cage. Its health was suddenly in the deep red.

It had **Stunned** over its head with a 15-second timer.

My gauntlet only had a 2% chance to inflict Stun on monsters. I'd never, not once, gotten the debuff to activate until now. With a baleful glance at the ceiling, I took two steps toward the tiny unmoving form. For a moment, I contemplated just punching it to death.

Time to pay the Daddy tax.

"If it makes you feel better, she was talking about you. You're the daddy," Donut said, looking down at the almost-dead boss.

"No, Donut," I said. "That does not make me feel better. That's the opposite of making me feel better."

I placed my bare right foot upon the small monster.

"Sorry, Ralph," I said.

46

THE DUNGEON GROANED. IT FUCKING GROANED.

I sighed as I wiped my foot on the metal bar of the cage. The entire dungeon rumbled as if it was experiencing a small earthquake. My HUD flickered. I felt dirty and sick. I rubbed my foot over and over, but the blood wouldn't come off.

The boss fight officially ended, and the distant door opened. The thirteen danger dingoes fled into the hallway, scattering away to the wind.

I looted the neighborhood map. Dozens of red dots filled the hallways. These were newly generated brindle grubs. I watched as the white dots of the dingoes continued to run toward the main artery hall, snatching up and killing the grubs they passed. The dingoes, as a pack, hit the main passage and their dots disappeared.

I wondered what would happen if they ran across another group of crawlers. Probably nothing good, at least not for the crawlers. Either way, they wouldn't bother us again.

"Let's see what's in this main room," I said.

We stepped over the slagged, still-smoldering remains of the kobolds. Most of their bodies had been destroyed. I picked through what was left, looting a few spiked helmets and gold coins here and there. One had a scroll of *Heal Critter* and a handful of pet biscuits.

The small gerbil cage lay on the floor, undamaged by the fire. I tossed it into my inventory.

The kobold who'd pressed the button to open the cages also had a key. I examined its properties.

Master Pen Key.

Opens the individual cages of both the fighters and the bait animals within the kobold fighting pits. This key is magically attuned to the kobold race. If you are not a kobold and attempt to use this key, it will only work once before breaking.

Choose wisely.

We stepped into the arena, and I was immediately assaulted by the stench of death. A small, round fighting arena stood empty. The dirt floor was stained red. Against the left wall stood a pile of bones as tall as the ceiling. Several dozen chairs made of hardened wood circled the arena. I picked them up and looted them all before approaching the line of cages against the back of the chamber.

The moment we approached the cages, each filled with a different type of monster, two achievements popped up.

New achievement! I'll Take the Ceramic Dalmatian, Pat!

You have discovered a reward room! Scattered throughout the dungeon, reward rooms offer crawlers items generally not available within loot boxes. Most reward rooms only allow one choice. So, if you're in a party of multiple people, tell them I said you should get the prize, not them.

Reward: Don't be a greedy bitch. The goddamned room is the reward.

New achievement! Menagerie!

You have discovered a pet reward room. From caterpillars who secrete vodka to basilisks who can turn mobs to stone, a good pet can make the difference between survival and the end of the road. Just remember what happened with Harambe. There ain't no zookeepers around to shoot the monster's ass if you bite off more than you can chew.

Reward: You have a key. It opens only one cage. Figure it out, Einstein.

"Well, shit," I said, looking over the choices. "I guess we're getting a pet."

"I get to pick," Donut said. "The thing said it was my prize."

"Yeah, Donut. It said the same thing to both of us. It's trying to get us to fight."

"Really? Well, that was mean." She gasped as she noticed the very last cage. "Carl, Carl, give me the key!"

There was a line of ten cages. None of the creatures looked particularly impressive. But then again, that gerbil hadn't looked too impressive, either. Still, I suspected since this was only the second floor and the first of these treasure rooms we'd come across, none of these guys were super rare or valuable.

I was hesitant about this. In most games I'd played, you could only have one pet at a time. Would that be the case here? If so, how hard was it to give up the pet? I had no idea.

The first animal was a parrot thing with a long beak, and it was easily the loudest thing here. Its dot was red. I examined it, but the system didn't give me any info other than its name. **Juvenile Riven Wing.**

The next was a green slime, then a rat, then a meatball with two legs and a mohawk called a **Tummy Acher.** Of the first four, only the slime and the rat had white dots. A row of equally pitiful animals followed, looking up at us, including a white-tagged brindle grub. I thought of those massive deadly Brindled Vespas and thought maybe that'd be a good choice.

But Donut only had eyes on that last cage.

It was a chicken dinosaur thing with pink downy feathers. The monster cooed up at the cat, making a chirping noise.

The thing looked pitiful. I immediately saw why Donut liked it. It landed firmly in the it's-so-damn-ugly-it's-cute category. It was probably seven inches tall. It stood on two legs and cocked its head at me. The damn thing looked like a raw piece of chicken with a few random pink-hued feathers attached to it. It had two tiny forearms instead of wings and a long serpentine tail. It squawked, opening its beaked mouth, revealing a row of sharp tiny teeth.

It was called a **Mongoliensis**. It was also red-tagged.

"Is it a boy or girl?" Donut asked. "How can I tell? If it's a boy I'm gonna call him Mongo." The chicken thing chirped at Donut. "If it's a girl I'm naming her Sissy."

"It looks like dinner," I said. "I think we should get the brindle grub."

"Give it a pet biscuit," Donut said. "See if its dot changes to white."

I sighed and pulled a pet biscuit out. I tried to toss it into the cage, but a blue force field appeared, blocking the treat. The chicken cried in outrage and slammed its head against the bars. All up and down the row, all the creatures started squealing and squawking.

If we were going to get a pet, I knew it would be for the best to let Donut have the creature. I didn't know for certain what attribute counted the most toward keeping it happy and not murdering us in our sleep, but I imagined charisma had a major role. And maybe strength. Donut outranked me in both. I weighed whether or not I should attempt to overrule her.

"If it's a girl, we can get her a little dress, and she can sit on my shoulder when we do interviews. Can't you just see it? I'll be like Paris Hilton with Tinkerbell."

"Donut," I said. "I really think—"

Warning: The cages will permanently close in thirty seconds.
Translation: Hurry the hell up.

"Carl, quick! Please, please, please! I'll never ask for anything ever again. I promise!"

I sighed. "It's going to attack us. I'll grab it, and you try feeding it."

I took the key, and I jammed it into the lock of the mongoliensis cage. I cracked the door, and the little bastard shot out. I grasped it in both hands. It started thrashing and attempting to bite me. The thing barely weighed anything at all.

I had to sit on the ground while Donut pulled a few pet biscuits from her inventory. They appeared on the ground in front of the thing. It continued to fight me, but it slowed down, eyeing the food. I eased my double-handed grip enough for it to peck at the food like a chicken. It took a few bites, then squawked.

The dot remained red.

"Carl, it's a boy! It's okay, Mongo. I'm sorry I said I'd put you in a dress. We'll get you a nice little bow tie. Would you like that?"

The creature snapped forward and bit Donut directly on the nose. She squealed in pain.

"Bad! Bad Mongo!"

The baby dinosaur, still in my grip, started screaming back at the cat while I tried to keep myself from falling over with laughter. Donut hissed and swatted it lightly on the head. The small monster squealed indignantly and snapped again at her face.

I examined the creature's properties.

Male Mongoliensis—Level 1

This is a pet-class mob.

This pet has not yet bonded with a crawler.

The stubborn and hotheaded Mongoliensis is not the type of pet to ever be "tamed." The best one can hope for is mutual respect. And even then they still might try to eat you if the fancy strikes them. While especially powerful, fast, and vicious when they are fully grown at level 15, getting them to level 15 is about as likely as a cheerleader from West Virginia reaching her 18th birthday as a virgin.

They will immediately attack any mobs they see. They will fight to the death.

Good luck.

"Goddamnit, Donut," I said. "I knew we should've gone with the grub."

"I'm not going to have a disgusting bug thing as a pet, Carl,"

Donut said. "You can't even put a bow tie on a grub." She reached forward and patted Mongo on the head. He snapped at her and attached himself to her arm. She yowled and shook her arm until he fell off.

"Well, we better figure out how to get this thing to 'bond' with you before we go to Mordecai's room, or Mongo here is going to teleport away the second we walk in there."

"Don't worry, Carl. Mongo and I are practically best friends already. Aren't we, Mongo?"

Mongo shrieked at the cat.

47

THE PROCESS OF GETTING MONGO TO BOND WITH DONUT TOOK THE rest of our time on the second floor. It also, for whatever reason, appeared to be endlessly amusing to the general public. The continuing fallout from the Maestro sex tape along with Donut getting her nose chomped over and over and over by her new "pet" seemed to be a winning combination, in terms of views, at least. Even though we faced no more bosses or major battles for the remainder of our time on this floor, we were far from idle. Zev was beside herself with our numbers, which apparently were exceptionally good for the second floor.

We received daily updates from the PR agent. The pet was playing well. Zev implored me to stop training with the slingshot. Nobody liked me using the "boring" slingshot, she claimed, not when I could toss a stick of dynamite instead. I ignored her advice and continued practicing with it. I managed to get the skill up to five. And while the tiny stones did very little damage, they had the ability to knock the Brindled Vespas out of the air. A single hit to one of the hornets' wings caused it to crash to the ground and make it unable to spit its acid. A follow-up magic missile from Donut—whose skill in the spell had risen to eight—usually killed them off. We didn't need to wander far when we had an almost endless supply of the level eight hornets to hunt.

The first thing we did after winning Mongo was go talk to Mordecai. The creature fit in the gerbil cage. Barely. It wasn't ideal, and it was cruel to keep him in there. But if I carried him in my hands, he spent every free moment trying to bite me. If we stuck him in the cage, it allowed us to take him into a safe room without having to worry about him teleporting away. That is, as long as we kept our fingers away from the bars.

"Don't ask me about that thing until you start the bonding process," Mordecai said. "The rules are a little weird about taming dungeon pets." In his cage, Mongo screamed and hissed at the guide. "Once you figure out how to remove his automatic hostility, which is the first step, come back, and I'll give you more info."

"Remove his hostility? Like how I did with the danger dingoes?" I asked.

"That's right. You can't bond with a creature when its aggro is activated. If you see that dot turn white, come back here, and I can help after that."

Donut and I opened up our loot boxes from the boss fight. Donut "coincidentally" received a spell book of *Heal Critter*. I received yet another potion of Determine Value (which had come from a looter box, not a boss box last time) and 1,000 gold coins. I wondered about that. There seemed to be a reason why the system kept giving these things to me. I drank it down, and I had a few new sort options for my inventory, including a new history tab. I would explore all that later. It still didn't tell me the monetary value of my individual items.

I also received an achievement for feeding the danger dingoes.

New achievement! PETA Enthusiast!
  You somehow managed to remove the hostility of an aggravated non-sapient enemy. That enemy then fought against other enemies to your benefit. The ghost of Steve Irwin smiles down upon you.
  Reward: I SAID THE GHOST OF STEVE IRWIN SMILES DOWN UPON YOU.

"Okay," I said. "So, let's talk about the third floor."

"All right, here we go," Mordecai said. He rubbed his furry hands together. "Here's the deal."

He indicated a pair of chairs, asking us to sit. I sat down, placing Mongo's cage on the floor between me and Donut. The guide seemed oddly excited about this. I noticed for the first time that he'd cleaned up his chambers. His bed was made. The shelves with the picture of his brother and the urn with his mother had been straightened and dusted.

Once we were settled, he continued. "You're going to go down the stairs, and you will immediately find yourselves back in this room. You will first choose your race, then your class, and then you will distribute your stat points. From there, I will give you information on class guilds, if applicable. Not all classes have guilds."

"How many choices will there be for race?" I asked.

"A lot. It is unique every season, and the both of you will have a different pool of choices. The class choices will depend on your racial choice. You know how in every new Olympics they introduce a few new sports, usually ones associated with the host country? That's how it is with classes. The base classes will always be available. Fighter, mage, rogue, bard, cleric, et cetera. But there will also be additional, more specialized classes available, including new, Earth-specific classes."

"What does that mean, though? Earth-specific classes?"

"I don't know yet. I won't see the list until you do. But you will have an incentive to pick one of these classes. They like it when crawlers pick the new classes because it's good for ratings. The system AI . . ." He paused, making sure I was paying attention. "Again, the system AI and *not* Borant will give you some recommendations based on your preexisting skills. These recommendations are generally good. However, these recommendations do *not* take into account how these choices might affect your standing socially. Does that make sense?"

"Yes," I said. "The AI might say it'll be best to turn into a rock monster paladin, and I'd be a badass, but it might also tank my views."

"Exactly. I will also be allowed to offer limited advice. After class selection, your stat points will automatically distribute up to the race and class minimums, and you will be free to distribute the rest as you please. However, you, Donut, can't distribute stats because of your Enhanced Growth buff. You'll want to find something that comes with a boost to constitution if you can. Got it?"

"Got it," I said. Donut grunted assent.

"Wait a second," I said. "What was your class? I know you chose a Changeling as your race, but what was your class?"

"I chose Arcanist, which allowed me to explore several different magic schools. Certain classes can further specialize when they hit the sixth floor. It was then that I chose the fire path. I was a Changeling Fire Mage Arcanist. It worked out well for me. I ended up a few levels behind people who went straight to fire magic, but I could still wield other magics without a big penalty."

"So you didn't pick one of the special classes for your planet?"

He frowned slightly. "I almost chose a skyfowl class, something called a Storm Commander. But Odette talked me out of it. My brother ended up picking it instead, on her recommendation."

I paused, my eyes immediately moving to the framed photo on the shelf. He'd mentioned his brother a few times, but I hadn't realized he'd been a crawler. I'd assumed he'd been lost during his planet's initial collapse.

"Finally, there's the matter of the third floor itself," Mordecai said, making it perfectly clear he had no desire to go down that conversational path. "I prefer to explain it when you get there because there's a lot to take in. It's not something you need to worry about just yet. Okay?"

"Sure," I said, standing. "Now . . ."

Thwum.

"Mongo!" Donut cried.

I'd stood too close to the cage, and the monster tried to bite me. He teleported away.

"Whoops," I said.

"Carl, you scared him!"

"I *scared* him?" I picked up the now-empty cage. "Well, that sucks. I guess it wasn't meant to . . ."

Donut bolted out the door, yelling, "Mongo! Mongo!"

"Goddamnit, Donut!" I cried, running after the cat. "Don't go out there alone!"

We eventually found the thing huddled in the main hall, crying like a baby, squawking at the top of his little chicken lungs.

"There you are! You're going to get lost! Don't wander like that!" Donut cried, out of breath.

The dinosaur looked up. The little shit looked like he'd been crying. His beady reptilian eyes grew giant when he saw us. He ran right to Donut, little arms out, like a long-lost puppy reuniting with his owner.

"It's okay. I'm here. Mommy is here," Donut said.

He rushed up and chomped her directly on the nose.

———

THE NEXT DAY CONSISTED OF GRINDING, KILLING BRINDLED VESPAS, and wrangling Mongo.

We quickly learned that only one thing stopped the thing from trying to murder me and Donut: seeing another mob.

If any sort of enemy came anywhere near us, the crazy chicken went absolutely apeshit. He screamed and snapped and tried to kill himself in an attempt to get to the creature. He was like a goddamned psychotic wolverine hopped up on bath salts.

Other than his ability to inflict punishing nose chomps, the dinosaur chicken remained mostly harmless. I was afraid to let him near any mobs, even simple brindle grubs, in fear he'd get himself stomped.

But in the end, that's exactly what we needed to do. It was the recap episode that gave me the clue. We were only on the program for a few short moments, but I learned something important. The four-eyed, orange-hued host of the show mentioned that Mongo was a pack hunter. That gave me an idea. After the episode, we went out and found a lone brindle grub struggling its way down a hall.

"You need to show him how to kill it," I said. "I'm going to let him free, and you two kill it together."

"You mean, I gotta use my claws?" Donut asked.

"Yep," I said.

She sighed. "All right. Who knew being a mother would be this difficult?"

I opened the cage, and Mongo shot out like a bullet toward the level two brindle grub, who squeaked and tried to crawl away. The little dinosaur leaped in the air, slashing with his clawed feet and chomping down on the bug. The health bar on the grub appeared, but it barely went down.

"Look, these guys are juicy on the inside," Donut said, coming up behind the two combatants. "If you cut here, all the stuff falls out and they're dead." She rolled the grub over and cut with her claw along the bug's stomach, like she was unzipping it. The grub shuddered and died, spilling white goo everywhere. Mongo shrieked with joy and began to vigorously devour the remains, filling himself up so much his stomach bulged afterward. The little dinosaur puked on the floor and then ate that, too.

"Christ, that's disgusting," I said.

"Good boy. Good Mongo!" Donut cried.

Mongo stood on top of the grub's remains and peed. Luckily the ban only applied to humans; otherwise we'd have summoned about 100 elementals that first day.

"Come on, let's keep killing," Donut said. The next hall down held three grubs. I followed at a distance while they rushed over and tried it again.

Mongo seemed to have been paying attention. He managed to kill the second grub by himself, slicing open its belly with the hooked claw on his foot. He bounced up and down with excitement after he did it.

By the time he'd finished off all three grubs, Mongo's dot turned from red to white. He still wasn't "bonded" to Donut, but he no longer attacked us. Actually, that wasn't true. He still attacked, but not as much. We didn't need the cage anymore. He followed us on foot, sometimes running ahead, sometimes hopping sideways and lagging behind. If we approached an unknown mob, I had to stick him back in the cage, however. He did not like that one bit.

Despite killing a dozen grubs, he remained at level one. We decided it was time to go back to Mordecai.

"So, pets," Mordecai said after we returned to the guild. "I'm limited in what I can tell you at this point, but I can now reveal you're on the right track. Keep doing what you're doing. That's the good news. The bad news is you need to hurry. If he's not bonded by the time the floor collapses, you won't be able to bring him with you."

We had barely forty hours left.

"Oh no," Donut cried. "Carl, we need to get back out there!"

"Just a minute," I said. "I have a couple pet questions. Can we have more than one?"

"It depends," he said. "There are multiple types of pets. The quick answer is no, you generally can't have more than one. But there are lots of exceptions. Some classes and some races allow for crawlers to have multiple pets. Also, if you have an especially high charisma, like Donut, you can also have multiples of certain types of pets. Also, pets with crawler IDs don't count toward that number. So if Donut had still been classified as a pet, you'd have been able to bond with another. Crawler pets and dungeon familiars are actually a different sort of thing. That's why that Lucia Mar kid can have those two dogs without any issues. There's also this one lady who brought like 15 goats in with her. She's still alive, and so are the goats. It's bizarre. There's this one show that is obsessed with her."

"Why isn't he leveling up?" I asked. "It's like he's not getting any experience at all."

Mordecai nodded. "Pet-class mobs are a little different. You got him from a treasure room, but it's the same as if you'd purchased him from a shop. Mobs that start out as a pet class will always be level one regardless of what they usually are when you find them in the dungeon. And they'll stay level one until they're bonded. Only then will they start to level. Once they do start gaining experience, though, they will grow rapidly. He'll get physically more mature each level up."

"The description says he's fully grown at level 15. Is that as high as he can get?" I asked.

"Oh no," Mordecai said. "Not even close. He just won't get physically bigger after that."

"How big will he get?" Donut asked, looking down at the chicken, who was running in circles around Mordecai's room, shrieking.

"I can't tell you," he said. "But that little cage you've been using isn't going to work for much longer. You need to do more than just bond with him. You need to teach him restraint, or he *is* going to die, and he might just take you down with him if he aggravates the wrong mob. Any attempt at stealth is out the window until he learns to behave himself." Mongo responded by running up to Mordecai and leap-attacking his leg.

It took us a good bit to find where he'd teleported to. He'd entered the hallway across from our current quadrant and was in the process of wrangling with one of those level three cow-tailed brindle grubs. He didn't quite yet have the chops to take one of those things out on his own, but the ferocious little dino was doing an admirable job of dodging the grub's tail swipes.

We spent the next several hours trying to train him with dog commands. "Attack" and "come" and even "lie down" worked really well. "Stay" was another story.

Donut was surprisingly patient during this time. It turned out Mongo was very food motivated, and he loved pet biscuits, which made him easier to train. After a full day, we managed to keep him from just outright charging every time he saw something. He'd snarl and squawk and hop up and down, but he wouldn't plunge headfirst into battle until Donut said the command, which had somehow evolved from "attack" to "sic 'em."

When the timer was down to ten hours, we had to start carving our way toward the stairwell. We didn't have a choice. Mongo still hadn't officially bonded with Donut, and I was getting pretty worried it wasn't going to happen.

We were now exclusively fighting the Brindled Vespas. Despite the dungeon halving the number of hornets in the dungeon, they were still everywhere. The mobs gave a decent amount of experience, and we both hit level 13.

Out of desperation, we finally allowed Mongo to participate in the fights.

If there were more than a couple hornets in a hallway, we didn't fuck around. I tossed in an explosive. But if there was only one or two, I grounded them with my slingshot, and Donut hit them with magic missiles. Sometimes a single missile wasn't enough to kill them. That's when we'd send Mongo in to enthusiastically finish them off. The little beast was getting good at using his claw to rip open the thorax of the downed bugs.

In the hallway just outside the stair chamber, the same hallway we'd run through a few days earlier during our fight with the rage elemental, Mongo rushed in to finish off a hornet monster. The Vespa grabbed at Mongo with his human-like hand, capturing the small creature. The mob had been mostly dead, but apparently not dead enough. It lifted the screaming and struggling chicken into the air and moved to toss him into its enormous, toothed mouth.

"Put Mongo down!" Donut screamed, flying across the hallway and slashing at the bug. I'd never seen her move that fast. She decapitated the monster with a quick slash, and all three of them fell into a heap on the ground.

"Carl, Carl, something happened," Donut said a minute later.

"I see that," I said, walking up. I felt an odd combination of relief and dread. "It finally worked. Congratulations."

On the minimap, Mongo's dot had turned from white to orange. "Wait, I can officially name him now," she said. "I have a new menu and everything!"

Mongo the Mongoliensis Level One (Pet of Grand Champion Best in Dungeon Princess Donut) has joined the party.

Mongo's title has been changed to Royal Steed.

"We did it," Donut cried, hopping up and down. "We tamed Mongo!"

Mongo also jumped up and down next to the cat. He squawked with delight, waving his little arms.

And then he bit Donut right on the nose.

SO, WITH SEVEN HOURS LEFT—ONE BEFORE THE RECOMMENDED time to descend—we camped out in the room with the stairs.

I sat on the ground playing with my menus while Donut and Mongo ran in circles around the large chamber, playing energetically. Donut was instructing Mongo on the art of pouncing. I watched, smiling. My heart felt heavy as I watched them. What would the next floor hold? How much longer could we survive?

I thought of Mordecai and his brother, of that time we'd caught Mordecai unawares. He'd been drunk, holding on to that framed picture. This game—this terrible, cruel game—left scars that spanned centuries. I thought of the cheering crowds watching this all from the safety of their homes.

You will not break me. Fuck you all. You will not break me.

As we waited for the timer to hit six hours, I thought back to that odd boss prize I received after killing the gerbil. I would've thought that defeating the boss in such a manner would've garnered me a better prize. The dungeon AI wasn't my friend. It wasn't on my side. I knew that. But surely I should've gained *something* good.

I pulled up my inventory menu. I had that new tab labeled

History. I clicked on it, and it was filled with pretty much the same junk I had now, but with the chopper and a few extra potions and scrolls and bits of things I'd used to build other items. Curious, I clicked to sort it by value.

I practically choked. Listed at the very top of my menu were three items I'd never seen before. I clicked over to make sure I didn't have them now. I didn't.

What the actual hell?

I looked about, afraid to say anything out loud. Was this some sort of bug? I went back to the menu and examined the three items. The tooltips didn't go into the same detail they would if I still had the items on me, though I could see their names and what category my inventory had placed them in.

Trans Tunnel 7C Orator Relay by Valtay Corp.—Inter-Tunnel Communications Device.

Valtay Perso-Shield Platinum Edition.—Tech-based Personal Shield.

Mag 3040 Valtay Corp. Pulse Pistol.—Tech-based Weapon.

The first item had a red exclamation point next to it. I hovered over the red mark, and a warning popped up.

Warning: The System AI governing this program has deemed all non-sanctioned and monitored communication devices illegal, and they will not work within the dungeon. You may own and sell illegal devices, but any attempt to use or circumvent dungeon rules will result in immediate disqualification.

I was completely at a loss.

"Somebody's coming," Donut said. "There's a blue dot moving toward us."

My first thought was Frank and Maggie. I jumped to my feet and pulled up the map. It wasn't them. The moment I saw who it was, though, I realized I knew exactly where those items in my inventory had come from. The realization hit me like a brick. *Well, that's a weird coincidence.*

"Agatha," I said. "Holy shit, she's still alive."

I had taken her entire shopping cart into my inventory during that boss battle with the Ball of Swine. So much had happened so quickly during that battle, I'd never actually examined the individual items of her cart. I'd never even thought to do it. I looked now, and sure enough all of it was there. The shopping cart. An inordinate amount of IKEA bags and cans of spray paint. Blankets. Clothes. And a goddamned "Pulse pistol." All three of the items appeared to be manufactured by the same company. The Valtay Corporation.

My mind raced. I thought of what Brandon had said. Agatha had been the one to set their old folks' home on fire, bringing everyone outside. The act had, temporarily, saved the lives of hundreds of people. But did she work for Borant? Had someone just given her that stuff, and she didn't know what it was? And why the hell hadn't she shown up on the recap episode? Should I say something?

"You ain't dead," Agatha said a few minutes later as she wheeled the squeaking shopping cart into the room. The woman was still level four, the same she'd been since the boss battle with the tusklings.

"Where have you been?" I asked, moving toward her.

"Don't touch me!" she cried, shuffling faster toward the stairs. "You're a cart thief. I don't trust cart thieves."

"Hey, I gave it back," I said.

She didn't answer. She just pushed her cart toward the stairs.

I was tempted to grab her cart again, but only for a second. Whatever this was, it was something well beyond my current ability to understand or process. And getting involved with it probably wasn't good for my health, especially when I didn't know what the hell was going on. *Never trust someone if their motivations aren't clear.* Odette had said that to me. Still, I was overwhelmed with curiosity.

I thought of that saying, *Curiosity killed the cat.*

Mongo screamed at Agatha, but Donut whispered a quiet command and the little monster held back. Agatha gave the dinosaur no heed. The stairs had already turned into a ramp thanks to the earlier descent by Brandon and crew.

"I see the others made it down," Agatha muttered as she pushed the cart forward.

"You should wait ten minutes," I called. "If you go down now, you'll lose six hours. Plus I need to talk to you . . . about your shopping cart." I added that last part without thinking, and I immediately regretted it. *Don't get involved, you idiot!*

Agatha paused. She gave me a sharp look. Through her rheumy eyes, I saw a warning there. *No,* those eyes said, *stop now.*

"I can fix the wheel," I quickly added. "It's squeaking. They can hear you coming."

She blinked, and the look went away so quickly I wondered if I had imagined it.

"No need to fix m'squeak, boy. Them critters already know I'm here. They just don't know what to do about it. You worry about you, and I worry about me."

She continued down the stairs, quickly disappearing from view.

ZEV: Are you guys okay?

DONUT: WE ARE FINE. ARE YOU OKAY?

ZEV: Okay, false alarm. I see you now. There was a brief outage there in the feed. It happens sometimes. Odette says she's ready whenever you are, so feel free to go down starting in seven minutes. I won't be able to talk to you until after you're done with the race and class selections. I guess I'll see you guys on the other side. Good luck.

CARL: How long was the feed out?

ZEV: Just a couple minutes. It's been acting funky all day. Don't worry. It's nothing unusual. People are always complaining about it. I'm on planet, and I still have feed issues.

Them critters already know I'm here. They just don't know what to do about it.

Christ, I thought. What sort of bullshit was this? I thought back to the inventory potion. The moment I'd discovered the items, Agatha had appeared. Was that a coincidence? Was she working with the system AI? I shook my head.

A week and a half ago, I'd been planning on kidnapping a prize-winning cat and then selling everything I owned in order to bribe my ex-girlfriend to keep her from suing me. And even that was more drama than I'd ever wanted to deal with. All of this . . . with the Skull Empire and everything else, it was just too much, too fast. How could we focus on surviving when we had all this other stuff to deal with?

I sighed. I watched the timer finally run down to six hours.

"Come on, Donut," I said. "Let's see what this third floor is all about."

"Do you think it'll be as exciting as the second floor?" she asked.

"God, I hope not," I said.

Mongo screeched.

EPILOGUE

"YOU DO REALIZE THAT THING IS GOING TO GET YOU KILLED, RIGHT?"
Odette asked after the conclusion of her show. Donut was currently
chasing Mongo around the studio. The little dinosaur kept running
headfirst into the invisible wall and screaming. Lexis, Odette's production assistant, had given the small monster a bow tie to wear on
the show, and he'd practically bitten off her finger. The tie had lasted
about three seconds before he'd ripped it off.

The taping had gone well. We'd started off by discussing the
whole thing with the rage elemental. Then we talked about Mongo.
Donut had trained him to perch quietly on her back, clinging onto
her fur. He'd behaved himself. Mostly. Odette had mentioned something about a magical pet carrier, which apparently was the dungeon's equivalent of a Poké Ball. They were supposedly expensive,
but it would allow us to put bonded pets into inventory without
harming them. I didn't care how much they cost. If we could afford
it, it was going to be one of our first purchases. No more shoving
Mongo into the gerbil cage and then sticking him in the bathroom
so we couldn't hear his shrieks while we slept.

I'd known what was coming next.

After the segment on Mongo, I'd finally gotten to see a shortened
version of the infamous Pork Boy Snick. Donut had found it hilari-
ous. The mysterious creator of the video had been very . . .
generous . . . with my proportions. I'd been half-expecting the video
to feature my feet prominently. I didn't dare say it out loud, but I had
this strange notion that the system AI might've had something to do

with the video. But if it did, the video showed nothing to indicate it. In fact, it had clearly been produced by someone more interested in the Maestro than me, as he was the obvious subject of the video.

"So," Odette had said after we watched the scene and the audience's uproarious laughter eased, "you are likely unaware of this, but *Death Watch Extreme Dungeon Mayhem* announced earlier that it was going into hiatus while the show restructured."

"I'm shocked," Donut said. "Quite shocked."

The audience laughed.

"King Rust of the Skull Empire, who recently arrived in Earth orbit, has been oddly quiet about the controversy. A spokesperson for the royal family has requested people stop referring to the prince as 'Carl's Naughty Little Piggie.'" The audience roared. "But so far, nobody seems to be complying." Odette turned to her audience. With her bug helmet, her face was expressionless, but I could hear the grin in her voice. "I would personally like to assure King Rust that I would never call Prince Maestro 'Carl's Naughty Little Piggie' or 'Pork Boy.' And I would like to encourage my audience to never sink to that level. Again, it's 'Prince Maestro' and not . . ." She held her hands out.

"Carl's Naughty Little Piggie!" the audience shouted, followed by peals of laughter.

"Anyway," Odette said, "what do you think about this, Carl?"

"Look," I said. "I don't know anything about the Skull Clan or Empire or whatever, or this king guy. I'm sure he has a perfectly nice family and kingdom." The audience laughed. "I don't want any trouble with him and his people. But his son is a dick, and I called him out on it. Nothing more and nothing less. I didn't mean to cause an intergalactic incident. I know nothing about the video."

"So, to be clear, it is a snick," Odette asked. "A lot of people seem to believe it's real."

"If I was going to turn gay, it wouldn't be with that guy."

The audience screamed. Odette nodded. "But you did challenge him to single combat."

"Yes, I did. And that offer still stands," I said. "I still don't know how any of this stuff works because you guys won't tell me anything." More laughter. "But I hope for the chance to face him one on one."

"We do, too, don't we?" Odette said.

The audience cheered. Someone shouted, "Glurp, glurp!" A minute later the whole audience was glurping.

Odette shook her head in mock disgust.

The show ended soon after that. Like last time, Odette ushered Lexis out of the room so we could talk for a few minutes.

"Is it worth it?" I asked, indicating the pet. "If he lives, I mean."

"You should've picked the Tummy Acher," Odette said. "The little round guy with the mohawk. They're very friendly and easy to work with. Plus they're rare, and people love them. Once they're full-grown, they are one of the best melee tanks in the game. But your Mongo is a solid choice. If you can keep him alive, he will be a vicious fighter."

"So," I said, "I gave your message to Mordecai. He wasn't too pleased with the idea of working for you."

She nodded sadly. "I saw. I watched you tell him. He had a few additional choice words for me after you left. He'll come around. Tell him I understand his feelings on the matter, and I would love for the opportunity to explain myself."

"What happened between you two?" I asked.

"We don't have time to go into it," Odette said. "But the short answer is I pushed him too hard, and he paid dearly for it. Anyway, you're about to hit the all-important third floor." She'd asked me on air if I knew what I was going to do, and I'd answered truthfully. I had no idea what was going to happen. Donut had lied and said she had it all planned out. "Do you really not know what you're going to do?"

"I don't even know what my choices are going to be," I said. "How can I decide?"

She nodded. "When I decided to stay human, it lost me several viewers, but not too many. You're in a tough position. Whatever you choose, make sure it has either a Pathfinder skill or some sort of advanced-mapping ability. Finding stairwells as quickly as possible will be crucial on further floors. It's not going to be a problem on this third floor. Also," she added, "make sure Donut goes first. That way you can tailor your class selection on hers. I would ignore the AI's advice for your race, but I'd take a careful look at whatever it suggests for your class."

"Hey," I said. "Do you know anything about the Valtay Corporation?"

She paused, cocking her head to the side. "Where did you hear about them?"

I shrugged. "Just curious. I heard it somewhere."

She smiled, but without humor. "Be careful. If they are somehow contacting you or trying to get to you, be very cautious. They're a corporate system government, and they're the ones who currently have an entire fleet parked outside of the Borant system, ready to collect on the debt. They were hours away from initiating a full-scale collection action when the kua-tin stopped them in their tracks by starting the season early. They're one of the most powerful entities in the universe. The next season is going to be run by them."

"Are they human?" I asked. I thought of Agatha. Was she one of these aliens? The idea seemed absurd.

"No," she said. "Not usually. They're a parasitic life-form. They do utilize human bodies, but their home world is aquatic, and they much prefer water-based hosts, such as the kua-tin or the gleeners. They're known for their technological advancements. Their version of *Dungeon Crawler World* is less goblins and trolls and more android death machines and pulse rifles."

I contemplated telling her about Agatha, but I decided against it. I decided it would be best to just stay away from the woman the best I could.

Mongo pounced and chomped directly onto Donut's tail. She howled and started running in circles with Mongo still attached.

Odette shook her head. "You're gonna want to level that thing up as soon as you can. But make sure Donut has proper control over him first. Those little nibbles and nose chomps are cute now. They won't be so adorable when he's full-grown."

"Do you know how big he gets?"

"You honestly don't know what he is?" Odette asked. "He's a pretty common creature across the universe. They always seed the human worlds with those guys and the others before the humans develop. Most human kids love these things."

"He's a dinosaur of some sort. I know that much."

"He's a dinosaur all right. Mongoliensis." Her eyes flashed in a similar way that Mordecai's did when he was searching through his menus. "Ahh, I see," she said after a moment. "The issue is the translation. 'Mongoliensis' is based off the scientific name. Your language had a more common name for those things."

The little chicken jumped up on Donut's back and squawked.

"You called them velociraptors."

I returned my gaze to the little monster. I'd been thrown off by the pink feathers and the beak. But now that she said it, I could see the monstrosity Mongo would soon become.

"I mean, it's obvious, isn't it?"

"Oh hell," I finally said.

She laughed.

Donut came up to us, breathless. "Carl, is it time to go yet?"

"There's one last piece of advice I'd like to give," Odette said, looking at the both of us. She paused, as if uncertain about what she was about to say. She'd changed on a dime, suddenly looking different, almost sad. "It's just a suggestion. I don't know if, morally, this is a good idea or not, but this will greatly increase your chances of survival. It's something to look for during class selection. It's generally only offered to crawlers with a high charisma, so if it's available, it'll be hidden somewhere amongst Donut's choices. The problem is, if you pick it, it's going to make someone very angry."

BACKSTAGE AT
THE PINEAPPLE CABARET

PART ONE

RORY

"RORY," THE GOBLIN SHAMANKA WHISPERED TO HERSELF. "RORY."

That was her name. *Her* name. She'd never had a name before. The idea of having one had never even occurred to her. It was hers. Nobody could take it away. Nobody could steal it. Not ever, no matter what they did.

She held on to the idea, clutching it against her own chest. Rory. Rory. Rory.

But the presence of this new discovery added questions. Why? Why had it not occurred to Rory that she *should* have a name? What had they called each other before? She couldn't remember. She banged her head against the wall. Just a little tap, causing her piercings to clink. She did that sometimes to jiggle out the thoughts.

Tap, tap, tap.

Boss man Damien had a name. Some of the protected ones, like Tiatha, Glennis, Mordecai, Helix. They had names. Foodz room Bopcas had names. Why was she just a number? And not just the same number, but a moving one? When the magical words appeared, when the boss man spoke with her, her reply would give her an ever-changing designation. Numbers and symbols she didn't understand.

One of the engineers had once suggested that the numbers changed based on where she was standing when she responded. Later, when she'd tested it, she thought maybe he'd been right. She felt bad afterward. The engineer hadn't even been that delicious. Maybe if *he'd* had a name, she wouldn't have eaten him. Maybe he would've started bathing. Names were important.

All around her, the others sat in a haze of smoke. Their raid against the llama cartel had been one of those okay-that-could've-gone-betters. While they'd successfully raided their processing lab and stolen their stash, a group of llamas had moved into goblin territory during the attack and killed the chieftain along with all the younglings and all the oldlings and all the preggos. Not good. Blown them right up.

So, Rory and the others had been forced to retaliate and do a whole lot of murdering of the llamas. Not just a raid, but a full-on scorched-dungeon campaign. They'd driven a bunch of the murder dozers right up to the kingpin's cavern and blown it all up with funpowder. Murdock had kicked the kingpin in the eggs, and Lorelai had cast *Does This Look Infected?* on him. Rory was planning on taking a bite out of his llama grandma, just to drive the whole don't-fuck-with-our-clan thing home, but she'd been too distracted by their haul. By the time she was ready to do the chomp, the walls were doing that spinning thing. So the llama grandma had gotten away unbitten. That was okay, Rory decided. The llama kingpin was dead. Their production facility was done. The clan had the stash.

And now they were sitting in the burned-to-a-crisp remains of their workshop, reaping the spoils of their conquest. And by "reaping the spoils," she meant tearing through the llamas' meth and the llamas' weed and the llamas' blitz sticks like a pack of rabid blender fiends. They'd looted enough to keep the whole family floating until level collapse.

Part of her registered she should be upset about the death of the younglings. That's why they did this, wasn't it? They fought to impress the boss man, and when he was sufficiently wowed by their crawler-killing skills, they'd move on to the second floor. And then they'd move to the third. Then the fourth and so on. The deeper they went, the safer they'd be. Never mind what that rat-kin shaman had once said to her. That the deeper mobs had their thinkers scrambled. That they didn't know they were in the dungeon. They didn't even know what the dungeon was. That they didn't have continuity from one season to the next. The deeper floors were different every time, and so the monsters had to change, too. They were like empty fun-powder sacks filled up with different stuff each time.

But did that matter? Maybe that would be better, Rory thought. Maybe they wouldn't be so afraid all the time. Maybe it would be nice not to know where they really were.

Now the younglings were dead. The preggos were dead. There was no more clan. No more family, except who was left in the room.

It would be nice to forget. To be an empty sack refilled with a new thinker that didn't know about that room right there filled with the dead.

Sober Rory would be especially upset about all of this, she knew. So the solution was easy. Don't be sober.

But even shaky Rory was starting to do the bad type of thinking. She kept seeing the chieftain, who was worried all the time. Him and that one youngling. The one with the yellow dress and the ribbon on her head and the gap between her teeth. The one who already knew how to cast *Keister Blaster*. Rory liked the way the youngling giggled when she cast the spell at a dumb regular goblin.

The little girl never had a name. That didn't seem right.

No, no, no, Rory thought. *No sad thoughts.* She needed to stay away from the blitz, which helped relive memories. *No, no, no. I have a name now. I need to be celebrating.*

She turned to a bomb bard who sat to her left, leaning up against the wall. He had a piece of dynamite on his lap, and between hits, he was in the process of tying a llama steak to the dynamite. He would throw the stick to cook the steak. Those bomb bards always liked their foodz cooked. And in really small portions.

"I have a name. My name is Rory," Rory said to him.

"Yeah? I ain't got a name," the bomb bard said. "How do I get one?"

"Someone's gotta give it to you. Princess Donut gave me my name."

The bomb bard seemed to think on this for a little bit. "Can *you* give me one?"

Rory also thought about this.

"Yes. You have a name now. Your name is Meat Stick."

"Yeah it is," said Meat Stick. He started wrapping a potato around the other side of the stick of dynamite.

Rory looked across the way at the other shamanka, Lorelai, who was in the process of kicking a regular goblin who'd lost his pineapple stick during the raid. The pineapples were hard to find. And they were important, too. She couldn't remember exactly *why* they were important. But they were. One couldn't just lose them and not get kicked.

"Lorelai," Rory called. "We're giving everyone names. You do that side of the room. I'll do this side."

Lorelai nodded. She turned back to the goblin, who was curled on the floor, sobbing. "You're Bootprint, Maggot."

Bootprint, Maggot looked up, smiling big. He was missing several teeth. "Thank you," he said.

She kicked him again. She then pointed to another goblin who'd also lost his pineapple stick. "You're next."

Next put his hands together. "Thank you, Lorelai!"

This was all interrupted when the magic words appeared in Rory's interface.

> **DAMIEN:** You idiots aren't supposed to attack neighboring
> quads. Not unless the crawlers go with you. I am much too
> busy to deal with this bullshit. Don't let it happen again.

Damien. The boss man. He was a human, but a different type of human than the crawlers from this season. He was always yelling at them for this or that.

Fuck him, Rory thought. *I have a name now. He don't know what it's like.* She mentally typed a response.

> **5X772*:** They was holding out, and they had it coming.

Rory blinked at the magic words. She had a name, but it didn't say her name. She looked up and whispered at the god who spoke the magical words, "I have a name now. It's Rory."

To her utter astonishment, there was a chime. She was pretty sure she was the only one to hear it. She blinked at that. She pulled up the magical words again. She couldn't send new messages to anybody, but she could still read the old ones. Her name had changed.

RORY: They was holding out, and they had it coming.

Yes! It was official, then. If the magic words god said it, then it must be true.

She elbowed Meat Stick. "We should celebrate. But you need to take a bath first."

"Uh," he said, looking sadly down at his half-prepared meal. He'd pulled out a carrot. "What about finishing giving all the guys their names first? Who's that guy?" He pointed the carrot at one of the engineers.

The engineer sat there, and he had his hat, a bowl with a bunch of little holes in it, held out in front of him. The stoned goblin was oohing and aahing as the light caught the little holes just right. The light came from the still-burning pile of coal.

"You," Rory said. "Your name is Spaghetti."

Spaghetti looked up. "I was kinda hoping to be Wallace."

"Fuck off," Rory said. "You're Spaghetti." She pointed at the next guy down. Another engineer, but with a padded helmet. "That one is Wallace."

"Yeah," Wallace said. "Don't be trying to steal my name, Spaghetti."

She was about to name another, but the magic words came again.

DAMIEN: Did you just change your name yourself?
RORY: I did. My name is Rory.

There was a long pause.

DAMIEN: Don't try to go anywhere. I'm sending in a team.

In the back of Rory's dumpster fire of a mind, an alarm bell went off. But it was ringing somewhere in that same I'm-just-going-to-ignore-you headspace that had told her that the llamas didn't use explosives. Not when they didn't have thumbs. Not when they could spit and vomit out lava.

Still . . . those alarm bells jingle-jangling in her brain were insistent. So insistent, in fact, that she spent a moment thinking about this.

RORY: A team? What sort of team?

Message not delivered.

She'd never seen *that* before.

She had a sudden memory. Long ago. Before the llamas were always next door to them, it'd been slash kobolds. The kobold leader had found a safe room, and he'd figured out if they all went inside and behaved themselves, they could stay safe. The chieftain had found out and thought it was a great idea. He'd decided to make the clan do the same thing.

. . . Until the "team" came jogging through the hallway. Big guys in heavy armor that didn't clank like real armor. It clinked and clicked like pottery. And it was different kinds of big guys. Sometimes human. Sometimes the big kobolds called gnolls. Sometimes other creatures Rory could barely fathom. But they all wore the same hard shells as they jogged down the hallway. She didn't know the details after that. Didn't know how they got them out of the safe room. She just remembered there were no more slash kobolds anywhere after that, and there was a lot of blood everywhere until the ratties came and licked it all up. The chieftain had decided not to move them after that.

"I think . . ." she said out loud. In her drug-fueled stupor, it was hard to form the words. "I think we might have hardshells coming in."

Lorelai looked up from where she was kicking Next. "What? What did you say?"

"I think hardshells are coming," she repeated. "Coming for us."

"Why? What did we do?" Lorelai asked. She had a blitz stick hanging from her lip. She looked down at Next and kicked him again. "What did you do?"

"I don't knoooow," the goblin howled.

Rory hauled herself to her feet. The world continued to spin, to sag around the edges. She tried not to look left. That's where the chieftain had lived. That's where the babies had died. Nobody was allowed to go in there.

"Everyone!" she shouted. "Gear up! We got hardshells coming in. They's gonna kill us, I think."

All around, slack-jawed goblins peered up at her through the smoke.

"Hardshells? Coming for us? Why they gonna do that?" Spaghetti asked.

"Next did something to piss them off!" another goblin said. Rory was pretty sure that was Bootprint, Maggot speaking, but she was already losing track of who was who.

"It doesn't matter what Next did," Lorelai called. Her voice was always louder and stronger than Rory's. Especially when she got to kicking. "If we got hardshells coming for us, then we gotta fight back."

"But they're untouchables, ain't they?" Wallace asked. "If we try to hurt an untouchable, we get the zip zap? 'Member when that one bard ran his copper chopper over that fish person's flipper? He just disappeared! He never came back!"

"No, you can fight hardshells," Lorelai said. "You can't hurt the boss man, and you can't hurt the boss man's boss people. The fishies. But the hardshells are wearing hard shells because they're soft on the inside."

So, they got ready for the hardshells. The bomb bards got on their choppers and got their boomers ready. The engineers all got on their dozers. The regular gobs jumped in the back of the dozers, all clutching onto their pineapple sticks. All except Bootprint, Maggot and Next, who didn't have pineapple sticks. They'd each picked up lengths of metal piping as their weapons.

Rory had a bad feeling about this. They were all probably dead. The hardshells didn't fight fair. They weren't like the crawlers, who usually didn't know the first thing about fighting. And the crawlers were usually crying. The hardshells never cried. They had their sticks with the electricity at the end. And in some rare cases, they had their lightning shooters.

But what else was there to do? Rory also prepared. She moved to the back of the room, the heat from the burning coal and dead younglings warming her back. The smell, at least, was pleasant. She had spells she could cast. Lots of spells, but only the ones at the top of the list worked. For fighting, her three go-tos were: *Never-ending Nosebleed. Hangnail.* And *Crackleskin.* She'd used that last one a lot on the crawlers. She'd used it on the llamas, too. That one always got folks to screaming.

She paused, looking at her list of spells. A spark of an idea was misfiring back there, and she desperately tried to latch onto it. There was another spell she'd used a lot, but it wasn't a combat spell. In fact, it was the spell she'd used, by far, the most.

It was called *Revenge.* She'd been taught that the spell was supposed to be cast on someone who was about to kill you, and it'd hurt them bad if they managed to do so. But the spell took lots of seconds to cast, so it was kinda useless. If you had extra seconds to cast it, then you probably had extra seconds to get to running. So most shamankas never used it.

But that wasn't right. They were wrong about what the spell did. Rory learned this a long time ago. The spell let you cast it on things, and it stayed cast on those things. It was an "enchantment." She'd learned that word from the rat-kin shaman. It didn't work on small things, but it worked on big things. So she'd cast it on the murder dozers when they'd built them. It made it so when the dozers blew up, the blast only went toward the idiot goblin who was responsible for making it blow up in the first place. That way they wouldn't lose a whole crew when an engineer tried to do loop-de-loops in the dungeon hallways with the things.

Just earlier today when they went about smushing the llamas, one of them had fireballed an engineer, and the machine had gotten to overheating. The whole thing had blown to bits, and the llama who'd cast the fireball . . .

And there it was. The idea.

By his left tit, Rory thought. *By his left tit. That . . . that might actually work!*

"Line up the dozers! Line them up at the entrance to the hall with the pipes facing out! And everybody get to the back! Off the dozers once they're parked! Spaghetti and Wallace, get over here! I need you!"

"COME ON OUT, YOU DIRTY LITTLE GOBLINS," THE GRUFF VOICE called, taunting. "We're not here to hurt you."

This was followed by a chorus of hyena laughs.

They had the hallway sealed up good and tight with a couple murder dozers smushed side by side. Only one way in. As far as Rory could tell, there were nine of the hardshells out there. The hallway outside the chamber was twisty, but it caught sounds good, and even with them whispering, she could hear everything they said. She didn't understand most of what they were saying, but she could hear it.

She was starting to come down from her high, which would cause the buzzing to come back. Things would get bad shaky on the outside instead of the good shaky on the inside. The good shaky wasn't all that good for fighting, but it was a mighty bit better than the outside shaky. Rory contemplated what to do about that. She decided to split the difference and take a swig of some toiletshine she'd bought off the slimes. It burned on the way down, but it kept the buzzing at bay. Long enough so she could hear what the hardshells were saying. She passed the bottle to Lorelai, who stood next to her, also listening.

"We're gonna have to clear this away ourselves," one of the hardshells said. A different one than the first. This one had a lady voice. She was a gnoll. They all sounded like gnolls to Rory. "I didn't bring any heavy ordnance with me. I'll have to call for some to be brought up."

"How long will that take?" the gruff one asked.

"Too long," the woman replied. "We have over 300 expulsions on the slate, with more added by the second. These guys are popping their restraints left and right. So everyone is busy."

"Gods," the gruff one said. "I hope this isn't an indicator of how the rest of the season is gonna go."

"It's already fucked," the woman gnoll replied. "Not only did they push everything out the airlock half-cooked, but they skipped the mob audit, like always. Figuring we ain't got anything better to do than to clean up after them. We're gonna be busy as fuck. Look at these stats. These guys in here are almost *twenty seasons* past their expiration. Anything to save a credit. Did you hear about the Street Preacher boss? That thing turned a soldier from Beta group into a literal pillar of salt."

"Wait," the gruff one said. "Are these goblins in here the same ones that ran into that crawler with the talking rodent thing that thinks she's a princess or whatever? They blew the boss to mulch without even stepping into the boss room. She had that line about the babies they keep playing over and over at the pub."

The woman laughed. "I hadn't heard about that, but maybe. It says the attached neighborhood boss is already dead, thank the gods. Killed by the crawler."

"Yeah. I think this is them. When we get back, you gotta watch the scene. It's a good one. Odette already had it on her show."

Rory and Lorelai looked at each other.

Rory felt a strange sense of . . . what? It wasn't anger. It wasn't rage. Was it . . . She didn't know what it was called. But it made her chest feel as if it was suddenly being filled with sand. It made her feel like she'd already been an empty funpowder sack and didn't even realize it.

Do you want to come with us? Princess Donut had asked that. Rory had said no. She couldn't.

And they'd responded by killing all their younglings.

That was how it was. Goblins killed crawlers, and crawlers killed goblins. Still, Princess Donut had been different. But she *wasn't* different, was she? Rory looked down at the bottle of shine in her hand, and she realized it wasn't enough. What they'd looted from the llamas wouldn't be enough, either. Not enough to keep the bad thoughts away.

"I still don't understand why we can't just have the AI take care of this for us," a third hardshell whined. "When they unlock themselves, they become dangerous."

"You know how this works," the woman gnoll said. "Especially this season, if the rumors are true. The less involved that thing is with judicial duties, the longer it'll last. What happens if it decides it wants to keep them around? Besides, don't you like having a job?"

The whiny gnoll just grunted.

"Hey," the gruff one said. "These things are just old-fashioned steam engines, right? They ain't got anything living inside of them. The relief valves are right there. If I twist this and we fall back, they'll eventually explode. Right?"

"Good thinking, Brewster," the woman said. "They can't have gotten too intelligent if they parked them with the valves facing out. Let's go ahead and—"

"Back!" Rory hissed. She and Lorelai rushed to the back of the room, not waiting to hear the rest. They dived behind the hastily erected pile of sandbags.

Normally, the dozers did take some time to go boom if you

messed with them wrong. But with a bit of fiddling and a re-up of the *Revenge* spell, which suddenly seemed much more powerful than it was when they first built these dozers . . .

Bam!

———

WHEN RORY CAME TO, EARS RINGING, PIERCINGS ON HER FACE ALL hot to the touch, and everybody all around groaning, the hardshells were gone. The hallway where they'd been standing was nothing but a long, charred corridor that didn't even smell like how people smelled when they got themselves blown up. It was like the directional blast had erased them from existence.

The murder dozers themselves were gone, too. Mostly. The sides of the machines, the sides that had been facing the goblins, remained standing there. But the pieces crumbled to the ground as Rory watched.

"Hey," Meat Stick said. "Has anybody seen my steak?" He'd left his uncooked dinner in one of the murder dozers. But it was gone. Vaporized.

"Do you think they're gonna be extra mad at me now?" Next asked, wringing his hands.

"Should we run?" Lorelai asked.

A strange blue shield suddenly appeared, locking them in the room. Not just closing them in the workshop, but blocking off the chieftain's chamber behind them, too.

Warning: This area is under emergency quarantine. Cleansing will commence in minus two. All Admin personnel must evacuate immediately.

The message came out loud. She'd only heard out-loud messages three or four times before, all in older seasons when crawlers went into the chieftain's chamber. And then the words were scrambled in her thinker. Come to think of it, the words of the hardshells were usually scrambled, too, except when they gave direct orders like "Get the hells out of my way."

But this time, she'd heard all their words.

The light of the room flashed red, and the message repeated. She didn't know what the word "quarantine" meant, but she certainly knew what "evacuate" meant.

"Where would we go?" Rory asked out loud, answering both the voice and Lorelai at the same time. That sand-in-the-chest feeling was still there.

And she suddenly found herself sitting on the floor.

Death was always a way of life in the dungeon. Goblins died all the time. Heck, they literally ate each other. Rory was always prepared to die. Always. And now . . .

And now.

Now, it seemed different. More important. Something had changed. She never wanted to die. She always wanted to live. And now that she didn't have anything left to live for . . . she wanted to live more than ever.

"Is it because I have a name?" she asked.

All around, the goblins were mostly ignoring her. They all knew what was about to happen. Lorelai was kicking Next again, hurling insults while Bootprint, Maggot helped, kicking him on the other side. Wallace and Spaghetti were hugging each other. Meat Stick had another stick of dynamite out, and he was affixing another llama steak to it. The rest of the never-got-nameds stood about, looking terrified.

What do you want?

She blinked.

These were magic words spoken just to her. But they weren't signed. The words just floated there.

"Wha . . . what?" she asked out loud.

There was no answer, but the words remained there, floating in her vision while the light of the room became an even darker red.

What *did* she want?

She thought of the younglings. Of the chieftain. Of the preggos. Even the oldlings. She thought of the goblins all around her. After all this time, all their work, what did they have to show for it? They were all either dead or were about to die.

All of this was for nothing. Nothing.

She thought of the little goblin girl with the yellow dress and the ribbon on her head.

RORY: I want her to have had a name. I want her to have been Keister Blaster.

There was no response. No chime.

She thought of the sand in her chest. She thought of how much heavier she suddenly felt. She moved back to the message.

RORY: I also want revenge.

Cleansing Commences Now.

———

THERE WAS A WASH OF HEAT, A BLINK, AND SUDDENLY RORY AND the rest of the crew were in a new place.

It was a giant, dimly lit room. She could see distant walls, but they were far, far away. Above her head, there was a ceiling, but it was very, very high. A strange terror filled her. She'd never been in such a wide, empty space. It felt too open, too wide, like she was suddenly falling. Her breaths came to her in surprised, ragged gasps as she looked about. The ground wasn't rock. It wasn't tile. It was a weird, shaggy substance. Soft to the touch. Like hair or fur, but not real hair. Not real fur.

She fought not to close her eyes.

I'm alive. I'm alive.

In addition to her own crew, there were others here, too. But they were all very far away, and there weren't many of them. All distant figures hidden in the low light of the gigantic room. She recognized one of them, however. The closest one. It was grandma llama. The one who had gotten away. It was her along with a small group of the regular bad llamas.

"Where are we?" Spaghetti asked.

Welcome, Rory. Welcome Backstage. You will reenter the playing arena soon.

PART 2 WILL APPEAR AT THE END OF
CARL'S DOOMSDAY SCENARIO.

ACKNOWLEDGMENTS

Wow. When I first started writing this series, I had no idea it was going to blow up like it has. I went from a guy who'd gotten his teeth kicked in by the pandemic to someone who actually gets to write silly stories about a talking cat for a living. It is a privilege, and I consider myself forever grateful that this is something I can actually get paid for.

This is where I'm supposed to thank my agent (Seth), my lawyer (Matt), my editor (Jess), all the copyeditors and marketing people and designers (uh, you guys), etc., and I do thank all y'all for believing in me. But I wouldn't have gotten to the point where I have an agent, a lawyer, and an editor if I didn't first have folks like *you*. The readers. The Patreon members. The folks who post on r/Dungeon CrawlerCarl on Reddit. The cosplayers. The perverts who send me concerning feet pictures. I couldn't do it without any of you. Writing is a lonely, solitary, sometimes soul-crushing business, and knowing there are weirdos out there who actually *like* what I'm doing? It's pretty damn cool.

Way back at the beginning of this book, there's a dedication that's written to Fiona the hippopotamus from the Cincinnati Zoo. (If you don't know the story, look her up. Born significantly premature. The hospital staff had to move the heavens to keep her alive. Today, she thrives.) Dedicating a book to a hippo might sound like a waste of space or a silly joke, but the truth is, I've always been fascinated by the stories of those who survive against all odds. I think in order to truly enjoy Dungeon Crawler Carl, no matter how dark it gets (and believe me, it's gonna get dark), you need to be the type of person who is able to cling onto hope, no matter how small that spark is. *You will not break me* is more than just a mantra. It's the theme to this whole series, and by dedicating this book to Fiona, I'm really dedicating it to everything she represents. Perseverance. Grit. Hope. And that's *you*. Hell, it's all of us after the shit of the past few years.

Okay, that sounds really sappy and way too heavy for a book series about a guy running around in his underwear. But damn if it ain't true.